Dedication
For Chupie

BY
THEA CONSTANTINE

STUMPTOWN
Published 2017 in U.S.A by Genre/Over The Edge Books

ISBN - 978-1-944082-31-4
Cover photography by Eddie Morgan / Eddie Morgan Photography
Stumptown logo/art by Cleo Hehn / @Cleohehn.com
Layout by Michael Ziobrowski / @XIsTheWeapon

overtheedgebooks.com

CONTENTS

Sometime in the Aughts

SPRING

Portland attracts the crackpots of the crackpots. The misfits of the misfits.
— Katherine Dunn, author Geek Love

Jolene stared out the window of the Greyhound bus. Only four more hours, and she'd finally be in Portland. As for "riding the dog," she could now confirm every hellish tale she'd ever heard. If things didn't work out, she'd simply have to walk back to San Francisco.

But she was absolutely determined that this time it would work out. This time was going to be different. For one thing, she wasn't Jolene Layne any more. From the moment she stepped off this freaking hellhole of a bus, she would be Jolie. Jolie Lane. She'd thought it over. It had a nice French sound to it and it was an absolutely valid contraction of Jolene. So it wasn't like a fake name or anything.

The name Jolene had been a gift from her mother. Her mother Patsy. Patsy had determined that her own name had been a major factor in the woes of her existence. According to Patsy, it was a lesson learned the hard way from the Grand Ole Opry. Look at Patsy Cline: a wonderful singer. An attractive woman, too. But Patsy Cline got left. Over and over. Listen to just about any of her songs. It was all there. And so did Jolene's mother. Get left, that is. So Mrs. Patricia Layne Thompson Thigpen McGuire gave her daughter the gift of a winning name. A name from her favorite Dolly Parton song, in which a Patsy-type of woman begs the beautiful redheaded Jolene to please, please give back her man. Jolenes didn't get left. It was one way to safeguard her daughter from inheriting the family legacy of heartbreak.

Getting left was the least of Jolie's problems.

***

Bubbles pushed past the last of the thinning crowd headed the other way. "Stupid fuckers!" she yelled back at them as she rushed to the slumped form on the bench at the far corner of the schoolyard. She squatted down to face the boy on the bench. Brian looked up at her. A huge shiner had already half-closed his left eye and his wire frame glasses lay twisted at his feet. Bubbles's stomach fisted, along with her hands.

"Oh God, I can't believe those freaks. I can't believe nobody helped you. Oh Brian, look at your poor eye." She leaned forward to touch him but Brian pulled away.

"Yeah, look at it!" he snapped. "Gee Brian, you should totally come out at school. It's really no big deal anymore, Brian. It's the twenty-first century, Brian. Everyone will totally get over it in a week."

Bubbles pulled back, eyes wide, as Brian continued, "Well, it's not the twenty-first century here at Lewis and Clark, okay? Maybe in Portland but not here. So just leave me alone."

"Oh, all of a sudden it's my fault? That's not fair. It only goes to prove that they're all just in the closet themselves, otherwise why would they get so upset?"

Brian leaned down, picked up his pretzeled glasses, and stood. "I don't know and I don't care. Maybe it's not your fault but it was never your problem either, okay?" He slowly turned and made his way back toward the gym.

Bubbles stood on the empty schoolyard as she watched Brian disappear into Lewis and Clark High. "That's not fair," she muttered. "It was kind of my problem."

Bubbles's mother never tired of telling complete strangers about how adorable she'd been as a babe in the crib, blowing enormous spit bubbles as she cooed and gurgled. It might have ended there if she hadn't fallen for the magic of the rainbows that lived on the soapy orbs that came from her first bubble pipe, a stocking stuffer in her seventh year. She'd moved from that to wands, and then to large hoops that she dipped in big bowls of Lemon Fresh Joy and water, urging each perfect bubble out bigger and bigger, more impressive with each pass of the hoop. She'd won first prize in the school talent show three years running.

The nickname stuck. Now at fifteen, a self-proclaimed Neo-Goth nihilist, try as she might, she could not shake the name. Perhaps if she'd come from a large city (as she thought she should have), she might have escaped. But here in Longview, Washington, she was Bubbles.

Dressed head-to-toe in black, pierced and tattooed with her ripped fishnets and knee-high Doc Martins, she felt about as bubbly as a coiled cobra. She was pretty sure if she didn't get out of this town, she was going to lose her mind.

***

It felt like a medium sort of day for Barkin' Jack, but it was too early to tell. So far not a scary day, but it didn't feel super lucky either. They'd kicked him out of the shelter pretty early. Was it today when he got out early? Yeah, today.

His feet had taken him out of the shelter by way of Union Station. They did that a lot. They liked to go to the Greyhound station too, but all in all, his feet seemed to prefer Union Station. On a good day, he could even imagine himself getting on a train and going back to being Jack Barker again. It wasn't that sort of day, but it was good enough to feel social. Barkin' Jack liked to greet newcomers to the city. If not him, then who?

***

Nat the Cat was out of Valium. This much was clear and Eleni was glad Max was driving. She didn't think she could have handled it nearly as well. If only she hadn't forgotten the remaining half of his Valium on the nightstand at the last motel. Poor Nat—he wasn't a seasoned traveler. There was something about the Siamese voice, too. It was in the same range as an infant's, or close enough. You couldn't ignore it. It ripped through your psyche and broke your heart. This trip up the I-5 was nothing like the fun-filled, carefree time they'd spent driving up the coast the first time they came to Portland.

Max figured they'd be there in about two hours. They'd already gotten the key from the landlord. He couldn't believe they were actually pulling it off. Two hours and they would arrive at their new Portland home.

Eleni couldn't believe it, either. They actually set a goal and made it within a month of their deadline. They decided they had at least one more adventure in them. Even if they were over forty. They'd cashed in what was left of the 401K from Max's job and blown out of LA; it would last them a few months if they were extra careful. Max was joining a new band with his friends Mickey and Bobby. Eleni had a few dreams of her own to pursue. Tonight they'd make a slumber party of it: lay their blankets on the floor and spend the first night in the house. Tomorrow, they'd sign up at the clinic and get their doses. They were going to make it this time for sure. This time would be different.

***

Barkin' Jack entered Union Station with its mish-mosh of Tudor walls, Spanish roof tiles, and New Orleans ironwork. It had the universal look and feel of what a train station was supposed to be, all wrapped up in one convenient package. He stood for a bit in the center of the main waiting area. Marble walls marked To Trains — From Trains — Tickets — Baggage. A large clock kept everyone appraised of the time. He turned down the hallway and slipped out a side door to the tracks themselves. He hummed along to the soundtrack of old blues songs about trains and stations as he walked up and down the tracks. Nothing coming in—nothing going out. He shuffled around a bit. Saw a guy walk toward him with a square badge on. Barkin' Jack beat feet across the street to the Greyhound station.

***

A sudden jerk and a hiss of brakes and Jolene's eyes flew open. Didn't it just figure? Thirty-five hours with no sleep and now when she just got comfy, she was finally at the terminal. Damn. At least she was in Portland. She fished around in her pack to pull out her brush and make-up bag and did the best she could while the bus lumbered forward toward the right gate. She squinted at the image in her tiny make-up mirror. Was thirty-two the new twenty-four? It sure didn't look like it today. She'd meant to call Jenny about a half hour before she arrived to come and pick her up. Damn.

***

He'd barely gotten thru the door of the Greyhound station when folks started to come out. He peered through the glass. More coming—a steady stream. Barkin' Jack positioned himself a few feet from the door.

"Welcome to Portland," barked Jack to a large Mexican family who smiled nervously as they went by. Another family came out, followed by a young couple. "Welcome to Portland," barked Jack. "You folks have a great time!"

Now outside the station, the young woman looked nervously at her fiancé as they made their way to the parking lot. "Did that man just bark at us?"

"Yeah, I'm pretty sure he did," replied her fiancé. "Funny thing is—I could have sworn he was saying something."

***

Jolie picked up her bag and dragged it toward the first available bench. She dug around in her pack until she came up with her cell phone. Dead, of course. Where the hell could she have charged it on that nightmare of a bus? Damn. She'd just have to go out and get herself a cab or something.

Hoisting her bags back up, Jolie headed for the door. As she stepped outside, she saw a funny little man with a bright red nose and a four-tooth smile.

"Welcome to Portland," barked Jack. "Have a wonderful time."

"Thanks—you too." Jolie went to find a cab.

***

"Three days? Are you fucking kidding me?" Max looked on in horror as he listened to Eleni's side of the call.

"Sorry, right...yes, ma'am...yes, I understand, but ma'am—we can't wait three days. They told us we could just continue treatment from the LA clinic. What? No. Nobody told us anything of the kind. Right. Well, be that as it may, we can't wait three days. Do you understand? Mmm hmm. So Burnside and what?"

Max turned away and shook his head. She was trying. You always had to give Eleni points for trying. She didn't give up easy. But this had hopeless written all over it. This was one of those bureaucratic lose/lose situations. One thing was sure, though—they couldn't wait three days.

***

The endless patter of drops on the metal roof never stopped and Daisy was cold, as usual. Bone cold. She'd been trying to stop complaining, tried to look on the bright side. The van sure was better than their old spot. It kept the rain off and made you feel safer—but she knew it was only a matter of time before its owner came around and kicked them out.

They'd noticed the van about a week ago and just sort of moved in the other day. So far, so good. Actually, Toby was the one to notice it. Toby had instincts that Daisy just hadn't developed. She had street smarts. But Daisy was learning—she had found a better methadone clinic than Toby's. They were nicer and faster than COMA. Of course, she'd had to find the Delphia clinic because she'd gotten kicked off the COMA program. Didn't matter; they were all a bunch of creeps at that clinic anyway. Of course, this meant they had to go to two different clinics every day. But it wasn't as if they didn't have any extra time on their hands.

***

Toby tried to tune out Daisy's whining. She'd whined all the way to her clinic and she whined her way on and off the Number 15 bus and onto the Number 6 and then all the way up Burnside. Blah blah cold, blah blah tired, blah blah sick, blah, hungry blah. She was still talking when Toby left her outside and went into the COMA clinic.

Toby spotted the figure at the dosing window. Whew, lucky. It was a new nurse today. The regular nurse would have noticed she had a group hold and that meant no dose until she made up the missing group. She hated the therapy groups at the clinic. They were all so stupid and the more dirty UAs you got, the more stupid groups you had to go to. She hoped her counselor would let her do a few one-on-one sessions to make up for a couple of her missed groups. He wasn't in his office but the woman at the desk said he was in today. Well, she could go back out with Daisy and just kick it for a while.

***

Jolie was pleased to see that although the neighborhood left something to be desired, the Broadmoor Apartments was an impressive building. The intercom system alone was the latest in high-tech digital display. But, as was generally the case with these things, it did not facilitate her entry to the building. Just as she was about to give up, someone walked out and she made it to the front desk. This, too, was fraught with all sorts of security measures and it took all her powers of persuasion to gain access. This was weird; a doorman was one thing but these people were crazy.

After signing in and waiting for Jenny to come and escort her upstairs, she was now finally face-to-face with her old friend in the tiny apartment. Jenny looked good. She'd put on a couple pounds and her skin was clear.

It turned out the Broadmoor was a sober-living house. Jenny filled her in about it. Portland, it seemed, was awash in such places. They had one-month drug programs, detoxes, halfway houses, three-quarter houses, and sober living. Even Jenny wasn't sure about all the differences. Clearly, there was something for everyone, Jenny assured her. They just had to find the right one for Jolie.

"Find the right place?" Jolie eyed Jenny as she nervously smoothed the morphine delivery patch under her jeans. "Can't I just stay here? I can pay some rent."

Jenny looked up at her with sheep's eyes. She licked her lips and looked unsure of how to begin.

"What?" said Jolie. "You told me last time we talked that we could share a room. What's up? Jenny?"

"You can totally stay tonight—that's no problem," blurted Jenny. "It's just like, not every night."

"Jenny?" Jolie was beyond tired, beyond confused, beyond disappointed.

Jenny spilled her tale. She'd been busted since they last spoke and the only way to stay out of jail was to enter one of these programs. She'd pulled some strings with a friend whose boyfriend was a bigwig in the recovery community. Most people had to jump through hoops to get into the Broadmoor, but Jenny had managed to get straight in and she thought she could help Jolie do the same.

"But I don't want to go to rehab," she said, screaming inside like Amy Winehouse.

"Shhhh!" said Jenny.

***

"The lady on the phone said maybe if we go see a counselor face-to-face we might get lucky," Eleni said as they pulled up in front of COMA.

"The county office of medical addiction?" Max murmured in disbelief.

"Something like that anyway," said Eleni. "Whatever it is, we're here."

They didn't have to ask which building it was. COMA had the depressive look of methadone clinics worldwide: an old dumpy bunker-like building with a discreet plaque outside that stated the clinic's name. You had to look twice. Inside was much the same story: ancient linoleum, fluorescent lights, several lines of people, and a couple of mismatched vinyl chairs.

They approached the counter and were told to have a seat. For a while, they just sat and checked out the scene around them. They could see the dosing window from where they sat. That was new. In LA, you had to go through a locked door to even approach a dosing nurse. That was about the only difference, however. The patients—or "clients" as they were now called (as if anyone really gave a shit)—

looked exactly the same as the ones at home. Indeed, it was all so familiar that it took them awhile before they even realized that no one had asked their names or told them who or what they were so patiently waiting for.

"Oh man," said Eleni. "We are so fucked. Nobody's gonna do a goddamn thing today."

Max looked as if someone just shot his dog.

"I'm going out for a smoke," said Eleni. "Wanna come?"

"What and lose our place?" Max gave her a smile.

Eleni laughed and walked out the front of the clinic. Thank God for Max. Even with all this, he still tried to cheer her up. She looked around for anyone who looked as if they might be able to help. With anything. A couple of runaway-looking girls sat outside with their backs against the building, a couple of large backpacks strewn around them. One of them looked up.

"Any chance we could bum a smoke?" asked Daisy.

"Sure." Eleni fished out an extra Marlboro as she lit one for herself.

Eleni eyed the two girls. Up close, they were a little older than she'd originally thought. Early twenties probably; one looked like Rebecca of Sunnybrook Farm fallen on hard times, the other had telltale pinned ice blue eyes under a shock of spiky black hair. They might just do. She launched into her tale of woe and need.

"Sounds like you could use some brown," Daisy said.

"Oh yeah," agreed Eleni. Five minutes later, the four of them were in the Volvo headed for Felony Flats.

***

Bubbles wiped her eyes. They had really started to burn something fierce. She'd logged on about six hours ago. First her e-mail, then a couple hours of World of Warcraft, then she'd hopped around various music sites and finally, onto her Facebook page. Thank God for that. She'd met a lot of really cool people online this year. Much cooler than any of the assholes in this godforsaken backwater. The only person she could talk to in Longview anymore was Brian but he didn't seem to trust anything she said to him anymore.

Well, one thing was sure: she was getting out of this town, and she really didn't think she could wait for graduation anymore. If there were more classes like her Psych class, maybe she could have dealt with it, but for the most part, they just spewed meaningless crap. Besides, what the hell was a stupid degree from Lewis and Clark High School going to do for her anyway?

Hmmm...it looked like one of the new guys she'd met online wanted to meet up with her. Well, tonight she was going to tell him yes. Maybe she'd tell him to meet her at Maggie's in Portland. She'd been dying to go there anyway. Who knew? If he was cool enough, maybe she just wouldn't come back. If he really looked anything like his pictures, she could almost guarantee it.

***

"Oh my God, Jenny. I just got off the phone with this bitch at that COMA clinic. She says I have to wait three weeks before I could get on the program with my Medicare. And three fuckin' days, even if I pay cash. Are they nuts? I can't wait three days. I'm sick NOW." Jolie clutched her little cell phone to her chest as she paced back and forth in the tiny apartment. It only took about three steps before she had to turn around each time.

"SHHHH...Jolene! The walls have ears here." Jenny's eyes darted around nervously, as if someone in authority was going to materialize right there in the middle of the room.

"I don't give a fuck," snapped Jolie. "You gotta help me, Jenny. This is your fault. And don't call me fucking Jolene anymore. My name is Jolie. Jolie—got it?"

***

Barkin' Jack made his way over the pedestrian bridge that spanned the train tracks and entered into a condo complex that sprawled from the train yard to the river's edge. There was a long public walking path where he could wander along the Willamette River for a few blocks. A few little rock paths here and there led right to the water's edge. Today, the water was filled with ducks floating gently in pairs. Side by side, they all seemed to enjoy an agreed-upon promenade, proceeding at a stately pace. Their very presence dropped Barkin' Jack's blood pressure and tension level a notch. Meeting-and-greeting could be stressful work after the first few minutes. Sometimes the longer he stood there greeting newcomers, the less he seemed to care. Ducks were simple, lacking the troubling complexity that his fellow humans all seemed to carry. Barkin' Jack wished he had some bread or something to share with them, even if there were signs along the path that asked people not to feed the animals. What did they know? If the damn ducks were full, they wouldn't eat. If they weren't, well then, why not?

He liked watching the geese, too; they were comical and stately at the same time. He enjoyed the honks and quacks that broke the silence near the boat slip. The ducks seemed to choose one area and the geese the other. Opinions got bandied back and forth. Still, he was willing to bet they got along better than two such different kinds of people would.

Thinking about bread for the ducks started Jack thinking about his own belly. By the light in the sky overhead, he'd bet it was getting on to lunchtime at the Salvation Army. Or, the Salivation Army as his friend Smokey called it.

"See Jack, we're all just like a buncha hounds in a lab. They ring that bell and we smell that food and then we all know to go and listen to some God-awful know-nothing sermon to get ourselves fed," Smokey had jeered.

"We're the Salivation Army and they need us jus' as much as we need them." A lot of the fellows thought Smokey was pretty crazy but as far as Jack was concerned, the man spoke the truth, even if it wasn't always comfortable.

Smokey lived in Forest Park these days. He'd gotten in with some of that crowd up there. Some of those guys hardly ever came into town anymore. You could get lost if you went in deep enough. Jack liked the park, liked to spend time in nature, but going in that deep frightened him. Jack needed to see the world around him, needed to see other people. A man got pretty isolated living the way he did. Any more isolation and he didn't think he'd be able to maintain even the tenuous hold he had on reality. Speakin' of which, maybe it was time to get out and see what was what.

***

"They were pretty cool," Daisy remarked as they left the bathroom at Fred Meyer, where Max and Eleni dropped them. Toby hadn't wanted to wait to do her shot.

"Yeah," Toby agreed. "Lucky they ran into us. They could have got majorly ripped off."

"Poor things—stuck in a new town, sick, no dealer."

"Yeah, I hope I don't have to deal with that shit at their age." Toby shuddered.

"Do you have anything left on your food stamp card?" Daisy pleaded. "I'm hungry. We could get those little mini cheese cakes. I'll get strawberry, you get chocolate?"

Toby frowned. "Doncha think we oughta wait a while? Not use 'em all up at once?"

"Aw, come on, aren't you hungry? You love the chocolate ones."

"I guess." Toby pulled out her card. They went back inside Fred Meyer.

***

"Thank God we ran into those two." Eleni flipped off her shoes.

"Yeah," said Max. "We could have been majorly ripped off."

"You got their phone number, right?"

"Yeah, they said to call them when we wake up tomorrow."

"Cool, that's a big time relief. Poor things," Eleni murmured. "Living on the street like that. Stuck in a freezing cold van."

"I know," said Max. "They're just kids."

***

"I'm afraid you're on your own tonight, Jole—uh... Jolie. I'm only allowed to have visitors twice a week, and they're going to get suspicious." Jenny looked down at her feet, too embarrassed to meet Jolie's eye. "I wish I could get you in tonight but they'll notice."

"Where the hell am I supposed to go? You told me we'd be roommates, that you had a place, that it was so great here. Did you think I wanted to come all the way from San Francisco just to be sick and homeless in a neat new location?"

"I know, I know, I'm sorry, it's just—everything changed after I got busted. You know it's here or jail for me. I have to play by their rules."

Jolie did not want to hear this, although she'd already figured it out. Hearing it straight out made it real. Made it unequivocal. Made her life—hell. Again.

"So where am I supposed to go tonight, huh? You got any suggestions?"

"Well, maybe you'll meet someone tonight, when we're out," Jenny offered lamely. "You know how it is—right? You never know?"

"Uh-huh," said Jolie. "You never know, maybe I'll meet someone...and maybe I won't, or maybe I'll have no choice? Is that it?" Jolie could feel the sick coming up all over her. Her nose was stuffed, her eyes watered and her bones felt as if they'd been peeled.

"Oh God, Jolie—I'm so sorry," Jenny whined. "I didn't mean for you to get stuck here like this."

"Oh, shut the fuck up." Jolie wished like hell there was somewhere to slam the door and run to.

***

Eleni looked down the tracks to see whether she could spot the MAX coming. She loved the light rail trains; they reminded her of the New York and London subways, although the MAX was all aboveground. Normally a MAX ride cheered her up but today all she could do was worry about the events of the last twenty-four hours. Things had definitely gotten out of hand.

First, there was the whole insanity with the clinic and their three-day policy. Back in LA, the counselor had just written down the name of the clinic and told them the switch would be no problem—ha!

Now, coming home after a grueling three hours of filling out forms at the Employment Development Department, she wondered what state she'd find Max in today. Yesterday, she'd found him sitting in the kitchen with his head in his hands. He'd just learned that his bass player was dead and his old friend Bobby, the band's leader, was in jail.

All those plans they'd made in LA. All those calls back and forth to Portland and it was all falling apart. As she stood there and looked at him with his dreams unraveling, the best she could come up with—was to call Toby and Daisy. This was not what they wanted. This was no different at all.

***

Barkin' Jack slipped back into the Greyhound station and headed for the restroom. On his way, he passed a little rack with free leaflets and little magazines for tourists. Barkin' Jack helped himself to one that extolled the virtues of Washington County. He enjoyed reading about the gracious living in the Portland area. The whole concept of gracious living intrigued him. Could you live graciously with no means of support? From what he read in most of these missives, it was an idea that had escaped notice. But Barkin' Jack wasn't so sure. Although the line between the "haves" and the "have-nots" was clearly drawn, there were areas of blur.

Once upon a time, the "haves" just purely pissed him off. Even seeing people stuffing themselves silly at a sidewalk cafe used to make him feel angry. Didn't they see all the people around them who were hungry, goddammit? Would it kill them to offer out half a sandwich or a slice of pizza? Or people going into the supermarket with their fat wallets. Coming out with shopping carts filled with food rather than all their worldly possessions. And woe betide the Barkin' Jack who might ask for a bit of change. Some of them just behaved as if no one had said a word. As if there wasn't a human being standing in front of them. Others had the nerve to get angry at him. Tell him to get a job. Well, he'd had a job, thank you, and it hadn't worked out very well at all. A job defending their thankless asses from a stupid war they cooked up to watch on TV while they stuffed their faces.

Time, however, had mellowed Barkin' Jack. The longer he spent out here, the better able he'd become to look after himself. He was no longer hungry all the time like he once was. He'd learned a bit about where to get a meal and who expected what from a man like himself. Now he was able to appreciate some of the freedoms that came with a life on the street. He certainly had more time to stop and smell the roses. It was just a shame about all the other things he had to smell.

***

Bubbles looked for Alison in the crowd that headed into Maggie's for Goth night. A respectable gay bar most other nights, Wednesday night was special. Wednesdays, the back room at Maggie's was Goth heaven (if that wasn't an oxymoron). So far, everything was going smooth as silk. She'd successfully snowed her parents into thinking she was safe at a sleepover and her sister's ID had gotten her in the door without a second glance. Even the buses actually got her here just when she wanted them to: not too early—not too late.

Alison and Raven were new friends she'd met at a Portland show last month, and they were exactly the kind of friends she needed now. They looked like she did and thought like she did. Nothing like the stupid know-nothing hicks she went to school with back in Longview. Raven didn't even go to school. She was an emancipated minor with a trust fund. Alison was home-schooled by her extremely cool mom.

Alison was almost positive that Nicholas the Facebook guy would be here tonight. The Nicholas who Bubbles had already had some pretty hot little chats and texts. Raven said she was pretty sure her friend Ash had slept with him one night. So he was straight and available. Just thinking about the whole thing made her crave alcohol.

***

Nicholas slid off the barstool at Kelly's and headed out. He could catch the MAX on the corner and make it to Goth night at Maggie's. He was really getting a little old for this shit. But what could a poor boy do? Ever since Honey had kicked him out, things had been a little lean. That was the problem with older women, or at least women his age. They just wanted so damn much. The little girls at Maggie's made him feel like King Shit. Maybe that girl with the bird name—Hawk, wasn't it?—and her little friends would be there again. And that cute new girl with the weird name who kept texting him. Wasn't she supposed to be there? Well, he'd find out soon enough.

***

"Hi-yee!" screamed Alison. Bubbles looked up with relief. Her friends. Thank God. She was beginning to feel like a real geek. Everybody here seemed to know one another. She was on her third PBR and her second shot of Jaegermeister. She figured as long as she kept drinking, she looked busy. At least the bartender was really sweet. Raven tucked her arm through hers. "How long ya been here?"

"Oh, not long," said Bubbles.

"I am so high." Raven giggled. "What was your name again?"

"It's Bub," said Alison. "God, Rave, I told ya five times already."

"Here you go, Ronnie." The bartender brought Bubbles the third shot she'd requested.

"Ronnie?' said Alison. "I thought you said your name was Bub?"

"It's the name on my ID," whispered Bubbles. "It's my sister Veronica's, so I just told him to call me Ronnie."

"Oh cool," said Raven. "I like Ronnie better than Bub."

"Really?" said Alison. "I like Bub better. It's so tough-guy. Like, Hey bub, hey buddy, listen buster!"

"Well..." By now, Bubbles was feeling no pain. "How 'bout you call me Bub," she looked at Alison, "and you call me Ronnie." She pointed at Raven.

"Works for me," said Alison.

"Sure," said Raven. "Hey, come in the bathroom," she continued. "We brought treats."

**

Jolie held onto the bar on the MAX train, stared at her boots and tried to breathe deeply without smelling anything. Man, she was drunk. They sure liked their beer up here. They'd already gone to a pseudo-biker bar, an oldies club, a fake English pub, and now they were on their way to Goth night at some gay bar, for Christ's sake. Hadn't Goth gone the way of the covered wagon? (Not in Portland, according to Jenny.) So far, all Jolie had to show for it was a couple of Vicodin and a beer belly. To make matters even more annoying, Jenny could not stop whining and worrying about whether someone was going to rat her out to the recovery community.

Well, she had news for Miss Jenny. She wasn't going to her nice warm apartment until Jolie found herself something to set her straight, and she wasn't cutting out of here until Jolie found herself a place to go too. Even if Betty-fucking-Ford hunted them down.

**

Bubbles leaned on the wall outside the club. She'd slipped out for a breath of air. Man, she was drunk. Being able to drink anyone at Louis and Clark High School under the table had not fully prepared her for serious bar drinking. And the hit of X that Raven gave her was seriously bringing on the whirlies. She did not want to blow chow all over the place like some amateur.

Alison and Raven still looked great, twirling around inside the club. The last time she'd checked herself out in the bathroom mirror, she had definitely lost most of her patina. She just hoped she looked more buzzed than fried.

As she turned to go back into the fray, something caught her eye. Coming around the corner. Could that be? Omigod, it was. She didn't know anyone else who looked like that. Hot. Kind of like that old rocker Nick Cave. Nicholas. Her Facebook friend. Her whirlies spun and then disappeared as she watched him head straight for the door. Headed straight for her.

**

Nicholas realized he'd copped more of a buzz at that last bar than he thought. But the fresh air helped. And the night was young. And so was he. Fuck Honey and all her "We're getting too old for this shit." Maybe she was. It was a fact: women wore their mileage earlier and a lot harsher than men did. Twenty-nine was the end of the line for most of them. But for a guy like him? Hell, it was just the beginning. He looked at the crowd gathered in front of Maggie's. An adorable little girl leaning against the wall looked up and gave him a familiar grin. Oh yeah, it was just the beginning.

***

Daisy was freezing—again. And starting to get wet. At least the van had kept the wet out. Portland could be so cold. They were back under the stairs by the waterfront. They'd arrived at the van the other day, just in time to see it being towed away. With half their shit inside. They'd chased the truck for a minute like a couple of out-of-control Labradors. The driver never even looked at them. So here they were, back under the stairs. She snuggled up to Toby.

Her partner, her best friend, her lover. During the day, it seemed pretty cool: the two of them together scamming, getting high, messing around. Free of all commitments. But out here at night, it didn't seem as if she'd exactly turn anyone green with envy. She leaned over and checked to see whether Toby was fast asleep. She opened up her pack and took out the letter again.

Dear Daisy,

I know things haven't been easy for you and I believe you now about all that stuff you said about Daddy. But he's dead now and he can't hurt you anymore. So now you can come home. I really need my big sister and Mom needs you too. She hardly comes out of her room so she can't make you mad anymore.

Gran comes and shops for us once a week...

Toby stirred and Daisy quickly shoved the letter back in the pack.

***

Jolie looked around at the scene outside Maggie's. She looked at Jenny. "Are you fucking kidding me? It's all kids here."

Jenny sighed. "I don't know what happened. It wasn't like this last time I came."

"How long has it been since you were here?"

"Oh, I dunno. Maybe a year?"

"Oh, for Christ's sake, Jenny. A year is like forever in nightclub time."

"Well, not everybody's too young. Look at him: he looks like a friggin' Wolf Prince or something." Jenny giggled as Nicholas walked by.

"Well now, that's more like it." Jolie smiled for the first time that night.

***

"Well, here's a familiar face." Nicholas hoped the familiar face would identify itself. Names were never his strong suit.

"It's me, ah Bub—you know, from Facebook? We, um, talked about getting together this weekend. I'm here with Alison and, you know, Raven?" Bubbles cursed herself. Every time she was nervous, she said "um" and "you know" every other word. The more she thought about it, the more she said it.

"Well, little Bub, it's getting pretty cold out here. What say we step in for a drink? That is, if you're not waiting for anyone?"

"No, no—a drink sounds great."

Nicholas reached for her hand. She didn't know whether he was going to kiss it or what. He just stood there looking at it for a moment and then he slowly turned it over to bring her wrist to his mouth and licked it. Just as quickly, he pressed it to his own wrist and held it there, all the while looking deeply into her eyes. When he let go, there was a perfect imprint of the entrance stamp on the inside of his wrist. He laughed.

"Now we're twins."

"Twins," agreed Bubbles happily. "Identical or fraternal?"

"I guess only time will tell. Which would you prefer?"

"I think we'd have to be fraternal on account of being male and female."

The doorman gave Nicholas the stink eye as he looked at his wrist. Lucky for Nicholas, the crowd behind them was too backed up for the guy to bother with him tonight. Nicholas grabbed her wrist again and they headed for the bar.

"Whatcha drinking?" he asked.

"Oh, just a PBR and, um, maybe a shot of Jaegermeister ."

"Sounds good. Same for me but with a shot of Jack."

"Ronnie," the bartender smiled up at her, "same again?"

"You bet. Make it two PBRs and a Jack as well." Bubbles loved the idea of having her own recognizable drink.

"Your wish is my command." He disappeared along the row of bottles.

"Ronnie, eh?" teased Nick. "Leading a double life?"

"It's, um, kind of a long story. Like, some people call me Ronnie, some people call me Bub."

And, she thought, if I play my cards right, no one will ever call me fuckin' Bubbles ever again.

***

It looked as if Barkin Jack's feet were taking him to the riverside again. It was typical Portland weather tonight: soft rain just enough to give you a chill, then it would clear up, and then more rain. It had been playing at springtime a bit. The cherry blossoms and daffodils had come out, and they had enjoyed a few really warm days last week but it was still late winter tonight. He'd meant to check in to the shelter but time got away from him and now it was too late. He loved the rows of cherry blossom trees that decorated the west side of the Willamette River downtown. Now there was gracious living. Just that little stroll along the water with tree after tree in vivacious pink beauty. All his, all for free.

He'd been up to Forest Park earlier to look for Smokey or Frank, one of the other guys he knew up there. He never found them, but he'd been surprised to see his friend Harry. It was probably seeing Harry that made him forget all about the time. He'd been both saddened and pleased to see her. Rumor had it that Harry's family had found her, taken her home, and that Harry was living in the lap of luxury up in Lake Oswego. Life on the street was much harder on women, in Jack's opinion. It seemed to prey upon all the things that made women so intriguingly different and from what he'd seen, it devoured most of them.

Harry was one of the few people Jack shared a bit of history with. She'd been a nurse in the war and had been there at the fall of Saigon like Jack had. Both of them just kids, both there only for the bitter end of a war that so many people thought was already over. It hadn't been a good war for Harry, either. All in all, she looked much better. Her short stay with her family had put the bloom back in her cheeks. But she told him that inside she'd just felt too stifled. Too much like a combination circus freak / charity case.

She said her people felt sorry for her for all the wrong reasons. She was opting for a break from her break. Jack could see how that might happen. He'd always liked Harry. Neither of them thought it odd that they could understand things about each other that those who had shared their lives with them could not. Not that they actually spoke of it. It was just something that occurred to them individually. Something they understood.

Now, Jack headed for the spot under the stairs where he sometimes sheltered for an evening. Tonight, however, two young girls were sleeping there. He left before he frightened them.

***

Jolie'd been about to give up on the beautiful wolfish guy, when all of a sudden he sauntered up to her. Up until now, he'd had that little Goth kid glued to his side. She was outside having a smoke (she couldn't believe they'd changed the smoking law a month before she'd arrived) when she felt him move in close.

"Any way I can buy or rent a smoke?" He smiled down at her.

Damn, he was tall. "Now how would one go about renting a smoke, I wonder?" Jolie hid her curiosity by focusing completely on the contents of her bag while she looked for her cigarettes. It never paid to let them see your interest.

"Well, perhaps indentured servitude would work better. You give me a cigarette, and I'm yours for whatever time you think might be fair trade."

"That could be interesting." She started to give him the smoke and then held it up for a moment. "Of course, how do you know I won't drive an unfair bargain, hmmm? I could put an awfully high price on my cigarettes."

He reached out and took the cigarette. "I guess I'll just have to trust you. And after all, you being a stranger in this town, a local boy might be just what you need right about now."

"How did you know I'm not from around here?"

"Oh, I know all sorts of things. I can be very useful."

"Well, maybe you can, local boy." Jolie gave him her best sly smile. "You got a name?"

***

They were all crammed into the stall in the ladies' room. Gay bars usually didn't spend much time fixing up their ladies' rooms. This one was a tiny one-holer with peeling gold flocked wallpaper covered in graffiti and band stickers. Raven had literally chased out the previous occupant. Bubbles loved this. She and Alison were still bursting into laughter every time one of them said "Boo!"; that was what Raven had shouted to the stall hog as she'd pulled her out of the tiny space, skirt still hiked up around her waist.

They were now fully amped and Bubbles was trying to get their advice between hysterics. "What should I do?" she kept asking them. He'd invited her back to his place, and she really wanted to go. She felt like she should trust her instinct. She might never get this shot at him again. She could see the other girls stalking him already.

"Well, do you want to go?" Alison asked.

"Yeah, I think so."

"Well, why not?" said Raven. "You're not like a virgin or anything." She said the word like most people say "warthog" or "cockroach."

"Um, of course not," she replied hurriedly. "A virgin. Right. Ha-ha."

"You know what I think?" said Alison.

"What?"

"Boo!"

And they all burst into hysterics once again.

***

Goddamn! Nicholas grinned. The only improvement on his evening would have been if that bitch Honey had been there to see him in action. This Jolie was something else: legs up to here—and smart, too. That little Goth girl he'd started out with was cute as hell (he hoped she wasn't still waiting for him) and now he was taking Jolie uptown to see a man about a little Mexican brown. Damn, who knew where the night would end?

***

Jolie leaned back in her seat. Could it be? Was her luck actually becoming something approaching fortuitous? Finally, a sign of some of that dope the Northwest was supposed to be full of. Not only that, but now she had a really fine-looking courier, too. She looked out the window of the MAX train as they zipped through the sparkling city. Maybe now she could look at it with something like hope.

***

It was now or never. Alison and Raven had found the party they'd gone in search of, so it was either stay and go home with Nicholas or leave with the girls. She looked over at Raven, who was flirting it up with a couple of really cute boys. What would it take for her to have that kind of confidence? Maybe getting rid of her virginity would be a good start. Everybody had been talking about "doing it" for the past five years up in Longview but that's all it was—talk. She was tired of hearing about it secondhand. It made her feel clueless and immature.

Well, it may not be a cure for everything, but it was certainly a place to start. She pulled herself upright and went to go tell the girls to go on without her. She was going to get a clue.

***

Jolie looked around the twenty-four-hour McDonald's with appreciation as she waited for Nicholas to finish his shot. Man o' man, did she feel great. It always surprised her when it really turned out to be as good as she'd anticipated.

A happy place, she thought with amusement. Such a happy place. She had that warm floating feeling that seemed to emanate in her gut, and then go coursing through her veins. My kind of place! She almost laughed out loud.

She could feel her hand swelling up where she'd missed part of her shot. It throbbed dully. But fortunately it was met with the painkiller aspect of the drug almost immediately. She held it out and examined it as if it were an object that was part of something else. The back of her hand had puffed up and looked a little bit like a Mickey Mouse glove, rounded and comical.

She reached for her pack to see whether she had anything to cover it up with. She was pretty sure she had packed some gloves in there somewhere. Where did it get to now? She looked around her, and then dove under the bench and searched under the table. Damn. She'd left her pack at the club. How stupid could she be? She looked around desperately for the time. She had to get back to the club before they shut their doors. A thin film of sweat seemed to instantly cover her face. Where was Nicholas, goddamn it?

***

It was all a terrible mistake. She should have known better; she was almost sixteen years old. What was she thinking? She sat on the stoop of a shop next to the club. She'd been dumped, ditched. Now it was going on 2:30 and she was all alone in downtown Portland. He wasn't coming back. All that shit he'd said was just that: shit. Now she had no way back to Longview, even if she could have gone home. Man. She could see her stepdad screaming at her: first for coming home at 4:00 a.m., and then for the inevitable sassing back when he'd said one stupid thing too many, and she couldn't take it.

She let herself chew on the fingernail she'd been eying all night. What was the point of keeping them nice now? She looked up and down the block. Everything was shut up tight. She pulled out her cigarettes and counted them. Six left. Fuck it! She lit one anyway. At this rate, if she smoked one every half hour, they'd be gone before morning. She got up and walked to the corner. If only there was a cheap hotel or boarding house like in the olden days she could stay there, but where was she going to find a place in Old Town for less than fifty bucks unless it was the Salvation Army? And even they were closed. Why hadn't she just gone with Raven and Alison? Now they were partying their asses off, and she was all alone on a street corner.

And if things weren't bad enough, who the hell were those guys coming up the street? They were loud and they sounded pissed off. She hoped if she drew herself into the doorway she might escape notice.

***

Figures they didn't get a cab 'til they were almost there, but Jolie couldn't waste any time. It was probably too late as it was, but she had to try. She remembered slinging the pack up on the back of the booth. She'd transferred so much crap into her purse that she'd mistaken the familiar heaviness for that of the pack. She hadn't wanted to look like a snail-woman carrying her home on her back.

That's what trying to look slick'll get ya every time, she chided herself. Now dream date was turning into a nightmare and blowing her high at the same time. There, she could see the club come into view. "Driver, just pull up over there." She pointed to the approaching corner.

The driver looked back at her with some concern. "You sure about that, lady?"

Jolie gave a snort of impatience. "Of course I'm sure. Why..." Her words drifted off as her eyes took in the scene. A couple of guys were shouting and pushing a young girl back and forth. She kinda looked like that little Goth kid who'd been stuck to Nicholas half the night at the club.

"Oh fuck—Bub!" Nicholas breathed out a whimper.

Jolie looked at him sharply. "Isn't that your friend from the club?" she demanded.

"Yeah, that's Bub...or Ronnie."

"Well, for Chrissake, we better go get her before she gets fuckin' killed." She looked at the driver. "Pull over!" she shouted.

"Now lady, I don't want any trouble."

Jolie looked back and forth at the two men incredulously. "What the fuck is wrong with you? She's a little girl." She leapt from the cab.

"Hey, you ASSHOLES!" she screamed. "Leave her the fuck alone."

The two men looked up sharply. "Who the fuck are you, bitch—her big sister?"

Nicholas stumbled from the cab. "Hey, hey, we don't want any trouble, man," he said in his best hippie-diplomat tones. When he looked at the two girls, they did look a lot like sisters with their shiny bangs and big doe eyes. Only Jolie looked bigger and somehow sturdier than her younger counterpart.

"I'm the bitch who just called the cops on you assholes," yelled Jolie. A strange detached part of her wondered just exactly why the fuck she was defending this stupid kid.

"Well, come and get her. Bitch." This came from the bigger of the two, your basic modern-day troll, complete with the obligatory black-knitted watch cap all Portland males seemed to come equipped with. The cab had long since screeched away, giving lie to the illusion of any support.

"Yeah, come and get her," Troll Number Two shouted and grabbed the top of Bubbles's T-shirt and ripped down sharply, exposing her breasts.

"Hey man, there's no need to—" Nicholas began as Troll Number One slammed a fist into his diplomatic upper lip.

"You son of a bitch." Jolie looked about desperately for a weapon. There was a newspaper kiosk—too heavy. A fire hydrant—immobile. A sapling someone had planted recently as part of the continuing greening of Portland's Old Town district. Jolie wrenched the sapling from its freshly dug plot and rounded on the two trolls, giving Bubbles the chance to break free and knee Troll Number Two in the nuts.

"Run!" Jolie knocked the astounded first troll to the ground. She dropped the unfortunate little tree, and the two girls took heel after they grabbed a gawping Nicholas by the collar.

"Run!" echoed Bubbles. As the three hit the corner of Broadway, a familiar cab arrived at the light simultaneously; Jolie wrenched the door open. "Thanks a lot for all your support, you fucker."

"Hey, I get paid to drive, not rescue young maidens," the driver sneered. "It's not much of a life but it's mine and I like it."

"Oh shut up and drive." Jolie sank back into the seat. "Tell the driver where we're going, honey." She looked at Nicholas. "I never can remember the address."

***

A scary day for Barkin' Jack. One of those days where everything just seemed wrong from the moment he opened his eyes. Actually, from the moment his eyes flew open, as that was how it began. He hadn't noticed that last night's destination had turned out to be no more than ten feet from the construction of a new MAX line. So the day began with a bang. Loud noises and his PTSD just didn't mix. So when the heavy machinery began to growl and something humongous hit the ground, so did Barkin' Jack—hit the ground and began to growl.

It must have taken him a full five minutes to grasp the reality of the situation and by then his nerves were shot. His feet were already powering him up Burnside and wouldn't even stop until he was well into the park. Finally, he stopped, hurled himself under a bush, and attempted to catch his breath. He was close to the spot where he'd run into Harry the other day. Was that yesterday? He couldn't quite recall exactly where they met, but it was around here. Stupid, he thought, as if she'd just stay rooted to the spot.

Time passed as thoughts of Harry floated by. When his heart hit a normal rhythm, he stood up and pressed on. As many times as he'd wandered round the park, he really had very little idea of where everything began and ended. It was huge. Frank had told him it was the largest forested area in an urban setting in the entire US. He could believe it. His stomach growled.

Once again, exhaustion led him to the base of a large tree and the park began to claim him. The wind rushed through the trees and the birds made themselves known to one another. Many kinds of messages were broadcast throughout the network of branches above. Mothers screeched away potential trespassers, and families and lovers called to each other. But there seemed to be more to it as it continued. It started with the crows. Their calls weren't like the melodious song of their avian cousins. Crows cawed. It could be a raucous cry or a sounding of alarm. A voice built to be heard at once.

As he listened to each caw, he made out more than a simple syllable. It was a command or a condemnation. Flaw, flaw, it seemed to say. Sick, sick, another bird agreed. Dead, dead, came the response from yet another species. Lost, lost, lost.

***

Toby stirred first. Waking up on concrete was nothing like waking up in a bed. No matter how she tried to pretend it was just like camping, it wasn't. She woke up sore in places she didn't know she had. She remembered the first night she'd been out on her own—wrapped in a giveaway blanket, she'd just stared at the pavement inches from her nose and shivered, partly from cold, partly from fear. She looked over at Daisy; at least she provided some padding. That girl lived to eat. Whether she ate to live remained to be seen. Together they had a better chance of fighting off those who would fuck with them. Of course, if someone really wanted to fuck with them, they were pretty much fucked. Almost as if she could read Toby's mind, Daisy shivered and pulled the blanket over her head.

Toby recalled a bit of gossip they'd picked up yesterday at the clinic. There were these guys going around in a van, picking up homeless girls and streetwalkers: pulling them in, raping and kidnapping them, holding them sometimes for as long as three days. They'd gotten the daughter of an older lady they knew from group. The woman cried as she told them to watch out. Her daughter just lay in bed now, curled into a ball, and wouldn't speak a word to anyone. Not even her mom. She'd been that way for a week now. Some of the other women said that another girl—a stripper—had been taken too. Neither one had gone to the cops on account of the fact that they both had a record for drugs or prostitution. They didn't want to deal with any further humiliation. Toby understood that. Considering what had happened to her the first time she'd been raped, it was almost like having it happen again. Just without the bruises. At least the ones you could see.

***

Nicholas woke in the night to every young man's dream: a pretty girl on either side. He slid up smoothly on the pillow and enjoyed this momentary peace. They sure were lovely. So alike in a big sister-little sister way. Offset just a bit: one with red hair and black streaks, one with black hair and red streaks. They looked so peaceful in their sleep. No one would imagine what insanity they were capable of. He rubbed his jaw, still sore from last night. He supposed this meant he had roommates now. Well, it wasn't as if he hadn't been considering that necessity anyway. They sure were a lot easier on the eye than any of the other candidates he'd had in mind. Only thing was, he was pretty sure they didn't have ten cents between 'em. Ah well, one thing at a time. He dove back under the covers.

***

Adrenaline: the drug you never asked for. It could turn you into super woman, lifting automobiles from the bodies of small children, but mostly it just fucked with you, made you think too much, made your hands shake and your stomach roil. Bubbles was chock-full now.

Once again it seemed as if she had made another life-changing decision in the way she made all her life-changing decisions: By inactivity. By doing nothing. All your life, she thought, they tell you about the hard decisions you'll be faced with. The truth was, life never really had the courtesy to stop and ask her how she might feel about things. Life never stopped long enough to ask her yes-or-no questions. She wondered whether this was unique to her. Probably not.

Well, now it looked as if she had left home. Not by leaving a note or packing her stuff up or doing any of the things she had imagined she might do if it came down to it. Just by not coming home, or calling, or communicating in any way.

She supposed she could remedy the situation if she did something right away. Made up a story, or just showed up and took whatever bullshit her stepdad might dream up this time. But that would mean walking out on what looked like a real adventure. If she just kept cool, kept her mouth shut and her eyes open, she might finally have a shot at all the things she'd always wondered about. Maybe that was the ticket—doing nothing. Maybe that's what allowed life the void space it needed to get busy with the ebb and flow of experience. Like now, for instance: Nicholas's hand ran up her leg, his fingers slipped underneath her panties. Maybe it wasn't the most erotic scenario she could imagine, but what the hell—if she just did nothing, it might just get the job done.

***

Jolie lay in the maelstrom of tangled sheets and pretended sleep. She listened to the familiar tussle next to her. It was hard not to laugh. Poor kid. Jolie supposed she should be jealous; after all, the guy had been in her sights last night and he was supposed to stay there, not go sniffing after little girls. But all she felt was relief. She was just too tired. From what she remembered of the end of the evening, the kid was in the same spot Jolie was. She was willing to bet they'd found a place to stay, if not forever, at least long enough to get something together. She'd seen the hungry look in Nicolas's eye, and she could bet there was a nice soft spot in his ego for a pair of damsels in distress, as long as he didn't really have to put himself out in any way.

She figured right around the time he finished up with—what was her name? Bubbie?—well, as soon as he finished up, Jolie could coax him out of the house to get some more of that stuff he got for her last night. Once that was taken care of, she could work out the rest of it. From the way it sounded, it wouldn't be that long.

***

Bubbles woke to a ray of sunlight stabbing her in the eye a few hours later. Her head pounded, her stomach roiled, and she felt really sore down there.

OMG. She'd done it. It. But was that really it? Because if it was, she now felt even more clueless than she had before. She struggled for more memories of the experience. Where was the feeling of womanhood, the earth moving, the secret knowledge she'd been assured would come with this monumental step? All that hype and it was just an incredible disappointment. Another supposed milestone that added up to a big fat zero. She rolled over and started to pull the covers over her head when she realized where she was. She'd been wrong. Something had happened— she'd started an adventure. She was now here in what could very well be her first apartment. In Portland. She could hear Jolie up and moving around. She slipped out of the bed and padded out to the kitchen.

She hopped up on the counter and watched as Jolie moved efficiently around the tiny kitchen and pulled coffee cups off the shelf as if she'd been living there all her life. Jolie poured out two cups of her cowboy coffee; she set one in front of Bubbles and then she took a big sip out of the other, and grinned at her.

"So kiddo, what do you think we ought to do about Mr. Nicholas?"

Interesting, Bubbles thought. Up until now, she'd really been thinking more along the lines of what he was going to do with them. He was pretty cute, but Bubbles could see where that kind of thinking could be a real problem now. Still, she wasn't at all sure that was where Jolie was going.

"I dunno. Do you want, you know, um, Nicholas? I mean..."

Jolie laughed but it was a nice laugh, which ended her stammering attempt at a question. "Nah. How about you, kid? You got it bad?"

Bubbles took a minute to respect the question. Nicholas had, after all, been the object of her desire for at least two weeks now and Jolie had seemed pretty interested herself last night at the club. But if they really were going to live here, especially now that she'd gotten a look at what Nicholas's attention span was like, well, it just didn't seem like a good idea at all.

"Nah," said Bubbles.

Jolie laughed again and held up her hand. Bubbles gave it a playful slap.

"So now what are we going to do? We're probably going to have to pay rent, huh?" Bubbles said.

"Well, first I'm going to get well," said Jolie. "Then we'll figure out the job situation."

***

Daisy sat cross-legged on the corner of 4th and Davis. She'd stuffed a sweater and a couple of T-shirts into the cover of her sleeping bag and stuffed that under the sweater and baggy Pendleton shirt she was wearing. Toby had neatly lettered a cardboard sign: PREGNANT—ANYTHING HELPS with a plastic dog dish underneath to hold offerings.

"Maybe you should take the dollar out," said Toby. "We look too rich."

"No." Daisy shook her head. "We gotta look like somebody cared. Nobody likes to be the first one."

Toby frowned. "Okay. I just think we look more pathetic with nothing."

"We'll try it this way for a while and if nothing happens, we'll take it out." Daisy pawed through her pack for her hand mirror. She wanted to make sure she looked just right.

"What if it were true?"

"Huh?" Daisy looked up from her make-up bag.

"What if we were really gonna have a baby?" Toby had a funny, almost longing look in her eye.

"Well...um," Daisy said carefully. She realized she shouldn't come out with the flippant remark that had sprung to her lips. "It'd be pretty hard, what with being on the street and all."

"Yeah," Toby murmured and then she seemed to snap out of it. "But she'd sure be a trippy baby, huh?"

"Oh yeah." Daisy nodded, relieved. "She'd be pretty cool."

Toby seemed not to hear her. She squinted at something over Daisy's shoulder. "Hey, isn't that Max coming up the block?"

Daisy looked over. Sure enough, it was Max and some other guy.

***

Max hated copping. Hated the running around the worst parts of town, hated waiting and waiting for some lackey to deliver the goods—usually some asshole you wouldn't normally piss on if they were on fire. Back home, Eleni took care of this end, but up here she didn't know her way around. The last two times she tried going on her own, it ended with her calling him from the Ross Island Bridge, half-hysterical, going the wrong way, and unable to find a turnout spot. This was hard to take for a girl who knew her way blindfolded around the maze that was Los Angeles.

So now Max, his nerves on edge, wandered through the huge and ornate arch on Burnside that was the entrance to Chinatown. It was a beautiful thing—a little kitsch, but it helped give what was an otherwise down-and-out neighborhood some style. The problem was that, although there was the gateway all painted red, green, and gold along with the cheerful red and gold streetlights within, there really wasn't anything in Chinatown but a few lousy restaurants. Even the famous Hung Far Low had closed down. Neighborhood associations had kept the sign going and stuck a Thai restaurant under it but now it was just a sign for something that didn't exist anymore, like Chinatown itself.

Max's paranoia grew. There'd been a big wolfie looking dude following him ever since he'd entered the gate. He almost considered passing the two girls up but it looked as if he'd been spotted already.

***

Nicholas was more confused than he'd been for a while. What the hell had he gotten himself into? It had been a little over a week since the girls transformed his bare little apartment into something resembling a chorus girl's dressing room. It was astonishing the amount of stuff Jolie had in that pack she'd left at the club that night (which, of course, he'd been sent to fetch the next day), let alone the suitcase that she'd had stashed at her friend's house.

He seemed to change his mind about how he felt on a daily, sometimes hourly, basis. Right now was definitely the down side of things. How had it fallen to him to cop Jolie's drugs for her? She was going to have to kick or find her own dealer. At least little Bub didn't have a drug problem.

He'd been on the way to the pay phone to call Carlos back when he spotted Toby. This could save him a trip down to Felony Flats on the MAX if he played his cards right. He'd noticed the skinny blond dude make a beeline for her. Somehow he looked familiar. Wasn't he...?

***

"Hey dude, didn't you used to be in American Lesion?" The Wolf-man spoke.

Max let out of breath of relief. At least he wasn't being stalked by some kind of new hipster-cop. He turned around and took his first real look at the guy. Man, he was tall.

"Yeah, that was years ago," he said to fill time while he checked the guy out further—he did have something familiar about him.

"Didn't you open for us in...?"

***

Toby shook her head. Just look at those two going on like some mutual admiration society, Toby thought as she watched the two of them. Portland really was a small town. As she moved toward them, she cleared her throat loudly to remind them of their original intent. "Bla-hem..."

***

Bubbles watched, both fascinated and devastated, as Jolie wound her way sinuously around Nicholas's hat stand. How the hell did she do that? She was both Eve and the snake. She twirled round the stand and rolled onto the floor; her legs scissored in rhythm to the tune bleating from the tiny speakers attached to the MP3 playlist she could only figure was "stripper oldies but goodies." Get your freak on, get your freak on…

Every time she tried to follow Jolie's lead, it came out awkward, silly, or just kind of gross.

***

Jolie looked at her with pity and frustration. The kid was cute as a button, but damn, she had no moves. Jolie wondered whether she'd ever been as young as Bub. What an awkward and bizarre name that was. It was like—not enough somehow. Just like her dancing. She switched off the MP3 player.

"Okay, why don't we take a little break now. I'm starting to feel a little sick anyway."

Bubbles tried to look sympathetic, but she was really worried. Nicholas had gotten them an audition at Hells Belles, a strip club where his last band had played fairly often. The owner had a string of gentleman's clubs, as well as regular nightclub venues. Nowadays it was trendy for bands to play both.

Of course, Jolie always seemed perfectly comfortable in her body. Bubbles couldn't stand the idea of people looking at her scrawny white body. Maybe if she'd been born with Jolie's body, it'd be easier. When she mentioned this the other day, both Jolie and Nicholas had laughed and said, "But you were, silly girl."

Bubbles didn't see it, but she couldn't come up with any other way to make enough money for rent either.

Jolie leafed through an old Rolling Stone. "Check out this picture of Lady Gaga." She held the magazine out for Bubbles to see. It showed Lady G sitting at the keyboard, wearing an outfit made entirely of soap bubbles. "She's a total poser, but that bubble outfit is great."

"Big deal," said Bubbles. "I was doing that in grade school."

"You what?" said Jolie. "No way."

"Wanna bet?" Bubbles headed for the kitchen. "Bet me."

"But I don't even think those were real bubbles…you're serious?" Jolie narrowed her eyes. The kid was serious.

Bubbles flipped on the tap and filled the washtub with dish soap and warm water. She looked around the kitchen and then headed for the bath. She brought out a double-sided hand mirror. "You think he'll miss this?" she asked.

"Nah," said Jolie.

Bubbles wrapped it up in a towel and smashed the mirrors out. She was left with a perfect hoop. "I need some smaller ones too."

Jolie got to work trying to make loops with twist-ties, and then she found a mini-magnifying glass and managed to get the lens out. After a couple of trial and errors, Bubbles went to work: giant bubbles, bubbles within bubbles, tiny bubbles. Jolie watched; a look of wonder glowed under her normally sardonic countenance. Encouraged, Bubbles stripped down to her panties and began to cover herself carefully in the soapy orbs, placing each one carefully in a circular pattern around her body.

"Damn, you really did it!" whooped Jolie. "That is so awesome."

Bubbles felt a calm slip over her she hadn't felt since she walked out the door of her Longview home. Entranced in the Zen of her bubbles, she didn't even hear Nicholas come in.

"Wow," he breathed as he stared at her in astonishment. "How cool is that?"

Bubbles's face flamed up. "Well, um, it's just, um, like you know," she stammered. Tiny pops zinged all over her body as her suit began to disappear.

"It's just your new act is what it is," purred Jolie. "A girl who can do that, she really doesn't have to worry about her dancing at all."

"No shit," said Nicholas appreciatively.

"We'll call you Bubbles," Jolie announced, looking proud of herself. "It's perfect."

Bubbles made a choking sound and ran from the room. Jolie and Nicholas stared as they heard the bedroom door slam.

"Hmm," said Nicholas.

***

Eleni laughed as Max filled her in on the details of his first rehearsal session with Nicholas and Bobby on the drive to the clinic. She was happy to see him looking more upbeat. She was feeling a lot better herself now they finally managed to get signed onto the methadone program here. They really put you through the hoops in Portland. No other city she'd ever been to had such an elaborate and demanding program. Back in LA, you saw a counselor maybe once a month, talked to them for fifteen minutes tops, and got your UA on a monthly basis. Here, you had to go to hour-long therapy groups every week and see a counselor twice a month for forty-five minutes each session. At least for the first few months.

Everyone working here seemed very earnest and quite mad. She and Max had only signed on two weeks ago and they had already changed Max's counselor twice. The groups varied in theme. There were "process" groups, where people shared about the difficulties of staying clean. There were groups for people who were addicted to Benzos; groups for men and groups for women. There were groups for single moms. There was a meditation group and an "art" group. Art group was supposed to include art therapy in the form of painting, making collages, and water coloring. To Max and Eleni, it seemed like summer camp for the chemically challenged.

If Max got this new job at the hardware store, he'd only have weekends off and she'd have to come here by herself. Of course, Max getting a job would be a good thing. She'd never realized how lost he was without one. He'd failed the drug test for the Beaverton gig last month. That had sent him spinning into a depression like she'd never seen. She was learning a lot about how they reacted to change these days.

She wasn't too happy with what was happening to her. She'd really thought her days of lying in a fetal position on the bed would be over when they moved here. But she felt tired all the time. Watching people in the group nodding out just made her crave dope even more. Eleni watched as a fellow artiste slumped lower in her chair and slowly, the woman's eyes and head began to droop, like a time-lapse film of a dying flower.

Eleni pulled her eyes away. Dammit, she wasn't going to give in. She wasn't going back to that infantile state again. She'd noticed a new restaurant that had opened just a block away. Some kind of vegan place. Miso Horny. She and Max had cracked up when they saw the sign. She'd also seen a help-wanted notice, too. Never having waitressed, she'd dismissed the idea at the time but the more she thought about it, the more appealing it seemed. The place wasn't that big; how hard could it be?

***

Jolie stood at the mirror and put on the mask. The perfect, sexy, hard face she'd learned to show the world. It took a lot more foundation and concealer these days—but in an odd way, some days it seemed as if her face would morph into the mask on its own with no cosmetic effort at all.

It probably started with Johnnie. God, how corny it had all been: small-town boy falls for exotic dancer—only to be destroyed. But no, that wasn't right, and it wasn't fair either. Johnnie had been a wonderful kid and really, she'd been a kid, too. Neither one of them had a clue as to what the real world was like. For all her pretense, she'd just been a little girl in a G-string and feathers. Kinda like Bubbles.

She remembered the anticipation and excitement she felt—meeting up with Johnnie after the clubs closed every night. Strippers and musicians kept the same working hours; it was a comfortable combination. And then one night, she came home and he was lying on the bed, face blue, unwakeable. She didn't know what he'd taken or whether he was going to make it. But he wasn't dead, not yet. She called 911—they took forty-five minutes to come. She learned that night never to say it was an overdose. They didn't care about drug addicts. She'd finally run downstairs and grabbed a meter maid who was tagging cars on the street. Begged her to please make someone come and save him; the woman had called in on her radio, but it was too late.

When they finally did come, the EMT bastard told her it was a DOA and they were going to seal up the room. Locked her out and kicked her out on the street. She'd cried a lot, but after that, she locked her face and her tears up, and she'd made damn sure no one was ever going to get in ever again. She wondered whether Bubbles would end up with a mask of her own someday. She hoped not. Sighing, she went to go check on the kid's progress and wondered whether she was doing her any favors.

***

Bubbles yawned as she came out of the bedroom dressed and ready for their audition.

"You have got to be kidding me." Jolie took one look, rolled her eyes, and sighed.

"What?" Bubbles was truly tired of Jolie rolling her eyes at her all the time.

"You look like a fuckin' bag lady. Can I just remind you that this is a strip club we're auditioning for?"

"Well, what the hell does it matter what I'm wearing if I'm just gonna take it off anyway, huh?"

"She's got a point there." Nicholas laughed from his perch on the couch arm.

"She has no fucking point and who the hell asked you anyway?" Jolie snapped.

"Okay, okay, geez. I'm staying out of it. I gotta practice anyway." Nicholas slunk out of the room.

Bubbles looked as if she was about to burst. Frustration seemed to radiate off her body. Jolie took a deep breath and tried again.

"Honey, look, you're going to get us turned away before we even get a chance, looking like that. Okay? Now we've practiced this stuff, and I think we've got a pretty good shot at getting this gig, which we need. Right? Do you have your little kit together? Soap, hoops, all that stuff?"

Bubbles held up a little black bag.

"Okay, great. Now lemme just find you something here." Jolie waved her back in the bedroom and opened up her suitcase to pull out bras, camisoles, T-shirts.

"Your bras aren't gonna fit me, you know."

"Yeah, you're probably right." Jolie stepped back and looked at her again. "I got it." She grabbed a white T-shirt out of another pack and ran into the bathroom. Bubbles threw herself down on the mattress.

"Don't get too comfortable. We leave in five minutes." Jolie came back with a box of Ninja Turtle Band-Aids. "Come here."

"What are you gonna do, tie me up?" Bubbles eyed her nervously.

Jolie ignored her. "Take that thing off," she said.

Bubbles reluctantly removed her oversized men's shirt. Jolie unwrapped four Band-Aids, stuck an X over each of Bubbles's nipples and held out the tight white T-shirt. "Now put that on."

Bubbles shook her head, but she put the shirt on. Jolie looked her up and down and gave a quick nod.

"You bring the CD?" Jolie asked. Bubbles held up the little black bag again.

"Okay, let's rock." Jolie held the door open. Bubbles followed. What else could she do?

***

Nicholas heard the door slam and breathed a sigh of relief. Now he could practice in peace. He hadn't been playing regularly or practicing much before he hooked up with Max and Bobby. What a spot of luck that was, running into Max that day. And Bobby had played with a lot of the bigger bands around Portland. They were older than him, of course, but Nicholas was used to being the youngest one in the band—he liked it that way. But he didn't want to look like an amateur. He didn't like practicing with the girls around for the same reason. He wanted to look perfect when he had an audience. Besides, someone had to start pulling in some bucks around here. He had a career to take care of.

***

A pretty good day for Barkin' Jack today. He'd come down from the mountain and had a terrific breakfast at Sisters of the Road with Frank this morning. He was indebted to Frank now. It had been Frank who found him mewling under a tree in Forest Park and who'd taken him to his secret hideout there. Jack didn't remember much of the first week he'd spent there but he'd been cared for by Frank, Smokey, and a few others he'd never met before. And now today, Frank had actually left the park, something he rarely did, and they'd gone for a meal together. What had touched Jack most of all had been the fact that neither Frank nor his friend Smokey had asked Jack to explain himself. They just understood. In fact, the only thing Frank had said to him today was that he looked so skinny he could smell the shit through his ribs, and that they were going out for a real meal.

Now he was back at the riverside by the condos, after stopping to greet passengers at the bus station. Jack didn't know why he felt it necessary to greet people. He didn't know why he did half the things he did. That's what made people like Frank and Harry so precious.

Jack looked out at the Willamette. Like most newcomers to the city, he'd originally pronounced it Willa-mette like moist towelette. But folks up here called it the Wil-lam-met like God-dam-mit. He followed the river in his mind to the place where it met the Columbia and made a T at the top to span Portland and divide it from Washington. A vague memory surfaced of a fishing boat and a man looking very much like himself, only younger, sitting next to him and baiting a hook. His dad? Jack shook himself loose from the fantasy. He tried to catch his reflection in the water, but it was full of ripples—the wake caused by duck feet and breezes. He walked a little farther to the landing, where a small fleet of ducks lounged about: some sleeping, some just sitting there. He reached into his pocket for a roll he'd saved from breakfast and set to work tearing it in little bits and tossing them into the water. Instantly the waterfront filled with ducks coming from God only knew where. Some left the water and came to beg right at his feet. The roll was running out as still more ducks came. Jack tried to throw the remaining pieces far out into the water to urge them back out. He'd spotted a small mother duck trying to catch a piece and being foiled over and over by her bolder, more voracious fellows. He found himself trying to aim the very last couple of morsels to her but every time she lost out to another sleeker, faster duck. He cursed them and her too. Dammit! It's for YOU. Go git it! Hey! Not you. YOU—come on, git it! Jack searched his pockets for crumbs or something else to offer but he had nothing left. The roll was gone. He looked down to see the flock slowly move back out to the water while the little mother duck just floated in place, patiently waiting for nothing.

***

On the other side of the Broadway Bridge, farther along the waterfront, Daisy sat cross-legged with a pile of lighters spread out on her jacket. Recently, an old Israeli vet had showed her how to fix disposable lighters in all sorts of ways: either taking the tops off and turning them further up to get the last bit of use out of them or switching the tops out on different kinds and getting one good one out of two broken ones. She and Toby had taken a mess of them to Crack Alley a couple of nights ago and sold them for two or three bucks apiece to desperate smokers. They'd ended up making enough to stay smoked out themselves and have McBreakfast the next morning. Of course, there wouldn't be any more action until well after midnight but it gave her something to do while she waited for and fumed about Toby. Toby, who had promised to come back after she went to cop. Toby, who she'd waited for until it was so late she had to sleep outside by herself. Toby, who could be lying in a ditch somewhere or laughing her ass off with another girl. Part of her was terrified that something had happened to her and part of her felt that something better have happened to her or else.

***

Eleni shivered as she smoked in the alley behind Miso Horny. Her stomach churned. She'd gotten the call last night. She was hired. They'd told her if she liked, she could come by and pick up a menu tonight to familiarize herself for the next day. When she asked Max whether he thought it was a good idea, he'd told her yeah, on account of she had to memorize it. Man, the things she didn't know.

She had stayed up until dawn, trying to keep the various dishes in her head. They certainly had a lot of them. She'd also been surprised to find out that there were meat dishes on the menu. The owner told her he had originally wanted a vegan restaurant, but he'd found the neighborhood just wasn't enlightened enough to go completely meat-free. She cupped her cigarette in her hand and hoped he wouldn't find out how truly unenlightened she was. She'd always avoided waiting tables before, partly because she could be pretty clumsy (especially when she was nervous) and partly because she was so bad at math. Figuring out 8.25% sales tax on the hoof was way beyond her scope. Here in Oregon, however, they didn't have sales tax, and the restaurant was so small she figured she wouldn't have to balance huge trays or anything.

She'd given up on the job initially because they didn't call back in two days, which she'd been assured was their hiring deadline. She found out from the other girl that they had, in fact, hired someone else but that the girl didn't call or show up her second day on the job. Oh well—her loss, my gain. She ran today's specials over in her head, along with her rap.

"Why, yes, ma'am, the soup du jour is Miso Horny's own miso spinach. Yes, sir, we serve only Oregon Green Farms 'Green meat' in our burgers."

Ugh—green meat? When she'd asked about that particular choice of words, she was assured Green Farms green meat had an excellent reputation and was a locally owned business. So it was wise to let the customers know they were a community sustainable outfit. Well, okay, she figured it was just part of the greater learning process. Man, the things she didn't know. She stomped out the cigarette, threw it in the dumpster and headed back inside

***

Bubbles was on her second double Greyhound and feeling no pain. They were celebrating. They'd both gotten the job. Jolie was teaching her all about the various cocktails here at Kelly's Olympian. Bubbles didn't have a lot of bar drinking experience. At least her sister's ID was working like a charm. No one had questioned it. She'd been scared at first, because if anyone took a good look at her, they'd see she had blue eyes, not brown like it said on the ID. But no one did. They just squinted at her and let her pass every time. She was going to have to get a new one soon. A real one or at least one with her picture. She'd almost told Jolie her real age the other day but in the end, she decided against it. Her skin still felt kind of sticky from the soap bubbles but her face had finally stopped flaming.

Looking back, it was kind of a kick how well they had done. First, Jolie'd done a little autoerotic number back-to-back with Bubbles, facing away from the stage to the tune of "Sisters Are Doin' It for Themselves." Then it was Bubbles's turn. She'd gotten some odd looks as she filled her little soap bowl up in the bathroom and carefully placed a few plastic bubbles in with them for sticking onto her most private parts.

She'd gathered strength from one of her favorite songs, "Peek a Boo," and launched herself out on the stage. She almost faltered and fled as the total silence from out front enveloped her and the goose bumps rose on her skin, but the familiar rhythm of dipping the hoop in the soapy water and coaxing out the bubbles sustained her as she placed the perfectly round little prisms up and down her body. She twirled and sent trails of bubbles out into the audience; little oohs and ahhs and a couple of unhs floated back at her. The next thing she knew, the song was over and the club was applauding. Some of the girls even came up and introduced themselves, and the owner showed them up to his office and gave them their schedule. Jolie'd given her a hug and told her what a great job she'd done. She'd almost blushed harder at that than she did on stage.

She remembered when Nicholas had first told them about the gig. She'd been full of questions for Jolie. Had she ever done it before? What was it like? Did she like it? Jolie had just rolled her eyes and told her it'd be okay as long as it wasn't too sleazy. Now with Jolie all loose and friendly, she asked her what she thought of Hells Belles. Did she think this was one of the sleazy ones? Jolie laughed and told her if it been one of the really sleazy places, she wouldn't have to ask. Then she said it wasn't the classiest place on earth but it was tame compared to a lot of the joints she'd seen in New York or even San Francisco.

"Well, like how?" Bubbles persisted.

"Like, you can keep your G-string on if you want. You decide how far you want to take it. And you don't have to do any special tricks with your body." Jolie'd said this last with a shudder in her voice.

"Like what?" Bubbles was intrigued.

"Like peel a banana and eat it."

"So what's so special about that?"

"Well, you don't peel it with your hands." Jolie looked at Bubbles and slowly lifted her eyebrows.

Bubble sputtered, "That's impossible. How would you? No!"

"Oh yeah." Jolie was enjoying herself now. "There was this one chick—she was a legend on Broadway. Man, she could peel fruit, smoke cigarettes. Some guy even told me he saw her blow smoke rings once—ha!"

"Oh man, you are fuckin' with me now—right?"

Jolie just smiled and blew smoke through her nose like a Chinese dragon.

***

Toby woke up mummified. She was wrapped in white and surrounded by white walls and it felt as if she was covered in bandages. She started to yell but something hitched in her chest: a gasp followed by a dull pain. She became aware of some kind of tube running out of her chest. There was an IV in her arm as well. Her mouth was so dry she could only produce a squawk. She wrenched her other arm out from the tightly tucked sheet and found a call button. The smells assailed her and informed her. Hospital. Alcohol, piped-in air, blood, sour, chemicals, starch. Hospital. Where was Daisy? Hospital. Intercom, beeping machines, squeaking shoes, phones ringing far away, voices, the hum of electricity and fluorescence. Hospital. Squeak, squeak. Nurse.

"You're awake!" Nurse stated the obvious.

Squawk

"Let me get you some water." The homely woman in white squeaked her way over to a table on wheels and poured water from a disgusting gold-colored pitcher into a paper cup. This she held tightly and urged Toby to take the smallest of sips, yanking it away every time she swallowed a drop. Toby felt the water going all the way down her throat into her chest and down to her empty stomach.

"Squawk!"

"If you drink too quickly, you'll just sick it all up."

"SQUAWK!"

"I'll get doctor." Nurse squeaked her way out.

Toby tried to raise herself up and quickly failed. She racked her brain. Why? Why was she there? Not an OD. More serious. Where was Daisy? Okay, she remembered going to cop. She remembered ducking to the bathroom at Fred Meyer to do her shot and then trying to get downtown in a hurry. A white van. Something triggered inside her. Don't get in. Too late, someone had grabbed her. Oh God. Now she remembered. She squirmed and tears rushed to her eyes. Oh, goddammit. Oh, fuck. Why do I always try to remember what I need to forget?

***

He could tell something was wrong the minute he walked in. Eleni just had that look on her face. What a drag; he'd been on such a high coming back from rehearsal. It was after midnight. What could have happened now? Couldn't anything just be really cool and fun for a while before something came along to fuck it up?

"What's wrong?"

"It's Toby. She just called from the hospital—some sick fucking maniacs kidnapped her, right off the street." She stopped for a minute and waved her hand in front of her face as if she was trying to physically ward off tears. "Oh, goddammit, Max! It's just awful. They beat her, raped her, and left her for dead by the side of the road. She doesn't know where Daisy is. She asked me if we could help her find Daisy. She's all alone."

Max looked at her in frustration. "Eleni, how the hell are we gonna do that? She's homeless—she could be anywhere. Toby was the one with the phone."

"I know, I know." Eleni's voice rose. "But what the fuck was I supposed to tell her? 'No? Sorry you're in the hospital with no one in the world—but I can't help?'" She started to turn away but Max reached out and pulled her to him.

"I know. I'm sorry; it's okay. We'll figure something out. God, this is awful. Where is she? Toby, I mean."

"Emanuel. I've got her room number and everything."

"Okay, we'll go see her first thing tomorrow. She probably needs some things anyway. We can find out more information when we get there. Maybe she'll have some ideas on where we can look."

"You should have heard her, Max. We barely know her, but we were the only ones she could think of. For some reason, we were the only number she could remember except the dope man, and you know how helpful those guys would be."

"Humanitarians."

"Actually, now that I think of it—Daisy might call them. I mean, if she's all by herself, she probably will. They might be willing to tell her to call us."

"You're right. That's where she'll go. They're closed for the day but they have bent the rules for us once or twice. If we buy something, and you know we'd have to buy something. Dammit, I really didn't want to talk to them anymore."

***

Daisy woke up slowly. Somehow, without even opening her eyes, she knew she was in unfamiliar surroundings. Big surprise. Maybe it was the smell. Old bananas and cardboard. She cracked a peek through her lashes. Where the hell was she? Stacks of cardboard boxes and plastic milk crates were all around her. Stretched out alongside her was a pretty cute guy. She raised her head. Mistake. She fell back on the mattress. It felt as if a cymbal had crashed in her ears. A cymbal? A drum. Drum circle. She'd been at the drum circle under the bridge last night. That must be how she ended up here. The drummer boy—riiiiight. Tequila. Lots of tequila. The smell wasn't helping. The boy rolled over and threw his arm across her. He had a funny name—Freddy? Freddy the Freegan. Shit. Toby was going to kill her.

***

Bubbles stirred another packet of sugar into her coffee. Coffee in the library. Back when she was little, they never let you have food or drinks in the library. Now the library had its own coffeehouse, so they had to let you drink it. Portland really was a pretty cool place. She was learning so much, doing so many new things, every day was like an adventure. So many new people.

Funny to think that even though she had people around her all day and all night, she was lonely. Even though she had to come to the library just to get away from Nicholas and Jolie, she was still lonely. She wondered what was wrong with her. I guess it's because I don't really know them. And they're so much older, too. Over twenty-five. Everyone in Longview kept telling her she'd be dead by the time she was twenty-five. From what she had no idea. If they could see her now. Ha! She was already starting to live the fantasy life she and Brian had always threatened to live when they left home. That was it. She just needed to check in with Brian, send him a message and try to connect. Her old accounts had to be closed down and she'd reconnected to them all under the name Troubles. She'd already had a chat with Alison on Facebook. She and Raven were going to meet up with her at the Fez this weekend. She really adored those two, but Brian had been her friend for years. It was a little dangerous contacting him but hell, they could only trace her as far as the library. He'd figure it out it was from her. She put down her magazine, and went to reserve a computer up at the front desk.

***

Nicholas did a little happy dance as he put down the phone. "Jolie! We got it! We got the gig!" He ran into the living room where Jolie was doing dance exercises on the floor. He scooped her up and danced her around the room. "You are a genius! My muse!"

Jolie laughed despite herself. "Come on—down, boy, down! All I did was tell ya about the show—you did the rest."

"Yeah, but I think you're my good luck charm. Ever since I met you, I've gotten lucky. First I got a roommate—two of 'em—then I found a band. Now we got a gig. You are my lucky star, my very own muse."

Jolene looked up at him. He really was good-looking; she could have done worse for a girl who was homeless just a couple of weeks ago. "Tell you what—I got a bottle of champagne from an admirer last night. We'll celebrate. Where's our girl?"

Nicholas looked into her eyes. "She's at the library or something. I think we might have more fun, just the two of us, eh?" He whipped out a fold of coke. "Somebody dropped this at the studio the other day."

"Dropped it, huh?"

"Well, sometimes we have to make our own luck."

"You got that right, driver. Let's see if we get lucky, huh?" They raced each other to the bedroom.

***

Well, finally, things seemed to be looking up. Max put down the phone. He couldn't wait to tell Eleni. They had their first gig. Max rubbed his back as he wandered into the kitchen. He hated Tuesdays when they received all the merchandise for re-stocking at the hardware store. Bending to count it in and then lifting heavy box after heavy box. His fellow employees always seemed to go MIA when it came to unloading.

A beer would go down good right about now. Max heard the phone ring again from the living room. Fuck it, let the machine pick up.

"Max? Oh, Max, are you there? Please pick up." Eleni sounded freaked. He ran in to pick up.

"Hey, hey, I'm here. What's up?"

"Did you get my messages?"

Max looked down at the blinking light. "Uh no, I haven't had a chance to—"

"Max, has Nat eaten his food? Throw it away, NOW! It's poison."

"What?"

"It's full of fucking E-coli!"

"E-coli? Hold on."

Max ran to the kitchen. Some meat was still in the dish, broken up into chunks. Just then, Nat walked in, mewed and threw up on the floor. Max dumped the food and ran back to the phone.

"Okay, I got rid of it, but Nat's barfing. What the hell happened?"

"Fuckin' green meat is what happened. I'm on my way home. Call the vet."

"We don't have a vet."

"Find one! Please, Max, this is serious." Eleni began to sob.

"Okay, okay, I'm on it. Be careful driving home, okay? Please?"

Max clicked off and ran back into the kitchen. Oh please, not Nat, he begged the God he didn't believe in. Please don't let anything happen to Nat. He looked down at the smallest member of the family. Nat threw up on his shoes.

***

Looking back on Saturday night, Bubbles felt really good. She'd met Brian and

Alison at the Fez. Raven couldn't come for some reason. For once, she felt as if she had the inside straight. She was the one who was living the life. She'd been so happy to see Brian, to see his little Harry Potter face. Brian bore a striking resemblance to the actor who played Harry Potter. Unfortunately for Brian, it was young Harry—not teen Harry. She could tell he missed her and loved every minute of their night out. Especially when Alison kindly saw through his pick-up act and introduced him to some of her cute gay friends.

Later, she had invited them all to the big debut show with Nicholas's band at the club and they all promised to come. She could tell that they were suitably impressed by all the changes she'd gone through, and to top it off, they were really happy for her. She just loved this town.

***

Eleni held Nat close to her heart as they drove home from the vet's office.

"Oh my God, Max—just look at him, sleeping like a baby."

"Probably the only time he's ever been in a car not screaming his head off." Max looked fondly down at the little cat as he snoozed his way home. "I really don't think I could take another night like this."

"Oh jeez, I forgot to tell you! I saw Daisy. She was dumpster diving with this weird dude at the restaurant this morning and I told her where Toby was. She didn't get any of the messages we left her."

"Is she going to see her?"

"She said she was. Max, if I didn't know better, I'd say her and Mr. Dumpster had a thing going on."

"Poor Toby. That's the last thing she needs right now."

***

Toby really thought she would start to feel better if she could only see Daisy. But now? Okay, maybe she shouldn't have been so weird with her, but what the fuck? Jesus, what the fuck did Daze think she was doing? It started out okay enough. But somehow it had all just gone to shit.

First, Daisy showed up at intensive care, almost a week late, with a Tupperware bowl of grapes and this John-the-Baptist looking motherfucker.

"They're from New Seasons," Daisy said proudly.

"Wow! You really sprung for me, hey?" Toby kidded.

"Well, not exactly..." Daisy giggled. "Actually, you have Freddy to thank for them. But they're from both of us."

"All the earth's bounty should be ours. Free for the taking," offered Freddy the Baptist or whatever his name was.

"Freddy's a freegan," Daisy announced proudly. "We get everything for free now."

"What? Just 'cause you don't eat meat?" Toby had asked reasonably. And been laughed at. Laughed at by both of them.

"Not a ve-gan, silly—a free-gan." Daisy went on to tell her about the wonders of this dumpster diving asshole. How he and his little buddies know where they throw out all the food. And when you can get to the donated clothing too fucked up for even Goodwill to bother with. And on and on. And then the conversation after Toby asked whether Mr. Freakin' Freegan wouldn't mind giving them a moment alone. Jeez.

"Don't be like that, honey," Daisy pleaded. "It's nothin'. Freddy's just takin' care of me until you get better. He's a really cool guy. You'll really like him after you get to know him."

Toby doubted this. As a matter of fact, she'd never been more sure of her complete loathing for another human being.

The final straw? When the idiot walked back in during their kiss and said, "Cool, I love to see the beautiful ladies getting it on."

Was it any wonder she threw the fuckin' grapes at his head?

***

"Just wait until you see the surprise Bubbles and I have for you guys. We're opening your show with a sparkle and a bang." Jolie had that I've got a secret look on her face. The one that could mean anything, Nicholas had learned. He watched her float around the apartment and gather up various articles of discarded clothing.

"Oh yeah?" He followed her disappearing figure into the living room but it looked empty. He turned to leave, and then heard a voice from the corner.

"Oh yeah, me and Bubbles are gonna warm up the crowd for you."

"Wait a minute, what are you guys gonna do?"

Jolie popped up Jack-in-the-box style from behind the couch where she'd snagged a pair of pink tights.

"Didn't I tell you? It's a surprise."

"I'll just get it out of Bubbles later."

"Oh no you won't." She giggled. "God, I bet you were the kind of kid who peeked at Christmas." She stuck her tongue out as she moved past him down the hall.

"It won't like, throw the rest of the band off or anything, right?" Nicholas dogged her footsteps.

"Believe me, they're gonna love it." She popped into the bath and came out holding several floaty robes. They stood in the hall for a moment. Nicholas gave her a pleading look.

"You know this is an important show—it's the very first one. We want it to set the tone."

"I know. We're going all out, believe me. I even invited Jenny and her new boyfriend."

"Wait a minute, Jenny?"

"Jenny? The one who invited me here to Portland in the first place, remember? The one who left me high and dry?"

"Oh yeah. The one who brought your stuff over a couple weeks ago? Cute little redhead?"

Jolie rolled her eyes and headed toward her room, leaving Nicholas to follow once more.

"Yeah, that's her, the useless bitch. Anyway, she promised to invite some people and Bubbles invited some of her little friends. We're packing the house for you. We're gonna show 'em how it's done, right?" Jolie shoved all the garments she'd collected into a pillowcase. Nicolas grinned.

"Man, you guys are the best. What would I do without my girls, eh?"

"What indeed?" Jolie handed the pillowcase to Nicholas. "You wouldn't happen to be headed to the laundry room anytime soon, would you?"

***

If anything still had the power to piss Barkin' Jack off at this stage of the game, it would have to be the time slicers. The arrogant and imperious way that time was viciously divided into minutes, seconds, and days was bad enough. But the morality of time was what really got up his nose. Early risers were Good—hardworking and resourceful. Late sleepers were Bad—slothful and lazy.

Doors were closed to those who did not live within the prescribed time frames. If Barkin' Jack wanted a shower, a bed, or a meal, he had to be certain places at certain times. Seeing as the moral time frame had absolutely no benefit to the homeless, it really seemed beside the point. Now, Barkin' Jack sat once more dirty, cold, and without a safe place to sleep all because of the time slicers.

***

Toby and Daisy finished a joint behind a Range Rover in the underground parking lot of the hospital.

"I swear I'm losing it, Daze. I gotta get outta this place."

"Well, I already told you we can stay at Freddy's. I know it's not perfect, but it's a roof, and I really don't think you should be on the street in your condition."

"What do you mean, my condition? I don't have a condition."

Daisy carefully knocked the head off the now tiny roach and placed it in an Altoid tin. She looked Toby square in the eye. "You know what I mean. Those fuckers almost killed you. Look at you, poor baby." She reached over and stroked Toby's cheek.

Toby couldn't hold back her automatic flinch.

"See?" Daisy said. "You even pull away from me."

Toby rolled her eyes. "It's just a little PTSD. It's going away. I don't really wanna stay at Freddy's. He's an idiot, Daze. We could try to get a room from welfare again. You could go down there tomorrow."

Daisy shook her head. "You just aren't giving Freddy a chance. Besides, they're going to cut you lose before we'd be able to get any kinda place to stay. It'd just be for a little while. Come on, Toby, do it for me?"

Toby looked around the parking garage. "I'll think about it. You got a cigarette?"

Daisy rooted around in her bag and started to remove its contents onto the floor of the garage. Midway through, she pulled out a flier. "Hey look, Max and Nicholas are playing at Hells Belles this weekend. I saw him and Eleni downtown. They said for you to come if you're better." She handed Toby a crushed-up pack of American Spirits. Toby fished one out and held it up for a light. She breathed in the smoke and started to cough.

"Fucking things taste like shit." She took in another drag. "But good shit." Daisy laughed and after a second, Toby did too. "Oh alright, so when are you gonna bust me out of this joint?"

***

Eleni and Max sat on the outside patio of the Florida Room. Max shook his head.

"So that's it? No mo' Miso Horny? I can't believe he's just shutting it down."

"He said it was the Meat Karma that did it."

Max put down his beer and stared at her. "He actually said that?"

"Yup. I think I might have started laughing right then if it hadn't meant we were all out of a job."

"Yeah, that'll definitely harsh your mellow."

Eleni poked the ice in her empty drink with a straw. "I know. I couldn't help picturing all these little cow spirits going Moo-ha-ha."

"Can you get unemployment?"

"I don't know. I don't know if I worked long enough or made enough money. Well, at least I can stay up all night tomorrow and not have to worry about getting up at the crack of dawn."

"Just make sure you leave the little cow spirits at home."

***

"Did you make sure Nicholas got everyone on the guest list?" Jolie and Bubbles were doing the changing positions dance in front of the bathroom mirror. Mirror to toilet seat and back.

"Yeah, I guess. Goddammit," Bubbles swore. "I stuck the fucking wand in my eye."

"Careful there, girl." Jolie concentrated on her own eyelid area as Bubbles scrambled for some toilet tissue to keep her work from running. "All we need is a blind stripper to fuck everything up."

"Thanks for your concern." Bubbles scowled. "Did you pack up my wands?"

"Not yet, but I got 'em all laid out and ready to go, along with the CD and the soap and everything, so don't be such a worrywart."

"A what?'

"A worrywart."

"What the hell is a worrywart, anyway?"

"Oh, just chill the fuck out. We're gonna be great, okay?"

"I guess. It's just I got kind of a weird feeling about tonight, like I forgot something important, or I should have done something about something. I don't know."

"Ah, it's probably just stage fright." Jolie worked her cheekbones and filled them in with blush and bronzer.

"Maybe. I hope so." Bubbles started to line her lips.

In four hours, she and Jolie would take the stage.

***

Brian bit his lip hard and wondered whether pretending to faint would help. If only he hadn't fallen for the oldest ploy in the world—get 'em drunk and take advantage—he wouldn't be here now. Here, being Veronica's car speeding toward Portland. If he squinted really hard, he could pretend it was Bubbles driving and not her fierce and scary big sister. She'd caught up with him at the tavern and milked him like the stupid cow he was: bought him drinks, pretended to be his friend and then turned on the tears. If only she knew her baby sister was okay, she'd be happy. So he threw her a bone. And she rammed it through his nose. Now he was taking her against his will to the club where Bubbles was performing that night. He tried to comfort himself with the fact that it was better than the call the cops option she kept offering them.

They'd reach Portland right about the time the show started.

***

Okay. Jenny knew life wasn't always fair. She knew that. But this was absurd. Here she was, doing everything right and it was all going wrong. She'd cleaned up. Cleaned up in record time for someone with a habit as bad as hers. She'd gotten a job in one of the worst economies ever. She was living sober and going to meetings. She tried to help others. She stopped lying, shoplifting, cheating, and gambling. She exercised and watched her figure. She didn't even eat meat.

So why was it that in the past week she'd lost her job, gained five pounds, had her rent raised, and then, if that wasn't bad enough, she just got dumped? Dumped during the coffee break of a Narcotics Anonymous meeting. The son of a bitch didn't even have the nerve to take her to dinner or coffee or let her down easy at her apartment. No. Just wandered over while she was reaching for the nondairy creamer and told her it wasn't working out. He had issues. No hard feelings. It wasn't her. It was him. Really. And then scurried back to his seat.

And now, apparently, she had to go see Jolene's new boyfriend's band all by herself. Jolene—now magically Jolie. Who was still getting loaded. Who had a job and an apartment and a perfect figure. Who helped herself to anything that wasn't nailed down. And drank too much. Who never did anything right. It made you think. It really did.

The club was probably just opening right about now.

***

Max steered Eleni into the club past an enormous bouncer.

"She's my guest," he said. The bouncer stamped Eleni's wrist with the imprint of a black cat.

"Nobody asks for my ID anymore." Eleni sighed.

"He knows you're with me, is all."

"I'm sure that's it," Eleni said.

Although they were early, the club was filling up nicely. Eleni looked around. It was a fairly small place and most of the tables and chairs had been lined up against the walls, leaving people to stand around the bar for the most part. Some of the crowd drifted around the stage area, where a girl in a G-string and Pippi Longstocking striped socks finished up a rather lethargic set. Back toward the front, Eleni saw two girls enter the club. Although they looked strangely similar, one strode with a sense of purpose while the other just drifted along. They made their way to the back and disappeared behind a curtain.

"Those are Nicholas's roommates," Max told her.

"Lucky Nicholas."

"Yeah, they're supposed to be a warm-up act for us tonight."

"Warm-up, huh? Could be interesting. Hey look, it's Daisy and Toby." Eleni waved and peered into the crowd to see who the girls were talking to. "Hey, isn't that...?"

"Yeah." Max rolled his eyes. "The fairy God Mexican—he's Bobby's guest tonight."

"God, Portland really is a small town, isn't it?"

Pippi left the stage and the sound system cranked up as the lights dimmed down. The club was packed.

***

Bubbles peeked out from behind the curtains. "Wow, there's a ton of people out there. I don't see Brian. Oh look, there's Alison."

Jolie took a look. "All the band's here. I think I see Jenny. Don't see any new boyfriend, though."

"Do we have enough time to go say hi?"

Jolie looked out at the bar clock. "If we make it quick."

***

It had been awhile since she'd been out seriously clubbing. Unless you counted the fiasco of Jolie's first night in town. Looking around to make sure she didn't see anyone from NA or AA, she slipped up to the bar and murmured her order.

"Jenny! You made it!" Jolie yelled across the crowd as she cut through like a hot knife. She grabbed onto Jenny's sleeve and pulled her way up to the front of the drinks line. Jenny was relieved to see her friend. Jolie was a loose cannon, but she was her loose cannon. She pulled Jolie into an embrace.

"'Course I am. I wouldn't flake on you, girl. You look good. A lot better than the last time we got together." A shimmer of irritation crossed Jolie's face and Jenny immediately regretted this last remark. Fortunately, the bartender chose this moment to bring her drink. Her electric blue drink. Jolie smirked.

"Hey, hey, Jenny, that don't look like mineral water to me."

"Yeah, well..." stammered Jenny.

"I'll never tell. Where's the new boyfriend? I thought you were bringing him."

"Fuck the new boyfriend."

Jolie laughed and threw her arm around Jenny's neck. "You'll have more fun tonight on your own anyway. Come on, I'll introduce you to the band."

Jenny knocked back half the blue drink in one sip and followed Jolie through the crowd toward a small knot of people.

"Hey guys, I want you to meet an old friend of mine." Jolie waved toward the tallest of them. "You met Nicholas, my roomie? And this is Bobby, right?" A lazy nodded grin and a set of well-muscled arms made this next candidate an attractive one. Jolie now squinted at the last two, trying to place them in her memory. "And Max, the amazing bass player? And I don't know your name but you're Max's wife, right? Elaine?"

Jenny looked at the woman in question. She had a friendly, relaxed air about her. From the way Max's arm draped around her waist, it was clear she didn't suffer from relationship problems.

"Close. It's Eleni."

"Hi, I'm Jolie." Jolie indicated Jenny again. "And this is Jenny." Just then a little Goth girl waved at Jolie through the crowd. "That's Bubbles. She's my other roomie."

The lights dimmed down further and the Goth girl looked a question at Jolie. "I think I better get backstage. You guys take care of Jenny, okay?"

Bobby smiled at Jenny and eyed her now empty drink. "You need another one of those? I was just going to get one too."

"Sure." A smile crept up Jenny's cheeks. She felt a hell of a lot better than she had ten minutes ago, that was for sure.

"Nice to meet you guys," she called back to the other three. She followed Bobby to the bar.

***

The house lights were now completely down and the stage lights dramatically dimmed to red only. Eleni turned to Max. "Looks like we're in for the first act. Do you have to go backstage yet?"

"Nah, not enough room. We should get up closer so I can keep an eye out, though."

"Sounds good to me."

As they wedged their way in toward the front, they'd gotten close to the edge of the stage when the lights blacked completely.

The DJ's voice boomed out like a sleazy comic. "And now ladies and gentlemen, Hells Belles own: Jolie and Bubbles...."

Up came the disco ball lights and Muse full-blast doing "Super Massive Black Hole." A now flashing stage revealed Jolie, dressed in silver boots and matching G-string, orbiting her pole and surrounded by a wash of floating bubbles blown by Bubbles herself in matching boots and bubble attire. The audience hooted and clapped appreciatively as the dance became wilder and the girls began their bumps, grinds, and twirls. It was a great effect between the strobing light and the flying bubbles. Eleni found herself entranced until a big redhead pushed into her. A terrified-looking little queen seemed to be trying to hold her back. Her face was contorted with rage and she screamed something, which was drowned out by the combination of the music and the appreciative hoots and calls of the audience.

The DJ had pushed up the light effect to full strobe and hit a few of the red spots on and off. Dollar bills were moving forward through the crowd and Jolie swooped in here and there to collect them with various body parts while the smaller girl just spun as if in a trance and sent more and more bubbles flying around the stage. Back in the audience, the angry redhead had shaken her escort's last attempt to hold her off. As she tried again to push her way forward, a tussle began when she apparently stepped on the toes of one of the women in the crowd. Eleni turned to take in the scene and caught a few of the epithets being hurled back and forth between the two.

"I don't care who the fuck you think you are, lady—these are four hundred dollar John Fluevogs you just stomped on."

And then from the snarling woman, "Fuck your shoes. That's my baby sister!"

Although this last was shrieked at such volume as to get the attention of most of the surrounding crowd, it had little effect on those in the outer vicinity. It had, however, been heard by one of the women on the stage to dramatic effect. Eleni's attention had turned back forward and was astonished to see little Bubbles stood stock-still. She peered into the crowd and did a cartoon take: looked into the crowd, back at the stage behind her, and into the crowd again. Then quick as a wink, she dropped the bubble wand and took off running backstage. Jolie had caught only a little of this as she danced but obviously sensed something terribly wrong had happened. She turned just in time to see her partner flee and after a confused moment, gamely took up the wand and finished the dance herself for the last few measures of the song. Then she took a quick bow, scooped up a few fallen dollars, and disappeared. Max looked at Eleni in wonder.

"I don't think that was supposed to happen."

"Moo-ha-ha."

***

In the midst of all the chaos, Brian had found a part of himself detach and step back to enjoy the madness. But the larger chunk of his psyche was in a total state of panic as he watched Veronica shove her way backstage after Bubbles. Looking about helplessly, he spotted Bubbles's friend Alison. She stood with another girl a few feet away. He made his way quickly over.

"Alison, it's me, Brian—Bubbles's friend."

Alison and her friend turned to look at him. Alison squinted a minute, and then said, "Oh yeah, hi. Hey, what's up with her?"

"Listen, you want to help? She's in big trouble."

"Okay, sure."

"Around the corner is a silver Prius. Let the air out of the tires. I'll explain later."

"Which way, right or left?"

"Left as you walk out of the club, left again midway up the side street—sorry, I don't know what it's called."

"You got it."

"Thanks, hurry!"

Brian made his way backstage to find Veronica.

***

It hadn't taken Jenny long to figure out all the players on the program tonight. The band, the dancers, a couple lingering pervs, the friends of the band, and who matched up with who. And of course, standing a little aloof from it all—the fairy God Mexican. She might have been out of commission for a while but her instincts were still intact. It also hadn't taken her long to talk Bobby into splitting a bag with her. But now, as he passed her the rig on his way backstage, she wasn't so sure she was making the right decision. Well, of course, she wasn't making the right decision but...it was true what they said: Once you clean up, you can never really look at it the same way. Once you know how out of control you really are, it doesn't seem so cool.

On the other hand, she could never believe it when people at meetings said they flushed their shit down the toilet or threw it away. It just didn't seem right. Throwing a whole bag of dope away seemed so terribly wrong. She looked down at the little balloon nestled in her bag. Nope. She just couldn't do it.

***

Jolie slumped against the wall backstage. She'd run up and down the block, looking for Bubbles to no avail. Fifteen? Jesus. Somewhere in the back of her brain, she knew Bubbles was younger than she let on. If she'd let herself think about it, she probably would have put it all together, but she hadn't wanted to. She had just wanted a partner in all this madness. Someone to make her feel not so alone in this town. Someone who was even more clueless than she was. A little sister. But now the real big sister was on the scene. She'd avoided that one like the plague. She didn't like the look of her at all. Maybe she thought she was doing the right thing by Bubbles. Maybe she was. But Jolie was willing to bet she didn't really understand her little sister. It was obvious big sis didn't have a lot in common with her. Not like Jolie... She shook her head as if to dislodge the thought. What was she thinking? She was better off without Bubbles. She really didn't need a fucking minor tagging along. She didn't need the extra baggage. She'd always worked best on her own. No one to hold her back. No one to disappoint.

She just wished she knew where the poor kid had run off to, half-naked in the middle of downtown Portland. A blast from the guitar shook her out of her reverie. A drum roll followed. The band was tuning up. It was showtime.

***

Bubbles found herself slumped against her own wall, one that held up an office building near Skidmore Fountain and the bowels of the Burnside Bridge. There was a MAX stop there and she contemplated getting on. It would have been the most logical thing to do if she had any idea where she was going but she didn't. Her feet ached; her ankle throbbed. She'd twisted it running away in her brand-new silver boots.

What a nightmare this evening had turned out to be. Nothing at all like she'd pictured. Now she thought of it, though, she realized she had felt something wrong. Like a premonition. She'd even mentioned it to Jolie. Jolie! God, what was she thinking now? Now that she knew how old she was and what a fake she was. Part of her felt like crying. Part of her felt like screaming. Most of her felt like jumping off a bridge. Or just slicing her arms up. She thought about how good the sharp sting of a razor would feel. Something she could just guide and control. Feel nothing at first, and then watch the blood appear, along with the sting. Like she used to do late at night in her bedroom in Longview. Well, that was over now. Everything was over. She had to get a hold of herself. Her life with Jolie and Nicholas was probably over. Her life in Longview was definitely over. Fucking Brian. He'd ratted her out. She didn't have a penny on her, so she couldn't even call Alison. Funny, she was probably there at the club where Bubbles had invited her what seemed like a million years ago.

Now she sat on the street, wearing nothing but a silver G-string, pasties, and thigh-high silver boots under a blazer she'd grabbed off the back of a chair as she ran out the back door. She checked the pockets of the jacket. They contained half a pack of Marlboro Reds, a couple of guitar picks, an expired MAX ticket, and a red-and-white stripy dinner mint. No matches, of course. No cash. She buttoned the jacket and checked her reflection in the glass of the doors. She still looked absurd but at least she wasn't completely exposed. She was dying for a cigarette. She desperately needed a light. There wasn't a bar, shop, or restaurant in sight. She pulled her shoulders back and took a deep breath; she forced herself up and out. She'd run far enough away from the club that the likelihood of running into her sister was slim.

A car cruised past and slowed to a crawl beside her. She stiffened and kept walking, her eyes focused straight in front of her. She realized with some amusement that they probably thought she was a hooker. Her smile faded as she took in her situation. How far wrong were they? What exactly were her options now? She thought about all the dates she'd been offered at the club. It seemed like most of the girls had their regular customers. The car disappeared round the corner. She found herself wishing she had at least asked him for a light. As if the idea had rolled forth on its own power, she heard the car come back around. The inside light was on and the driver rolled the window down as he pulled over. They made their requests almost simultaneously. Bubbles ran around the back of the car and disappeared into the passenger seat. The automatic locking mechanism clicked into place. Bubbles looked at the illuminated clock on the dash: 1:16. It was now officially her sixteenth birthday. The car took off.

***

The drama seemed to have played itself out, Eleni thought as she looked around. At least the band was keeping it together. The first song was a little less solid than she had heard it on the rehearsal tapes Max listened to when he practiced, but after that, they seemed to be getting hotter and hotter and the club came alive again as people responded to the music. The bouncer had finally ejected Bubbles's big sister. Eleni felt bad for the both of them. She didn't have any siblings herself but she could imagine how worried Bubbles's sister might be. But she couldn't help thinking that she really should have handled the whole thing a little more sensitively if she'd expected her sister to go anywhere with her. She'd obviously dragged that other kid with her into the middle of the confrontation against his will, and the way she'd shrieked at everyone in the club, yikes! Eleni didn't think she would have found the idea of coming home with her very appealing at all.

She found herself standing alongside Jolie now while they watched the band. Eleni noticed that although she'd slipped on a skirt and T-shirt over her costume, she still managed to capture the attention of every male she came near. And yet, Jolie seemed oblivious of it all. She looked pretty miserable, even as she tried to lose herself in the music. She was obviously worried about her friend. Eleni liked her for this. She'd always appreciated loyalty in female friends. On stage, the band had changed up from their more manic numbers into an almost hypnotic space. The audience was still fully with them and swayed in unison. Maybe the evening could be salvaged after all.

***

Huddled in a corner under the Burnside Bridge, Barkin' Jack dreamed in Technicolor. He had wild, visceral, vivid dreams tonight, although he woke often. Foremost was a series of inexplicable visitations by a teen-angel dressed as Barbarella. Shaking himself before he rolled over once more, he curled into a fetal ball and tried to get back to the Land of Nod.

***

Brian could feel himself start to relax a little as the whiskey hit his stomach for the third time. He and Alison and Raven were up on the roof of someone's apartment building. Moon-bathing, the girls said.

He'd caught up with Alison, and they'd left in the middle of the set. The band was pretty good but neither of them could stay still after the whole thing with Bubbles went down. Veronica had screamed at him and threatened him with police and parents as she waited for the AAA to come and fix her flats. Brian just walked away. He just didn't care what she did or who she told anymore. He'd had it with Veronica. He'd had it with his parents. He'd had it with the kids at school, and he'd had it with Longview. Alison said he could stay with her tonight, and he'd just have to figure it out from there. He wanted to find Bubbles. He'd have to find out where Nicholas and Jolie were tomorrow. But that was tomorrow. Right now, Alison handed him the bottle. Right now, he was just going to have another drink and catch some rays.

***

Jolie grabbed someone's drink off the table and slugged it down. Yuk—watery. She grabbed the one next to it. Much better. She turned her attention to the band. God, Nicholas did look good up there. Being on stage gave him an authority he didn't usually command. They all looked much more...interesting? Formidable? Powerful? Maybe all three. That was the magic of rock 'n roll. Max's wife stood near her. She seemed nice. Proud of her husband. Like they were a little unit. Where was Jenny? Come to think of it, she hadn't seen her for a while. Did she bail? It seemed unlikely, the way she cozied up to Bobby. Nicholas was at the mic now, in between songs. He seemed to be searching someone out in the crowd.

"And this one goes out to Jolie, my very special roommate."

The band plunged into "Wild Girls," one of their originals. Awww. He really was pretty sweet sometimes.

***

Eleni had to pee. She really hated walking off in the middle of the set. She didn't want Max to think she was bored or didn't care. But the fact was she had to find the bathroom and fast. If she waited 'til the end of the set, it'd be swamped with women. She looked round and saw a flight of stairs going down with a sign for the restrooms. She squeezed through the crowd and cautiously slipped down the steep steps in her heels. You could break your neck on these suckers if you didn't watch it, she thought. When she found the door with the silly she-devil picture on it, she pushed. Something blocked it. She knocked and pushed again. The door gave a bit more, but it felt as if something was still in the way.

"Hello?" No answer. She gave another shove and peeked round to see what was in the way. Boots, legs, the bottom half of a woman in leopard-skin boots.

Oh shit. Eleni shoved her way into the tiny space and saw the rest of Jenny slumped in front of the stall. The cooker was still on top of the TP holder and the rig was on the floor. By now, Jolie's friend was pale blue.

***

Toby watched the band with increasing difficulty. She liked them, they were really good, but her ribs ached with every breath she took. She had discharged herself from the hospital too early, and she knew she had no business being out in a nightclub, but if she had to sit around with that moron of a freegan one more minute, she was gonna kill him. Contrary to Daisy's prediction, she did not like him any better than she had the first time she met him, which was not at all. She still had half a bag left, and she was gonna have to do it before she went home. It just hurt too much to wait. She signaled Daisy, who happily bopped to the music.

"I'm going downstairs."

"'K . Want me to go with?"

"I'm okay."

Toby took a deep breath and felt slightly better just anticipating the relief. As she reached the bottom of the stairs, she spotted Eleni backing out of the bathroom, looking as if she'd lost her mind.

"Toby!" Eleni grabbed her arm and pulled her toward the doorway. "Thank God. You have a phone? We gotta do something."

"We?" asked Toby, but she came a little closer as she said it.

***

Sweat blocked Max's vision as he banged out the last few bars of the last song. He'd already pushed his shades up on top of his head as they kept slipping down his nose. What a night. Now Nicholas was up at the mic, doing his "bye bye" number and thanking the crowd. All in all, the show had gone pretty well. He couldn't wait to get his hands around an ice-cold beer. Where was Eleni? He looked out in the crowd as he unplugged the bass. She was conspicuous by her absence. Then he heard the sirens approaching full bore.

***

Jolie was just headed down the steep steps to the bathroom when Eleni appeared at the bottom. "Jolie, thank God," she'd hissed. "Come here." And promptly proceeded to take her to another circle of hell located in the ladies' room.

"Oh fuck, fuck, fuck! Jenny? Are you fucking kidding me?"

"Toby called the paramedics. She might make it. She's still got a pulse."

"Look you guys, I hate to abandon you, but I just can't be here, okay?" Toby had been holding Jenny up in an attempt to keep her lungs clear.

"Thanks for making the call. You might have saved her." Eleni moved in to take Toby's place holding Jenny's body upright. Toby shrugged uncomfortably and apologized once more before she disappeared up the stairs. Eleni indicated the limp body now in her arms. "Is she a real good friend of yours?"

"Yeah, I guess." Jolie took another look at the figure in Eleni's grip. "Oh God. I guess I better go with her to the hospital, huh? Between this and Bubbles, it's not like I'm gonna have a job at the end of the evening anyway."

Eleni looked at the slumped form in her arms. "Well, it'll go a lot better for her if you do." She put a finger under Jenny's nose. "She's still breathing. That's really good."

Jolie stepped forward and took her turn keeping Jenny's body from hitting the floor once more. Eleni squeezed her way out of the tiny cubicle and gave her a look of sympathy as she started up the stairs. Her steps slowed as she reached the top.

Then she turned back.

"Look, do you want me to come with you?"

"Oh God, would you?" Jolie felt the band of desperation wrapped around her solar plexus loosen up a notch.

"Lemme go find Max." Eleni disappeared up the stairs just as Jolie heard the sirens approach.

***

Agent Orange
A US military code name for a mixture of two herbicides, 2,4-D and 2,4,5-T, used as a defoliant during the Vietnam war between 1961 and 1971. The herbicides were unintentionally contaminated with the highly toxic chemical dioxin, which is believed to cause cancer and birth defects in animals and has been established as a cause of chloracne and porphyria cutanea tarda in humans. See also dioxin.
—Mosby's Medical Dictionary, 8th Edition

Contrary to popular opinion, Barkin' Jack didn't actually bark at people. It would never really have occurred to Barkin' Jack to bark at anyone. Well, hardly ever. Barkin' Jack did, however, have chronic bronchitis and an increasingly persistent cough. It was a condition he'd returned home with, along with a small piece of shrapnel buried in his neck.

Jack's voice was an experience in itself. It reminded one of broken glass, rubbish disposal systems, and ancient blues musicians. His cough, however, reminded one of nothing else so much as a bark. This particular morning, Barkin' Jack woke up a barking fool.

"Ark, ark, ba-rrrrk, bark." Barkin' Jack doubled over with the sheer force of his lungs' rebellion.

A nearby sleeper took offense and yelled, "Motherfucker, what the hell is wrong with you? Who the hell elected you the neighborhood burglar alarm? Shut the fuck up and go back to sleep!"

Unfortunately, it just wasn't that easy. Barkin' Jack eased himself up off the pavement and moved on in an effort to avoid any more than insult to his injuries.

***

God, she hated hospitals. Jolie had avoided them whenever possible, even at the risk of seeming like a real flake at times. She just didn't do well within the atmosphere of linoleum, fluorescence, and pain. The smells alone were enough to make her want to bolt for the door. Eleni seemed to have very little problem maneuvering them through the red tape and walls of confidentiality. She'd even volunteered Jolie as a distant cousin to Jenny (just in case they gave them the old "family members only" runaround, she'd said) and seemed familiar with the various medical protocols. For now, Jenny was stable. Now the only thing left for them to do was wait.

"Come on, let's go smoke." Eleni tapped her shoulder on her way out. Jolie joined her as they passed through multiple sliding glass doors. Shhhh. Shhh-unk. The doors made their electric comments as they passed. Eleni didn't seem to notice.

She was busy digging through a voluminous shoulder bag in search of nicotine. They moved down to an approximation of the ten or twenty-five feet they were supposed stay away from the entrance.

"I friggin' hate these places. They make me itch." Eleni breathed out a cloud of smoke.

"Really? You seem so together. I wouldn't have remembered to say half the things you did."

"Yeah, well, unfortunately, I've spent a lot of time in these places." Eleni seemed to drift for a moment as she thought of dark times. Then she sort of snapped to and looked at Jolie again. "But, thanks."

"No prob." Jolie dug through her pockets and came up empty. Eleni held out a Marlboro.

"Wow. Thanks again." Jolie accepted gratefully. The two women smoked for a bit, lost in their own thoughts. Jolie looked up.

"Funny place to make a friend."

"No shit," Eleni agreed. They looked at each other and laughed.

***

Nicholas staggered out of Max's car. His legs were not doing him proud right about now. He snickered and sketched a comic bow toward the taillights as he made his way to the steps. Then he fell on his ass. From time to time, Nicholas had been accused of not being determined enough, lacking in the drive and the ability to zero in on what he aimed for. Honey and her band of naysayers would have been amazed at the determination he commanded as he attempted to mount the steps of his apartment against all odds. Like the man said, one step forward, two steps back. One leg up, one leg down.

Boy, it had started out to be a hell of an evening there. Clearly, it was his equipment bag that held him back. He tossed it up ahead of him, where it slipped off the top step and fell back down, only to send him tripping back over it.

Okay, keeping the bag. Yup, before it all went to hell, we had 'em eatin' outta our hands. Okay. One, two...Damn...One, two... He stumbled again and decided to lay his head down, just for a little break.

Jolie pitched herself halfway down the very same flight of stairs and tripped over Nicholas's body three hours later after Eleni dropped her off in front of the building. After a few choice words, she had hauled him into the apartment with the idea of helping him into the shower to rinse off the grime and various bodily fluids he'd acquired in his trek home. This was cut short by the discovery of their little roommate asleep in the tiny stall under a torrent of water.

***

Jesus Christ, it looked more like an emergency room in here than it did at the fuckin' emergency room. Jolie had an Ace bandage wrapped around her wrist from where she'd sprained it when she fell over Nicholas. Nicholas had a black eye from his battle with the front steps. And Bubbles had scraped half her skin off after trying to pumice and loofah herself clean of whatever it was that she did last night. Her face and arms looked as if she'd lost a battle with an alley cat while skateboarding.

Whatever it was, was bad.

She'd come home ready to rip Miss Bubbles a new asshole for running out on her like that, but when she'd found her lying there in the shower, blood running off her abraded body, for a minute she thought the kid was dead. And in that moment, her heart felt a lot more broken than it had in quite a while. Bubbles had come to as Jolie dragged her out from beneath the icy spray of the water. And as she looked up into Jolie's anxious eyes, she'd begun to shake with sobs.

Nicholas had been, of course, useless, although his presence had served to bring Bubbles back to her senses more quickly than if it had just been Jolie with her. She's got her pride, Jolie thought. She didn't want to be seen blubbering away in front of everyone. In this, they were an awful lot alike. It was one of the things that endeared her to the kid. But it had also effectively ruined the moment that Bubbles might have automatically spilled what happened to her. Now, she would have to wait awhile to find out. Jolie knew it was more than just her big sister showing up at the club. This made things a lot more complicated for Jolie. She had decided to lose the kid like a bad habit. Cut her loose. She really was excess baggage. But damn, could she really do this to her now?

***

Freddy's squat was really not working for Toby. She had tried. She thought it might get better when she felt a little more up to speed physically, but all getting better had done was allow her to spend more time away.

If she stayed out all night or came in after midnight, Daisy got all huffy. Which was weird, because other than that, there was no further indication that they were anything more than friends anymore. As a matter of fact, Toby had asked her more than once, why exactly, was it that she did make such a big deal out of it?

But Daisy would just roll her eyes and be all like, Duh.

Well, Duh wasn't gonna cut it anymore. Toby would rather sleep under the fuckin' bridge than hang here anymore. And the truth was, she didn't have to sleep under the bridge. She could stay with her old cellie Kitty, who'd just gotten out of jail last week. Maybe Kitty wasn't as cute as Daisy and maybe Toby didn't have the same feelings for Kitty that she did for Daisy, but maybe that was for the best. It just didn't pay to let people get too close.

***

Why did Toby have to be such a damn bitch about everything? Why couldn't she just hang out and enjoy having free food and a roof over her head? Maybe it wasn't like a mansion or anything, but it was free and it was a lot more comfortable than the sidewalk.

Things had taken a turn for the better as far as Daisy was concerned. She was back on the clinic now that she had a real address for her Oregon Health Plan. Her abscesses were finally starting to heal up and her hair had stopped falling out. There were just a couple things that had her worried. First thing was she sure had put on a lot of weight lately. It didn't make a lot of sense either, because Freddy brought home such healthy food for the most part. She'd never eaten so many vegetables in her life. The other thing was, she thought for sure she should have got her period back now that she wasn't strung out anymore. Without the interference of hard drugs, she was usually regular as clockwork. Yeah, that was a worry alright.

***

"Thanks for coming with me." Jolie reached into her bag for a smoke and noticed Eleni making the same movement at the same time, as if they were synchronized smokers or something. Of course, at 10:30 a.m. on a Saturday, the sidewalk in front of the clinic was crowded with smokers, jokers, dealers, squealers, and everything in between.

"No prob." Eleni exhaled gratefully. "I had to see my counselor anyway."

"It's the last of my dancing money. If I didn't do it today, I don't know when I could have gotten it together again."

The smokers visibly tensed as a counselor came out of the bunker-like building. Speaking with the shrill voice of authority, she moved among them and shooed them like chickens.

"Walk and talk, people—move it along."

Jolie and Eleni scattered with the rest, floating through the murmurs of "Fuckin bitch," "Jesus Christ," "What the fuck?," and "Gah."

Eleni laughed as they cleared the clinic's boundary. "Dang, now what were you saying?"

Jolie paused to think for a moment and shook her head. "Just bitched out about money shit."

"Me too. I need a job like, yesterday."

"If something doesn't come up fast, we're not gonna make rent."

"Doesn't Portland have, um, more strip clubs per capita than anyplace else?"

"Yeah, that's what I hear. Of course, I gotta find somewhere that hasn't already heard about our last show. Between Baby Bubbles running offstage and Jenny turning blue in the bathroom, well, you know…"

"Yeah, that was some night. It's not really fair that you got canned, though. I mean, the band did really great and you didn't do anything wrong."

"Guilt by association. Club owners had enough lawsuits and shit in the nineties. Of course, they covered their asses by saying they had to let someone go and I was the latest hire. But I've been blackballed, there's no doubt about it—at least in all the clubs that guy owns."

Eleni nodded sympathetically. "Yeah, there was some really great bands in LA that couldn't get gigs because of their audiences. How is Jenny, by the way?"

"She's okay. She's back in with her twelve-step buddies. She won't say it, but she doesn't want me hanging around—more guilt by association." Jolie's stomach growled audibly. "You hungry?"

Eleni laughed as Jolie rubbed her tummy. "Yeah, definitely getting there." She stood still for a minute and took in their surroundings. "Isn't My Father's Place right up the street? They're cheap and you can get a drink. I think my budget might stretch that far."

Jolie grinned and looped her arm through Eleni's. "Sounds like a plan."

SUMMER

*Satisfaction of one's curiosity is one of the greatest sources
of happiness in life. – Linus Pauling*

Barkin' Jack sat with Harry at the Outside In. It was the second day they'd showed up there. If it wasn't for Harry, he probably wouldn't have bothered, but Harry said she was worried about his cough and if he stopped to think about it, Barkin' Jack wasn't thrilled with it either. By all rights, he could have gone to the VA, but the last time Barkin' Jack had been there, it was a bad day and Jack had bitten a nurse. No matter what his friends said, Jack was certain that she'd remember and do something awful to him. As he recalled it, she'd already tried to do something awful to him before he'd even bitten her.

The way the Outside In worked—kids came first. It was originally created to help homeless kids and at-risk youth in general. It was one of the few places where the more problems you had, the better service you got. After the kids got treatment, you were served on a scale of how bad off you were physically and financially. The homeless were considered the next priority. Outside In had all kinds of services: from helping kids get off the street to tattoo removal for gang members. Harry had been looking into volunteering her nursing skills there so she had a few friends at the free clinic.

Unfortunately, the heat wave had brought in all kinds of people, suffering everything from festering infections to heat stroke. Most folks didn't realize that the heat could cause almost as many problems as the cold for the homeless community. Even with the crowd, Barkin' Jack's cough had cleared a liberal space around them. The two sat in companionable silence, broken only by the occasional flurry of barking coughs from Jack 'til they finally called him into one of the patient care rooms.

***

Max was lying on the couch, watching public access when Eleni came in from her job interview. She wore a suit and she didn't look happy.

"It was fucking knife sales."

"I thought they said it was a customer service job?"

"That's exactly what they said, but when I got there after getting lost about five times on the fucking Ross Island Bridge, it turned out to be knife sales."

Max frowned. "That's just wrong."

"No shit! I'd call the Better Business Bureau, but they've got all these people who say they're just the happiest little knife salesmen in the world, so it probably wouldn't do me any good."

"That sucks."

"First, there were the insurance people who wanted me to pay them money to have a job, now there's knife sales disguised as customer service. The temp agency says my typing or keyboarding or whatever the fuck they're calling it these days isn't fast enough. I'm never gonna get a job."

Eleni threw her purse across the room and pulled her blouse off and kicked off her sensible shoes. "And I hate this fucking outfit! I never want to see it again."

Max watched sympathetically while she ripped the rest of the outfit off and finally collapsed on the floor. She looked at the TV.

"Oh, is that the guy with the lobsters on his head who talks in that weird language?"

"Yeah, Von Hummer."

Eleni scooted in closer. "Oh, I like him."

***

In Alison's tiny apartment, Bubbles felt more comfortable than she had in a while. She didn't have to worry about sounding like a clueless kid. There really was something to be said for having a peer group, people your own age. And Brian was here. Seeing him—someone who shared her history—made her feel better. She couldn't believe what he'd done to protect her, either. They were still laughing about Veronica finding her Prius with four flat tires.

You really found out who your friends were when the shit hit the fan. Alison, Raven, and Brian had all really been there for her at Hells Belles that night. But now poor Brian was homeless and that was a problem. She couldn't put him up at Nicholas's apartment. She felt as if she was on pretty thin ice there herself. Alison and Raven had been wonderful about letting him do the couch surfer thing, but still, it made her feel like she'd been inadequate. Watching him joke with the girls now, she saw that strangely enough, despite his situation, he looked a lot better than he had before they'd left Longview. He even seemed to have lost most of his puppy fat.

Alison had asked her to come by to help solve Brian's current housing predicament. Now, midway into their second bottle of wine, Alison pulled out her tiny laptop and clicked away. She seemed to find what she wanted and waved the two of them over.

"C'mere and look at this." Alison indicated the Google map onscreen. There was a strange area of expanse with tons of tiny wavy lines that ran through it.

"What exactly are we looking at?" Brian asked.

"Well, I'm thinking, it might be your new home."

"My home?" Brian looked lost.

"Where the hell is this place, the Martian home-world?" Bubbles squinted at the strange landscape.

"It's my Uncle Charlie's cabin. Well, it's where the cabin is. Funny thing, it's actually not that far from Longview."

"Won't Uncle Charlie mind Brian staying there?"

"Uncle Charlie's been dead for like, ten years. My mom inherited it when he died, but since she left my dad she never uses it. It might be kinda dusty and stuff but I know where the key's stashed. It wouldn't be forever like, but you could stay there 'til you found something else."

"Really? Wow. Really?" Brian thought about it. It could be a real adventure. He used to go to a kid's camp in the woods every summer when he was young. He'd even done the Cub Scout thing.

"How would we get there? It looks pretty far from the bus lines."

Alison whirled over to the phone. "I can call Icky Dicky. He's a geek, but he'll drive me any where I want. I might even be able to borrow his van. Yeah, that'd be cool. We'll all go up for the weekend. Have a little party. Brian could bring his stuff and get set up. I'll be able to show you where everything is and stuff. Whadaya think, guys? You up for a little woodland adventure?"

***

Brian quickly reviewed his options: A) He could try to bum up the money for a cheap hotel every night. B) He could go back to Longview and face his furious family and probably get beat and grounded for the rest of his life. C) He could take his chances and go to the cabin.

"C!" Brian cheered.

"C?" Alison and Bubbles asked.

"Yeah, C. C is for cabin. I'll take the cabin. Door number three."

"That's the spirit!" Alison said. "We'll come up every weekend and take you to town. You'll love it up there. It'll be fun."

"Yeah, it'll be totally fun!" Bubbles pumped a fist. She felt better knowing Brian wouldn't be on the street because of her. She really hoped he'd be able to deal with living in the woods. He wasn't very butch. But then again, Girl Scouts camped out and they weren't very butch either. The idea of a party really appealed. She hadn't cut loose in a while. "We'll have our own little mini Burning Man!"

"Great idea," Alison said. "Let's figure out what to wear, then we'll call some people."

"Okay," echoed Brian. He hoped his voice didn't sound as hollow to the two girls as it did to him. All alone in the woods, not a cab or bus for miles. It was a little unsettling. He could hear his stepfather's voice: There's something wrong with that kid, Marsha. He don't act like a normal kid. He's like a little sissy-boy. And his mother's timeworn reply: Oh, he'll grow out of it. He's just a little delicate. Well, he'd show them. This would be the perfect opportunity. He took a deep breath.

"Okay. Perfect. It'll be fun." Yeah, that sounded better.

***

Daisy lay on her back and stared up at the wall behind her. The boom-box on the shelf had a conservation sticker on it. She stared at the word "Earth" and realized it had the same letters as "Heart." That was cool. And it could be "Threat" if you added a T or "Art" if you took away the H and the E. Man, she was stoned.

Freddy had a little patch in a garden collective way out in the sticks somewhere. He grew marijuana and tomatoes. She figured he'd put in the tomatoes just to cover up the pot plants, but those tomato plants were the healthiest freaking plants in the world. They had bowls of the fuckers all over the place and Freddy had baggied up a ton of them and handed them out to everyone who came by whether they wanted them or not. He could be so sweet. Did she love him? She wanted to. Did she love Toby? She wasn't sure about that anymore either. Why did shit have to be so complicated?

When they were together on the streets, she and Toby had been a team. They did everything together, shared everything and told each other everything they felt, everything they thought. Now she was pregnant, and she hadn't told either one of them. Obviously it was Freddy's. That was one thing about Toby. She wouldn't have had to worry about getting knocked up if she would have stayed true to her. She rolled over and reached for the cigarette pack on the nightstand. It was all crumpled up and the last one was broken. She snapped it off at the break, emptied the tobacco out of the filter end, and expertly fitted it back together.

As she lit the cigarette, she climbed out onto the roof. She loved it up here. If she walked out to the end, she could see the water. She looked over the city and thought she really had everything she had wanted: a place of her own, as much pot as she could smoke. No responsibilities. Everything free and easy like Freddy always said it should be. So why was she actually contemplating having this kid? It wasn't as if she was anti-abortion. She'd had one when she was sixteen and had been thrilled to get it. She remembered it felt like exorcising an invasive species. It had been terrifying having something inside her she'd neither wanted nor asked for. Something she could not rid herself of on her own. She'd slept with so many guys that summer she didn't even know whose kid it was anyway. But this time, it didn't feel so bad even though she still hadn't meant it to happen. This time it felt kind of warm and friendly. Could she do it? Could she actually pull off the whole mom thing?

She wondered what Freddy would think. Somehow she didn't think he'd mind. She'd watched him playing Frisbee with some kids in the park yesterday. He was so natural with them. Like a big kid himself. She had never felt terribly grown up either. Wouldn't that be good? To be in the same head space as your kid? And what would she tell Toby? She walked to the edge to look at the river and saw that the bridges were just opening up to let a big ship through. She loved the way the different bridges all came apart and went back together. Maybe it was a lucky sign.

***

Three o'clock was dead time at Coffee-stop. Perfect for taking advantage of free Wi-Fi and two dollar happy hour cappuccinos. They'd pushed the chairs together as close as possible as they all tried to peer into the little screen on Eleni's ancient laptop.

"Man, you got it made if you're an engineer. Look at all these listings!" Eleni ran her finger down a Craigslist page.

"Well, you're not an engineer," Jolie said. "Let's see what they've got for undereducated artists and runaways."

"Oh you think they might have a special category for that?" Eleni said. "That would save us a lot of work."

Bubbles moved up and pointed at a listing. "What's a human billboard?"

Eleni leaned in and scrutinized the ad. "Good question."

"Nine dollars an hour, pays by the day. I like the sound of that. You don't think it's anything kinky, do you?" Both girls looked at Jolie.

"What?" Jolie said. "I'm the expert?"

"If the rubber suit fits..." Eleni said.

"I can't believe you guys!" Jolie huffed. Then, "Well, if it makes you feel any better, I've never heard of anything like that."

"Goodie!" Bubbles chirped and leaned in toward the ad. "Where do we sign up?"

***

Day 1 – Human Billboards

"And to think—I thought being a stripper was degrading," Bubbles said. She stood on Interstate and held a giant cardboard pizza that said Had a piece lately? in bold black letters. She'd been instructed to hold it at waist level.

"I don't know how much longer I can take this." Eleni held an enormous red arrow. She'd been instructed to keep this pointed toward Genaro's Slice o' Heaven.

"Well, now we know what a human billboard is." Bubbles sighed.

"I don't think there's enough liquor or drugs in the world to make us forget this." Eleni's sign kept slipping, and pointed every which way. The light changed and the bus that had been idling next to them roared off and blew a huge cloud of diesel flatulence into their faces.

"How long have we been here now? It's got to be time for a break." Bubbles's tone was somewhere between a whine and a whimper. Eleni dug in her pocket for her cell phone, trying to keep the arrow squeezed between one arm and her side as she peered at the time. Her eyes widened. "Oh Jesus, it says 11:15—this can't be right."

"YEAH BABY! I'll take one right now!"

Eleni turned around to see one of a group of fat teenagers leaning out of a car. His friends howled their approval.

"How'd you like this up your fat ass?" Eleni held the giant arrow up as they screeched off. The time was now 11:16.

***

Toby lay curled in a fetal ball. She wished she could return to the Land of Nod and realized that no matter how crappy and tired she felt, she couldn't sleep anymore. Maybe if she had her wake-up shot she'd feel better.

She lay there a few moments more and listened to the sounds of the loft around her. Didn't sound as if anyone was moving around. Probably all up and out already. It was probably afternoon by now.

She grabbed her jeans and padded into the bathroom, reached under the sink and got the spoon out from behind the baking soda box, pulled the balloon out from the tiny pocket in her jeans and unwrapped it. Carefully, she shook out her shot. She fished the little bit of white she'd saved out of the big pocket and she set it on the edge of the sink, where it promptly rolled off into the trash. Fuck, great. She plunged her hand in and snatched it out; something fell out onto the floor. Plastic. One of those home pregnancy tests. Oh. My. God. Daisy.

Toby looked at the window on the stick and saw a little smiley face. Did that mean yes or no? She pulled out the instruction paper and checked. That would be a yes. Congratulations, you bitch, you're pregnant. My girlfriend is pregnant.

Oh man, and it just couldn't be anyone else but Freddy the Freegan, could it? Could it?

***

Human Billboards Day 2 – Corner of Interstate and Lombard

Bubbles frowned at her cardboard pizza. "Do you want to be pizza today? I could do giant arrow."

"I don't know." Eleni whirled the arrow in her hands. "I think I'm finally getting the hang of this thing." She turned to Bubbles. "En garde!" She pointed it one-handed now, toward the pizza.

Bubbles held the pizza shield-style. "Yaaaah!" she howled in ninja-stance as the two began to duel for the appreciative crowd at the bus stop.

"People!" A new voice cut through the scene like a cleaver. The two turned and faced their job recruiter. His face wore the self-serious expression of a lifetime hall monitor. "What exactly do you think you're doing out here? There is no excuse for this."

Eleni saw the light of a thousand snappy comments jockeying for position flash behind Bubbles's eyes as she turned to face him. Eleni held her hand up toward him in submission.

"You're right—there really is no excuse for this." She turned to Bubbles and aped a cowgirl twang as she said, "I think it's time to hang up our weapons and get the hell outta Dodge, pardner."

"A-yup," said Bubbles. And with that, they laid down their cardboard props at the hall monitor's feet and walked away.

"You know, I really find it amazing that you're over forty sometimes," said Bubbles as they waited for the MAX.

"Imagine my surprise," said Eleni.

***

Max was pissed. This was the second time Bobby flaked practice and this time he hadn't even called them until they were already there at the rehearsal space. He was bitching to Nicholas as he wrestled his amp back into the car. "That's my whole evening shot. I could have done something else tonight. It's my only day off this week. Now it's too late to get anything together."

Nicolas was thumbing down the messages on his cell phone. "Maybe not, dude, maybe not—you never know." He clicked his way in and out of texts. "Well, nothing for tonight so far, but it looks like there's a big party next weekend. Remember my roommate? Little Bubbles?"

"How could I forget?" Max said, sourly remembering their being eighty-sixed from playing Hells Belles.

"Looks like she and her friends are throwing a party out in the country somewhere. She sent a map and everything."

"Won't it just be a bunch of kids?"

"Not if we invite enough adults it won't."

"I suppose I could ask Eleni if she's up to it. She's been kinda down with this whole job-hunting thing."

"Yeah, Portland's not the place for getting your dream job right now. Tell ya what, you call Eleni; I'll make a couple calls and see what I can shake up. We could all use a little blowout. It'll be like when your dad used to take the car out and drive it over a hundred to clear out the engine—just a little blowout and we'll all be good to go again."

***

You could still smell the ghosts of cigarettes in the old smoking section side of My Father's Place. It had been one of the last places you could enjoy three different oral fixations at once: food, booze, and smokes. Now it was down to two. Eleni and Jolie were taking advantage of these in the form of Bloody Marys and French toast. Eleni dragged the last triangle of French toast through her maple syrup.

"I'm so glad it's finally cooling off. One hundred and fucking six degrees last week. I thought I'd seen the last of that shit when we left LA."

"I know. Everyone in San Francisco kept saying how much colder it would be up here. How tired I'd get of the rain. HA!"

"What did you do when you lived there? Same as here?" Eleni moved on to her orange slice as she opened up the little circle and nibbled at it.

"Yeah, pretty much alternated between waiting tables and taking off my clothes."

"I had my first waitress job last month. It was a trip. I don't think I want to do that again. I wasn't very good at it. I kinda hate dealing with the public face-to-face like that." Eleni shuddered. "And that gig with Bubbles? Don't get me started. But it's hard to get temp jobs here. They don't have all those huge office buildings full of law firms and ad agencies and stuff. I don't know what the hell to even look for anymore. I've had so many bizarre jobs in my life, and it used to be kind of fun just going from one thing to the next while I made my movies and took all kinds of art classes. But now when I think of what I really might be able to do that could be interesting, nothing seems to call out to me. I still don't even know what I want to be when I grow up, and I'm already middle-aged."

"Don't feel too bad. I don't either. I look at Bubbles with her whole life spreading out in front of her and it makes me feel—well, not really jealous but, I don't know. Is wistful the right word?"

Eleni considered it. "Yeah, I think wistful just about nails it. I know what you mean. It's like I look at people younger than me and think about how much stuff they have to look forward to and how much weird stuff they don't know yet. That never used to happen to me. How is Bubbles? She's still living with you guys, right?"

The waitress chose this time to indicate their empty drinks. Eleni raised a conspiratorial eyebrow. Jolie gave her the nod.

"Yeah, Bubbles is still with us but she's been spending a lot of time either out at her friend's house or just sitting in the corner with her nose in a book these days. I think something's going on with her, but she's kind of a mysterious kid. I worry about her sometimes. She reminds me too much of me. It's like you said, all this stuff she's got to learn. I just think, oh fuck—how the hell's she gonna survive it all?"

"She's lucky she's got you in her life, though. I wish I would have known somebody who could kinda show me the ropes, tell me what was what. I had to bumble through it all in a big cloud of cluelessness."

"But acting like you knew everything anyway, right?"

"Yup, acting like I invented it."

Both women laughed and turned their attention to the fresh drinks that had arrived. Jolie looked at Eleni.

"You know, it's really nice to have someone to talk to like this."

"I know, especially someone who's had the same kind of background as me. Someone who won't, like, think you're deranged if you tell them all the stuff you've been into. Or even the stuff you think is interesting."

"It's a strange little world we come from, in a way. Not everybody gets it and there's no point trying to explain otherwise. Either you know or you don't."

***

It was gonna be like old times, just the two of them hanging out for the evening. It was supposed to be fun, but Daisy found her hand shaking as she applied her mascara. Should she tell Toby about the baby tonight? Or would that just be a big bummer better saved for another day? She hadn't even told Freddy yet.

He was off somewhere dumpster diving for the camera of a PCC student making a documentary film about freegans. Daisy was going to be in it too, but tonight Toby had gotten tickets for a show at Dante's. Daisy had a couple hits of E she'd gotten from a girl at the clinic and some of Freddy's homegrown. It would mellow them out. Make it more like it used to be before everything got so weird between them.

***

Conspiratorial mutterings woke Bubbles from a sound sleep. She raised her head up from the couch.

"You sure she's not gonna wake up?" Eleni's voice.

"Nah, kid sleeps like the dead," Jolie replied.

"Can you do me? This is the only place left." Eleni again, followed by more mutterings and what sounded like flesh being slapped.

Bubbles stretched the kinks out of her body and rolled off the couch to take a look. In the kitchen, Jolie was bent over Eleni's foot with a needle. Eleni's outstretched leg had a pair of tights wound tightly round her ankle. Eww.

"Eww," Bubbles said.

Eleni shrieked, and Jolie inadvertently poked her foot with the needle. After another yelp, they both turned on her and Jolie began to curse.

"Goddamn it, Bubbles! What the fuck are you doing sneaking up like that?"

Bubbles glared right back. "I wasn't sneaking—I was just walking into my own kitchen. You guys were sneaking!"

Eleni looked sort of embarrassed but Jolie wasn't done.

"I am not sneaking. It's my kitchen too. Now what do you want, anyway?"

Bubbles ignored the question, and asked Eleni, "Is it worth it? That looks really painful."

Jolie rolled her eyes. "Oh for fuck's sake."

But Eleni raised her hand up. "No, it's a valid question. How's she gonna learn anything if she doesn't ask?"

Jolie smirked. "Right, Eleni, go ahead then: Heroin for Dummies."

"God, you are such a bitch. Anyway, the answer is yes and no. In the short run—yes. In the long run—no."

Bubbles sidled up and examined the paraphernalia on the table. "Can I try some? I want to see what it's like."

"NO!" they answered in perfect unison.

***

Toby's common sense told her she was just spinning her wheels, but an even bigger part just couldn't let go. She missed Daisy. Not seeing Daisy as she still did at the loft now, but being with her in the special way they used to have. The two of them as a team. Just the two of them. So she was going to give tonight her best shot. Maybe if Daisy saw how good it could be, she'd forget all about that moron Freddy.

Should she tell her she knew about the baby? Or would that just be a big bummer better saved for another day? She'd just sold a pile of T-shirts she'd shoplifted to some rich high school kids, and she had a little cash. Maybe she could get some brown for the two of them. Maybe some white, too? Duck into Fred Meyer and do a big fat speedball just before they went to the club? That would get them feeling warm and cozy. She pulled out her cell phone. God, what the hell was wrong with her? Her hand shook.

***

Bubbles punched up Raven's name on her cell phone.

Raven's drawl was there immediately, as if she'd been waiting for her call. "Buh-bells, what's up, girl?"

"Not much. I was just wondering if you could hook me up with some brown.

"Whatcha doin' right now?"

"Wow. Excellent timing—eck-sa-lent. I'm at Tommy's. Let me give you the address."

***

Thirty minutes later, Bubbles found herself gazing around approvingly at Tommy's tiny apartment. He'd chosen an outdoor motif: AstroTurf, lawn furniture, a broken umbrella table, and a birdbath completed the look. On the floor, a family of stone rabbits, an impressive variety of garden gnomes, and a pink flamingo fought for elbow room in the tiny space.

Tommy, a pedi-cab driver, was Raven's latest future ex, and the man they'd chosen to find Bubbles her first bag of dope.

"Now this is a one-time deal, right? I don't really do this for people but since you're Raven's friend." He gave Raven a puppy-eyed look of devotion.

"I told you, Tommy can find anything in this town." Raven patted his hand and then gave him a firm push to the lower back. "Now, hurry up so we can have some fun."

An hour later, they all lay on the floor, feeling the first effects of the brown powder they snorted.

"You know, I can see what people like about this stuff, not like I'm planning on making a habit out of it." Raven smiled as she painted blue eyes on a stone rabbit with nail polish.

"Yeah," Bubbles agreed. "I feel pretty damn good." She laughed and reached for a garden gnome when her guts gave a lurch. "Whoa, all of a sudden my stomach doesn't feel so hot." She stood up, making things a whole lot worse. "Tommy, where's your bathroom?"

"Through that little hallway. I share with the place next door."

Bubbles took off, barely able to get the seat up in time. As the last of her stomach contents fled her body, Raven appeared next to her, looking gray.

"Shove over, would ya?" She promptly lost her lunch.

"You finished in there?" Tommy appeared behind them, hand over his mouth.

"Yeah," Bubbles said. The two girls headed back into Tommy's room with the serenade of his retching behind them. Lying on her back in the "grass," Bubbles decided she wasn't sorry she'd tried this, but she sure as hell wasn't going back for a second helping anytime soon.

***

Eleni considered the huge stack of books in front of her and sighed. "You know, I can only afford one of these—maybe two if I get cheapies."

Jolie considered her slightly smaller stack and sighed. "Yeah, me too."

They sat at a long table full of readers in the already crowded coffee shop at Powell's Books. Despite the rain, outside the little room felt overheated and steamy.

"Well, what do you have there?" Eleni pointed at Jolie's stack.

"New paperback Terry Pratchett, a Kelly Link, Elmore Leonard, Elizabeth George, and an old Paul Bowles collection."

"Well, I've got the Link at home and the George on my pile, so one of us could get that and then we could go in on the Pratchett."

"Cool!" Jolie piled their choices into one stack. "This is one of the benefits of getting clean—books." A bearded man to the left of Jolie gave her a long look as her pile invaded his space. She quickly re-piled. Eleni smiled. A group of loud tourists came in, shouting into cell phones and each other's faces, and the noise level rose to unacceptable. The low murmur of the room grew quieter and the tourists seemed to finally notice the massive stink eye power of thirty bookworms focused on them. They huffily gathered their packages and left.

"I love this place," Jolie said.

"Yeah, I always say Powell's is half the reason I moved here." Eleni eyed the discard pile.

"Hey, absent-minded professor and street poet just left. There's a corner table—let's grab it."

"Who just left?" Jolie grabbed her books.

"Absent-minded professor and street poet." Eleni laughed. "I tend to name people in my head."

Jolie looked out the window at the retreating forms of the poet and professor.

"God, they really do look like that—the bald one with the glasses, that's the professor, right?"

"Well duh," said Eleni. "Don't you ever do that? I look at people on the MAX and I make up little stories about them. I see a guy walking his dog and I start to think about what the guy's thinking and then what the dog's thinking."

"What the dog's thinking?"

"Well, yeah, I mean he has his story too."

"I think maybe it's time for you to stop reading and start writing maybe," Jolie said.

Eleni looked at the stack in front of her again. "I think you're right."

**

Barkin' Jack made his way out of the shelter. He had managed to bed down there two nights running so he figured he had to be on the mend by now. Except he really didn't feel that much better. Last night, he'd had a couple of coughing fits that were so bad he'd had to smash his face into the thin pillow in order to keep the noise from getting him booted out. Several people had complained the night before. This was just another reason why Barkin' Jack hated to stay in these places. Did they think he was doing it on purpose? Like it was a choice? Some examples of humanity just weren't worth investigating. Jack decided he'd go see whether anyone interesting was arriving in Portland today. It wasn't far to the bus station.

**

"Well, this should be interesting. A cabin in the woods. Did you go to parties like this when you were young?" Eleni asked Max.

"No, not really. I played some big rave-type gigs out in the boonies, but we never really went to parties in the woods. I'm not sure I even want to go to this one, to be honest." Max looked up hopefully from the computer where he'd been printing out the map.

"You never want to go anywhere right before it's time to go there." Eleni laughed as she hopped around on one boot and looked for the other. "I feel the same really, when it comes down to it, but I'm really curious to see what it's like. If it sucks, we'll just split."

She pulled several single shoes out from under the desk. "Have you seen my black patent-leather motorcycle boot?"

"Is this it?" Max pulled a boot out from under the kitchen chair.

"Yes!" cried Eleni, pulling on the lost mate. "Perfect. Now if I can just find the keys, we're outta here."

**

Bubbles read the text message Alison sent her with relief. It looked as if finally the whole thing was coming off without a hitch. Brian and Alison were already at the cabin, and she was on her way to Raven's to meet up with the rest of the crew. Icky Dicky was coming to get them in half an hour. Raven was over the moon about some new hip hop boy named J that she'd met at a party. Apparently, he was coming with them and bringing a friend along. Despite Raven's hints, Bubbles really wasn't too interested.

Two of the Maggie's Wednesday night regulars, Chris and Courtney, were coming too. Bubbles had always secretly viewed them as cartoon Goths. Like the ones on South Park. They were just too Hot Topic in her opinion but Raven and Alison seemed to like them.

Bubbles looked up at the ornate brownstones and Victorians around her as she approached Raven's apartment. It was a really beautiful, well-maintained old building and Bubbles remembered something about Raven's family having a lot of old lumber money. Northwest Portland sure was different than regular North. She could hear the music the moment the old elevator doors opened, even though it was at the very end of the hall. She humped up her sagging backpack and headed for the door.

***

Brian felt he was maturing. For instance, he knew that all this fuss wasn't really so much about him as it was about having something to have a party about. Nevertheless, it was fun. He'd spent the last half hour helping Alison decorate—a process which consisted of helping throw black sheets all over everything and filling several vases with dried dead flowers or stems with thorns. Now he was trying to polish a tarnished old cocktail shaker he'd found in a cabinet with toothpaste while following one side of the phone conversation that Alison was having with (he was pretty sure) Raven.

"Well, duh." Alison twisted a loop of hair through her fingers. "Hip hop boys, really?" She squinted as she said it, and her nose wrinkled.

"Make Icky Dicky bring them." She held the loop tighter.

"Whatever." She pulled her finger carefully out and watched as the curl sprang forth.

"No way!" She grabbed for another loop. Her eyes grew large as she listened and twisted.

"You didn't..." She carefully unraveled this loop and began again with another.

"No way!" Twist.

"But how?" Unravel.

"Get the fuck." Twist.

"No way." Unravel.

"Okay, okay." Twist.

"See ya." Unravel.

Brian looked at her expectantly as she slapped the little phone shut.

"So? What was that all about?"

Alison looked at him with a confused expression. "What was what all about?"

Brian said, "The conversation you were just having?"

Alison shrugged. "Oh. That was Raven and them. They're coming over."

Brian sighed and continued to polish the shaker.

***

Barkin' Jack found that he had stumbled down to the waterfront without realizing it. He looked out at the cold gray landscape, the bare trees, the one brave hunched-up jogger who ran beside the slate blue water. No ducks, no dogs. Shivering, he turned and made his way back toward the bus station. He moved past the new Saturday market, past the old Saturday market, past the Salvation Army; he passed the screaming Jesus man who moved quickly as he dragged a sandwich board along with him, he passed bald Elvis who was inexplicably singing a Neil Diamond song, and then coincidentally passed the storefront of the twenty-four-hour Church of Elvis. He waved at a few familiar faces in front of Sisters of the Road. Every now and then, he would have to stop to catch his breath and let go of a dozen ripping coughs. He passed Dirty Pie Pizza (although he had never understood why anyone would want to eat a pizza like a dirty pie) and he stopped to admire a row of little pink smoking rabbit statues in a storefront window and he noticed the new Green Line rail train zipping by, didn't look so new anymore. When he looked up and saw the familiar tower of Union Station, he had reached the bus station just in time to greet a load of passengers fresh off the bus from San Francisco.

"Welcome to Portland," barked Barkin' Jack. "Good to see you."

***

Looking around her, Bubbles thought if she could design an apartment of her own, it would have looked just like Raven's place. It was like the dwelling of an urban Edwardian/Egyptian princess: eggplant walls and tarnished golden woods, heavy velvet curtains, ivory skulls, and wrought iron chandeliers. And sprawled atop a pile of silken embroidered pillows, Raven held her little court. Chris and Courtney were there already, and brown-nosed Courtney actually sat at her feet. Sheesh. On the fainting couch and floor respectively, were the two new arrivals J and Trey. J really was just as handsome as Raven had told her he was. Bubbles wondered whether he'd disappear as quickly as poor pedi-cab Tommy. J looked a little like an Egyptian prince himself, lounging in baggy jeans and a "Fuck tha' Police" T-shirt. He had a secret little smile. Trey, on the other hand, sported a perma-smirk and a "Club 187 Cop Killa" shirt. He looked her up and down before he returned to his examination of Raven's CD collection.

"Buh-Bells." Raven popped up from her nest. "Hey everybody, this is Bubbles." She threw one arm around Bubbles and stuck a pipe in her guest's mouth with the other. "Bubbles is an awesome dancer," she announced. To avoid any further comment, Bubbles sucked on the pipe for all she was worth. Trey looked up from the pile of CDs he was perusing.

"Oh yeah? What kinda dancer?"

Oh Jesus, she did not need this. What the fuck was Raven smoking? She looked down at the pipe in her hands, which answered her question. Was she ever gonna get away from the whole Bubbles rep? She was literally saved by the doorbell as everyone's attention was pulled away briefly toward the entryway. Icky Dicky had arrived.

***

Barkin' Jack slipped into the restroom of the Greyhound station. He hadn't had a chance to clean up at the shelter that morning, and he felt grubby. He was still so tired. He set the hot water running and looked into the mirror. Today, it was like looking into the face of a stranger. Salt-and-pepper hair stuck up in an odd frame over his forehead, like tufts of grass. One…two…three lines cut across his forehead, like newly dug rows in a garden waiting to be planted. His eyebrows were two perfect semi-circles over bright, glassy blue eyes, which gave him a startled look that seemed to match his state of mind. Tiny red lines grazed across the whites of his eyes and made their way in a darker shade around his nose.

Had his nose grown? Could a man his age still grow a bigger nose? Funny, because the rest of him seemed to have shrunk.

Jack pumped the odd foamy soap from a steel dispenser and thrust his hands under the now lukewarm water to splash it up on his face. After a few such immersions, he ran his still wet hands through his hair and attempted to slick it back off his forehead. He pulled some rough brown paper towels from the towel dispenser and folded them up; he ran them under the water and then pumped soap on them. He attended his armpits and the back of his neck with the makeshift washcloths and tried to rinse and dry himself as well as these circumstances would allow.

Another glance in the mirror told him that he'd made very little headway, although now he looked a little like a drowned rat. Another bout of coughs doubled him over and he held one of the towels over his mouth to cover both the cough and the noise. When he drew it away, it was spattered with blood.

***

Daisy woke with a huge metal helmet on her head. Her mouth had completely dehydrated; there was no moisture in it at all. As a result, her tongue had turned to leather. She attempted to lift her head up but the helmet was too heavy. She drifted. Sometime later, she awoke again and found that the helmet was gone, but now her legs wouldn't move. As she fought to pull her head upwards, she saw that her pants were down around her ankles and held her legs fast. When she tried to swing herself up, it seemed the metal helmet had reattached itself. This time she fought the desire to flop back down and took a quick peek at her surroundings. Thank God. She was at home in her own bed. She inched her way up to the makeshift nightstand and downed the flat soda that sat there. Although it tasted pretty horrible, the liquid felt wonderful on her parched mouth.

She wriggled her legs free of the underwear/jeans manacle and sat up. Holding her aching head in her hands, she racked her brain for information about the night before. Jesus, fucking Toby had lost her mind. She remembered they'd started with speedballs in the bathroom at Fred Meyer and had moved onto the hit of X and the joints that Daisy brought. There was something about a bar in there and a pitcher of beer. Then there was Toby raving about being followed by a van. They hadn't made it to the show. Or had they? No, right. They wouldn't let them in the club.

Then that creepy girl showed up. The one with spots. And Toby got mean and said all those awful things about Freddy and the baby. Then they were in Crack Alley and they were with all those people in that building. And Toby was being so paranoid. She even started acting as if Daisy was in on some insane crazy plot she couldn't even understand. And then she'd just disappeared. What a fucking bitch. She'd just left Daisy there with all those scary people. It was a fucking miracle she'd made it home. Well, fuck her. That was the last straw. Daisy really didn't care where Toby was this time. She could just fucking stay there forever.

***

Toby dreamed of the ocean. The waves crashing up onto a rock where she sat. The tides coming closer as she slipped on the hard, craggy surface where she was perched. She was feeling something close to hysteria, a sense of some unspeakable doom. As the water came in once more to claim her, she shouted and became aware of her dream. She could stop this. She struggled to open her eyes. To pry them open and allow her to escape. She was shrieking to herself, "Wake up, wake up!" Then she made one more valiant attempt at opening her eyes and to her amazement, succeeded.

"Hey, you okay?"

Toby found herself looking up into a vaguely familiar face. It spoke again.

"It's just—you were thrashing around and making these little squeaks. I thought you were gonna wallop me pretty soon with your arms flyin' around like that."

Toby looked around her. She could still feel the rocks and hear the ocean. After a few more moments of consciousness, she realized what she heard was the sound of cars—lots and lots of cars. She was under a tarp somewhere near the freeway. And the face was...Pony! The past twenty-four hours began to flicker in and out of her memory. She'd started the evening with Daisy. Daisy—where was Daisy? She looked around behind her and could see no evidence of anyone else.

She hadn't seen Pony since the two of them were kids in juvenile hall back in Washington. Even back then, Pony had been a bit of a mystery. What was Pony doing here? What was she doing here? God, it was cold.

Pony knee-walked to one of the shopping carts that held up the tarp and pulled a pack out from under it. She pulled a little bag out from that and extracted a well-used crack pipe, which she quickly loaded up with a stash from her pocket. After taking a couple of hits, she popped another large rock into it and handed it to Toby. "Here, this'll warm ya up."

Toby reached for the pipe gratefully. As her head began to clear, she glanced up at Pony, who looked prettier every minute. She decided to play it cool. "So wow, Pony. Whatcha been up to?"

***

She'd been called Pony for so long there was practically no one left who knew her by her real name. And the world Pony lived in now was plenty real enough without having to dig that shit up.

It probably started around her "cafe au lait" birthmarks, the most obvious of which was the one on her forehead. It was diamond shaped. Very much like the markings on some types of horses. Then there were two others on her torso that looked almost palomino. Not like she knew much about horses. Didn't matter—it fit.

Pony looked over at the latest addition to her tent. It had been quite a while since she'd had any sort of partner or even a friend. And she could tell that Toby was checking her out too. She wondered which version of her Toby saw. No one ever saw the whole picture. People saw what they wanted to see. What they needed. What suited the picture of themselves they liked best. What would Toby see? What would she want her to look like?

***

Barkin' Jack checked into the shelter just as they were locking the doors. The prune-face battle-ax at the door gave him the stink eye and muttered something about rules and respect. Barkin' Jack stuck his tongue out when she turned around but unfortunately too many people laughed. When she turned back, she glared at him with such a promise of comeuppance he nearly shuddered. Jack shuffled over to see whether there was any good free stuff in the bin or maybe a snack to be had. The only things he found to eat were some old instant hot chocolate packages and a bag of taffy one of the staff had probably brought back from a vacation on the shore.

He grabbed a handful of them and went looking for a cup and some hot water for the cocoa. He ended up using warm water from the tap and a not too dirty mug from a temp agency.

As he looked around for a cot, he saw he wasn't the only one who'd gone without dinner. Watching people having various amounts of success or failure with the saltwater taffy and their rotten teeth or dentures was better than television. Old Selma snapped happily away, her dentures falling off her gums and back on again. Jed was just sucking on them for a while, extracting the flavor and occasionally whispering to them. One young fellow cursed as a black tooth gave up the ghost and lodged itself in a big purple wad.

As he sat on his cot, Jack pulled tiny bits off one piece at a time to savor them; the sugary juice soothed his throat while the taste cast his mind back to a time long ago without any clear memories but a warm feeling nonetheless.

***

Since the first wino stumbled out of his cave, society as a whole had just shaken its head in wonder as to why anyone would choose to live such a life of degradation. Since then, there'd been a lot of sound research into the fact that most people don't actively choose such things, and how heredity and brain chemistry can play a major role in addictive behavior.

Those who have, for whatever reason, joined the ranks of the chemically addicted will tell you that no matter what does end up happening to your life in the long run, that first and foremost when it works, it really does work.

For those stolen moments—it feels fucking fantastic.

Right now, Toby felt fucking fantastic. Did it matter that she lay on a questionable mattress under the freeway? Did it matter that she had no job, no home, no place to call her own? Not right now. Right now, as the cocaine charged through her body, that body of hers was alive in every fiber of its being. That body had just experienced complete nirvana, and that mind floated in the stars.

Pony looked down at Toby's body stretched out before her like a feast. Despite Toby's cute boyish looks, under the baggy T-shirts and jeans was the body of a woman. Perfectly round, exquisitely firm breasts. Neat lean torso, and long, long shapely legs with the tightly muscled calves of a dancer. And like a feast, Pony had been to the table over and over and over again. One of the really awesome things about sex between two women was multiple orgasms and unlimited capacity. No waiting for some pesky organ to refill like a toilet. They had been at it for something like a week now, on and off.

The "on switch" that coke provided had been flipped off for no more than an hour or two here and there. Normally neither woman was much of a jabber jaw, but in this state they had pretty much caught each other up on their mutual childhood histories, adult disillusions, and current hopes and dreams. And the "on switch" did not stop at the mouth (or at least its role as an instrument of verbal communication) it traveled down. It kept them in a constant state of sexual readiness heretofore exclusive to wet dreams.

To Toby, this was nothing short of a miracle. Sex between her and Daisy had long been nonexistent, and even at the beginning had been mostly a friendly game of mutual masturbation. An act of comfort and consolation. In her younger days, it was something either taboo with curious straight girls or stultifying sincere female jocks. Then there were the years of clubbing and going home with women who she could never have identified later in a clean, well-lit room.

So this was the reason all those desperate men picked her up? This was what they'd been looking for? And probably got no more than a flicker of what she was now feeling. A spark to light their otherwise desperate lives. Wow.

***

For the first time that week, Barkin' Jack didn't make it to the shelter on time. The battle-ax's eyes shone triumphant as she blocked his way in. Although her voice came through syrupy sweet with regret, Jack knew he was paying for his face-pulling moment of rebellion last week. As he turned to make his way out, Smokey Joe ran up the stairs.

"Too late," barked Jack. Smokey rattled the handle nonetheless and was met with a resounding silence. He shambled to the foot of the steps where Jack sat and began to rip apart the cigarette butts he kept in a plastic bag in order to make a fresh one.

"Where d'ya think you'll go now?" He looked up at Jack, who stood now.

Jack shrugged. "Not sure—guess I'll find something."

"I got a place," Smokey said. "I only came to the shelter for a shower and that can always wait another day. I can take you with me, but you gotta swear not to tell everybody else."

"Okay," said Jack. He hadn't been looking forward to finding another spot.

"You swear?" Smokey peered at him through the acrid smoke of his now finished roll-up. "You gotta swear."

"Sure, sure." Jack held his hand up witness style. "I swear never to tell, okay?"

Smokey held his eyes a moment longer, searching for the truth of his statement. After a few moments, he seemed to accept Jack's word.

"Okay, come with me—but remember this is my place. Don't nobody know 'bout it, but me and you."

Jack followed Smokey through downtown and into a more residential part of town. They walked and walked until Jack figured he couldn't tell anyone where the place was even if he'd have wanted to. Just as he was beginning to doubt the existence of the place at all, Smokey motioned him to cut through one backyard, and then another. Finally Smokey gestured to him to follow and they came upon what once must have been the guest or carriage house to a larger place, now gone. There was a large lawn in the place where most of the other houses sat side by side, and set deep in at the back of the lot was a tiny cottage style house.

"Go round toward the front. I'll let ya in." Smokey disappeared through the basement window. Jack made his way quietly back to the front, placing his feet as carefully as possible. It was dark and he didn't want to go pitching over anything and making a racket.

***

Daisy was touched by Freddy's reaction to the news of the baby, which was to pick her up and swing her around in the air with a whoop. At that moment, she released an enormous breath of relief that she hadn't realized she'd been holding in since the day she stopped kidding herself about the pregnancy.

"Oh my God, he'll be here in time for Mardi Gras," Freddy whooped. "That is so magic."

Mardi Gras? Daisy thought. And then—he? She put the thoughts away as quickly as they came. The important thing was that they were going to have a baby. There was no longer any doubt about it. Now she could make plans and decisions about the baby. The only problem now was, she wasn't quite sure what sorts of plans and decisions you were supposed to make when you had a baby. There was probably a ton of stuff you were supposed to do. Toby was supposed to help her. She'd promised her that she'd be there for her. But Toby was gone now. Now it was all up to Daisy.

***

When he got to the front of the house, Smokey held the door open wide and grinned even wider.

"C'mon in."

Jack did just that and surveyed his surroundings. He was in a tiny living room space of what was once a really charming little place. A galley kitchen and a small built-in breakfast nook lay to the right. To the left was a door, which Jack presumed led to the bedroom. Jack wandered over and took a peek. Sure enough, there was one more tiny room, now furnished with an old mattress and an overturned milk crate. A tin lid sat on top, filled with ashes. Candle stubs were stuck here and there around the room. Clearly this was Smokey's inner sanctum.

"You can bed down out here." Smokey appeared at his shoulder. Jack could tell by the timbre of his voice that Smokey didn't want him getting any ideas about the bedroom. That was okay by him.

"Sure thing."

Jack turned back to the main room and gave it a second look. An old slightly sprung plaid couch dominated the space with a matching chair across from it. Third-hand pieces of furniture someone decided were not worth the trouble of moving. Jack was glad for the little bit of illumination from the streetlight outside. It was otherwise pitch dark in here.

"I brought ya some of these." Smokey appeared again, carrying a couple of candle stubs and an old wine bottle to use as a holder.

"You wouldn't happen to have a light, now would ya?" Jack smiled.

Everyone knew if there was anything Smokey had, it was a light. Smokey had gotten his name from his obsession with keeping his tobacco habit thriving. Smokey knew every outdoor smoking area behind every office building in the downtown area. Since the new laws had forced the smoking community outdoors for good, every business had its little hidey-hole where the last citizens of Marlboro Country could be found. These provided an endless supply of butts and half-smoked cigarettes that Smokey harvested on a daily basis. He kept them in plastic vegetable bags from the grocery store. His fingers were permanently gray from digging into ashtrays half the day with yellowed tips from the unfiltered roll-ups he made. Jack had made a friend for life when he'd given Smokey a carton of cigarettes he'd found in an abandoned squat last summer. Smokey had accepted the gift with such reverence it still made Jack smile to think of it.

The miasma of smoke and ash and the reek of the butts that followed Smokey Joe always made Jack think of Pigpen in the Charlie Brown comics. Now Smokey sat half swallowed by the old armchair and rolled away, stopping briefly to give Jack a pack of matches extracted from a handful he had in his pocket.

With the candle lit, Jack examined the room further. There were several unexpected treasures left by the previous tenant, including a stack of paperbacks and book club hardbacks left on the built-in shelves. Some crockery still resided in the cabinets, and the stove and fridge would have worked had there been any electricity. Jack chose a copy of Best American Short Stories and went back to join Smokey.

"This is some place you got here. How the hell did you find it?'

"Old Army buddy of mine used to live here." Smokey paused in his rolling with a faraway look in his eyes. "I came by to visit one day and he was gone. It was raining cats and dogs and I took a chance and let myself in. I kept checking in here and there and nobody hung a sign out or moved in, so I stay here a lot now. It'd be perfect 'cept for no water and no way to cook. So I go to the shelter for my showers and such, but this is home base." He gestured proudly with his roll-up at their surroundings. Then he leaned in toward Jack.

"You know, I been bursting to tell someone about this place but you can't trust most folks you meet on the road." Smokey leaned back, exhaled another plume of smoke and pointed to Jack with the butt. "I don't forget who's been good to me, though. You could'a sold that carton a' smokes for some real cash but you remembered me. So I'm gonna extend a permanent invitation to stay here any time you want. Okay, buddy?"

Jack felt truly touched at this gesture and said as much to Smokey.

"Just don't tell anybody!"

***

"Here she is, folks—your chariot awaits." Icky Dicky gestured toward a large, dirty white, windowless, serial killer type van. Everyone stood around on the sidewalk and stared at it for a moment.

"Eww," Raven said. Then, "I got shotgun."

Bubbles clambered into the back with Chris, Courtney, and the hip hop boys. Whatever had been back there originally was now ripped out, giving her the feeling of being in a huge washing machine. She tried to anchor herself around the wheel well for traction but quickly slid into J the moment the van left the curb.

"I got this from a guy who used to move equipment for X and Social D down in LA," Icky Dicky said, hoping to impress.

"Who?" said Trey.

"Really big in the 80s." Chris rolled his eyes.

Bubbles had finally curled herself into a hard tight ball with her heels dug into a dip in the corrugated metal floor to steady herself. This was starting to be a drag.

***

Under the freeway, love blossomed. Under the freeway, there was a state of abandon neither girl had ever experienced. Declarations of love and raw sex that went on and on. It would have been paradise if they hadn't needed to finance the fuel that kept them going day after day.

But they did.

In Pony's case, this meant going down to 82nd Ave. or one of the other popular pick-up streets and selling herself.

They had tried going as a team, but since Toby's abduction, this had become unbearable, as they had found out when Pony had to pry Toby's fingers from around the neck of an abusive john. Whether she was willing to admit it or not, her abduction by the men in the white van had changed her. So Toby shoplifted and ran whatever scams she could come up with, given her limited resources.

For many new couples, this state of affairs might have driven the romance out of the relationship. For Pony and Toby, it only served to bring them closer together.

***

Bubbles sat in the back of Icky's van and watched the hysterical flash of the red and blue lights as they pulsed through the van. It was a silent cacophony of light to match the maelstrom in her head. Icky Dicky was outside the van, as was Raven, each being questioned by their very own police officer. She looked at J and Trey with their "Fuck tha' Police" and "Cop Killa" T-shirts. Why, oh why, on this, of all days, they had chosen to wear those T-shirts? And why, oh why, were the police waiting so long to ask the rest of them to get out of the van?

At least it had given them time to swallow the rocks and buds the guys had with them. She'd swallowed a couple of the big rocks and wondered whether she'd begin to feel it soon. She was pretty sure you had to smoke crack for it to work. Chris and Courtney had eaten most of the buds but she kept running her tongue over her teeth to make sure there wasn't any big green specks clinging to them.

Now, she could hear some action outside. Courtney crawled up front and looked out the window.

"There's another car here now," she said.

Well, that made sense, Bubbles thought. There were seven of them. Now Trey climbed up front to look too. "Oh shit," he said. "K-9."

"Motherfuck." J ran his tongue over his teeth.

Bubbles tried to run a quick inventory of all the drugs they'd used in the van. Had Raven spilled anything when she rolled that joint? She pulled herself up to the window and watched the two sets of cops with the dog. They now headed toward the van. What could that dog smell?

***

Daisy's mind felt as if it had slipped the leash and now soared around on its own journey, zipping away from her body—this new, strange, swelling body—and leaving it down below in front of the bonfire. The constant boom, boom, booms of the deeper drums seemed to hold it close to the earth while her mind zinged around with all the other ratta-tat-tats, ching, ching, chings, and paradiddles weaving in and out through the airwaves that surrounded her.

She was at the Sunday drum circle, under the Hawthorne Bridge with Freddy. She liked it down here, hidden away by the river. Daisy watched as a pretty blond hippie girl swayed and danced to the beat. The bells around her ankles chimed every time she smacked her feet on the ground. Daisy liked the other drummers, the fire, the feeling of wildness right in the middle of the city. When Freddy first told her about the drum circle, she thought she might even try to give it a whirl herself. But now, as she sat here with the fire in her eyes, she knew she could never keep the beat.

***

Jolie slammed the last and final kitchen cabinet she'd searched. "Who ate my last ramen?"

Her stomach felt like a tiny shriveled thing, her legs ached, and something in her back had been twanging painfully ever since she'd tried an ill-advised back arch onstage the other night. The head cold was still with her full force. She stomped into the living room to face the object of her rage.

Nicholas sat, eyes glued to some stupid reality show, one of the latest in the Be an assistant to some overblown has-been series.

"Nicholas, goddamn it." Jolie grabbed the remote and snapped the assistant off, mid-grovel.

"Hey, I was watching that." Nicholas gave his best offended party glare, somewhat ruined by his quick glance down to the empty bowl that peeked out from under the couch.

"That's too bad. You can finish watching it after you go to 7-11 and get me another ramen."

"Can't you have something else?" Nicholas said.

"Like what, Nicholas? Like what? Coffee grounds? Mayonnaise?" Her voice had risen to a shriek that surprised even her.

"Okay, okay." Nicholas rummaged around for his tennis shoes. "I'll get your damn ramen—don't have a heart attack."

Jolie just stood there with her arms folded, eyes blazing, foot tapping. Nicholas, sensing no quarter, ducked into the closet to find his favorite jacket. Its absence reminded him of another missing object.

"Hey," he called, braving one last contact with Jolie. "Have you heard from Bubbles today? Or Max and Eleni? Aren't we supposed to go to that party?"

Just then the doorbell rang.

***

The vibe between Nicholas and Jolie was decidedly chilly. Eleni wondered whether Max had noticed it. Jolie kept sniffling and Eleni wondered whether she was sick sick, or dope sick, or had been crying. The whole thing made her uncomfortable. Over an hour in traffic with the two of them in this glacial state was gonna be a nightmare.

"Can we stop for cigarettes?" Nicholas asked. Max pulled off the freeway at Mall 205. Right near the parking lot they always waited for the fairy God Mexican. This felt like a sign to Eleni. Maybe not from the heavens but a sign nonetheless. She tossed out the first volley.

"This is right where we always met..."

"Yeah."

"You know...just one last..."

"Couldn't hurt..." A voice from the backseat.

Eyebrows lifted. Jaws clenched. Eyes pleaded. Shoulders shrugged. Lungs sighed.

Nicholas returned. The cell phone engaged. Eleni guessed the party in the woods was on hold for a while.

***

Daisy sat in the window, looked out at the city and wondered whether there was any way to get rid of that bitch without looking jealous. Just thinking about it made her want to scream. The bitch in question being Atlantia—the girl with the silver bells on her ankles. Who was now tinkling away as she so helpfully prepared steamed vegetables in the kitchen. In Daisy's kitchen. In Daisy's place, with Daisy's boyfriend Freddy. The father of Daisy's baby.

When Freddy first brought her back from the drum circle, Daisy hadn't been smart enough or clever enough to see the signs. God, she could be so dumb. She should have noticed Freddy's fascination with Atlantia's stupid hippie past.

"Atlantia's parents are Rainbow people," he'd announced. "She's like a third-generation Rainbow child. Her great-grandparents were at Woodstock!" And Atlantia had just sat and smiled that creepy little self-satisfied smile of hers and pretended interest in Daisy's baby. She even had the nerve to offer to help deliver it. Said her mother was a mid-wife, and she'd grown up attending birthings. Had Daisy thought about where she might want to bury the placenta? Eww. And all the while, Freddy had just sat there grinning away as if she was just the most amazing thing to hit the planet.

And then the bitch had gotten right into their bed, too. All the while with that creepy, loopy smile. Said she hoped they didn't mind. Hoped they were cool with her relaxed attitude about things. "I guess I just grew up with so much 'if it feels good, do it' all around me, I have to stop myself sometimes and make sure everyone's like, cool with it."

Well, Daisy wasn't cool with it. She wasn't cool with it at all. But she'd pretended she was. She just couldn't bear the idea of being the uptight one. And now the bitch was in her kitchen, no doubt preparing a healthy vegan meal for her and her baby. As if she really gave a flying fuck about them. She'd acted all shocked when she saw Daisy come home with Burger King French fries. "Daisy, are you sure that's a healthy choice for your baby?" As if she cared. As if Daisy didn't know that all she wanted to do was to make her look bad in front of Freddy. Which, of course, she had.

What had that two-faced fucker said? "Yeah Daisy, now it's not just your body you're poisoning. You really have to think about that."

Well, she wasn't the only poisoner in that house. Maybe somebody really ought to think about that.

***

It felt like the cold gray concrete bench beneath her leeched all the warmth from her body. Not storing it, just leeching it away and making it disappear before anyone or anything could benefit from it. So this is a holding cell, she thought. Most of the women around her looked as if all the warmth had been leeched out of them a long, long time ago.

Bubbles knew instinctively to keep to herself. She had seen a sobbing Courtney being led away somewhere by a shovel-faced female sheriff, and wondered when they'd come for her. She still didn't know exactly what they'd found in the van and no one would answer any of her questions. At least her parents were out of the picture for now, even though a part of her wanted her mother more than she had in a very long time.

She'd told them she was twenty-two years old and had no ID. She tried to lean back and rest. She didn't dare fall asleep in this place. God only knew what the hell would happen to you if you did. She felt a little woozy and jittery from the stuff she'd eaten in the van, but at least it seemed to be helping her stay awake. One woman already wore the nondescript prison smock you eventually got if you didn't get bailed out. The one they gave you after they sprayed you with bug spray and searched your body inch by inch. Jolie had told her all about that. The smock woman started to scream for someone to give her money for the phone. Several cops had walked by; one even paused to look at her for a moment but then moved on. The screaming woman got angrier and angrier. Bubbles watched in amazement as the woman finally leapt across the room and, balancing against the bars, removed her lower right leg and smashed it into them.

Bang, bang. "Motherfuckers, give me my mother-fuckin' phone call." Bang.

Wow. What would the kids at Lewis and Clark High School have to say about this? she wondered. She couldn't wait to tell Brian.

***

"I can't believe this. Nobody's here yet. Nobody!"

Brian stared at the table where he'd set up the little snack buffet. Two bottles of champagne sat in the silver buckets he'd spent the better portion of last night polishing to a shine. There was beer in the fridge. Vodka and some mixers. Fresh lemons and limes. When he'd set it all out three hours ago, it had looked so festive. Now it just looked sad.

"Hey, I'm here!" Alison snapped. She'd been lounging on the sofa in front of the fire for so long he'd practically forgotten she was in the room. He knew she'd figured it was the best possible background for the Chinese silk pajama outfit she wore.

All dressed up and no place to go. He felt bad for her, too.

"Sorry, I didn't mean..."

"I know," said Alison. "I guess maybe some people got their signals crossed, but I can't understand why at least Bubbles and Raven aren't here. Do you think their ride fell through?"

"I don't know. You'd think they would have called. Have you checked your cell phone?"

Alison rifled through the bag at her feet. "Shit, no service."

"So, they could have been trying to get a hold of us all this time."

"Yeah, I guess." Alison looked a little happier. "Well, okay! That's probably it. They're just stuck by the side of the road or lost in the woods or something."

Brian giggled. "That must be it. Or maybe they've been eaten by bears. Lions and tigers and bears, oh my!"

Alison perked up and scooted to the edge of the sofa. "Yeah, that's cool. Just as long as we know they didn't forget about us and go someplace better." Alison laughed and downed the beer at her feet. "So can we finally open up that champagne?"

Brian sketched a little bow and extended his hand toward the table. "After you, madam."

***

Jack tried his best not to disturb Smokey, but his coughing was uncontrollable. He doubled over as another attack left him gasping for air. Just when he thought his chest had calmed down, another wave hit him. Tears watered out of the corners of his eyes as he sucked in as much air as he could between coughs.

He looked up to find Smokey Joe staring at him from the doorway, a look of concern in his eyes. "You okay, partner? Sounds like you got the whooping cough. You seen anyone about that?"

Jack fell back on the couch. "They just said I was supposed to rest up. They gave me some pills but I lost 'em."

"Antibiotics?" Smokey asked.

"Guess so. They were green and black."

"Must have been the Keflex," Smokey said knowledgeably. Jack looked up at him, obviously surprised.

Smokey grunted amiably. "You smoke like I do, you seen 'em all. We're gonna have to get you somethin' for that, partner. Ain't gonna get better on its own. Not that far gone. Don't suppose you got insurance?"

Jack looked at him blankly for a moment, and then doubled over one more time as another series of coughs wracked through him.

Smokey nodded. "Alrighty then, looks like we're going to the fish store." Smokey shuffled back into his room for a minute and then headed for the front door. "You just stay put, buddy. We'll have ya right as rain in no time."

Jack extended his thumb upward and continued to cough. After the door closed and the coughs subsided, he paused to consider the last few minutes. Fish store? He shook his head and fell back once more, exhausted.

***

Just a little fun, okay? That's all she'd wanted, just a little fun and to maybe relieve some stress and chase away the blues. Was that too much to ask? Apparently it was. Goddamn Nicholas. Goddamn fucking lightweight. She watched as Jolie took her turn marching him around the room and kept him from falling out again.

No sooner had she done her shot, than Nicholas up and turned blue. They'd spent the last half hour hauling him into the shower, slapping his pretty face and trying to keep him from going under.

Relieve some stress, huh? Her hands were still shaking and of course the whole thing had pretty much blown her high.

She'd seen the desperation mirrored in Max's face as they both tried to revive him. Knew he was also thinking about how everything could come crashing down around them if Nicholas flat-lined. Portland. Their new home. Everything they'd tried so hard to find that was finally in reaching distance. She knew she was being insensitive, but goddammit, would this shit never end?

***

Max looked around the room. Only a few months and it already looked like a dump. Wet towels were everywhere: on the floor, on top of piles of clothes neither of them seemed to find the time to put away. Ashes had escaped the tiny ashtrays on all the table tops. A glass of bloody water sat on the nightstand. Jolie and Nicholas just looked like another big pile of laundry heaped on the bed. At least Nicholas seemed as if he was back among the living.

This is it. He thought, This is the last night I spend hauling someone in and out of the shower. I'm done.

The room had gotten so quiet. After all the cacophony and hysteria that had just happened, it seemed everyone was lost in their own thoughts now. Were they all thinking the same thing he was?

A burst of music somewhere in the corner made him jump. He almost laughed as he saw Eleni suppress a shriek.

"My phone," Jolie explained and cast about for the source. By the time she pulled her purse up from the side of the bed, it had fallen silent. "Pay phone," she muttered when she looked at the screen. It burst into song once more as she stuffed it back in her bag.

"Goddammit!" She put the offending object to her ear. "Yeah? What? Yes, I'll accept the charges."

Max watched her blanch as she received whatever information came through the airwaves.

***

Toby slipped out from beside Pony as quietly as she could. Try as she might, she just couldn't sleep anymore. She reached for her jeans, slipped them on. Pony muttered something in her sleep and rolled over into the warm spot Toby had left.

Toby's stomach gave a growl so loud it almost made her laugh. There's one good reason I can't sleep, she thought. She felt in her pockets for change and came up with two crumpled bills, a quarter, and three dimes. Enough to get a Coke and hopefully talk her friend at the pizza place out of a slice.

She wrote BRB in eye pencil on the back of a band flier in case Pony woke, and then she took off. It really was shaping up to be a nice day out. She passed a couple in shorts and sandals. Didn't matter if it was only fifty-five degrees out. If the sun was shining, Portlanders liked to pretend it was still July.

As she headed for the front door at Rocky's, she noticed a familiar figure seated on one of the benches. It was Daisy, stuffing herself with a topping heavy slice. Some things never change, she thought.

***

Daisy looked at Toby's grinning figure as she plopped herself down next to her. On the one hand, she felt as if she really ought to snot Toby off for dumping her in the crack house that night. On the other hand, it was so nice to have somebody to tell her problems to. Somebody to understand.

This morning, after deciding she simply could not, would not, face another meat-free, sugar-free, flourless, odorless, tasteless fucking dish of Atlantia's, she'd managed to sneak off to Rocky's.

And after a while, she'd been so glad she hadn't blown Toby off either. It was worth as many slices of pizza as it took to finally have a hand in dealing with what she'd come to think of as the "Atlantia syndrome." If anyone could figure out a way to get rid of that sexy, grinning witch, it was Toby.

***

Could anything else go wrong? No, No, No! Jolie's superstitious nature went into overdrive. Forget I even thought that!

But things were already looking pretty black from where she sat. First Nicholas almost dying and now Bubbles was in jail. And they said bad luck comes in threes. Well, at least the kid was smart enough to have lied about her age.

She had spent the past three hours trying to bail her out, calling the girls from the club about a bail bondsman and drumming up the cash, as well as talking Nicholas into using his guitar and amp for collateral. The bastard hadn't even wanted to do it at first. It took all kinds of whining and reminding him that Bubbles's rent money had kept a roof over his head last month. The thought of Bubbles in a cell made her stomach twist into a big hard knot.

***

It had taken everything in her, every scrap of strength not to break down crying on the phone to Jolie. Tears had even slid down the sides of her face as she wrapped up the call, but she kept her voice steady. She'd done it by imagining what Jolie herself would do. She couldn't imagine Jolie turning into a bawling child the minute she got arrested.

In the end, the tears had been the hardest to stop when she realized that Jolie was going to help her. That she did care. Bubbles hadn't been sure. Now she knew, and the thought of Jolie sent more tears quietly trickling down. She held her breath so as not to make any crying noises.

What would happen? She looked around at the other women in the holding cell and imagined the countless others in the jail above. What would happen if we let all the tears we all held in here come flowing out?

Would it make a puddle? A stream? A river they could all float away on? Just float on out of here. How many tears would wash them free?

***

So cold. Jack hadn't been this cold since...? There was a memory there: he's in a ditch and there's snow all around him, and he's young, just a kid; he sees his hands in little red mittens. When was that? Who was he then? Jack felt that tickle down in his lungs as the cough began to scratch its way up. Another wave of coughs started, hacked and ripped their way out. Each volley made him wish he could just pass out again and sleep. Sleep. His chest hurt, his head ached, and his feet were blocks of ice.

I guess I'm still alive, he thought. You have to be alive to hurt this much.

Jack heard a noise in the bathroom and started to panic until he realized it was Smokey letting himself in the window.

"Hey buddy, it's me." A waft of stale tobacco surrounded him and Smokey Joe stood in the doorway. "Jeez, partner, looks like I got here just in time. You look like shit!"

***

Jolie slammed back into the room and tossed her cell phone down. "Just when you think things couldn't get worse, get a load of this—they lost Bubbles. They can't find her! Those idiots!"

Eleni looked at Jolie incredulously. "What do you mean they can't find her? She's in jail. That's the one place in the world where you're absolutely guaranteed to stay where you are. That's why they call it jail."

"It's insane. I mean she's there, but they've screwed it up somehow. It's the fucking computers. They can't find her in the system. If the computer can't find her, she doesn't exist." Jolie paced back and forth as if her movement would affect the world around her.

Eleni shook her head. "The poor kid. I bet she thinks everyone's just blown her off. I mean, that's what I'd think if nobody came to get me. I'd be afraid they'd all forgotten about me."

Jolie stopped short and finally flopped down on the bed next to Eleni. "I remember one time this boyfriend of mine spent my bail money on dope. I was sitting there for days thinking he was off getting the money together, and he was spending it as fast as my friends were giving it to him. After a while, I decided nobody cared, that I'd been forgotten completely. You see girls like that in there. The ones no one comes for, not even the pimps."

Eleni shuddered. "Yeah. It's the scariest place in the world. It's like you're out of real time. You're in a void space. You feel like the whole world is carrying on without you—and it is. Can't the bail bondsman do anything?"

Jolie sighed. "I don't know. He says he's doing his best, but I can't help thinking we're not exactly priority number one. I do intend to keep nagging his ass, though."

"Squeaky wheel," Eleni agreed. "Just keep at him. It's the squeaky wheel that gets shit done."

***

"You know what always cracks me up?" Toby took a long sip of her Coke. "Guys who act like they're all totally sexually open, up for anything and in touch with their feminine side. They just love threesomes until someone suggests two guys and one girl. Then it's a whole different story."

Daisy looked at Toby with interest. There was a message there. Toby laughed as she picked the pepperonis off Daisy's third slice.

"You might want to investigate how Mr. Freddy the Free-Lover feels about that. A different kind of threesome."

Daisy tried to picture Freddy making out with one of the guys in the drum circle and giggled. "Oh Toby, that's it, isn't it?" Daisy hopped up and hugged her so hard, Toby gasped.

Daisy shook her head and grinned as relief swept through her. Her old friend had come through for her one more time. It was so beautifully simple. Just turn the tables, sit back and watch the fun. Now, she just had to come up with the perfect candidate. Tall, dark, and preferably vegan.

***

Smokey fussed with his pack for a moment and then brought out a wrinkled paper sack.

"Okeydokey, lemme just get ya some water."

Jack heard him clomp off, heard him bumping around with his water bottles and followed the clomps back in his mind until they brought Smokey into view holding two little boxes and a glass of water. "You got any allergies?"

Jack gave it some thought. "Just shrimp—can't eat shrimp."

Smokey laughed as he read the fine print on the boxes. "Well, I got—let's see, EM Erythromycin and TC Tetracycline, and they might be made for fish but they ain't fish. So you'll be alright."

Smokey opened both boxes with pictures of what looked like giant goldfish on them and started popping pills out of the push-packs. "We'll try 'em both to start with. Gotta give you quite a few as you're a hell of a lot bigger than a guppy."

He handed Jack a hand full of pills and the water glass. "Now drink it all down. It'll help keep yer stomach from acting up."

Jack looked at Smokey desperately. "Are you sure this is okay? Fish pills?"

"Don't you worry there, partner—they work like a charm. Now just you take them and drink all that water down." Smokey watched Jack as if he knew Jack had considered trying to stuff them under the pillow.

Oh well, Jack figured, can't feel much worse than I do already. He swallowed the pills and drank all of the water.

***

Poked and prodded in the most humiliating places. Sprayed with bug spray and disinfectant like a pound puppy. One size five flip-flop hit her mid-foot. The other, a size ten, felt like trying to keep her foot in a ski with no straps. She now wore a little plastic wristband with her number on it too. It was a very long number.

She had endured the ritual by removing herself to the role of an observer. Noted the details for later contemplation. It would make a great story if she had anyone to tell it to. She was beginning to wonder whether she would ever have anyone to tell anything to for a very long time.

She had been so sure she'd be out by now. She wasn't just in holding anymore; she was in jail. Real jail. Not detention, not juvie. Jolie had promised her she'd get her out as quick as she could. It was coming up on forty-eight hours in this place. Where was Jolie?

***

Brian stood on the pathway and waved at Alison's disappearing car. It reminded him of when he was a kid and his grandma and grandpa would leave after spending the holidays. The whole family would walk out with them and stand there waving until the car was long out of sight.

Now he stood there with the same feelings he'd had back then—as if he'd lost something. He was really alone now. Alone in the woods. Just like the beginning of every fairy tale he'd ever been told.

He turned and walked back into the cabin. I'm such a baby. Think about poor Bubbles in jail.

Alison had finally been able to get in touch with Courtney, who'd given them the news about the ill-fated excursion to the party. Of course, even though they were over eighteen, Raven and Courtney had been rescued by their parents. No one seemed to know where Bubbles was, except that Courtney had caught sight of her briefly at the police station.

He and Alison had called around to all the juvenile facilities but no one had any information. Brian was pretty sure she must be in real live adult jail. He was a minor with no car and no credit. There wasn't anything he could do for her. For the time being, they were both totally alone.

***

Pony rolled over, patted the mattress for the familiar form of Toby, and came up empty. She reached out further and dragged her jeans over to fish in the pockets for her cell phone. She squinted at the tiny clock on its face: 11:30 a.m. Might as well get up.

She gave a little snicker when she saw Toby's BRB note. Toby wrote everything like she was texting. Be right back. From where? And when did she write this note? No matter; if Pony knew Toby, she was off begging food from that pretty new girl behind the counter at Rocky's. She'd head down there and see whether Toby was slick enough to get an extra slice for her.

***

Art Group at the clinic. They were supposed to put together a collage with imagery showing their dreams of what life could be like once they got clean. Eleni and Max cut random photos out of National Geographic and People magazines.

Eleni had been amazed at the simple, almost childlike images that formed around her: sunbursts, families, cars, children playing.

The counselor told them to consider this theme of their clean and sober dreams during the process part of the group. Eleni's ears had perked up when one of the girls started talking about a free writer's resource in Portland. Apparently they even had free workshops. Her friends had always told her what a great story-teller she was, and once again she'd wondered whether her dream of writing could really become a reality. Wondered what kind of stories there were in this very room. She bet they were much more interesting than their collages.

She'd cornered the girl after the group broke up and jotted down the number.

***

Brian caught sight of something moving out of the corner of his eye and turned around in the doorway just in time to see a baby deer leap past and drop out of sight behind the foliage. Maybe this wasn't such a crazy idea after all, he thought. This is a magic place.

He'd paused once more to take in the cabin's central area: the woodstove in the fireplace, the beamed ceilings, the wonderful vintage wing-back chairs and sofa. All mine for now. He felt a shiver of excitement go through him and headed for the kitchen area.

"Hmm...now what's for supper?" He spoke aloud as his mind turned toward the practical. He rifled the cabinets. As if in answer, his question was met by a low growl from the corner.

***

Jolie paced up and down 5th Street, smoking and waiting for the MAX. Try as she might, she could not get Bubbles out of her head. She would not be able to think straight until the kid was sprung.

Why did this kid matter to her so much? She'd gone out of her way to shed as much personal baggage as she could. Wasn't that part of why she was here in the first place? She'd cut all her ties in San Francisco, broke up with the "better than nothing" boyfriend, even started fights with a few of her girlfriends just to get them off her back.

So what was it? The kid could be sullen, secretive, downright snotty at times. Was it the steady look in her eyes when she asked Jolie a question? As if she was sure Jolie would have the answers? Or was it how it began? With Jolie saving her from those creeps in the middle of the night?

She remembered something she'd read in a book of Japanese fairy tales. That if you saved someone's life, you were responsible for them forever. It hadn't made any sense to her then. Why is the one who saves the one responsible? Shouldn't it be the saved one? But now it made sense to her. Now she got it. For better or worse, Bubbles was hers.

***

Brian froze. Slowly, he'd craned his head forward in the direction of the growl, his shoulders hunched up around his ears. He caught a glimpse of a golden eye, watched as it flashed red in the shadow.

The growl came again. Even deeper now.

Omigod. Omigod. Omigod. What the hell could it be? What the fuck am I doing here? What am I gonna do?

His thoughts kept flashing past like a teleprompter across his frontal lobe as the adrenaline coursed through his body. He realized he held his breath and managed to suck in a little air between his teeth.

No one's gonna save you. It's you and him, nature boy. Okay. What would my he-man stepdad do? Oh God, he'd probably beat it to death with something in his tool belt. That's never gonna work.

He watched in fascination as a huge rat tail snaked out from under the water heater. Omigod.

Giant rats? In the woods?

I suppose it's more afraid of me, than I am of it? Right. But maybe it really is scared. Let it out. That's it! Let it out. Brian slowly backed away toward the door. Quietly, he turned the handle and opened it wide. Then, he scurried outside.

Damn, I wish I had a cigarette. He sat on a log and watched the front door. After what seemed to be an eternity, he saw a possum slink out the front door and dash out toward the woods.

A possum! Jesus. A possum.

What's the difference between an opossum and a possum? Are they the same thing? he wondered idly as he slowly made his way back into the cabin.

Later, in bed that night, he reviewed his day. All in all, he'd done okay. Things were going to be just fine. He smiled as he snuggled into the thick down comforter. Just as he was falling away, he heard something scuttle under the bed.

***

Veronica sighed. She would be so happy when Denise, the office manager, came back from vacation. She did not like doing the mail for her department. She'd put it off on the way in, and now she had to hustle before her boss came in and discovered he had no morning paper. She took the stairs down to the mailroom and grabbed the bin for her floor.

Back at her desk, she looked at the huge mass of banded letter envelopes, piles of larger manila envelopes, and stacks of magazines and newspapers. She'd do the magazines and papers first. Her boss wasn't the only one who started his day with the crossword. The Wall Street Journal, USA Today, Seattle Post-Intelligencer (what the hell was an Intelligencer anyway?), the Times: all the usual suspects. Now for the trashies: the Inquirer, the Star, and something new, too: Busted? What on earth was that? It looked so trashy she just couldn't help but take a peek. All these awful people. Face after face. People who'd been arrested last week. Most looked like zombies, eyes half mast, hair every which way. My God, the make-up on some of the women—and the men!

She felt a twinge of pity as she looked at some of them, though. A dazed and battered middle-aged woman looked out at her, face devoid of all hope. One young girl reminded her a little of her sister. Wait a minute. Was this some kind of nasty joke? Her heart began to pound so hard she put her hand up to her chest.

There was Bubbles, her baby sister in the flesh but the name under the photo was...Veronica Louise Byrnes. Panic hit her as she snatched up the paper and jammed it under her desk. Who had seen this? She tore through the stack. Were there any more copies?

***

For the first time in months, Barkin' Jack slept uninterrupted by coughing fits. He still had a way to go before he'd hit a hundred percent, but he wasn't afraid of dying anymore. That in itself had been a surprise. Jack hadn't realized that he cared one way or the other.

For the first time in quite a while, he'd started to think about what he might do when he got better. It would be a relief to get out of this bare little room for a bit, that was for sure.

Smokey Joe had been such a good friend to him. Jack really didn't understand why. As time had gone by, he'd been astonished to see Smokey return day after day. He brought Jack soup and water and those funny fish pills. Spent money from his tiny government check. Every day.

What was in it for him? That's what Jack could not fathom. If he'd learned anything on the streets, it was that people did the things they did in order to fulfill their personal needs. What did Jack have that Smokey needed?

***

They followed the matron double file up the courtroom steps. Bubbles was reminded of grammar school days where they were always told to look out for their neighbor. Her neighbor in this instance was a used-up crack whore who looked forty-five but was probably twenty. She saw the Portlandia statue at the top of the stairs but instead of a trident, she held the scales of justice.

Soon they were led into the courtroom and lined up on hard, blond wood benches. The bailiff appeared and said, "All rise."

Bubbles looked up to see the judge appear from chambers. Long black judicial robes, familiar hair-do... "Mom?" Oh my God, her mother was the judge? How could this be? She'd never been anything but a housewife. Actually bragged about never working a day in her life. As if being a galley slave and hand servant to her stepfather wasn't work.

Judge/Mom settled herself high above the proceeding. Then she looked down from her high bench and straight into Bubbles's eyes. "Oh Bubbles, I am so disappointed in you."

Bubbles opened her mouth to speak, but no sound came out. She tried harder and harder to make herself heard.

"Shut the fuck up, bitch. What the hell is wrong with you, girl?"

Bubbles opened her eyes to see the face of an unhappy cellmate hanging down from the bunk above.

"Sorry," she mumbled.

"We got court tomorrow. I need my rest. Don't need you down there yellin' like a fool."

"Um, sorry," Bubbles muttered into the darkened cell around her. "Good night."

***

Eleni waved at Max as she put down the phone. She looked intense.

"Max, we got a little emergency here."

"Ruh-roh! Now what?"

"Grab a jacket. I'll fill ya in on the way. It's Bubbles. We're coming to the rescue."

"Oh joy. The thought plickens."Max grabbed a jacket, took one last longing glance at the couch, and headed out the door.

***

Jolie shifted her weight from foot to foot with nervous energy as she waited in front of her apartment for Max and Eleni. She really wanted to kill that asshole bail bondsman. She couldn't believe he had the nerve to calmly ring up and inform her that Bubbles had been found and was headed for court right now. "If you hurry you can probably be there when she arrives."

And when was that? She'd heard him shuffling papers in the background. "Let me see, looks like 11:00 a.m."

Oh great, only just about half an hour from now. The bastard! It was 10:35.

***

The bus ride might have been fun if she wasn't so nervous. Everyone seemed to be infused with manic energy. Pickles, one of her cellmates, was telling hilarious tales about the last judge she'd been up before—who she knew to be an extremely kinky client of a friend of hers. Apparently, a muttered, "Who's a good doggy?" under her breath was enough to get them released that day.

Pickles had taken a liking to Bubbles, introducing her around and even encouraging the other girls to help her look her best for court. Last night they'd gotten together and made tons of little rag curls using toilet paper twisted and tied around small sections of her hair. She woke to find that after undoing them all, her hair stood straight up from her head—not baby doll curls, but an insane halo-fro of red and black.

Some of the other girls amused themselves by making obscene gestures at passing male motorists. Bubbles wondered whether this bus trip to court meant she was no longer an unknown quantity in the system or whether this was just part of the over-all insanity. She was certainly getting an education.

***

Veronica concentrated on her breath as she finished the mail. She'd learned that when she was stressed, she literally stopped taking in enough air, and her breathing became so shallow that she had panic attacks. Well, not this time. This time she was going to calmly and coolly grab her little sister and throttle the life out of her.

When the mail was neatly and properly sorted she called Joy, the HR lady, and told her that there had been a death in the family and she'd need to take a few personal days—effective immediately. Then she tidied her desk, grabbed her bag and headed for the Prius while she thumbed her Blackberry for the number. She hit the familiar icon when she found it. She took another deep, cleansing breath.

"Butchie? It's Veronica. Listen, I need a really big favor."

***

Pony gave herself to the beauty of the day as she walked over the Burnside Bridge. She could see the Ferris wheel and tents setting up for another festival—Labor Day? Maybe. It didn't really matter; Portland was always ready to celebrate. The trees were beginning to show yellow and red leaves and the roses were giving one last burst of color before the summer's end.

She moved on up Burnside, past Chinatown and myriad bars and street missions toward Rocky's. The spring in her step remained until she saw Toby being squeezed half to death by Daisy, her ex-girlfriend.

Pony slowed her steps considerably as she approached the pizzeria. She was tempted to just turn around and flee. Get a hold of yourself, girl. She made herself wait at the crossing. They always leave; they always leave. The familiar tune ran in and out of her mind.

Pony watched as Daisy grabbed Toby for one last enormous squeeze before she ran off, and Toby looked over and saw her standing there, waiting at the light. And then Toby waved—and smiled. She seemed easy, not in the least self-conscious.

Well, that was different.

Pony crossed and after a cursory hug asked, "So, um, wasn't that Daisy I saw a minute ago?" Ugh. She could not believe that little wimpy voice just came out of her.

Toby laughed. "Yup, that was Daisy alright."

Pony looked at her face and saw nothing but Toby looking back at her. When she spoke again, her voice sounded stronger—back to normal. "So, what was she up to?"

Toby threw her arm around Pony and started forward. "Oh man, you're not gonna believe this latest."

Wow, just like that—no long ass explanations, weird pauses—no guilty looks! Pony tucked her arm around Toby's waist and fell into step with her. She's not leaving. "Really? What's she up to now?"

The two women headed for home, breakfast forgotten. The streets were full of people, glowing with a last blast of summer warmth.

"Oh cool, the bridge is up." Toby raced ahead to see the Burnside Bridge split in the middle, each side slowly coming back together over the water as a huge container ship sailed through. Pony caught up and grabbed her hand.

"C'mon, let's follow the ship down the waterfront."

They took off. It was a ritual they never tired of. The Broadway, Steel, and Hawthorn Bridges lifted up in the middle to allow passage underneath. The Burnside and Morrison each split in the center. Only the Marquam, the Fremont, and the Ross Island were high enough for the really big ships to sail through without moving.

They followed the path until they found a good lookout spot and gazed out over the Willamette as each bridge went through its paces and waited until they could no longer see the ship.

Pony had managed to acquire a Popsicle along the way, and they shared it back and forth as they walked home.

"Still warm enough for ice-cream—Indian summer." Pony offered out the last little bit on the stick to Toby. But Toby stood stock-still.

"What the FUCK?"

They had come to the spot beneath the underpass that had served as Pony's home for the past six months. Pony just stared as her mind tried to take in the absence of the lean-to, the mattress, the table, boxes, tarps, and carts that had once made up their love nest. It was all gone. As if it had never existed. As if she had never existed.

***

Now in the waking world, Bubbles sat on the cold, shiny, blond wood bench and watched the judicial process unfold with a mixture of horror and fascination.

"Bonnie K. Hamilton, how do you plead?"

"Guilty, Your Honor."

"Bail has been set at five hundred dollars, remanded to custody." Bang went the gavel.

"Next."

"La Shonda Williams, how do you plead?"

"Guilty, Your Honor, with extenuating circumstances."

"Bail has been set at five hundred dollars, remanded into custody." Bang. "Next."

On and on it went, with the occasional variance of someone being released on their OR (own recognizance) or the occasional not guilty plea, which didn't seem to make any difference to the outcome.

Although the prisoners had entered the building through the back and into a holding cage, Bubbles knew that there were dozens of other courtrooms in this building. She thought about the scenario in front of her taking place in an almost identical fashion all around her. Above and below, on either side, people's entire lives were being determined in thirty-second interactions with a complete stranger. It was now 10:45. Was it possible to be bored and frightened at the same time?

***

Jack's temperature was finally a steady 98.6. He was, however, suffering from cabin fever. As he wandered around the abandoned house, Jack wondered at its history. Who had lived there before? How old was the place? Who owned it now?

In the kitchen, he noticed that the table was actually an old desk. Jack idly opened the drawer. There were some take-out fliers, rubber bands and garbage ties, expired coupons, and underneath, an old manila envelope addressed to a Mrs. Joseph Fratelli with an address in Idaho. It had been taped up at some point and re-taped. Inside, Jack found a stack of report cards and some old class photos. The report cards were all for Joseph Fratelli Jr. Young Joseph was a steady C student with the occasional B in English and Ds in Math. Apparently, Joseph had suffered from Poor Citizenship and had great difficulties with sitting still and remaining quiet while in the proximity of his neighbors.

Jack shuffled through the photos. The first one was black-and-white, featuring class and teacher with a little plaque in the corner reading:

Cherry St. School
Mrs. Garvin's B1 Class
1964

He studied the earnest little faces lined up according to height with the smallest ones in the front row. His eye fell on one grinning little guy with a buzz cut and two missing front teeth.

No, could it be? Well, look at that—a tiny Smokey Joe. Joseph Fratelli Jr.

***

"Jesus, it should be way past the morning rush. What's up?" Eleni peered into the distance as they sat stock-still on the freeway.

"I don't know—accident?" Max sat behind the wheel, a still counterpoint to Eleni's fidgeting.

Eleni leaned across Max to see out his side. "Can you get over to the left? Maybe we should take the I-5 to the Morrison Bridge."

"That takes us way out of the way. The 405 is the best route."

Eleni sat back, and then leaned in and turned on the radio, hoping to find some kind of answer.

Max dug the cell phone out of his jacket pocket. "Here, I think you better call Jolie. We are definitely running late."

The time was 10:55.

***

Friday drum circle. Daisy waved the joint away on the third go-round; she had to keep her head somewhat clear. She was on a mission. After her enlightening talk with Toby, she'd been weighing the pros and cons of various candidates. Finally, it looked as if she'd found her man. A regular at the circle, Rafi kept coming up aces, no matter how she shuffled the deck. He was perfect.

She'd interviewed an ex-girlfriend, who'd told her, "He's so beautiful and so sincere. I know it sounds funny but he's soothingly stupid. It's so relaxing. You just don't have to worry about anything stressful or heavy when you're with him."

Men liked him too. The general consensus seemed to be, "Rafi? Righteous dude." Tall, dark, and vegan: what more could she ask for? Now she just had to get him to come home with them.

***

"Are you sure that's legal?" Butchie asked. "We'd be taking a minor over a state line and all."

Veronica barely spared him a glance as she powered down the I-5 and ignored the breathtaking scenery that flew by.

"It's precisely because she's a minor that we can do this. She's a runaway and she's sixteen. She has no rights at all in this matter."

"It just feels weird, is all," offered Butchie. His face had taken on that labored and troubled expression which in Butchie indicated deep thought.

Veronica caught his tone and changed tactics; she leaned over to squeeze a massive thigh. "Sweetie, she's my little sister. I can't just leave her out on the streets with all those awful people." She made a little gurgling sound in her throat, which she hoped would sound like the beginnings of a tearful breakdown. "After all, you did say if I ever needed help I could depend on you. You did mean it, didn't you?"

A misty rain had begun to fall, giving the car an intimate, secluded feel. Butchie rose to the occasion in more than one way. As she carefully guided her hand up his leg, he considered the situation anew.

"Well, if you really think it's okay, babe."

***

Toby started forward and searched the area that had once been home. She'd begun to sputter her outrage. Her voice floated in and out of Pony's consciousness.

"Who the...what the...how dare they...If I find..."

Pony hadn't moved since she'd first laid eyes on the spot. She just couldn't seem to connect the dots. Soon, Toby noticed the silence that had gathered around them. She walked over and put her arms around Pony. After a few moments of total rigidity, Pony's body began to soften. It softened to the point where Toby was the only thing that held her up. Then Pony cried for the first time in years.

***

Jolie wanted to jam a stick into the spokes of every bicycle that passed her. It was all their fault. Another fucking Portland public bike ride. Supposedly, Max and Eleni were just a few blocks away but with all the streets blocked off re-routed and detoured, she had no idea how long it would take for them to reach her. On top of that, all the blocks around the park were clogged with people attending an organic beer fest. Bikes and beer. This would have never happened in California. It was already 11:00.

***

Bubbles stared at the elaborate braids of the woman in front of her as the bus jounced them back to the jail. She was FREE. Only a little more paperwork and mindless cattle bullshit and everyone assured her she was good to go. She understood none of it. The judge had deemed her time lost in the system to be time served. And someone had finally posted bail, which had paid the court costs. It had to be Jolie. But where the hell was she? Many of the other women had friends and family waiting for them at the courthouse, waving to them across the aisles.

She didn't even understand the charges against her. Drunk on drugs? What the hell was that supposed to mean? Pickles told her it was just your basic under the influence charge. She said they always pulled it out when they couldn't find anything else. Pickle's boyfriend, Cecil, would be waiting for her when they got back, she said. If no one showed up, she could give Bubbles a ride back to town.

Jesus, she had no idea how to get from wherever the hell the jail was back to the apartment. Where the hell was Jolie? It was 11:10.

***

They had now circled the block in front of the courthouse for the sixth or seventh time. The streets were cool and damp but the car felt muggy. Eleni knew if she changed the radio station one more time Max was going to lose it. What was it with Portland and the Red Hot Chili Peppers? They didn't even play them that much in LA. It looked as if Max had finally found a parking space but now Jolie was back out and ran up to the car, waving her arms.

"Don't bother to park!" she screeched. "She's gone. We need to get down to the jail before they let her go." Jolie wrenched open the back door and hopped in.

"Where is it?" asked Max.

"It's near 121st and Stark, and they're on their way back already."

"Do you think we can really make it there in time?" Max nailed Jolie with unnerving eye contact.

Jolie pressed her hands together. "I really don't know but...please, you guys? I know it's a long way, but I've got to try."

Okay," said Max. "Hold on tight now." And he hit the gas one more time.

***

Joe was real glad he'd told Jack about the house. Turned out he needed it real bad. Worse than even Joe himself did.

And life had fallen into a funny pattern. Joe would get up and give Jack his pills and sometimes he'd even brew up some cowboy coffee and they'd drink a cup. Then Joe would go out and do what he did. Maybe get some breakfast at Sisters, visit all his buildings and get his cigarette makings and whatever else they needed, maybe stop at the park or Pioneer Square, although he didn't really like it there much now—you couldn't even have a smoke without some cop up your butt. Then he'd come back and they'd have something to eat (if there was anything to be had) and he'd give Jack his night pills, and damn if old Jack wasn't looking better every day.

Joe had been scared when he saw how sick Jack was. Like what if Jack up and died there at the house? Then what? He might even be blamed for it. But luckily Jack didn't die. He was getting better. Even said he wanted to get to a shelter for a shower this week.

Yes, Joe was really starting to get comfortable here in the house and he knew Jack was too. It sure was a shame it wasn't theirs.

***

Daisy sat under the overhang of the window and watched the soft rain start to float in. She felt dreamy and happy again. Just like she did before the Atlantia syndrome. She grinned to herself as she reviewed yesterday's triumphs once more.

They'd begun to lock up Freddy's favorite produce dumpster behind the gourmet fruit and vegetable shop. That had left them with nothing but a few rather sad-looking Safeway carrots and canned water chestnuts all week. Even the earth mother herself had been at a loss to make anything out of them. When Daisy waltzed in with two bags of fresh, hot French fries, she'd been greeted very differently this time. Freddy and Rafi had fallen on them like they were manna from heaven and then, they'd fallen on Daisy with gratitude. She wasn't sure which felt better: the approval from the boys or the really nasty look that had left Atlantia's perfect face all twisted up and definitely uncool.

Tie that up with Freddy's disappointing inability to find his feminine side with

Rafi the other night (thank you, Toby!) and the writing was on the wall. Atlantia's star was falling and Daisy's was once more ascendant.

***

Lines and lines. Line up to give back their clothes, to get back her clothes, to get back her property and then—out on the curb, kicked loose. Bubbles had stuck close by Pickles throughout the process and now they stood side by side and sucked in their first breath of fresh, clean, free air.

Pickles dropped down to sit on the curb and go through an enormous shoulder bag. From it she plucked a pack of cigarettes, a lighter, and a cell phone. After she offered Bubbles a cigarette, she then pulled out her make-up bag and got to work while she chatted away, occasionally offering an aside to Bubbles.

"Mmm hmm, mmm hmmm. He's on his way."

"Na uh, oh no. Keep your eye out for a silver SRX."

Bubbles puffed away. The first cigarette in over a week made her lightheaded. Cars and cabs went by, slowing down until they found their passengers, and then pulled up and sped away. A group of girls headed off toward the bus stop, laughing. If only Jolie would show up.

It was nice of Pickles to offer a lift, but she wanted her people, her friends here now. Not strangers. No more strangers. She'd been living with her breath held for a week now. She was so tired. The area around her had begun to get more crowded. People coming and going. A huge, silver Cadillac SUV came into view. Was that an SRX? Bubbles didn't know from makes and models. She turned to Pickles just as the woman launched herself up from the curb and waved. The car slowed and she heard the steady boom of a bass float out its sides. Pickles grinned as the driver's head turned in her direction.

"Cecil! Cecil, over here!"

Bubbles took another big drag, flicked away the butt, and followed Pickles to where the massive car had pulled over.

***

This part of town always made Eleni squirrelly—the "high numbers," they called it. One look at the faces around her in the car made her realize she wasn't the only one with trouble in mind. Good thing they were on a mission. Getting Bubbles was the number one plan right now.

"Shit, shit, I think that was it. Can you turn around?" Jolie called out.

Sure enough, after Max doubled back, the jail came into view. Eleni watched as several cars wound around the building.

"Looks like everyone's headed back there." She pointed toward the area where a row of cars pulled over and picked up passengers. Several women on the curbside craned their heads to see whether their car held any promise. Up ahead, she saw a large black woman and a little frizzy-haired girl headed for a huge SUV.

Jolie rolled down her window and stuck her head out, trying to see a familiar face in the crowd.

"Wait a minute, is that? No. Oh my God—it's Bubbles. What the hell did she do to her hair? Bubbles! Hey Bubbles!"

Eleni watched as the frizzy-haired girl turned at the sound of Jolie's voice. Sure enough, it was Bubbles. She would never have recognized her without her trademark Cleopatra haircut, but Jolie had spotted her. Max headed toward her when a silver Prius cut him off.

***

As she headed for the car, Bubbles wondered whether she'd even be able to direct Cecil to the apartment. She really had no idea where the hell she was. Well, at least she was free. Just then, she heard her name called; it was Jolie's voice. Yay! Then all hell broke loose.

She'd really thought she might be hallucinating at first. There was Max and Eleni and Jolie, who hopped up and down and waved, and then out of nowhere, there was her sister and some guy who looked like a refugee from WWE Smackdown. What the hell was Veronica doing here?

Then the wrestler grabbed her and her sister hissed in her ear something about going with them or ending up back in the jail for ID theft, and she was in the Prius, headed for Longview, Washington.

FALL

Portlandia sits on her perch high above 5th Street, the second largest bronze statue in the US, second only to Liberty.

The tourists are bundled up. She can always tell the ones from the Southern climes. They shiver and waddle, wearing clothing more suitable for the arctic than Portland on a fall day. The natives mostly stick to sweaters and hoodies. Macho teenagers wear shorts and T-shirts. Most of the birds are gone now—a relief, although the pigeons never seem to go anywhere.

An intense young Asian girl with huge black-framed glasses sits on a ledge below and sketches her. Two homeless men in the park pass a bottle back and forth and peel the pages of an abandoned newspaper apart to fold and stuff inside their pants legs to provide an extra layer of warmth. The coffee house across the street does a brisk business. A few brave smokers sit outside, faces hovering over their cups, and grab puffs between sips.

The bike cops have switched to their heavier winter uniforms, making them look a bit more official.

The wind picks up a pile of leaves and makes a tiny whirling twister, the leaves joining together to spin as one. The dance of the city reels on.

***

As she stared up at the intersection between two cracks in the motel ceiling, Toby tried to figure out what day it might be. She was pretty sure they'd lost at least a week, maybe more. She had wanted to take Pony away from the ruins of their lost home, wanted to escape the pain of losing their tiny niche. Now it felt as if she'd lost more than just some bad memories. Her head hurt and her upper arm felt hot and funny. She figured she'd probably sprung a couple of new abscesses. The shower was running in the bathroom. God, she hoped it was Pony in there. She drifted back to sleep.

***

"Whatever it was that just happened, I think I need a drink." Max leaned against the steering wheel.

"Definitely," Eleni and Jolie said simultaneously, and then began to laugh.

"I mean who the...what the...how the hell?" Jolie spluttered.

"I know." Max shook his head. "I know."

***

Halfway home, and Veronica hadn't shut up once. To the tune of nauseating soft rock song after soft rock song, she spouted her inanities. The wrestler just sat there like the big, stupid galoot he undoubtedly was.

"Mother's been worried half to death you know; I swear she's lost fifteen pounds. This hasn't been easy on her marriage, you know. Of course, I'm sure you never thought of that. You never think of anything but yourself."

On and on, as steady as the raindrops on the windshield. Bubbles stared out the back window. Pretty close now. They were passing the weird Christian billboards that signaled less than ten miles before they hit the Longview off-ramp.

"Don't you have anything to say for yourself?"

The car was silent, with the exception of Jack Johnson bleating out his latest hit. After a few more moments, Bubbles spoke up.

"Could you turn that stupid, fucking pretentious, hippie bullshit off, please?"

Veronica rolled her eyes and huffed. "Honestly, I don't know why I bother."

Bubbles closed her eyes. "Neither do I, Veronica—neither do I."

***

She was in a bus station, and she had to pee like crazy but she couldn't find the bathroom. Finally locating an unmarked door at the back, she entered and found a tiny employee bathroom. The most disgusting bathroom she'd seen in ages. She wondered whether she could hold out any longer when a man came in and yelled at her. Someone was in the other stall and was peeing and peeing and peeing. The telephone rang.

Toby's eyes snapped open. Oh, right: hotel room. The phone continued to ring. She rolled over and grabbed it.

"Checkout time is 11:30, Miss Smith. Would you like to reserve the room for a second day, ma'am?"

Toby glanced around for a clock. "What time is it now?"

"It's 11:25, ma'am."

"Okay, just give me a couple minutes. We're checking out."

"All right then, thank you, ma'am." The woman hung up before Toby could reply.

The shower was still running in the bathroom. Ma'am? Miss Smith? Toby guessed she must have rented the room in that name then. Either she or...

"Pony? Pony?"

Toby jumped up and ran to the bathroom. When she flung open the door, she found Pony curled in a seated fetal position on the shower floor, rocking back and forth. A thin stream of pinkish, watery blood came from between her legs. She looked up at Toby, eyes wide like a child's.

"Oh Tobe, that last guy, I think he hurt me."

***

Watching her mother and Veronica greet each other reminded Bubbles of trying to make her Barbie dolls hug and kiss. You'd put them together, but they were so stiff they just kind of clacked against each other. Nothing bendy, nothing soft. Clack, clack.

Hello Mother—air kiss—clack. Veronica—clack, clack.

Then her mother just stood back and looked at her. Bubbles felt her mother's eyes take in the tiny black skirt, strategically torn T-shirt, and the wild, frizzy cell block hair-do. She took it all in, emitted her trademark sigh, and summed it up in five words.

"Oh Bubbles, I'm so disappointed."

Gee, where had she heard that before?

***

Somehow, as the shock wore off, Jolie had ended up with Max and Eleni in a dark booth at My Father's Place. The three of them had been strangely quiet, slowly perusing their menus, and then ordered drinks and breakfast. Only after the drinks had been served and their plates set down did they all look up and begin to speak at once.

"So what the fuck...?"

"Who the hell...?"

"What happened...?"

They tried again. Jolie kept mum and let Eleni speak first.

"Wasn't that her sister? It was, wasn't it?"

It was what Jolie had figured too, but it was still unpleasant to hear it confirmed.

"Yeah," she agreed. "Had to be. I only ever saw her that one time in the club, but who else would do that?"

Max and Eleni recognized a rhetorical question when they heard it and just shook their heads. The quiet of the restaurant seemed to highlight the insanity of what had taken place just an hour ago in the jail parking lot. Jolie started in again.

"So what the hell did she do with her? Did you see that guy? What a freak. I mean, they fucking kidnapped her. Can they do that?" She tried to keep it steady but her voice got shakier and angrier as she went on. "I mean, that was not a voluntary thing on Bubbles's part. She did not want to get in that car. They fucking kidnapped her. That yuppie bitch and her white trash wrestler boyfriend stole our Bubbles!"

"Yeah, I guess they did." Eleni tried to piece it all together while she talked. "It was a kidnapping, but on the other hand, she is a kid." She took a long swallow of her Bloody Mary.

"So can you kidnap your sister? I mean, it's a weird situation. She is a minor. As crazy as it sounds, Jolie, I think it might not even be against the law."

Max stared down into his beer as if a better world might be floating in the bottom somewhere, just out of reach.

Jolie shook her head. "Well, it might not be illegal, but it's just fucking wrong. I can't just forget about her now. We've got to do something."

"Do you think she'll try to get in touch with you?" Eleni asked.

"Yeah, if she can, she will."

"What can you do, Jolie? It's not like you're even related."

"I don't know what I can do either," Jolie said. "But I'll figure something out. That bitch is not getting away with this."

The waitress approached and Max caught her eye. "Okay then, in the meantime, another drink sounds about right, eh?" Max offered.

"Good thinking," Jolie agreed. "We'll start with that."

***

For years, Bubbles had nurtured a dramatic fantasy in which she was a failed alien experiment left on the planet to die. Although she'd since come to grips with the unlikeliness of this theory, she was still at a complete loss in terms of a satisfactory explanation for how she ended up in her family.

If her mother was any more passive, she'd be a speed bump. Her biological father had been a workaholic engineer who died of a massive stroke when Bubbles was nine and her current stepfather Ken was a passive-aggressive, angry engineer (what was it with Mom and engineers?). And Veronica? Well, Veronica was quite simply a creature of pure self-love.

She'd given the whole family thing some thought during her introductory psychology class. Sure, she had certain reservations about the diagnostic process but she did enjoy entertaining herself by pegging her family into DSM IV categories. Veronica fit neatly in the border between narcissistic personality disorder and sociopath.

Their relationship had always been about how Bubbles could augment Veronica's life. Sister as accessory. Something to put in a baby carriage, or dress up, maybe earn a few bucks to watch. And for a long time, it seemed to work out well enough for her. But eventually, Bubbles was like a pair of shoes that kept running away or going out of style: frustrating and inconvenient.

Bubbles could never figure out why Veronica didn't just shove her into the back of her mental closet and move on. It would have been so much easier on the both of them. But Veronica had other plans. Most of them having to do with getting a handle on creating a smaller, more subservient version of herself.

Last year, she'd given Bubbles a Louis Vuitton bag. As if anyone who had even met her for five minutes could see her carrying such a thing. Bubbles had briefly considered trying to write "I HATE" over each of the little LVs on the nasty thing, but in the end she'd just tossed it in a Goodwill bin.

Later, Veronica complained that she never saw her sister carry it and let slip how much she'd paid for it. It had taken every bit of strength in Bubbles's body to stop herself from shaking Veronica to death. God, the things she could have bought with that cash. Not that big sis really laid out real dollars; knowing Veronica, she'd probably just slipped the charge onto her latest boyfriend's VISA card.

And now she'd actually hunted her down and kidnapped her. So what the fuck did she want now?

***

I feel so stupid. It was my fault. I should have never gone with them. I just wanted another hit so bad, ya know?

Toby stood in the ER bathroom as another doctor/nurse team was in seeing Pony. Pony's words just chewed a hole in her guts. Pony's fault? Wasn't it enough they'd almost ripped her apart? Left her to die?

All that was enough to send Toby round the bend, but then to look at Pony and know that she actually blamed herself?

Toby had kept cool until she got out of the room but now she couldn't seem to stop the tears and the shakes that kept on coming. Tears for Pony, tears for herself, tears for the fact that what she wanted more than anything else right now was another hit.

***

Bubbles shuffled down the beige hallway festooned with family photos in which her presence slowly faded away into—ugh!—the pink and black bedroom in the beige house. Bubbles thought she'd never have to see this place again. Her parents' house was a study in beige, beige and white outside, all the way down to the flagstone path. Inside: all tans, buffs, and off-whites. Vaguely Scandinavian. Her mother and stepfather in beige, too. Her stepdad's sandy hair and chinos. Her mother the only person she'd ever met with beige hair.

Bubbles knew her physical presence in the house constituted a messy spot. Like a walking, breathing pile of cast-offs.

The only exceptions to the beige theme were the girls' rooms, as her mother called them. Her bedroom and Veronica's were done in pale pink. Bubbles hated pale pink even more than beige. Hated the frilly Laura Ashley crap her mother hauled in there too.

Last year, she'd had enough. Bought a can of black paint and went at it with a vengeance. Unfortunately, she'd only gotten one and a half walls done when her mother came home and flipped. Her stepfather confiscated the paint and she was grounded for over a month. Her mother had left the room that way as a punishment supposedly, but Bubbles knew it was really because they'd given up. She was just the mess they wanted to go away.

***

Jack felt weirdly naked today as he sat on the bus. He couldn't believe how long it had been since he'd been out. The fall leaves were everywhere. Hadn't it still been summertime when he came to the house with Smokey? He looked over at Smokey Joe now, watched him bouncing in his seat as he looked happily out the window at the passersby. A ditty from his childhood came to mind: "The wheels on the bus go round and round, round and round, round and round, something, something, something." And then, "The people on the bus go up and down, up and down, up and down." He couldn't remember what they did after that.

He slumped down in his seat and clutched the torn upholstery. He wasn't prepared for how big and bright everything seemed, even on this overcast day. He felt vulnerable, like a sitting duck. Sounds were extra loud too. Not just normal loud.

Something disturbed in his ears. What was it? Sad. Sobbing, wet noises. He glanced over and saw a young Hispanic girl with a baby. It was coming from there. It wasn't the baby crying. It was the mother. The girl just sat there and clung to her child while fat tears ran down her face. The child seemed oblivious of his mother's pain, just clung to her and stared out in that unfocused way that infants did. It gave Jack the creeps. No one else seemed to notice.

***

Bubbles sat in the last stall of the girl's bathroom at Lewis and Clark, once more feeling as if she was caught in some déjà vu hell. After her time in the city, it felt absurd to be back in high school again. Waving away the smoke cloud, she was about to leave the stall when the two girls came in.

"Eww, someone's been smoking," one of them brayed.

Bubbles recognized the voice immediately: Brianna Taylor, cheerleader / moron extraordinaire.

"Omigod, it's ger-oss," echoed Chloe Johnson, Brianna's sycophant shadow.

Bubbles slowly climbed on the seat to avoid discovery.

"So is your mother going out of town this weekend?" Brianna asked. "'Cause I kinda already told Todd we're having a party."

"No way!" wailed Chloe. "I got in so much trouble last time, Bree."

"Oh don't worry, I promise I really will help you clean up this time. Really—promise."

A Muse ringtone went off and Brianna snapped her phone open. "Ya? Shut up! Ya?" She prattled on.

Just then Mrs. Murchison came in. "Ladies? Don't you have anywhere to be this period?"

The two girls scurried off like cockroaches when the light snaps on. Pretty soon, Mrs. Murchison was gone too.

Bubbles slipped out and checked her hair. As she reached for the faucet, something caught her eye. Lying on the sink was Brianna's hot pink metallic iPhone. The corners of Bubbles's mouth lifted for the first time in days. She picked up the little phone, slipped it into her right boot, and left the room. Perfect. The phone would probably only last for about another day before it got switched off but it was hers for now. She got busy texting Brian.

***

After her disastrous debut at Hells Belles, the best Jolie had been able to manage was a regular gig at the Golden Giraffe (a gentleman's club, it said in smaller letters under the sign). It wasn't the bottom of the barrel, but despite its claims, no one here could be accused of being a gentleman by any stretch of the imagination.

She'd been amazed at the variety and pure scope of all the clubs in Portland. For such a small town to have so many was pretty odd to begin with. And then to top it off, it seemed as if everybody had some special talent—that simply taking your clothes off was a thing of the past. There were girls who juggled, girls who juggled flaming objects, girls who sang karaoke, girls who sang in bands, girls who had blogs and wrote books, girls who did magic tricks. Just working the pole was no big deal, although there were also girls who taught housewives to pole dance as a sideline. The whole thing made her brain hurt.

Riding the MAX home, she stretched her aching legs out and wondered just exactly what in her life had changed since she moved here. Although the methadone kept her habit at bay, she still craved dope. She still danced in the clubs. She still didn't have anything resembling a relationship.

And she still didn't know what she wanted to be when she grew up. She remembered the dreams she'd had when Jenny had first invited her up here. She'd pictured the two of them finding a cute little apartment, and then maybe getting a job in a clothing store, maybe going back to school—City College—getting a kitten or a little white rat that would ride on her shoulder. It hadn't been world-shaking stuff, but it had seemed really possible. Now it felt like someone else's dream.

***

Brian adjusted the wonky lid in front of the window, checked the computer. There, he had a weak signal. He'd made the device in order to piggyback onto a Wi-Fi signal from the ranger station. Fitted the receiver into the lid, creating an antenna effect. To his amazement, it worked. Not perfectly, not one hundred percent dependably, but the fact that it worked at all filled him with satisfaction.

His woodland world had taught him so much about what he was capable of. In a place he never would have dreamed he'd end up, he'd finally begun to understand himself and most importantly, begun to stop judging himself so harshly. He didn't think he'd ever look in the mirror and say "I love you" like those affirmations his sister was always taping up all over everything. He didn't think he wanted to have a love affair with the mirror anyway. He just wanted to be comfortable and slowly he was getting there.

The drawback was loneliness. He'd gone into town every weekend with the girls at first. Portland might not have the scene that say San Francisco or even LA had, but compared to Longview, well, it might as well have been Babylon. He'd considered bringing a guy up to the cabin a few times but found that he didn't really want to wake up with a stranger in his bed, in his cabin. That was new, too. He never thought he'd prefer to be alone. To choose it. Didn't mean he wasn't lonely, but he slowly realized that someone wasn't always better than no one.

When he logged on to his Facebook page, he skimmed through various invites and causes. Delete, delete, delete; the process was so automatic he almost missed it. Won't you join my, help me get my, help us fulfill our, So and so wants you to like... private chat message. BRIAN HELP. Help?

Oh my God. Bubbles. Bubbles back in Longview. Kidnapped? He needed to talk to her friend Jolie. He'd never met her, but Bubbles thought she hung the moon. And she was an adult; she'd be able to do things he couldn't get away with. If she was willing to help. He tried to remember everything Bubbles had told him about her, where she was or where she worked. One thing was sure: he had to find a way off this hill ASAP.

As tempting as it was to wait for the weekend when Raven and Alison were coming by with the car, Brian knew he had to get to Portland now. If the shoe was on the other foot, he would not have been amused at a four-day convenience gap in his rescue. She'd already been there too long as it was. He grabbed his duffel and began to pack.

***

Nicholas nursed his beer and stared up at the ceiling, at all the motorcycles hanging down. Man. I'd love to haul that old Indian down, hop on, and disappear into the wild blue yonder. He paused briefly to fully indulge in the fantasy but the noise of the other patrons and the video poker machines slammed him quickly back to his far duller reality.

Kelly's Olympian was one of the oldest bars downtown and had revamped its image years ago by cramming vintage motorcycles, old gas pumps, and filling station gear into every available space. Normally, Nicholas didn't spend money on beer in a place like this, but the apartment felt seedy and desolate without the girls' energy to distract him from everything that was wrong. It was a dump. The location had really been the only thing to recommend it in the first place. He didn't know whether Bubbles even lived there anymore and Jolie always seemed to be off on some mission to get her back.

He didn't like just being part of the daytime clientele here at Kelly's. He wanted to be here at night, playing with a band. Not the same old crap—something fresh, something new. Like that tune playing now. Bobby had disappeared once more. Nicholas figured he was either strung out or in rehab. He realized that he'd been feeling depressed all week. The music didn't help, as beautiful as it was. Strange stuff for Kelly's. Then he realized it was coming from outside. He set his empty glass down and wandered out.

There on the corner of 3rd and Washington stood a girl with an open violin case in front of her. The violin itself was perched on her shoulder and the most amazing sounds floated up and danced in the air around her. The case slowly filled with dollar bills. Even the blasé lunchtime crowd could tell this was something special.

Now there's someone who could definitely chase the blues away, Nicholas thought as he approached the vision.

***

As he stood in the middle of nowhere, Brian got his map out and scanned it in earnest. It had fire roads marked in red, state highways in green, and all the waterways in turquoise. If he followed the turquoise line of the creek, it would lead to the highway, where he could hitch a ride to Portland.

After he'd left the cabin and started down the path, he noticed how little the world around him resembled the map. If only the hiking trails were yellow, like on the map, it would be so much easier. As it was, the ground beneath his feet was covered in wet fall leaves. Lots of colors here: yellow with black rot spots, red, scarlet, orange, faded green and brown.

He looked at the map again. Okay, a right here—and that should take him to the creek. A soft drizzle had made his glasses fog. He sure hoped it wouldn't start raining for real or he was blind.

Everything seemed to belong but him. Squirrels scampered here and there, lush tails held high as they navigated branches and tree limbs. All sorts of birds called to each other from the branches above. Chipmunks shot by on the forest floor, clearly headed in the right direction. Moss covered the trunks of the trees like sleeves with ferns nestled in the shelter below.

Okay, this looked like the place where he was supposed to turn left. That gate was probably the fire road, so he'd go left there. The drizzle was now officially rain. He heard his tennis shoes squish and the droplets sounded loud on his nylon hoodie. His mother was always going on about how they were one-sixteenth Cherokee. Unfortunately, it looked as if it wasn't going to do much good here in Chinook territory.

***

Jolie blinked as she tried to adjust her eyes to the darkness of the Alibi Lounge. Eleni had texted her to meet at the tiki bar for happy hour and good news. Peering past a palm frond, she heard Eleni's voice cut through the gloom, "Jolie—over here!"

Jolie spotted Eleni off in a blacklit corner; Max smiled at her from behind a large pineapple festooned with swords, straws, and maraschino cherries. Eleni held up her coconut shell filled with more plastic toys and a no-doubt lethal alcohol count. As she hugged Jolie one-armed awkwardly around the neck, she'd burst into a monologue.

"Taste this! You want one? They're awesome, or try Max's—it's really good, too. They're on me! Remember that temp agency way the hell out in Beaverland, and the lady said she was gonna call me and then nothing? And remember the story about the guy in the dumpster? So they're gonna have a reading—you gotta come. I'm gonna start training the day after tomorrow—it's in Southwest. It's market research."

"Whoa, whoa!" laughed Jolie. "You are way ahead of me. Let me get the waitress. I need to catch you guys up."

Two Scorpions, one Mai Tai, and a Zombie later, Jolie was able to determine that Eleni's luck had finally taken a turn for the better. Her temp agency had come through with a job and the writing program she'd joined had accepted a story for their yearly anthology.

"You know what this means, Jolie?" Eleni had said. "It's your turn now. Your luck's gonna change. It's gotta be—right?"

But later that night, Jolie wasn't so sure that's what it meant at all.

***

When they brought her lunch tray in, Pony realized she'd been lying there worrying for two hours straight without coming to a single decision.

The arrival of the outreach lady had been a complete surprise. It was the result of some new program to help abused street women and prostitutes. Pony had been a little weirded out by the labels. She didn't think of herself as a prostitute. She didn't like the victim status that abused woman implied, either. She was just someone who had to turn the occasional trick and the last occasional trick had turned out to be a little psycho.

But it wasn't that stuff that had her so spun. If sticking on all those labels made them happy, well, she didn't really care that much. It was what the woman had offered. Safety. A place to live and get clean. The stuff of dreams. At least that's what it seemed like at first. But then there was the question of Toby. And that's where things got nightmarish.

Because it didn't seem as if they cared that much about what happened to Toby. The woman told her Toby could apply and stood a good chance of being accepted, but even if she was, they would not be allowed to live together as they had been. And Toby apparently didn't carry the at-risk status she did. Maybe if she would have reported the guys in the van right after it happened, but she hadn't. And now, even though Pony hadn't reported the guys who hurt her, she had special status. All because of some asshole trick with a razor-spiked cock ring. The woman told Pony that she had to save herself before she could help anybody else.

Pony didn't know about that. She just couldn't help feeling as if it was a bunch of excuses to make her feel better about dumping the one person who really loved her.

In twenty-four hours, she would be discharged from the hospital. She had to make her decision tonight.

***

As they got off the bus, a kid on a fancy bicycle almost ran Jack over. They passed 5th Street and the rows of carts filled with plastic bags, people lined up for a meal, tables with folks hanging out and drinking coffee, and more people leaning up against buildings not doing much of anything at all. Jack almost tripped over a young woman who squeezed pus out of her leg and scraped it off with a twig. A dirty faced child ran up and grabbed Jack around the thighs, and then realized his mistake and ran howling off to his mother.

Smokey's cheerful attitude was the only thing keeping Jack from turning around and getting right back on the bus for home. On the face of it, his jitters seemed paranoid. He really didn't have a reason. He just felt wrong. He'd never been particularly psychic. If he was, well, he wouldn't be here now, would he? And he didn't want Smokey to think he was just some crazy old duff. Anyway, he really needed a shower and they were free at St. Francis today. Jack resented paying for a shower in a city surrounded by water. Maybe after he got all cleaned up, he'd feel better. Maybe.

Squeaky clean, Jack thought as he rubbed his skinny, pink-flushed body with a battered but clean, white towel. He'd really lost weight during his illness but he knew he was truly on the mend now. It felt good. Maybe things were looking up. He didn't have the heebie-jeebies anymore. He took a bottle of lotion out of the little bag the church people had given him. It had little tiny hotel bottles of shampoo and conditioner, which he'd used already. He didn't ordinarily use body lotion but he figured what the heck?

He rubbed it all over, head-to-toe, and when he was done, he smelled like cucumbers and lemon. A definite improvement on the odor he gave off coming in. The door swung open and a red-faced man with a woolen cap pulled down halfway over his face stood there and scowled at him.

"You 'bout done in there? There's other people waiting, ya know."

Jack just stood there and stared at the guy until he became embarrassed enough to leave. Oh well, nuthin's perfect, thought Jack as he gathered his things. The feeling of paranoia had lifted a little but Jack still felt antsy, as if things weren't quite safe.

***

Nicholas pulled the covers up, snuggled in and grinned happily. Gisarra was off in the shower, leaving him time to dream. Gisarra—what a beautiful name. So perfect for her.

She'd told him she was from South America, had a husband in New York but they were just friends now. The marriage stayed put only to keep her in the country legally. She'd landed in Portland two days ago. Nicholas couldn't believe his luck. Someone would have grabbed her up for sure by the end of the week.

Just last week, Max had said they needed something special for the band. They'd discussed the merits of getting a synth player or even a sax. He couldn't wait to call Max and tell him they had a violinist. The more he thought about it, the violin was really the only choice. Nicholas scratched his crotch, rolled over and fell into a deep sleep.

***

Toby drifted through the Park blocks—the emerald green oasis that she barely noticed anymore. It ran through downtown Portland and remained cool even in the summer. Tired walkers, office workers, and students found benches to sit on and there was some actually decent public art to look at from time to time. Now in the fall, it was filled with bright red, orange, and yellow leaves above and below.

None of this was on Toby's mind, however. She had nowhere to go, nothing to do, and nobody to do it with. She even envied Pony being in the hospital a little. At least she belonged somewhere.

Toby headed toward the hospital slowly. She knew it was lunchtime now and she didn't want to have to watch Pony eat. She was too hungry and she knew Pony would see it and insist she eat her lunch. She might be desperate but she wasn't desperate enough to take the food out of Pony's mouth. She racked her brain for something to do to kill the time. She wandered up Burnside and decided to check in at Rocky's pizza to see whether she could bum a slice again. It had only been a few weeks since she ran into Daisy here, but damn it seemed like a very long time since the day they'd sat there, chatting happily away about Daisy's problems. A familiar figure lurched out the door as she was about to enter. Oh God, it was Niner.

"Toby! Now if you ain't just the girl I'm lookin' for..." Niner held out his skinny tattooed arms.

Niner had gotten his name from a youthful addiction to the game of mumblety-peg, which had left him with nine fingers and nine toes. Toby knew it wasn't a great idea to get involved in whatever it was Niner was offering. On the other hand, what the hell else did she have to do?

"What's up?" Toby knew that by asking this question, she'd as good as agreed to whatever Niner had brewing.

"Ray Ray's back. He's out. Jay kept the old place for him. The old stomping grounds on Flanders, remember?"

Oh no, Toby thought, that place. Those memories never left her consciousness for long. Ray Ray had been her first real dealer.

"Sure," she said.

They marched up Burnside into the trendy Northwest neighborhood, marched over the freeway overpass. Niner's shambling, slightly crooked gait made her feel as if she were marching in some doomed parade of the dysfunctional. This area was the perfect combo of rags and riches. Trendy shops side by side with welfare hotels and the Goodwill. They turned off Burnside to walk down beautiful tree-lined streets with multicolored Victorians and restored Craftsmans all around them as they headed for the familiar garage door.

Niner pounded out a secret knock—a dot-dot dash-dash-dot kinda thing—and the door opened.

***

Daisy never realized how many changes went on when you were pregnant. Her feet were swollen, her shoes didn't fit right, her nipples got sore, and she barfed round the clock. Not just in the morning. She felt invaded. So she'd signed up for a freebie young mother's yoga class in the park. She'd noticed people who did yoga always looked slim and healthy.

She thought most of the girls there were hopelessly normal-formal. Even the two pregnant fifteen-year-olds seemed positively well-adjusted. Was she simply pregnant because she'd been too fucking flaky to even get an abortion together? Because she needed a friend who would never leave? Or was it just to prove she could do better than her mother had? That she could protect her child from being exposed to things a child should never know about? Like her father.

***

Max and Eleni flopped into their usual booth at My Father's Place. A Thursday morning ritual: go to the clinic, get their weekly take-home doses, and then breakfast at MFP. Before the smoking ban had taken effect, the fact that you could have a cigarette with your incredibly cheap French toast had made it a clear favorite. Now, it smelled a little better but Eleni was glad they kept the lights down low.

What you could see through the darkness was an eclectic decor. Musical instruments, prosthetic legs, KISS masks, and other items hung from the ceiling. The walls were covered in portraits of long dead presidents, and women in Gibson girl hair-dos. Vintage cigarette and liquor ads, and old tobacco tins and cigar boxes were nailed up alongside them. Lincoln had something awful smeared across the glass on his portrait. They had both talked about switching to a different coffee shop, but somehow every Thursday morning they ended up back here.

Dee, their favorite waitress, arrived at the table. "The usual?" she asked.

"You bet." Eleni nodded. This consisted of French toast for Eleni, spinach and cheese omelet for Max, split a side of sausage links, and keep the coffee coming.

"I went down another milligram on my dose," said Eleni. "I'm down to thirty-seven. Pretty good, huh?"

"That's great," said Max. "That's more than half your original dose."

"Yeah," said Eleni, "I'm not gonna rush it this time—this time I'm getting off and staying off." She smiled and pulled a keno slip out from the little holder.

"I notice my numbers keep popping up. Do you have five dollars?"

She sketched in the little boxes. "Oh, and my training is done on Wednesday. By the time we're here next week, I'll be a full-fledged recruiter."

***

Bubbles left detention and ducked out through the teacher's parking lot. These days, she wanted as little to do with her classmates as possible.

Soft bedding and hot meals had begun to soften Bubbles's shell of late. It had been nice to open a fridge full of food, to open a drawer full of clean, folded clothes. She'd almost forgotten the price tag that came with it: the long looks from her mom and stepdad. Long looks she couldn't even begin to decipher because they seemed to be exchanged at the slightest remark. Could you pass the orange juice? would be punctuated with an eyebrow lift or meaningful glance over the cereal boxes. She didn't even have to bother trying to freak them out anymore. They seemed to be on perma-freak. Had Brian gotten her message yet? she wondered.

She stalked the familiar streets of Longview toward home. She hadn't traveled much, but she imagined it was probably interchangeable with hundreds of other little towns throughout the country. Strip malls. Car lots. Banks. It had none of the beauty or life of Seattle to the north or Portland to the south. The stench of the paper mill was everywhere today. She had almost forgotten that sickening scent. The place was closing in on her. Why was she here?

She ducked into a Starbucks and breathed in gratefully. The smell of fresh brewed coffee replaced the sour chemical stink. She reached into her pocket and pulled out a crumpled dollar and a handful of change. Just enough. As she walked to the counter, she recognized her barista.

"Bubbles?" Brittany asked.

"Britt, it's you!" Bubbles looked at her old friend with frank curiosity.

"What are you doing here?"

"I came back." Britt gave her a bittersweet smile.

"But I thought you left for good—went to LA. You were one of my inspirations!"

Brittany gave her another kind of smile, not so sweet now. "Yeah, well, as you have obviously learned, Longview has a way of getting its hooks into you."

"I guess so." Bubbles looked at her friend's tired face and felt herself fighting not to recoil from her. "Well, um, anyway, good to see ya."

"Yeah," Brittany said. "Great."

Bubbles grabbed her coffee. It took every bit of nerve in her not to run out of there.

***

"Nicholas! I can't find my boots—Whoa!"

Jolie had barged into the bedroom, expecting to find only Nicholas. Instead, there was a very strange exotic creature, sitting there in nothing but her thigh-high boots and holding a violin. Nicholas was conveniently nowhere in sight. Bootsy looked up at her from beneath thick lashes.

"Oh, you live here too?" she said in a vampy foreign accent.

"Oh yes, I leeve here and my boots leeve here too. Take them off—NOW!"

Gisarra gave a shrug and laid down her violin carefully as she pulled off Jolie's boots, which slipped off her thin legs much more quickly than they did Jolie's.

"These are very nice." She dangled them out to Jolie, who snatched them back quickly.

"Um, where's Nicholas anyway? He just left you here?" Jolie asked.

"Oh Nick, he is getting cigarettes, he said. I am Gisarra."

Although Jolie spent her working day ninety-nine percent naked, she had to admit she was impressed with this girl's attitude in the altogether, which would have had left Jolie far less assured.

"Well, I'm Jolie. I live here. So does our other friend Bubbles but she's..." Jolie paused. Kidnapped went through her mind. "She's out of town," she finished.

"Ahh," said Gisarra.

Jolie sat on the edge of the dresser. "So, you play violin, huh? You any good?"

"I am, I think. Yes. Very good."

Jolie fished out a cigarette and lit up. "Let's hear it."

***

Bubbles eventually found that when you're always floating in a sea of passive aggression, you can learn to be sensitive in all sorts of ways. You learn very quickly how to read people. Veronica had simply been too nice for the past two days and Bubbles knew that meant trouble. Even when she'd gone out of her way to push Veronica's buttons, her sister had remained cool. That scared her. Doing something as simple and logical as asking her would never work, not with Veronica.

Which meant it was time to get snooping. Bubbles logged on to Veronica's laptop and poked around in her files. One, marked Letters, had some pretty funny stuff, but nothing to explain this strange state of being.

Hmmm... Seemed her e-mail was password protected. Bubbles got it on the third try. Veronica's birthday backwards. You are so predictable. Bubbles rolled her eyes. She could now see a flurry of letters to their mother. That was odd, considering how often they saw each other. Bubbles settled in and began to read. What a drama queen. Jesus. She wrote as if she were the heroine in some nineteenth-century novel.

"Mother, I am at my wit's end," wrote Veronica. (Short trip, thought Bubbles.)

"Bubbles will not listen to a word of sense from me. I simply cannot go on with this."

Ruh-roh.

***

Max was just stuffing his Handy Hardware shirt into his pack and preparing to buzz in when Nicholas appeared at the door of the studio.

"Max! Perfect! Bobby's upstairs already. Come on up."

Max knew if Nicholas had actually scraped together the cash for the rental space, it must be something big. Now, whether it had anything to do with actual musical talent remained to be seen. Nicholas was amped and took the linoleum stairs two at a time.

Max's step remained unhurried.

The rehearsal space was freezing as usual. Bobby was stretched out on the old sprung couch, talking to the guest of honor. If nothing else, she was easy on the eye. A gypsy beauty. Everyone grabbed a beer as cursory introductions were made. Nicholas stood and threw an arm out in Gisarra's direction.

"Okay everyone, here she is. All I'm gonna say is: prepare to be blown away."

The band set up and began to play one of the songs Nicholas had worked on with Gisarra. She let the song begin as usual and waited as they established the sound. Slowly her electric violin came in; she wove her notes through effortlessly and naturally. It was done so perfectly, adding the mood and tone they'd worked so hard to achieve, that Max realized he couldn't imagine ever going back to playing it the way it had been before. The song finished but the band kept playing—jamming now. Max's guitar began a musical conversation with Gisarra's violin. They played their influences, made musical jokes; they melded their styles and then broke away into a stream of melodic consciousness that transcended anything they could have possibly tried to put into words. When it was all over, they grinned like fools. The room buzzed with adrenaline. They could all feel it. It was the beginning of a whole new adventure for the band.

***

Toby's head jerked up from her nod as the MAX car stopped and the words La Linea Roja rattled into her consciousness. Shit, missed her stop.

When she jumped off the car, she looked around and got her bearings. Jesus, she hadn't been this loaded in a long time. Trust Ray Ray's dope. It was always the best, just like old times. What time was it, anyway? She peered into the window of a shoe repair. 3:30! Damn, she'd told Pony she'd be there around lunchtime.

Oh well. She continued on toward the hospital, feeling warm and buffered from the world. A little old man sat on the sidewalk cross-legged, his back to the wall of a shut-down storefront. He had a blanket spread out before him with a strange collection of very cheap items: a package of Kleenex, a cheap fake Chinese vase, several tiny plastic dinosaurs, a giraffe, and a little rubber tiger. Toby picked up the tiger. "How much?"

"Twenty-five cents for two."

"I just want the one." She fished out a quarter and pocketed the tiger. It would be a perfect gift for Pony.

***

Bubbles had always been the stronger of them; there was no doubt about it. When he'd seen her plea on Facebook, the desire to be the one who saved her was overwhelming. Action man. He realized now that he really hadn't thought the whole mission through. She'd told him to find Jolie at the Golden Giraffe in Portland. It wasn't like her to ask him for anything, either; it was one of the things he most admired about her. But this request was turning out to be a lot harder than he'd ever imagined. He was officially lost now and unless he grew fins, he didn't know how he was going to get to the highway. He didn't even know whether he could find his way back to the cabin either. He kept trying to pull his hoodie out so it would keep his glasses from fogging over but it kept collapsing. His glasses were now definitely crooked.

The only time he had ever been to the creek was to get fresh water after he'd read that article in Cosmo: "100 Ways to let Mother Nature be Your Beauty Supply." Now, he was almost staggering to keep upright. Leaning against a tree to fix his hood again, he thought he heard something different in the sound of the rain. Could it really be? The sound of an engine?

***

Eleni read from the screener verbatim as she'd been taught to do during her training. There was every possibility she was being monitored for quality assurance right now. She'd gotten through the initial introduction pitch, and the explanation of the study and the times, and the woman seemed to be sticking with her. She crossed her fingers under the desk.

"If you could have lunch with any famous person, living or dead, who would it be? Where would you go and what would you ask them?"

"What?"

"If you could have lunch with any famous person, living or dead, who would it be? Where would you go and what would you ask them?"

"What does that have to do with technology?"

"Well, nothing really; it's just to see how creative you can be. You know, just for fun."

"Anybody, living or dead?"

"Right."

"Well then, I guess I'd have to say the Lord," the woman said.

Images of the Charlton Heston style God of her Technicolor childhood calmly eating tuna sandwiches came unbidden to Eleni's mind. She shook them off and pressed on.

"Great! And where would you go with the Lord?"

"Well, I don't know. Anywhere he wanted, I guess."

"Well, just say you wanted to take the Lord to your favorite place in Beaverton. Where would it be?"

"We always like the Olive Garden. I guess we could go there. Yes, the Olive Garden."

Eleni's mind made the switch from tuna sandwiches to never-empty pasta bowls as she furiously scribbled the answers down on the screener in pencil. After dialing for two hours, she finally had a real candidate. "Terrific. And now, what would you ask the Lord while you were having lunch at the Olive Garden?"

"I think I'd ask about my grandma. You know, like is she happy in heaven?"

"Oh, that's a great question." Man, she was getting good at this. "So, the Lord, the Olive Garden, your grandma. Perfect."

"That would be nice."

"Okay, well, looking at your answers, I'm happy to say, it looks like you'd be an excellent fit for this study. So I'm going to read you our invitation verbatim just so I don't forget to tell you anything." Eleni turned to the final page. "So like I said in the beginning, the study's on Friday the 23rd—"

"This Friday?"

Eleni looked at the giant calendar pinned to the wall next to her desk. "Right, this Friday."

"Oh, I can't do this Friday. Don't you have any other day?"

Oh God, no. "Like I said in the beginning, it's a one-day study from 4:30 to 6:30 Friday."

"Gosh, I'm sorry. It's our son's football game that day. We never miss a game."

No, no. Are you kidding me? "Right. Well, let me give you our number just in case anything changes."

Eleni rang off and logged into break time. Looking down at the screener, she wondered, Is it really me? Is all this totally normal?

***

Toby made a quick right as she got off the elevator and avoided the fat bitch at the nurse's station. Ever since she caught the two girls smooching one day, she'd looked at Toby as if she were a lower life form. Rounding the corner, she saw an unfamiliar, serious-looking woman leaving Pony's room. Who the hell was that?

She stumbled into Pony's room. Toby held up the little tiger. "Rrrr! Guess who's here?"

Pony looked up at Toby's loaded, disheveled form. "Toby, we have to talk."

Uh oh.

***

Brian's heart leapt even as he told himself not to get his hopes up. But he could hear it more clearly with every step. It was the idle of an engine. He saw something move in the trees up ahead. It was definitely something—someone. A person. A human being! A human being by a stream. He'd found the water! Now he saw an old VW bus painted like a palomino pony. It had little plastic horses glued all over it. In front of it stood two more people.

They were an interesting group. One was a really beautiful girl who wore what once must have been a really pretty muslin and lace dress. At her side was an equally beautiful boy in tattered jeans and a soaking wet flannel hoodie. The boy by the stream was dressed in patchwork leather and filling a plastic water bottle. He had waist-length dreads that sort of resembled dried horse shit, but he was wearing a pleasant smile too.

"Hello," said the girl. "I'm Atlantia. We're looking for the Rainbow people. Have you seen them?"

***

Toby hadn't cared which way she headed when she'd left the hospital. She felt as if someone had removed her heart and her stomach or something. Just empty, numb. Pony was going off to that program and it meant Toby was alone again. Completely, totally, one hundred percent.

She went to the park and dry swallowed the last bar of Xanax pulled from the tiny pocket of her jeans. Slumped down under a tree, she had tried to figure out what the hell she was going to do. She must have drifted, because now she could hear someone standing over her, breathing loud. She was afraid to open her eyes.

Slowly, she slipped her hand into her jacket pocket and gripped the knife she now carried. She decided to play dead and just try to get a glimpse through slitted eyes.

Oh for Christ's sake, it was nothing but a big yellow dog! It must have sensed her coming to consciousness, because its tail wagged. She opened her eyes all the way and sat up.

"Well, hey there fella, whose dog are you?" She looked around the park. She checked the dog's neck, but there was nothing but a piece of rope around it. A frayed length hung down as if he'd broken free from somewhere, but not too recently. It was old and worn. The dog continued to stare, tail wagging. It cocked its head.

***

Pony had held her eyes open and steady until she heard Toby's footsteps disappear down the hall. She pulled her knees up tight to her chest and circled them with her arms, let her head drop. Then she let the tears roll down her cheeks. It hurt so much she couldn't believe it.

When Toby had staggered in three hours late, something had snapped. Well, not really snapped. It was as if life came into focus for a minute, and she knew with the same kind of surety she had in her dreams that if she didn't put the brakes on, the car was going to spin out of control. That if she didn't take this chance, she would be the one to blame. No one else. But she could also see, with equal clarity, that she wouldn't be able to go back if she went forward. Things would never be the same between them.

Why couldn't things be simpler? Easier? Why did they always have to be so fucking hard? She saw the people around her every day, coming and going. None of them ever looked as if they had to deal with the kind of shit she did. Was it all an illusion? Were all those people suffering too? Was everyone in pain all the time like she was? Or was she really just one of the unlucky ones?

***

Toby walked around the park to look for the potential parent or parents of this dog. A couple of little Latino boys raced around by the swings.

"Is this your dog?" she asked. They just stared at her. "Um, perro...yours-o?" Jesus, what an idiot she sounded like.

The little boys smiled and came to pet the dog, but they shrugged and shook their heads to indicate that it wasn't theirs.

She circled the park again, but so far, she could not see anyone else who looked as if they were missing a dog. The yellow hound tracked her every step.

"Now, wait a minute, fella," Toby said. "Stay!" The dog just continued to follow, smiling now. His tongue lolled out of the side of his mouth like a jauntily cocked hat.

***

Saved by the Burners! It could only happen to him, thought Brian. It seemed Atlantia and her friends Rafi and Boo were on their way into the California rainforest after picking up a van in Seattle for Mardi Gras, which was coming up right around the corner too. They had apparently missed one gathering here in Oregon already and were trying to get down there as quickly as possible. Unfortunately, despite the cold and rain, the van kept overheating and they had to make frequent stops to fill the radiator. As far as Brian was concerned, it was a car. A nice warm car. He didn't mind the delays at all.

He knew he should be grateful and just enjoy his good fortune, but he couldn't quite relax. Because as he sat in the humid, leather- and patchouli-scented van on his way to Portland, he realized he had no idea where the Golden Giraffe was, and had no idea what Jolie's reaction would be to his rescue mission.

Did she have any idea who he was? Would she want to rescue Bubbles? And even if she was willing to help, what the hell were they going to do? He had zero money, zero wheels, zero bright ideas.

A familiar skunky scent began to fill the van. Atlantia handed him a tiny wooden pipe. "You partake?" she muttered, trying to speak and hold the smoke in at the same time. Oh why the hell not? Brian reached for the pipe.

***

Toby had crossed the length of the park several times and had even gone up and down the blocks surrounding it to look for Lost Dog signs on the telephone poles. A sign for a lost, beloved, elderly cat had her tearing up, but she'd seen nothing indicating a wish to be reunited with this hound.

She looked down at the dog. "Look, dude, it's nothing personal, but I just can't have a dog." She stopped and attempted a harsher tone of voice. "Stay!"

Without so much as a blink, the dog continued to smile and follow. Maybe she should call the pound? But if no one reported him missing, they might have to put him down. No, better to just lose him somehow and let him take his chances on the street like she did. She eyed a corner bar down the street and decided to head inside. He'd have to stay out. They'd make sure of it. Of course, she couldn't stay there any longer than it took to use the bathroom because she didn't even have enough money for a drink. It was worth a try.

One pair of freshly washed hands later, the dog caught up with her a block down from the bar.

***

On the morning Pony left the hospital, the heavens opened up and dumped over an inch of rain on Portland within an hour's time and just kept on pouring it down. No matter what people said about rain in Portland, this one was exceptional.

Victoria, the woman from the shelter, had showed up early and brought Pony a fresh pair of jeans and a sweater to wear. Pony appreciated the gesture. The clothes she'd come into the hospital with were pretty messed up. But this outfit made her feel weird. Like an impostor.

Victim-wear. Were you a victim just because you got cut up inside? After it happened, the main thing she kept thinking about was how stupid she'd been. Everyone knew you weren't supposed to do doubles by yourself. Especially if they were both guys. She'd seen it as a failure of her street smarts. Toby was the one who kept saying it wasn't her fault. Pony still had a hard time with that. Sure, it wasn't right that those two assholes should do that to her. The really perfect solution would be to beat the holy crap out of them. Cut their nasty little dicks off so they couldn't do that to anyone again. Make them be the victims for a change.

She watched Victoria as she drove them toward the shelter and wondered what her story was. She looked so serious all the time even though she seemed to be a kind person. Vicky-the-victim-lady. Could she have had any experiences like Pony's? She sure didn't look as if anyone could get anything over on her, but you never knew. Looking out at the rain on the windshield, Pony worried about Toby. Where was she? Was she safe? Was she dry? What was she doing right now?

***

Toby sat under the shelter of a bandstand at the park and shivered in her thin jacket. It was sort of nice to have the dog there for extra body heat. She had to think of a way to get rid of him, though. She was in no position to be a dog owner. She was having a hard enough time taking care of herself.

Two large jock type guys ran their way, laughing as the rain soaked them. They were obviously looking for some shelter too. Toby felt the dog's body stiffen beside her. The poor thing had gone totally rigid. What was wrong? Toby looked around and realized it was the men. The dog looked at one of them, a muscular bearded man, and whimpered. A thin stream of urine trickled down from between his legs.

Toby put her arms around the dog and hugged him tight. "Aw fella, was someone that mean to you? Someone like him?" Toby ran her hands along his shivering body as her own cast of leering faces bobbed up into her consciousness. She shoved them back down and concentrated on the dog. She didn't want him feeling that too. The dog slowly relaxed as she stroked him. Toby got up and called for him to follow. She didn't want to subject him to someone scary like that, even if it meant losing their dry spot. She took off her belt and looped it through the rope around the dog's neck to create a temporary leash.

"Come on, fella. Let's get outta here," Toby said and they ran toward a sheltered bus stop. "You never really forget, do you? Don't worry, little guy. Toby's not gonna let no one hurt you anymore, okay?"

***

The water stops were getting more frequent, and Boo the driver thought they might have a slow leak in the radiator. After a brief confab, the group decided to get some sealant, and stay over in Portland that evening to give it time to take.

Atlantia had some friends they could crash with she said, and Brian was invited to spend the night with them as well.

Brian reviewed his situation and decided that as much as he wanted to get going, some time to dry out and get his thoughts together wouldn't hurt. Atlantia directed them into a warehouse district in SE and pretty soon they arrived at their destination, a loft space at the top of one of the old warehouses. A tall, friendly, shaggy-looking boy welcomed them into a huge room where a very pregnant young girl sat on an old couch. Unlike her boyfriend, she seemed less than pleased to see Atlantia. Brian backed up a bit. Perhaps she noticed his discomfort because she looked over at him and gave him a sad little smile.

"Wow, poor things, you're soaking wet!" She looked at the group, and then looked back at Atlantia. "I thought you were going to California or something."

Atlantia flipped her long blond locks. "Oh yeah, we're just here for one night. We're meeting my mom at the gathering."

The pregnant girl positively beamed at that, and waved them all deeper into the room. "Well, that's great! Are you guys hungry? Freddy, can we feed these people?"

The shaggy boy smiled and took things out of an old paper sack. "You bet. I just did a Whole Foods run."

The pregnant girl looked at Brian and patted a spot on the couch beside her. "Come and have a seat. I'm Daisy. What's your name?"

***

Standing at the bus stop with the dog, Toby racked her mind for somewhere the two could go. She saw the bus approach and noticed it was the Number 6. The box of nuts, Daisy used to call it. Daisy would probably take them in, at least for a night. She hadn't exactly been too polite to that idiot Freddy when she left last time, but she hadn't been too horrible either. She hopped up the little steps of the Number 6, but the driver refused to take the dog. "But it's a service dog," Toby improvised.

The driver looked skeptical. "You got a card?"

Toby flipped him off and pointed the dog in the direction of the MAX. They could just slip into one of the back cars and nobody would bother them. Maybe she could get one of those harness looking things for the dog later. All the service dogs seemed to wear them.

***

This time of year, just after Halloween, when the holidays got going, was really the worst if you were homeless, thought Smokey. If it wasn't all the shiny things in the shop windows reminding you of everything you could never have, it was all the billboards and ads about home and family. About being warm and having enough to eat.

He did like all the people being nicer, though, even if it sometimes made him feel like a poster for the have-nots. One woman had actually pressed a dollar bill into his hand this morning. He'd just been standing at the MAX stop and she assumed he was panhandling.

Things were looking up, though. This would be the first year he'd had some kind of roof over his head in a long time. Even if it wasn't exactly his roof. As he passed another brightly lit window display, a thought occurred: maybe he and Jack could make their own little Thanksgiving. They didn't have a stove but maybe he could figure something out.

***

Toby hopped off the Yellow Line with the dog in tow. I'm gonna have to find a name for you, fella. She looked down at the dog. She wondered whether the dog had a name for himself. She remembered a fairy tale from her childhood in which all the animals had secret names that only they knew themselves. The names had given them power.

Maybe we better not show up empty-handed, huh, fella? Toby inexpertly attached her belt loop to a post outside the market to secure the dog. A few tugs would be all it would take for him to get loose, but it was the best she could do for now.

"Okay, fella, be right back, okay?"

The market was packed with holiday shoppers. Just how she liked it. She stopped in front of the Bowser Boutique section and stuffed a leash, collar, and a complicated halter looking thing into her baggy pants. Then she cruised the wine section and managed to fit a bottle of wine and some Irish cream into her jacket. She paid for a fifty-cent candy bar and was back outside in minutes flat. The dog was right where she'd left him, tail wagging happily.

***

Strange as things were, Brian began to enjoy himself. He'd followed Daisy and Freddy into the makeshift kitchen and offered his considerable cooking skills to the mix. Soon they were whipping up roast potatoes, fresh green salad, and Tofurkey cutlets. Freddy had scored a crate of the vegan turkey alternative as the stores geared up for the Thanksgiving holiday.

Sometime during the prep, another guest had appeared. A girl with a big yellow dog and some fairly decent wine. Her name was Toby, and when she found out Brian was a dog lover, she peppered him with questions and had him laughing with stories about her newfound charge who just wouldn't take no for an answer. Looking around the room, he found himself liking all these strange people who had taken him in, no questions asked. They all sat around on the floor to enjoy the food and afterward, they passed around another couple of pipe-loads, drank Irish cream and told stories.

I think Bubbles would like these people, even if they are hippies, Brian thought and vowed not to lose touch with his newfound friends.

***

Smokey Joe looked around the house and grinned his widest grin. He'd actually pulled it off. The table was covered with a red sheet he'd found at the bins. A borrowed poinsettia and a wine bottle with a candle in it made the centerpiece. He'd given blood three times this month and scraped up enough for a pre-cooked turkey and mashed potatoes at Fred Meyer. He'd traded forty roll-ups for a bottle of cherry brandy to share afterward.

He felt kind of bad for sending Jack on a fool's errand to pick up a nonexistent letter at the drop-in center, but he'd had to get him out of the house. He couldn't wait to see the look on Jack's face.

***

After a rather Spartan vegan breakfast at Daisy and Freddy's, the Burners were kind enough to drop Brian at the Golden Giraffe. And after the goon at the door squinted at his fake ID for a while, he was allowed to pass through into the darkness.

Now, he couldn't keep his eyes off the disco ball. It was the biggest one he'd ever seen. All those tiny pieces of mirror all over it, flashing, glinting. Some gadget in its mounting made it spin, throwing light and sparkle everywhere. And though he knew it had no place within the realm of good taste, he thought it was fabulous. Wouldn't it be great to have a jacket like that? Or a pair of boots?

The walls that were lit by the disco ball were painted a flat black. Proof once again that nothing was tackier than a nightclub in the daytime. Besides the disco ball, the main focal point was the stage that the girls danced on. It was slightly raised and someone had mounted huge black chains along each corner to give it the appearance of being suspended above the floor, although you could clearly see the platform if you looked.

But the Golden Giraffe specialized in illusion: The illusion that its clientele were gentlemen. The illusion that the girls onstage were enjoying themselves. The illusion that they were thrilled by the pathetic, horny bleatings and gropings of these playboys.

Brian saw one girl's face and flinched. Her eyes were glazed; her smile a painted-on rictus. Two poles were mounted on the stage, but no one spun on them now. His foot was stuck to something on the floor. As he looked around for a napkin, he noticed another girl up on a table in the corner. She stood tall and moved as smooth as running water. He would have loved to take her photo just as she was, with that faraway look in her eye. Every instinct he possessed told him that he had just found Jolie.

***

It was cold outside and Barkin' Jack walked home quickly, hoping to generate a little body heat. He was worried about Smokey. He'd been acting strange all week, secretive. And now he'd sent him crosstown to get a letter no one had ever heard about. Who the hell would send Smokey Joe a letter anyway? Everyone he knew lived on the streets. His ears were so cold now they'd begun to burn.

Jack turned the corner and noticed smoke coming from the chimney. Damn! Smokey oughta know better. They didn't want to draw any attention to the fact that someone was staying in that house.

He had his mind halfway made up to give Smokey the rough side of his tongue when he opened the door and saw what awaited him there: the turkey and potatoes on the festive table, glasses filled with a dark red liquid, and a crackling fire behind Smokey Joe, who stood in front of it all like a happy puppy.

"Happy Thanksgiving!" cried Smokey.

Jack's eyes filled. Quickly swiping at them, he looked at his friend and wondered what on earth he had done to deserve this. Nothing at all that he could think of.

"Happy Thanksgiving, Smokey," barked Jack. He wasn't the least bit cold anymore.

***

Years ago, Jolie had slept with a self-proclaimed rajah who had gone to great lengths to explain astral projection. Halfway through his speech, however, she lost interest as she realized that the current state she was in—pretending to be interested in what he was saying, while her mind floated off and wondered when he would leave—was all the explanation she needed. Although she couldn't even remember exactly what the rajah looked like anymore, the phrase had stuck with her, and she always mentally referenced this phenomena as astral projection.

Three p.m. was the slow time of day at the Golden Giraffe. The girls didn't have to work the poles so hard and could mostly get away with lying around on the stage, posing, unless they got called for a table dance, which was Jolie's situation.

So she was up there in a state of astral projection, her body bumping and grinding away, occasionally treating the guy to a swoop down "oomph" jerk of her pelvis into his face. She did all this while her mind worried on the problem of Bubbles once more, as well as the rent, her clinic bill, and whether or not she'd be going out that evening. The set was finally winding down when she noticed a kid in the back staring at her and rolling his eyes toward the door as if he was trying to get her attention somehow. He didn't even seem old enough to be in this place and she wondered what the hell he was doing. As soon as she got down and collected her tip, he made his way over.

"You're Jolie, right?"

Jolie stared at the little guy curiously and nodded slowly.

"Well, I don't know if she ever talked about me, but I'm Bubbles's friend Brian." The kid stuck his hand out. "And boy am I glad I finally caught up with you."

***

The closest place Jolie could think of to go where they could sit around indefinitely was Voodoo Donuts on Sandy Blvd. She wasn't quite sure whether she wanted to invite this kid back to the apartment.

Now settled in with a Stumptown coffee and a chocolate glaze, she started to warm up to him—he had guts, even if he did look like that kid who played Harry Potter in the movies. After they left the club, she realized that she did remember Bubbles telling her tales about Brian. She even remembered seeing him once at Nicholas's disastrous Hells Belles debut.

She studied his serious little face as he told her his tale of Bubbles's predicament and his mad trek through the wilds of Oregon. About halfway through, as he described falling flat on his face, his glasses either fogging up or escaping his face completely, she tried hard to hold back a giggle. The idea of this poor little guy playing macho woodsman was too much.

He'd caught the sound of her held-in snort and after an initial attempt at appearing wounded, he laughed along with her. The further he got into his tale, the more they laughed. When he got to the part about being rescued by the hippie kids, they were carrying on so much people at other tables began to glance their way.

After they'd calmed down a bit, Jolie looked at him. "So I'm thinking we better get up there, Brian. What do you think?"

Brian was so relieved he almost cried.

***

Toby was still calling him Fella. She wondered whether that's what he thought his name was already. Would he get confused when she finally came up with the perfect name? Did he have a secret dog name? If she changed it in real life, would his secret dog name still exist?

She looked down at the yellow hound, and his tail wagged. Had anyone ever been so happy to see her? Her heart did a little squeezy thing. All she had to do was look at him and his joy was unmistakable.

"You've been cooped up in here too long, haven't ya, Fella?" As if he understood every word completely, he jumped to his feet, tail now a blur.

She wasn't used to having someone that dependent on her. Daisy had been close, she thought with a grin, but even Daisy didn't have to be walked twice a day. Freddy had told her about a dog park just three blocks down. She decided to give Fella a well-deserved treat.

She spent ten minutes looking for the leash before she decided to forget it. That's what they did at dog parks, right? Let them have a little off-leash freedom?

Fella was more than happy to skip the bondage act and followed obediently at her heels till they came to the large open field area that made up the park.

Sure enough, there were all kinds of people there with all kinds of dogs. Little snappy Chihuahuas, big Labs and Danes, a couple of Shepherds. Fella was ecstatic; he spun around in circles and looked back to check whether she didn't think they'd just died and gone to heaven too. Toby tossed the nasty old tennis ball she now kept with her, and Fella tore after it, his ears flying back as he ran back to her. She tossed it again and fumbled in her pack for a cigarette.

"EXCUSE ME!" A harsh, strident voice grated in her ear. A large woman with a mass of gray curls strode up to Toby and barked out rules and questions. She held a yappie little gray poodle.

"There's no smoking in the dog park. Where is your waste bag? Where is your scoop? Is that your dog?" She jabbed a gnarled, pink frosted finger at Fella. "Where is his leash?"

***

Pony honestly didn't think there had been as many bizarre rules when she was in jail as there were in the halfway house. And they all seemed to contradict each other.

Like they really wanted you to open up and talk about how you felt. On the other hand, she had already seen two women get booted for doing just that. They encouraged you to make friendships and care for one another, but then you were apparently supposed to snitch off your buddies without a second thought if you saw them doing something they weren't supposed to be doing.

You were supposed to be yourself but they were always going on about what was wrong with the way you did things. There had been so many days when she had been tempted to tell them all to shove it up their ass and walk out that front door forever. But she was also getting a taste of what could be. For the first time since she'd hit the streets, she was thinking she might be able to have a different kind of life. One where she could make the rules. One where she could call the shots. One where she didn't have to keep her head down all the time. Maybe she had to learn about rules. So she stayed.

***

Click, click, click, turn, click, click, click. Butchie listened to the sound of Veronica's shiny black heels march back and forth. They took on a military cadence in his mind: left, right, left. He was perched uncomfortably on a delicate barstool in Veronica's perfect kitchen as he watched the object of his desire wear a hole in her designer linoleum. She was perfectly put-together as always, not a wrinkle in her suit despite a long day at work, and the pacing little black shoes gleamed. Her blunt cut hair fanned out and snapped obediently back into place with each turn.

"I don't understand that girl. You'd think she'd be grateful for all I've done but nooo—not Queen Bubbles. She just sits there, nose in a book, pretending I don't exist."

Butchie's half-open mouth closed briefly while he thought of the appropriate response. "She's different than I thought," was what popped out.

Veronica stopped mid-click and turned to face him. "Really? And how did you think she'd be?"

Butchie didn't like the way she looked at him at all. He shook off her stare by looking at her feet and shrugged. "I don't know. When you had me out there, looking to see if she was going to school and stuff...she's not the same as those little girls at Lewis and Clark..." He tried to find the words to explain but eventually, his attention span failed him as he began to wonder what might happen to his toes if he tried to stuff them into such tiny points like the ones on Veronica's shoes. Her right toe, the subject of his reverie, began to tap menacingly. He forced himself into the present once more.

"I guess I thought she'd be more like, just a little...teenager."

"She is a teenager. How can she be more like what she is?"

This had all the earmarks of a trick question as far as Butchie was concerned. "I don't know. Never mind. So is she gonna be staying here every night?"

Click, click, whirl, click, stop, stare. A really weird stare this time.

"I don't know. I suppose she'll have to for a bit. I haven't really thought it through. To be honest, I really thought I'd have more support from Mother. I've left five messages—not a word."

Butchie looked up. "So your mother doesn't want her either?"

Click, whirl. "What? Well, of course, she does. We just thought it would be better for Bubbles to stay here for a while. With someone closer to her age... What do you mean, either? Did you not see what I went through to rescue her? After all that, I thought she'd be a little more grateful."

"For being kidnapped, you mean?"

"We did not kidnap her! We rescued her. I don't even know why I bother trying to talk to you. You are completely insensitive. I should have known, once again, I'm all alone in this. That's how it always is. I should be used to it by now."

"But—"

Whirl, stamp. "Oh, shut up, Butchie!"

***

Hopping off at her stop, Eleni felt pretty good. The job was such a disappointment. They'd actually given her a lecture and sent her home early for explaining something to a confused focus group candidate. Frustrated, she'd come close to stopping at the dealer on the way home. But she hadn't. She'd gotten through it. She could face Max without feeling the wrench of guilt and shame at one more failure.

Seconds after her key unlatched the door, Max popped out like a champagne cork and attempted to twirl her around the tiny entrance way.

"We're going on tour!"

"What?"

Max took her by the hand and plopped them both on the couch. Excitement radiated from him. "The band—we're going on tour. No, wait, okay—let me back up. This guy from Don't heard an MP3 of some of the songs. He said he was blown away. They're going on a West Coast tour and one of the other bands had to drop out. We're just waiting on Bobby but it's ninety-nine percent in the bag. We go up and do Vancouver BC and Bellingham, then turn around and do Seattle and Spokane, a couple of places way up in Northern California, then San Francisco, Berkeley, and LA."

"That's so fucking amazing, Max!" Eleni threw her arms around her grinning husband. "You so deserve this. Oh, baby, congratulations!"

Max's grin grew even wider as he finally let go of her. "So that's my news. You're home early—how was your day?"

Eleni cast her mind back on the events of the day: the horrible job stuff, her almost-relapse. "It was weird as hell but I'm okay. I'll tell you about it later. Now, let's hear more about this tour."

***

Jolie looked over her shoulder more than once on the way home from the club. She had the creeps, big time. It was one of those evenings that made her wonder whether most men really did hate women.

The club had been packed. On payday Friday, the Golden Giraffe was only too happy to cash payroll checks, extend happy hour, and stiffen up the watery drinks. Things had gotten loud and ugly fast. The bouncers really earned every dime of their pay on Friday nights. After her last set, she'd made the mistake of letting one of her regulars buy her a drink. Management always encouraged this kind of fraternizing and an ice-cold beer had sounded really good to her after four hours on her feet. It had tasted really good, too, and she'd started to relax, joking around, just kicking back and having fun. Fun—until her friend had grabbed her hand, and tried rubbing it over his hard-on like it was a handy sex toy. She pulled away and he grabbed it again, crushing her fingers as he did it, and she realized that there would be no punch line to this ugly joke. She jumped up, almost falling over the table in her hurry to escape. He blocked her exit and hit her with a stream of vitriol, a hidden rage streaming out of him that freaked her a lot worse than his actions.

"Fucking whore. You know you want it. You think you're too good for me, bitch?" On and on it went. She'd frozen for a moment and stared at this nice guy who'd always called her darlin' and remembered all the girls' names. Then she'd practically run out of the club. Her hands were still shaking when she reached the apartment. She looked both ways before she let herself inside; she collapsed on the couch and wished the place wasn't so fucking empty. Wished that Brian hadn't gone to visit his new friends, wished that Nicholas and Gisarra weren't out celebrating their new tour, wished most of all the Bubbles was still around. She tried telling herself it wasn't as if she hadn't experienced this before—every dancer had nightmare stories about guys like that. But it didn't seem to matter—this time it had gotten to her. It made her feel small and hopeless as she had when she was even younger than Bubbles. She didn't want to play exotic dancer anymore. She didn't feel empowered, or as if she owned her sexuality, or as if she was a talented burlesque performer, or any of the things the girls talked about when they wanted to feel as if they were in on something great. She felt used and abused and it wasn't fair. It was never fair and it never would be fair. When the tears trickled down her cheeks, she was glad at least no one could see her.

***

Over the river and through the woods. It was Bubbles's kind of day. Gray and brisk, with the last fall colors standing out beautifully against the softly smudged background. As she stood on the ferry boat, on the way to her grandmother's house, she looked out on the Sound and realized she should have felt better than she did. After all, Longview was so close to Portland, there was no way they could keep her there. Only a few more days before she'd be reunited with Jolie. She'd just play along until this visit to Grammy June's was over and Veronica called off her pet goon and then she'd hitch or bus her way back if Brian couldn't get hold of Jolie and a car.

Grammy's was actually Auntie Jane's place now. Poor old Grammy June had died eventually and left her old-maid daughter the family home. It just seemed weird not to call it Grammy June's anymore. Even if it had been a long time now. Aunt Jane was her favorite family member, although Bubbles had never been able to fathom how she lived such a hermit's life. Bubbles had fond memories of special lunches and teas in her garden. Jane had bought them matching tiaras once and she'd made them real English Earl Grey tea with scones and clotted cream, cucumber sandwiches and fresh jam. She'd recommend books for Bubbles to read and listen to her stories in a way no other adult ever had. So why was she so nervous?

A few seagulls clung to a buoy. One of them shouted out their peculiar call, somewhere between a scream and a dog whine.

Over the river and through the woods. The funny little childhood song went through her head. Over and over.

Veronica's mood seemed slightly hysterical. She was doing the nice thing again. The best Veronica usually got was smug, self-satisfied. She was an emotional vampire. Veronica didn't do happy; she did something more like sanguine.

Over the river and through the woods. Something was wrong. Bubbles wished like hell she knew what it was.

***

Barkin' Jack was so deep in his own head that day he almost didn't notice the police cars near the house. He'd slowed his steps and did his best to go invisible, a skill he'd almost perfected after over twenty years on the street. He'd gotten as close as the hedgerow next door when he saw what was happening to Smokey. As he stepped forward, Smokey had chanced an instant of desperate eye contact to shake his head to warn Jack away.

Jack was never sure how long he'd stumbled around town after that, and how it was he ended up in the park.

***

Daisy snapped off the tiny TV. Freddy had recently managed to jury-rig a cable connection to the little television (his latest freegan "find"), allowing Daisy to channel surf once more. She'd just seen a segment on the local news featuring someone called the Safety Mom. The Safety Mom had scared the crap out of her, and it had nothing to do with small, easily swallowed objects.

Am I supposed to identify with that woman? Now that I'm going to be a mom myself? Am I supposed to be like the women on the orange juice commercials? How the hell does a person become a Safety Mom? What if I wake up one morning and all I can think about is those plastic things you stick in light sockets? How much vitamin C my household needs to consume? What is motherhood going to do to my head? Will it change it—like it changed my body? Was that woman just a normal girl like me once? Did she have friends who she went out dancing with? A boyfriend she got kinky with? What if I wake up one day and I'm a Safety Mom?

Another thought hit her like a blow to the gut. What was my mother like before she had kids?

There had always been that unspoken resentment hanging between them. The one about her mother's life being full of an unmet potential. A potential that motherhood effectively killed. Was it that unmet potential that died and made it so easy to ignore what went on late at night in Daisy's room?

***

It was three days before they found out what Barkin' Jack had seen. Harry had never seen Jack like this before. He looked as if he were watching a movie: just sat there completely silently and stared straight ahead. He didn't speak. He didn't react to heat or cold. He didn't seem to need food, although he had accepted a cup of water yesterday.

One thing Harry understood, though, was that Jack wasn't just staring into space. Jack had seen something and apparently he was still seeing it. Whatever he'd seen, it hadn't been pretty. It frightened Harry, made her want to drag it out of him before it hurt Jack anymore, but Frank asked her to wait with her questions and let Jack take his own time with whatever it was. Harry had seen the wisdom of this and sure enough, it had been the best course of action, because this morning Barkin' Jack let rip. Told them what he'd seen and what he couldn't get out of his head. It had been hard to understand him but after she figured out what he was saying, she wished she hadn't heard it at all.

***

There were a lot of new holes in his perforated memory. How did he get out from behind the bush? How did he end up in the park again? How did Frank find him? How did Frank find Harry? Jack didn't know, and he guessed it didn't much matter anyway.

If only he could forget the part before that. Seeing the cops haul Smokey down when he was dangling half-in and half-out of the window of the house. Seeing the Taser throw all those bolts of electricity into his body. Seeing him flying up from the sidewalk like a fish on a griddle. Then the pleading look on Smokey's face, urging Jack to go away. Seeing those cops' big bodies block his vision as they circled round Smokey, their legs drawing back and shooting forward, landing each vicious kick. And then the lights, blue and red, blue and red, and then them sending the paramedics away. They sent them away! And then they threw Smokey's body into that cage in the back. If only they'd let the ambulance take him or even if they'd left him there for Jack to take care of. Why couldn't Jack forget that part?

Now, Harry was here and Frank was here. Now they knew, too. Now he really couldn't make it go away. He'd tried, but this one had him beat. And he knew the thing he was supposed to do was to tell someone else. Someone who could do something about it.

***

If it hadn't been for the light streaming in the windows, Bubbles would have thought it was four a.m. or something. It was that quiet. All the frills that surrounded her reminded her where she was: the guest room at Grammy June's. She sat up and peered at the pink plastic alarm clock on the nightstand. Wow—ten thirty. It was rare to be allowed to sleep that long in her family. Usually someone would have stuck their head in by now and made some kind of noxious comment.

Last night's holiday dinner had been the predictable passive-aggressive feast with her mother playing martyr, Veronica playing saint, Bubbles cast as ingrate sinner, and poor Aunt Jane trying to pretend she didn't notice all the subtext.

She swung her legs round and sat up, snatching at the robe at the foot of the bed. It was cold, winter cold. She hoped her sister had made coffee. Auntie Jane favored a brew that looked like tea and tasted like warm water.

As she padded downstairs, she was struck once again by that wrong feeling she'd had ever since she got on the boat to the San Juans. Maybe it was just the quiet that seemed to permeate the house. Come to think of it, why didn't she hear Mom and Veronica's chatter? They both generally created a wall of pointless sound wherever they were. Auntie Jane literally jumped when she entered the room.

"Bubbles! You startled me." Aunt Jane looked like a cartoon bunny in her fluffy white robe. "Can I get you something to eat? I can make pancakes, or we have some lovely eggs from the farm down the road. How about some oatmeal? You always liked my oatmeal." Aunt Jane's eyes darted around behind her John Lennon glasses; her hands wrung and worried the dishcloth she held.

Bubbles took the whole scene in for a moment and slowly reached for a chair. Without taking her eyes off her increasingly worried aunt, she sat down and took a deep breath. "Aunt Jane, where is Mom and Veronica?"

***

Art Group at the methadone clinic had become part of Max and Eleni's weekly schedule now. It was, in Max's opinion, the least touchy-feely of them all. Max truly hated any kind of open-your-heart-to-a-room-full-of-completely-fucked-up-strangers therapy. At least in Art Group you had something to do. Now that Jolie was getting clean, she had started to come with them.

Everyone could be so damn sincere or high-strung, like Drippy Dawn in the corner there. Jolie's irreverent attitude had landed them in trouble a couple of times, but Max couldn't help but enjoy the humor she brought to the situation. It was hard to believe they only had another week before he and Eleni stepped off. They were now down to three milligrams each and Jolie wasn't far behind.

Between the tempura paint and the suspicious glare of the counselor, Max felt as if he were in some kind of primary school of the damned.

This week they were supposed to make a collage based on their dreams. Jolie was drawing mustaches on movie star's faces. She looked up with a grin.

"Okay, I got a Christmas joke."

"Do tell," Eleni said as the rest of the room's ears perked up.

"Okay, there's these two guys in a bar: a rich guy and a poor guy. It's the holiday rush—they've both stopped in for a drink. Poor guy asks, 'So, what did you get your wife for Christmas?' Rich guy says, 'A fur coat and a Mercedes—if she doesn't like the car, she can always wear the coat.' Then he asks the poor guy what he got his wife. Poor guys says, 'Pair of slippers and a dildo.'

"'Really?' says the rich guy. 'Yeah,' says the poor guy. 'If she doesn't like the slippers, she can go fuck herself!'"

They all busted up as Drippy Dawn shrieked, "That's not funny," and burst into tears.

***

It wasn't so much the stuff that Freddy did to make her mad that drove her so crazy; it was the stuff Freddy did to make her happy. For instance—her favorite thinking place on the roof now provided a bird's-eye view of the latest present Freddy had brought home. She looked down at it now. The "Art Car" seemed to grin back up at her. Seemed Freddy had been so impressed by the palomino van that Atlantia and her friends had shown him, he needed to create a vision of his own. For Daisy and the baby. He completely ignored the fact the damn van breaking down was the reason they had shown up in the first place. One of his fellow freegans had offered him an old beater and Freddy was off and running, dreaming of the artistic statements he could now make with their very own lemon.

What made things even worse, was that Toby—who generally sneered at Freddy's freegan philosophy—had taken an interest in helping to fix the thing up. They were currently in the kitchen, trying to figure out a way to make wings out of old fenders and get it ready for Mardi Gras and Burning Man. She was six months pregnant now and nobody seemed nearly as excited about that. She gave the car one last filthy look and slipped back inside.

***

"I knew Veronica was being too nice!" Bubbles said with a sense of odd satisfaction. Aunt Jane had laid it out for her. She was now stranded on an island in the San Juan chain in the Strait of Juan de Fuca. Her mother and sister had sailed out on the morning ferry. The last regular ferry of the season. Getting out of here was going to be a lot harder than hitching a ride down the I-5 corridor.

"Look, if it's any consolation, I was dead against it, you know." Aunt Jane gave her a small conciliatory smile. "I hope you're not too angry with me."

Bubbles gave a deep sigh and looked at her aunt's worried little face. Somehow she couldn't be angry with her Aunt Jane. If anyone knew the pressure her mother and sister could bring to bear, it was Bubbles.

"No, it's okay, Aunt Jane. It's just...why couldn't they just have left me alone? Veronica went out of her way to snatch me up when I was perfectly happy, and then she couldn't wait to unload me on someone else. I was fine, Aunt Jane. I was happy. Why does she do these things? She's such an ass."

"Your sister doesn't like things to get out of control. She never has. She used to label her toys, remember?"

"Oh God, that's right!" Bubbles laughed despite herself.

Jane covered Bubbles's hand with her own and gave it a soft squeeze. "Look, I know this really isn't the ideal way for us to begin. I'm really not used to living with anyone myself..." Jane trailed off, obviously trying to gather her thoughts together into words.

"This is such an imposition. It's so typical of them not to care who they inconvenience." Bubbles climbed aboard her soapbox happily.

"No, no, that's not what I meant. I'm actually really glad to have you. It's no secret you've always been my favorite." Jane smiled when Bubbles blushed and ducked her head. "What I meant was, despite the way it began, perhaps we can find a way to make this a positive thing. A chance to get to know each other, maybe as adults this time."

Bubbles stared at her aunt for a moment. Adults? Did she really mean that? Or was it just another come-on? In the long run, she guessed it didn't really matter. She was stuck here until she found a way to get off this damn island. Better the carrot than the stick.

"Okay, Aunt Jane. That sounds good. I'd like that." In a funny way, Bubbles knew she meant it when she said it. The two women moved awkwardly toward each other and tried out a hug. It felt pretty good.

***

Brian almost didn't open the e-mail from jbookmobile@email.com. When he did, he realized it was a hastily written note from Bubbles on her aunt's e-mail account. It was now going to be even farther away and harder to reach her than before. Why did it seem that every time things started to look up, something like this had to happen?

***

Bubbles sat in Aunt Jane's garden with her book and cigarettes. No smoking in

Aunt Jane's house made the garden a perfect place for her to spend time. But it was more than just a place to smoke. She'd loved this garden since she was a little girl. Loved the reflecting pool with the little stone Buddha. She remembered when Aunt Jane had first brought the little guy home from some exotic vacation she'd taken. She'd let Bubbles place a penny under him before she'd set him down for good. It was supposed to bring luck.

Now, curiosity propelled her over and she lifted him up to check. Sure enough, there it was: blackened by time and moisture. She squinted at the date. 1996. The year she was born. She was suddenly conscious of a shadow above her. As she looked into the water, she saw Aunt Jane's reflection look back. In the gauzy gray morning light with her hair mussed, glasses off, wearing a green kimono, she looked familiar somehow.

"Wow, Aunt Jane, look in the water." Bubbles pointed down. "We really look so...similar."

Aunt Jane gave her a Mona Lisa smile now. "Mmm. Quite similar," she murmured.

***

Bubbles found herself at the reflecting pool in the garden again. Just she and the little stone Buddha. But no, that wasn't exactly right. There were birds in the trees above, each giving out their unique calls and songs. Aunt Jane's cat came slinking by now and again. There was the chit-chit of squirrels. So much noise in the quiet.

She'd run the gamut of emotions since she'd found herself stuck here. Rage and abandonment, a sense of betrayal mixed with bouts of scolding herself for ever expecting anything with her family to be straightforward. Now she was just confused.

Her entire reason for being was locked up in her move to Portland and her need to get back. She felt as if she'd been on the verge of learning so much. Finding her reality. Finding the real world.

But now, out in Aunt Jane's garden, she felt good. Felt safe and happy just watching a leaf float down from above, watching it hit the pond and then sit right on top of the water, so lightly. She felt as if her happiness was a small betrayal in itself. This wasn't what she was meant to do. Wasn't where she was supposed to be. She'd been tricked into coming here, after all. She didn't belong here in the quiet. She hadn't made enough noise.

***

The sidewalks were crowded as they made their way down Alberta Street.

"Shit, I forgot it was Last Thursday," Jolie muttered as they split single file to avoid a stilt-walker.

"Wow, this is awesome." Brian's hips began to move to a steel-drum band on the corner. "What's going on?"

"Oh, it's just Alberta Street's answer to the First Thursday art-walk downtown. Now every neighborhood's trying to grab a Thursday and out-art each other. Thank God there's only four of them." Jolie expertly sidestepped a drunken couple while she grabbed Brian's hand to steer him away from becoming part of a Capoeira demonstration.

"Stories?" A pretty blond girl who held a wooden box full of postcards and little hand-drawn pictures approached them. "If you've got five minutes, I can tell you a story—just pick one." She held the box out.

"Well..." Brian moved toward the box.

"No thanks!" Jolie said quickly and pulled Brian away. "Look, kid, this is serious. We gotta talk." She led him to the door of a small corner bar. "This looks good."

They found a dark back booth and Jolie went to the bar to get their drinks, avoiding any ID scrutiny a waitress might involve. Brian looked at his surroundings. He still loved the idea that he was now a part of this fascinating city. The walls were bright red and covered in found art, melted Frisbee lamps, and band posters. Jolie set an overflowing pint glass in front of him and the two of them took an appreciative sip. She didn't seem to notice how special everything was. But then again, she obviously had something on her mind and it didn't look as if she was too happy about it. She seemed to be gathering up her thoughts for a minute before she finally looked up at him. "I've been doing a little research on this place Bubbles's aunt lives. It doesn't look so good."

"What do you mean, doesn't look so good?"

"That sister of hers found the perfect place to dump her. It's a really small island. Way the fuck up there, past Seattle. After the first of the year, they don't have regular ferry service until the springtime. I can't figure out a way to get us there without calling major attention to ourselves. Looks like the only way to get to Bubbles right now is to swim."

WINTER

Silence is so accurate
— Mark Rothko

Spent most of my life in recovery
So tell me, tell me babe
Why are you killing me.
— Dead Moon, Killing Me

***

Bored, bored, bored, bored, bored, bored bored bored bored bored bored bored bored.............

Bubbles filled her journal page with the word. She finally gave up on the second page and flung it down on the couch, where it promptly fell to the floor. Crawling over to pick it up, she noticed a box underneath. As she pulled it out, she saw the words PHOTOS AND CLIPPINGS written on the lid. She opened it.

Bubbles looked up to see whether Aunt Jane was around. She'd last seen her heading out to the garden where she often spent hours doing whatever it was people did when they gardened. Feeling only slightly snoopy, she peered into the box and examined the contents.

There was a pile of yellowed newsprint, clippings, bits and pieces. Pages torn from magazines and weeklies. Underneath all that was an unsorted mass of photos of all kinds: Polaroids, snapshots, strips of photo-booth pictures, a few studio shots.

Picking up one of the clippings, she saw it was an old About Town piece from some defunct weekly rag. Various bands she'd never heard of coupled with a few that were now legend and a photo at the bottom of two old-school punk girls arm in arm who glared at the camera. The fine print below read, "Kitty Vacant and Jane Drain at the Nuns show Saturday." Could the one on the left with the safety pin through her cheek possibly be Aunt Jane?

She set the clippings off to the side. Bubbles dug through the photos. There were lots of people she didn't know, most of them looking strangely stylish in a punk sort of way. Mohawks and Nohawks everywhere. Some of them looked super 70s retro with shags and tube tops or glitter and feathers. And throughout them all, Aunt Jane appeared. Here she was among a litter of beer cans, arms thrown around a group of drunken friends; in another, she and a girlfriend pointed up at the Hotel Chelsea; and here, most bizarrely was Aunt Jane in a photo booth, tongue stuck in the ear of a grinning boy with a huge skull earring. Was this some sort of CGI madness? Or was there something huge about Aunt Jane's past that she didn't know?

Back at the reflecting pool, Bubbles paced, chain-smoked, and wondered about Aunt Jane's secret life. Why had no one ever mentioned it? Didn't anyone else in the family know? What was her mother doing when Aunt Jane was running around the country doing all that awesome stuff? She couldn't imagine her mother having any part of it, that was for sure. All the pictures she'd ever seen of her mom when she was young showed her as a slightly prettier, every bit as boring version of the woman she knew now.

She was fascinated with all the other people in Jane's pictures, too. Where were they? Many of them looked like people you still saw in the clubs downtown. Of course, they'd all be really old by now. She drifted back through the French doors and into the living room for one more peek at them. When she pulled the box out once again, she flipped through and found some of the ones she'd seen with Jane and her friend Kitty. Where was Kitty Vacant these days? Had she packed it in to live the life of a librarian like Jane?

She sat there, holding the photo in her hand and staring off into space when she heard a voice behind her.

"My God, look at us. I'd forgotten just how young we all were."

***

Eleni sat at her ancient laptop, trying to format her newest short story to suit the guidelines for her latest submissions: one for an anthology, one for a chance at four weeks at a writers' residency retreat.

She'd just gone through her list of submissions for the last six months, checking off all the pieces that got rejected. Glimmer Train, Stellazine, Wordstock, All-Story, Nu Re-Vu, Granta—check, check, check, check, check. Actually, Nu Re-Vu had been interested but they'd gone out of business before her story got published. Typical. She wondered whether it still counted on her resume. Well, she was keeping it in. She couldn't afford to lose a single credit.

Trying to live a writer's life was so different than anything she'd done before. So much of it was solitary. All her years in guerrilla filmmaking had her disciplined to a group effort. Writing required a single effort—self-discipline, something that she'd even wondered whether she was capable of. But people did it. It wasn't magic; it was just hard work. She was determined to figure out how.

Coming home from her market research gig every day, it was hard to get back in front of the computer screen again. All she wanted was to curl up with someone else's book. But when it worked, when she really got going and her characters talked back and actually helped her write—well, that was a genuine rush. It was (dare she say it?) a natural high.

Looking at the residency guidelines again, she wondered what it would be like to just sit out in nature for four weeks and write. No day-job bullshit, no grocery shopping or traffic. To be without the general exhaustions of everyday life—that would be heaven. On the other hand, there would be no Max, no Nat, no support group or writers' community. Scary when, now more than ever, she felt as if she needed all the help she could get. Oh well, she had a snowball's chance in hell of being accepted.

***

Mary scuffed through the living room into the kitchen. She looked down at her feet. Second day in her flop-mops. Not a good sign.

After what happened across the street, she hadn't felt much like going out. 'Course, staying in didn't really mean she could hide. Seemed as if that little man followed her everywhere. She'd even stopped watching her news programs 'cause of it.

Her stomach growled. It took signals like that to make her eat now. Eating wasn't much fun when your stomach was tied up in a knot all the time.

Turning on the radio for company, she looked in the fridge: water, condiments, some cheese, a head of really old lettuce. She closed the door and pulled a can of soup out of the cabinet. As she squinted at the label, she flicked on the lights. She didn't like to open the windows on this side of the house anymore. Kept the curtains drawn and the blinds snapped shut.

"Joseph 'Smokey Joe' Fratelli." The name sailed out of the radio and hit her in the gut. There he was again. Right there. He wasn't ever going to go away. Not till he had some justice. It was as simple as that.

The radio sang out again. "We'd like to hear from you. The lines are open now at 559-4000."

She repeated the number: 559-4000. She walked toward the phone. 559-4000. When she picked it up, she dialed the number. She didn't know what good it would do, but she just couldn't sit here any longer. She was going crazy.

***

KBOO Public radio 10:30 a.m. — Marian Blake's PDX — In Depth

If you're just tuning in, we're focusing on issues of police brutality here in Portland, specifically the recent case of Joseph Fratelli Jr., who was declared dead on arrival at the emergency ward after being detained by police in front of a vacant house earlier this year. Hello? Do I have a caller on the line?

"I lied."

"Excuse me?"

"I live across the street from that house. They asked me if I saw anything. I lied."

"Excuse me, caller. Are you talking about the vacant house in this case?"

"They asked me if I saw anything. The police. I said no, but I did see." She paused. "I saw everything."

"Can you tell our listeners what you saw?"

"That little man, he didn't fight back at all, but they beat him. He pretty much lived in that house. Everyone knew it, but nobody said so. I keep thinking about it. They beat him worse than an animal. I don't think they would have stopped if they hadn't heard the ambulance coming and that means I ain't the only one who saw them either."

"So you're saying there's more than one witness to this assault?"

"There's a whole street full of folks that saw it—but who wants to get beat like that little man?"

***

Jack missed Smokey more than he'd ever believed possible. People had been popping in and out of Jack's life for as long as he could remember, but none of them had left such an empty space before.

The funny little guy had insinuated himself into his life unbidden. Even though half the time he got on Jack's nerves, Jack really never thought he wouldn't see him again or have a chance to say good-bye.

Jack's feet took him back to the house again, against all of the common sense in the rest of Jack's body.

Jack's feet knew he just had to take one more look at the place. If only to assure himself that it had all really happened. And maybe, just maybe if the coast was clear, he could find some little part of Smokey to take with him. Maybe those report cards and school photos.

His heart pounded harder and harder the closer he got. It was getting hard to breathe, as if he had been running a long time or climbing uphill.

He could see one of the bright yellow ribbons stretched across the doorway. POLICE LINE DO NOT CROSS. Another length had blown off from somewhere and lay dragged and muddy on the lawn. A curtain twitched across the street.

Barkin' Jack continued on past the house. He tried to casually take in the neighborhood, see whether anyone was out on the porch or looking out their windows. He circled back and slipped in along the side of the house. His body gave an involuntary shudder when he looked at the window where he'd last seen Smokey, half-in and half-out and being pulled down by those cops. He blanked his mind and shoved the vision far back where all the other scary stuff lay piled up. In three surprisingly elegant moves, he was in the house once more. He looked around the place and headed for the kitchen. There was the table; the red sheet they'd used as a holiday tablecloth still covered the top. A guttered candle and a pile of Smokey's butts sat in a metal ashtray at the table's edge. Jack opened the little drawer once more. The envelope still lay among the pile of useless items. He took a quick peek inside; his fingers flipped through the contents. Then he re-sealed it and, holding it close to his chest, climbed back outside.

A police car rounded the corner just as he hit the sidewalk. It slowed and sidled along next to him. Jack felt the adrenaline surge through his veins as the fear swallowed him whole. The car stopped just a few feet away; the door flung open and blocked his path.

"Excuse me sir." The tone of voice belied the light comment.

Jack stopped dead and waited for the ax to fall. It made a funny kind of sense to him that he'd end his days just a few feet from where Smokey had breathed his last.

"There you are!" A tiny gray woman in fuzzy slippers bounded out of the house across the street. She looked directly at Jack. "I've been waiting for you. Guess you got lost, eh?"

"Do you know this man?" The policeman looked the little woman up and down. Her voice caught just a little as she said, "'Course I do. He's here to see me."

Jack stared at the woman and tried to understand what was going on. He didn't know why she was doing what she was doing but she looked a hell of lot less scary than these cops did.

"Absolutely," Jack said.

"See," said the woman. "I don't know what you're doing bothering an old man like him when there's violent crim'nals running the streets." She glared at the cop and took Jack's elbow. "Come on in now. I'm not paying to heat the neighborhood." She looked back at the cop once more. "'Less you need him for some reason?"

"Well, no, not if—" began the cop.

"That's what I thought. Good day to you." With that, she piloted Jack into the little house and slammed the door for good measure.

Now safe inside, the woman leaned her back into the heavy door and let out a long breath. She held out her hand, which trembled in the air. "Oh my sweet Lord," she said. "I can't believe I just did that."

***

Jack's feet piloted him west toward the Salivation Army. They knew it was dinnertime and did a better job of getting him fed than his poor stomach could manage. Along the way, he spun his meeting with Mary around in his head. She'd appeared out of nowhere, pulled him to safety and proceeded to drop a bombshell on him. A witness.

Can I get a witness? So many of the old blues songs he remembered had this query. Can I get a witness? Oh yeah. Now I got a witness. Oh yeah. And what the hell was he supposed to do with her? Maybe she could help him get a little justice for Smokey. But at what cost? Not just to him, but to her. They were two very marginal people. An aging blue-haired, blue collared, Social Security recipient and a homeless vet. Not exactly the folks you'd expect to go toe-to-toe with the justice machine.

He could now spot the line outside the Salivation Army. He slowed his feet to a halt and considered it. Hungry as he was, he just did not want to stand in another line today. Well-meaning folks would ask questions about Smokey. Others would just natter on about the same things they always did: Getting ripped off, beat up, screwed around. Some new scheme for getting a job, an apartment, a government check.

He dug around in his pockets and came up with three dollars and sixty-eight cents. Enough for a slice with no trimmings up the street. He ducked away before anyone could spot him and headed for the pizza joint. There was a line there, too, but at least he didn't know anyone here. By the time he got to the front, there was only one really ancient looking slice left in the case that he could afford. He paid for it and took it with him to the waterfront.

Can I get a witness? It was a quiet time now by the water. Just getting dark. The joggers and tourists and families with kids were all gone. Only the occasional dog walker or a lone soul like himself. A harsh wind blew up little wavelets on the still gray-green water. The pizza was stone cold now too. He got busy with it anyway.

***

Bubbles looked down at her hand that held Kitty's picture and the box of keepsakes open with its contents hanging out. Several possible excuses flew through her head, each one more absurd than the last. Might as well just go for the truth, she thought. It was the least messy of her options at this point, and they had promised to be honest with each other, after all.

"I'm sorry for snooping, Aunt Jane. It really was an accident finding this."

Jane still had one eye on the photo Bubbles held. It seemed to take a minute for Bubbles's words to penetrate her consciousness. She slowly looked over at Bubbles. "I'd almost forgotten about these. It's been so long since I looked at them."

Enthusiasm trumped guilt for Bubbles every time. She looked down at the collection. "They're incredible. This is the stuff all my friends wish they'd been around to see. If I had been there, I'd be telling everyone about it. How come you never did? How come Mom never told me?"

Jane gave her a funny little smile. "I don't think your mother knew too much about what I was up to in those days. I don't think she'd have been too interested anyway. We're very different people."

Bubbles narrowed her eyes. "Yeah, I can see that. But how come you never told me?" That was it, really. The thing that bugged her the most.

Jane looked at Bubbles standing there with her hands on her hips; her lower lip jutted out a little, jaw stiff. She'd gone from sheepish to defiant in seconds. Jane smiled. "You remind me so much of..." Her voice drifted. "Me, Kitty... Oh, come here." Jane moved over to the couch and patted the seat next to her, knowing curiosity would force Bubbles to abandon her combat stance. When they were both seated, she tried to find the words.

"I always wanted to tell you more about my life, but I really didn't know how to do it without sounding like one of those awful people who try to be hip with the younger generation. You know, 'When I was your age, young lady, we walked ten miles in the snow to get to the X-ray.'"

Laughter melted the tension level.

Bubbles held out the photo of Kitty she still had in her hand. "What happened to Kitty? You guys seem so tight. Is she still around?"

Jane's face froze; her body tensed. Then, just as quickly, she seemed to slump; her body turned in on itself. "Kitty's gone. She's dead. She died a long time ago."

"Oh." Bubbles didn't know what to say. The standard I'm sorry seemed even more false than usual. While she still searched for something to say, Aunt Jane jumped up, muttered something about leaving her tools in the rain and disappeared out the French doors into the garden.

Bubbles looked at the suddenly Jane-free space next to her. Now what the fuck was that all about?

Just when it looked as if she was going to get some answers, too. Story of my life, she thought. You think you're finally going to figure it out and boom—nothing.

She looked at the photo of Kitty in her hand. Weird to think she was gone. She certainly didn't look as if she had any idea she was gonna die soon. Bubbles got up and placed the picture carefully back in the box and put the lid back on. Then she shoved it back under the couch and headed for the kitchen.

***

Jane could see Bubbles moving around in the kitchen. She felt like a complete ass, standing out here in the wet garden. Not enough sense to come in out of the rain. But right now it felt like the right place to be.

She'd been as surprised as poor Bubbles probably was to her reaction. All of a sudden, it was as if her throat had closed up, and she just couldn't talk about Kitty. Anything else, but not Kitty.

That world had begun and ended with Kitty. When Kitty was alive, nothing seemed too bad, too hard, or too permanent. So they lived in a squat with no hot water—big deal! Neither of them had any kind of permanent job, and they ate nothing but potatoes, so what? It was a lark; they were young and beautiful.

And Kitty had been beautiful. Even when she tried to look tough and fierce under a ton of white make-up, black lipstick, and safety pins, she was incapable of being anything but fresh-faced Kitty. And corny as it sounded, the beauty went all the way through.

Which, as Jane knew, was not always the case. Like Jake. So handsome that people just automatically painted in a soul. Colored it into the outline when there really wasn't anything there at all. That was bad news for Kitty.

***

Stiff, so stiff. Jack woke from a dream of being frozen and left to fossilize in a mountain cave. He'd found a relatively safe space under the bridge after his pizza dinner last night. Safe from prying eyes but not safe from the elements. He still felt as if he were encased in the ice of his dreams. He tried a toe wiggle and got a slow but satisfactory response. A breeze off the river brought on a shiver and jerk of his body. Time to get moving. Movement=energy=body heat. Coffee would have hit the spot but he didn't have any money left. He wasn't too far from that hippie bookstore where they had free tea, though.

The scent of patchouli hit him as he entered the little shop. Fuzzy images of black-light posters, paisley bedspreads, and huge twisted glass pipes floated past in an instant as he headed for the little table in the back. He gazed at all the different tea bags in the basket: ginger, chamomile, lavender lotus, kava-ginseng, goji berry, acai-pomegranate, peppermint, tummy mint, red bush, kiwi morning. No Lipton. He finally settled on something called Morning Thunder, one of the few that didn't cheerfully tout its lack of caffeine. Jack tossed a bag in the cup, added water and after an unsuccessful wrestle with the honey-bear, added three packets of sugar. He took a tongue-scorching sip and looked around.

The woman at the counter was engrossed in a large paperback. Tiny wires dangled from her ears down to a little box clipped to her arm. Jack spotted a beanbag chair in the far corner, out of her line of sight. Carefully holding his teacup up and out from his body, Jack lowered himself into it and grabbed a book at random off the shelf. The beans shifted underneath him and molded themselves around his stiff, tired body. He was going to have a hell of a time getting up, but for now, it felt great. Jack looked down at the book in his lap. Tapping into Your Inner Life Coach. Life coach? Jack opened the little book and began to read.

***

Up in her room now, Bubbles sensed something familiar and comforting tickling at her. Smoke. Cigarette smoke. Impossible. Aunt Jane didn't smoke. Didn't like the smell, she said. But then again, Aunt Jane was full of surprises.

The day had passed slowly and more awkwardly than any since she'd first arrived. Both of them had holed up with solitary pursuits: reading, listening to music, or Net surfing. Dinner had just been stupid and weird, with Jane chattering about nothing and Bubbles murmuring mono-syllabic answers to perky, pointless questions. Bedtime couldn't come soon enough for either of them. But now, Bubbles sat wide awake in the dark, trying to understand what was going on. Pandora's Box came to mind. Somehow she'd managed to stumble on something much more complex and powerful than she realized.

And wasn't that just fucking typical, too. Why was nothing as simple as it appeared in this stupid world? The older she got, the more life seemed to be about paying attention to what people didn't say rather than what they did. To reading between the lines, body language, sarcasm and subtext. Well, fuck that. Bubbles threw on her robe and went downstairs to see where the smoke was coming from.

***

Pony sat in her third group of the day. "Groups" seemed to be the lifeblood of Harmony House. There were twelve-step groups, rap groups, counselor-led groups, groups about being a survivor, empowerment groups: the list went on and on.

She'd heard more tales of woe than she could even begin to process. The stories overwhelmed her, haunted her dreams. She found it incredible that all of these women weren't babbling idiots but for the most part, they seemed surprisingly clever, funny, and strong—a strength she thought was at odds with their past. And then there was Trisha. In the three weeks that she'd been here, she'd yet to hear Trisha say more than three or four words at a time.

But Trisha's eyes spoke volumes. They were a startling pale blue, huge and framed with thick black lashes. They looked both surprised and terrified at the same time. But sometimes when Pony was in a group like this, they seemed to deepen in color, seemed to acquire a mistiness and a depth that made you want to see inside. To jump into the lake of sadness and swim.

***

Bubbles could see the red glow of the cigarette in the dark. Saw it drop away, the sparks making a tiny shower as she squeaked open the French doors. She spoke into the dark. "I hope you didn't waste a perfectly good cigarette on my account."

"I..."Aunt Jane stuttered, and then she looked up sheepishly. "I'm afraid I did."

Wow, this is hysterical, Bubbles thought. Never thought I'd see the tables turned like this. Aunt Jane looked so guilty. But she also looked so sad and lost. Bubbles couldn't quite enjoy that. Well, I guess it's also time to see what happens if you don't act like an ass about it. Too bad, though; it would have been fun. She dug her pack out of her pocket.

"You want another one?"

Aunt Jane thought about it for a minute. "No thanks. They didn't taste as good as I remembered. You go ahead, though."

Bubbles opened the red and white pack, selected a cigarette and lit up, drawing the smoke deep into her lungs. "Tastes okay to me."

"Well sure, it's still new for you. Still fun."

"I guess." Bubbles rolled her eyes and smoked. The yard felt different at night. All the familiar sights and sounds changed. It was more about the sky and the stars than what was on the ground. She looked back at Jane, who seemed to be working something out in her head while she looked at the moon. Then with a sudden turn, she looked right back at Bubbles. "That's what makes being your age so memorable. Otherwise, adolescence would be pure hell from beginning to end. We'd all probably just block it. But in between the confusion and all the hard stuff, there's also all these new things you discover." Jane paused briefly and then her words spilled out double-time. "I just couldn't wait to get out there and see what there was to do. To try everything I was interested in. And I remember that it seemed like everyone and everything was determined to keep me from seeing anything."

Bubbles laughed and nodded. "Yeah! It really is like that. What's up with that?"

"I guess it's because there's some really scary stuff out there and no one wants to see anyone get hurt by it. At least not the people you love, the people on your watch."

"Is that why you never told me about you? To protect me?"

Aunt Jane paused, got that spacey-thinky look again before she answered. "Not really. It was more because I couldn't protect you. Because I didn't have any answers."

Bubbles ashed her cigarette into a bush, and then changed her mind and carefully stubbed it out. "Okay. Well, what if I don't want any answers? I'm tired of answers." Her voice sounded harsh even in her own ears but she didn't care. She just wanted to know what the hell Aunt Jane was so fucked up about.

Aunt Jane looked at her for a minute, and then, with what sounded like a little pride in her voice said, "Good question. Good answer."

"So? Talk to me, tell me..." Bubbles locked her stare onto Jane's face.

"Tell you?"

Bubbles sighed dramatically. "So tell me. Tell me everything. Tell me how you started out here, why you went out there, how you ended up back here?"

"You're not going to let this one go, are you?"

Bubbles grinned. "Nope."

Jane put her hands up to her head, grabbed her hair on both sides and mimed pulling it out. They both broke up laughing as the sky opened under a thunderclap, and it began to rain.

***

Barkin' Jack looked up from the book he'd been reading and wriggled a little in the beanbag chair to get his circulation going. He needed a moment to digest the contents of the chapter he'd just read. From what it said, he was able to understand that there were these people called life coaches and people hired them to make themselves feel better. To say, "Rah-rah for you!" If his understanding of the English language hadn't completely dwindled away, all it took to be a life coach was having the balls to say you were a life coach. People paid these life coaches to say things like, "You are enough," "You are a fabulous person," "You should really do whatever it is you do," "You are a star." Somewhere out there, people were clearly making more money than they knew what to do with.

Jack shelved the book and peeked out to see what the woman at the desk was doing. She was still reading her book, undisturbed by customers. He wondered whether she had a life coach. He'd be willing to bet Mary would be fairly astounded by the whole life coach thing too. He reached in his pocket and felt for the telephone number she'd given him. She'd said she felt bad about not telling the truth, not speaking up about what happened to Smokey, that she'd been ashamed of herself. She'd asked him where he could be reached. Barkin' Jack had no real answer to that question.

***

"Shoes, dildos, and computer parts?" Toby looked down at the three boxes Freddy had hauled out of the storage space under the stairs.

"Yeah, I been holding on to this stuff for over a year. I knew it would come in handy for the right project. It's the perfect reflection of Portland and the freegan lifestyle as a whole."

Toby foraged through the box of computer parts and pulled out several pieces of motherboard. "I guess some of these might look cool." She laid some pieces across the hood. "Maybe."

Freddy grinned. "You're seeing it—right? Found objects—you know?"

Fella bounced down the stairs, stopping briefly to give the dildo box a good sniff. Toby clapped her hands twice. "Fella, get the hell out of there!" After she had the dog back safely by her side, she gave the collection a final once-over. "Okay, we'll need a ton of silver spray paint and I ain't touching those things. Got it?"

***

They'd managed to get half drenched just getting from the garden to the house. Hastily kicking off their shoes, they grabbed towels from the linen closet and collapsed in the kitchen. Bubbles checked her image in the side of the toaster.

"I look like I stuck my finger in an electric socket—it always does that if I don't straighten it right away."

Jane cocked her head and squinted. "I don't know, it's kind of cute—very 80s."

Bubbles grabbed the kettle. "We'll have cocoa. Just like when I was a kid. We'll have cocoa and you'll tell me a story." Bubbles smiled pointedly.

Five minutes later they sat, blowing on their steaming mugs. Jane rubbed her forehead as if she could massage her thoughts together. Bubbles just sipped and stared at her.

Jane shook her head. "It's not that I'm holding back—I honestly don't know where to start."

Bubbles leaned back. "Tell me about Kitty."

Jane nodded, looking grateful to have found a page to start on. She took a breath and went for it. "Okay, Kitty. I'd never been that close to anyone but my mother before we met. She was my best friend. We'd been friends since third grade and we'd been planning our escape from this island for just that long. We'd dream about our very first apartment. We knew we'd leave home together. From the day we met, our paths were permanently intertwined. We'd draw pictures of our dream place. I remember the first versions were heavy on white shag carpet, princess phones, and pictures of cats.

"The summer before we left school, we both got jobs at the mall. I worked at the movie theater and Kitty did the make-up counter at the Broadway. We saved up enough for the first and last on an apartment in Portland. We both enrolled at PCC. We loved the life on campus, although our grades rarely reflected our enthusiasm. Our parents weren't thrilled with the idea. My mother wanted me at a proper university—not for an education, mind you. She actually used to tell your mother and me it was the best place to get your MRS."

Bubbles looked up. "Your what?...Oh—eww!"

"Eww indeed. My family's views were pretty old-fashioned but Kitty's situation was even worse. Her family didn't want her in school at all; her father thought it was a waste to send a woman to college. Said there was no point when she'd just end up married and having babies. You can understand how exciting it was for us. There was too much to see and do. Portland might be a small town by New York standards but it was a huge new world for us."

"Yeah." Bubbles sighed. "I know what that's like."

"It was the late 70s. The glitter scene had pretty much died down. People were roller skating in discos. We'd just been playing our old Stones and Velvet Underground records, wondering what came next—and then punk happened."

Bubbles's eyes glittered. "That must have been incredible."

Jane nodded. "It was an amazing time. We threw ourselves into it. It was a small enough scene then that you practically knew everyone involved. We started doing fanzines for local bands, then we got a shot with one of the new 'weekly' papers that was just starting up doing a sort of 'around the town' thing about the club scene. Down the Drain—with yours truly—Jane Drain." Jane mocked a little bow from her sitting position and they both cracked up.

"We all made up these new names and identities. Kitty started taking photos for me with an old Polaroid, then graduated to a real 35mm camera. We were off and running. We wanted to go everywhere, see everything. We got our hands on a dirt cheap old Fiat and started taking road trips. First San Francisco and LA. Then cross country to New York."

Jane's eyes seemed to lose focus as the memories flashed by. Then they hardened and got oddly flat looking.

"We met Jake in New York. Brought him back to Portland. Biggest mistake we ever made."

***

Jolie stared unhappily at the Guide to the San Juan Islands they'd gotten from the library. Tapping the photo on the cover with one long red fingernail, she turned to Brian. "There's no easy way here, kid. I've been on the Net, looked at the maps, and now I've read this thing from cover to cover. The only way to get to her is by renting a charter. There's a ferry that runs from summertime 'til mid-December, but after that, you're on your own. We're screwed."

Brian stared at the red ceramic coffee cup in his hand. In the silver gray morning light, it looked unnaturally bright. He shifted his attention back to Jolie. "Well, is there any way we could get a charter? I mean, people can't just be exiled there all winter, can they?"

Jolie just shook her head. "Okay, say we get the money together and get someone to take us out there. Then we have to hunt her down and get her out of her aunt's house and back onto the boat without anybody noticing. Do we just tell the guy with the boat just hang on a minute while we kidnap our friend? Let's face it—we don't exactly just fade into the scenery."

"But—there's got to be a way." The words sounded foolish the minute he spoke them, but he couldn't hold them back. Visions of his mad trek through the forest, his rescue by Atlantia and her friends, meeting Daisy and Toby and Freddy, his hunt for Jolie through the strip clubs of Portland: it had been the biggest adventure of his life. And now, to see it all go to waste because of a stupid ferry boat? That just plain wasn't fair. It wasn't fair at all.

***

Bubbles raised a finger. "Wait, I've been so curious about this ever since I found it." She came back moments later with the PHOTOS box. "Is this okay? Are some of them here?" She studied Jane's nervous expression.

Jane nodded quickly and reached for the box. "Okay, where were we?"

"Jake," said Bubbles. "Wait—let me see something." She reached for the strips of photo-booth pictures and pulled out the strips of Jane, Kitty, and the boy with the skull earring. "Jake?"

Jane's eyes went wide and then she laughed. She tapped a nail at one full face of the boy grinning like a pirate. "That's Jake alright. Pure charisma. He was something new. We all loved Jake at first. As I said, the whole scene was still very small in those days. Everyone knew everyone in Portland, so Jake was an unknown quantity. A big city New York boy and a total original. At least we thought he was. For a while. Then I started to notice things that I thought maybe I'd heard before." Jane looked frustrated for a moment. Bubbles waited patiently and allowed her to frame her thoughts.

"To Kitty, Jake was a total genius, an innovator, and he was—unless you'd read Burroughs or Genet or Rimbaud. And his music was the freshest thing ever—unless you took another look at your Velvet Underground records, and then that flat wry voice began to seem familiar. It's funny—he did turn us on to some great things, but through discovering them, I started to realize he just wasn't all that original after all. But Kitty didn't see it, wouldn't see it—even when I finally just up and pointed it out. I know she thought I was being bitchy or jealous." Jane broke off and peered into the middle distance.

Bubbles felt as if she looked hard enough, she might see Jake and Kitty too. In the flesh. Finally, she asked, "Were you?"

***

Pony huddled out in the rain with her fellow smokers. Break time at the Wednesday night NA meeting in the park. She'd actually liked this speaker. She'd been a hooker and a hustler but she didn't have that sort of "I found Pink Jesus" thing like some of them. She looked great and sounded as if she was having fun. Maybe she'd ask her for her number. Everyone at the house had been on her to get more numbers and find a sponsor. It just seemed so weird talking to total strangers about all your personal business. Walking toward the ashtray, she caught a glimpse of a familiar figure across the parking lot. No. It couldn't be. Could it?

Under a huge umbrella and under a leafless maple, Toby stood with a funny looking yellow dog. Pony quickened her step and headed for the two of them.

"Hey." Toby's familiar drawl had its usual intimate feel. As if no time had passed.

"Hey." Pony looked down at the yellow dog, who cocked its head at her, curious. She carefully offered her hand for sniffing. The dog took her offer and his tail wagged after he'd gotten a whiff. Pony grinned at Toby. "My replacement?"

"Nah, just a really good friend."

Pony looked nervously back at the crowd outside. "You really shouldn't be here."

Toby shrugged. "Just taking my friend for a walk in the park. No law against that."

"Right. At nine o'clock at night in the pouring rain."

"And I wanted to give you this." Toby tilted the umbrella over them and gave her a quick, deep kiss. "Okay, gotta run." She tugged on the red leash and the two disappeared as quickly as they'd come.

"Not fair," Pony muttered at the place where Toby and the dog stood moments ago. But there was a noticeable spring in her step as she headed back.

***

Jane's attention snapped back. "Was I jealous? Probably. It definitely changed things for us. We'd lost the apartment by then. We ended up squatting in this huge underground basement of an office building in what's called the Pearl District now.

Let me see..." She flipped through some shots of various partying friends to one of a huge wall with a big red Anarchy A covered in a circle of graffiti. Jake and Kitty sat on a battered couch underneath it, looking considerably more hard-core than the earlier pictures. "It was part nightclub, part rehearsal studio, part crash pad. A bunch of us moved in—we called it the Slab Lab. Jake and Kitty lived in one of the rehearsal rooms and I lived on the club floor—just a little space behind the curtain, really. It was pretty great at first—living in an art space like that. But things got harder and harsher and pretty soon everyone started getting a lot more serious about their drugs. The stuff we only did once in a blue moon was around every day. Coke, pills, and then heroin. Jake was the first to really acquire a habit. He hid it pretty well initially. Kitty was right behind him. I remember she was still such an innocent, didn't understand what was happening to her body. She kept complaining she had this flu she couldn't shake. I was just as dumb. Kept shoplifting aspirin and Nyquil for her. Then people started dying. First, a girl I didn't know that well. Then there was Suzy, one if the girls who lived at the lab."

Jane did another quick shuffle through the party people and finally pulled out two of the photographs. They were group shots—the kind that reminded Bubbles of several she and her friends had taken over the years: grinning faces, beers or hard liquor bottles in hand, arms around each other or piled on top of each other.

"I think that's Suzy." Jane pointed to a scowling blue-haired Goth girl with heavy black kohl around her eyes, one of a type you might see out at a show in any of the past three decades. She pointed to another of a group of four on the couch in the Slab Lab. "And there's Suzy, me, and I forget that guy's name—Dave maybe? And Kitty." Bubbles picked it up and examined it. Seeing Aunt Jane in her punk drag still kinda freaked her out but what was even freakier was seeing Kitty in this one. She looked awful, beyond decadent. Bubbles would not have recognized her as the same girl in the earlier shots—she looked totally burned out. Suzy looked much the same as she had in the last shot, but in this shot she was actually sort of smiling. Bubbles set the photo down and Jane quickly shuffled it back into the pile.

"Suzy was a lot of fun, kept everyone's spirits up around the lab, but she overdosed one night after a show. I think that's when the whole unit began to disintegrate. I tried to keep it together but Kitty lost interest in the paper. She got so involved in Jake: his habit, his band, his writing. She rarely took any photos that didn't feature him in some way."

Bubbles began to look at some of the larger black-and-white shots that were obviously Kitty's work. She found it interesting that armed with this new knowledge, Jake's sneer seemed both more posed and authentic at the same time. Creepy.

"I had to nag her to get her to do the stuff for the weekly column, which was the only thing we had coming in cash-wise. School had totally fallen apart. Then my mother—Grammy—had her first stroke. I had to come up here and take care of her. I was gone for over a month. I think Kitty was beginning to have her fill of Jake because she'd started calling me every day, wanting me to come back. It wasn't easy for her to do, either. This was before cell phones. It broke my heart, hearing her stuck in some phone booth in the middle of the night, begging dimes and quarters while trying to act like everything was going great. But I couldn't leave until my mother was able to care for herself."

Jane took a sip of the cocoa and set it down quickly. Her face registered surprise at how cold it had become.

"Kitty was in a jam. She wanted to go back to school but her parents wouldn't help her with any money and I didn't have a dime. She'd skipped on her loans so she couldn't go back to PCC until they untangled everything and she just wasn't together enough to face all that bureaucracy. I was getting ready to go back there and try to see if I couldn't help her get back on track. I was halfway to the boat when I saw the ambulance headed toward the house. Grammy had another stroke. When I came home from the emergency room, there was a message on the machine. Kitty was dead."

A tiny gasp filled the room and it took Bubbles a minute in the silence to realize it was hers.

Jane nodded. "An overdose. I couldn't believe it. We'd talked together the day before. Then the calls started coming in and I knew it was true. I thought I'd have the chance to at least say good-bye but her parents had her cremated. There was no service, no burial site for me to go pay my respects. It was like she'd been erased. I tried to stay in touch with her family, but I could tell I just made them uncomfortable."

It was Bubbles's turn to shake her head. "God, how awful. What did you do?"

"I unpacked my Portland bags and stayed at my mother's house. I never thought I'd stay there for good. But then Grammy's health got worse—she became paralyzed on her left side. She needed someone there all the time. Your mother was just out of high school and headed for college. It made sense for me to stay, I guess. So, here I am." Jane raised her hands, palms open. Then she scooped up all the photos and clippings and set them back in the box.

"And you never went back?" Bubbles asked.

Jane shrugged. "Well, not long after I left, the Slab Lab was condemned and boarded up—there was really nowhere to go 'back' to. Even if I'd wanted to."

"You didn't stay in touch with anyone?" Bubbles asked, amazed.

"Oh, at first I got some calls, but you know how people drift apart. We didn't have cell phones or Facebook like you do now. Stone-age technology, you see. And of course, so many of them are dead now." With that, Jane reached out to put the lid back on; it caught and then snapped into place.

It reminded Bubbles of closing a coffin somehow and she knew that question time had run its course. She tried for a few more quick answers.

"How about Jake? Did he die?"

Jane's face clouded briefly. "Yes. I did hear about Jake dying. He didn't last long after Kitty. I was still on the grapevine long enough to hear about that. After a while, I went back to school for my library science degree. Between taking care of Mom and studying, I really didn't have the time or inclination to hunt anyone down."

Bubbles leaned into the table, her arm propped up on her elbow and chin in her palm. "Did you tell my mom all about this stuff? Or your mom?"

Jane just shook her head. "No, I didn't really think they'd understand. Do you?"

Bubbles shook her head. "Nah, I don't think they'd get it at all. At least not the important stuff."

"No, not the important stuff."

Jane looked at Bubbles, and Bubbles thought she'd never seen her aunt look so young or so sad before. She put her hand over Jane's and the two of them just sat there for a while.

***

"I think the Lord sent you here, Mr. Jack. I think he means for us to get justice for your friend."

That's what his new friend Mary said. Jack was pretty sure the Lord didn't have as much to do with it as his restless feet did, but it did seem as if his feet kept takin' him back around that neighborhood. Logic said it was just because that was where he used to hang his hat. That his feet were just a little confused about where they lived now. And if Jack just happened to decide spur of the moment like to look in on Mary, well, that was just good manners, wasn't it? Now as he approached the house, he wasn't too surprised to see her out on her porch, waving.

"Oh Mr. Jack! I'm so glad to see you. I've been wondering when I'd see you again."

Jack muttered something about feet while Mary ushered him into the little house. Her eyes briefly darted around for witnesses to this unlikely caller.

The place was as he'd remembered it: spotlessly clean and filled with pointless do-dads he was afraid of knocking over. Moments later, he found himself nervously perched on the edge of a curly wooden chair, a glass of lemonade in his hand.

"I've done some thinking, Mr. Jack. And some praying on this matter. I talked to my daughter-in-law about it. She's a paralegal. That's practically a lawyer. She says we need the district attorney to help us. Says they got them a whole special department, just for lookin' into this kind of situation."

Jack cursed his feet silently. District attorney? That wasn't the sort of person Jack mingled with. That sort of person belonged to the other world—the one Jack didn't live in anymore. Jack stood up fast. So fast the curly chair tipped over behind him. Muttering something unintelligible, he made for the door and dragged his traitor feet with him, leaving Mary with her mouth gasping soundless words, looking like a freshly caught fish.

***

Barkin' Jack dragged his feet away from Mary's house. It seemed to take all of his energy and concentration to keep them moving. Jack didn't feel safe to let them stop. He just kept them going and going 'til finally they could go no more.

He threw himself down on someone's lawn and looked around. Looked like Laurelhurst maybe, kinda fancy. What was he doing here? Was it just those two words—district attorney—that had him so riled?

He'd been serious about getting justice for Smokey, hadn't he? Mary could help, but wasn't it up to him? He was the one. It was up to him.

What had he thought justice would involve? He hadn't really let himself think too much about that. Surely there had to be some other way. Or was there? Maybe he'd known all along that it would be something like this, and it would have this very effect on him.

And now, what would Mary think of him running out that way? Not good. Not good at all. He lay back on the grass and closed his eyes. He just wanted everything to go back the way it was. He drifted.

Jack sensed the subtle light change; felt more than saw the curtains behind him twitch. He got up before anyone could take offense at his presence on their lawn. On their property. Property. Jack didn't like the sound that word made. Didn't like the feel of it in his head. He moved it out—fast.

There was a giant golden lady on a horse in the middle of the road, had her own patch of grass. She was up on a concrete block. She wasn't going anywhere, that was for damn sure, but she shined wonderfully. Joan of Arc. Joan D' Arc. Joan Dark.

Jack moved on. By the time he hit Belmont, his feet wouldn't stop bothering him. Wouldn't stop hurting. Jack didn't want to sit on the sidewalk but his feet had other ideas. Jack slid down the wall near the fancy market. What would he say to Mary? Could he go back? Would she want to see him again after today? People were hard, too hard. People made Jack's head hurt.

"There you go. Make sure you get something to eat now—okay?"

Something flapped in front of Jack's face. It was a bill, a five dollar bill. Jack looked up into the face of a bearded man. A friendly face, weathered and surrounded by curly gray-white hair.

"I been there, man. I been there." The man reached forward and gently set the bill on Jack's knee. Seeing the look of confusion on Jack's face, the man said, "Just pass it on when it's your turn, man." Then he walked away.

***

Jane took a sip of tea and winced at its cold, bitter taste. She'd been sitting at her desk since 3:00 a.m., wrestling with the bomb that she'd received in the form of an e-mail. A silent little bomb thrown by her little sister Eleanor.

It was typical of Ellie to throw Jane a curve like that in writing. Not even a phone call. With e-mail, there was no messy emotional baggage to deal with. No troublesome opinions to get in the way. No back-talk.

Boot camp. They wanted to send Bubbles to boot camp. Had, in fact, enrolled or enlisted her already. Eleanor "hoped she'd understand." She didn't understand; she couldn't begin to understand why anyone would want to put such a clever, unique kid like Bubbles in an environment like that.

To make matters worse, she wanted Jane to keep silent about it. To give Bubbles no advance warning. They'd discussed it (she and stepdad Ken): "We've decided it would be for the best," Eleanor wrote. No consideration for the relationship Jane was building with her niece. No discussion about the fact that Jane had promised Bubbles a mutual trust, one that meant she'd be honest with her. Now she was expected to cheerfully lie to her face. Business as usual. Just another strategy they were trying out. Just like when they'd dumped the girl here on the island.

Bubbles wasn't Jane's child, Eleanor had been quick to point out. Although she was grateful, she really was, Jane must realize that she couldn't begin to understand the pressure of raising a daughter. Especially one like Bubbles.

Well, maybe that was true, but try as she might, she could not justify such a betrayal. She just couldn't be a party to this.

***

Daisy stared in wonder at the automobile before her. Two months in the making, during which she'd been strongly dissuaded from peeking. Toby and Freddy had proudly led her out with instructions not to look up until they gave her the go-ahead. Now that they had given her the thumbs-up, she could only stare open-mouthed. The battered old Dodge had been transformed out of all recognition into—well, into...

"It's a Dildosaurus-rex." Freddy stepped back from the car and grinned ear to ear.

"It's the only real smart-car." Toby laughed.

They had painted over the beige beater with bold stripes of green in several different shades. Two of the biggest dildos she'd ever seen were mounted on the hood on either side just over the headlights and looked like tusks. Across the roof and down the trunk, a line of about twelve more smaller ones gave it a spiny back armor. Motherboards and computer circuits covered most of the doors. Along the length of the body, shoes that had been sprayed silver were placed in pairs, with little black dotted lines leading from one to the next to form the steps of a ballroom dance.

"It's..." Daisy gave up and tried again. "You think you can really drive it? Does it actually run?"

"You bet it does," Freddy said.

"Purrs like a kitten," Toby added. "We tuned her up."

It was about the strangest looking automobile Daisy had ever seen but when she looked from one face to the other, she knew that car had accomplished what she could not. Toby and Freddy were a team now. The best of friends. They had finally discovered all those qualities in each other, the similarities that Daisy had tried to tell them about for so long.

Daisy took a deep breath and with one hand on her stomach to include the baby's presence, she said, "Well hell, what are we waiting for? Let's go for a cruise!"

***

Mary glanced at the front door. She'd had one of her notions again. This one told her that she was going to have a visitor today, so she'd taken a little extra care tidying up the house. Corners and baseboards and such. There wasn't really any reason for company to call today, but she'd done a little baking too. There was nothing like fresh cookies with a cup of tea in the afternoon. She had just taken the cookies out of the oven and set them by the window to cool when the doorbell rang.

***

It was only polite, Jack mused as he walked up the block. He'd been a guest in her home, and he'd just up and walked out. So, it was only polite to return and apologize for his bizarre behavior. He really didn't know whether he could have a meeting with the DA and such, but he could certainly try to be decent company. Of course, she could ignore his call today. Just not answer the door. That could happen. Or she might actually be out visiting herself. That was a possibility that Jack half hoped might be true.

Jack approached the little house and noticed that the blinds were drawn. That was a good sign. He could then just tippy-toe away and still have the good feeling of having done the right thing. He noticed the little button next to the door. He pressed his ear close to the thick wood of the door but he couldn't hear anything. He waited for a moment and then pressed the bell.

***

When Bubbles found Aunt Jane in her office the next morning, she could tell her aunt hadn't moved from her desk since last night. She looked totally depleted. And when Bubbles asked her whether they could talk about what was wrong, Jane sat her down and told her all about the letter from Mom. Just like that. It was incredible.

As nervous and upset as they'd both been by the news, Bubbles found herself strangely energized. She was so proud and happy about her Aunt Jane's honesty. Until then, Jolie had been the only adult who'd been willing to listen and really stand by her. Now she had Jane too. For the first time in her life, she had real allies. Maybe they still weren't quite sure what they were going to do about the situation, but whatever they did, they were going to work it out together.

Aunt Jane came back to her seat at the kitchen table across from Bubbles. "Tell me more about your friend Jolie."

***

Mary snuck a peek at the funny little man balanced on the edge of her bentwood chair. They were just sitting now, quietly enjoying her tea and cookies. He had that gray-brown coloring that people who lived rough seemed to get. But she was happy to note that he didn't look particularly dirty, and he didn't smell. He'd offered an awkward apology for his dash out the door yesterday, and she'd been careful to accept it as such while brushing it off as perfectly normal behavior.

She asked herself again what she was doing entertaining him. They were not the kind of folks who generally crossed paths socially, let alone spent time together. They likely had little in common and the man spoke so seldom, that if they had it would be years before she found out. But they did have Smokey. Or his ghost. And maybe that would have to be enough. The more Mary thought about it, the angrier she got.

Mary had been taught like most women of her age to banish her negative opinions, and to either stuff her rage into a tight, quiet little ball or deny it altogether. For most of her life, she'd managed to do that very well. But now she felt it was a little odd to be living in fear of the opinions of her elders. Elders who had been dead for years. Because she had joined the ranks of the elderly. She was one of them. Those who had always seemed to have the emotional luxuries denied to her. And murder? To condone murder was a sin. Whether those policemen had meant to kill him or not, a man was dead. And if she and this strange little man were the only ones who seemed to care, well then, so be it. It was just going to take patience.

***

Jack couldn't remember the last time he'd been entertained by a lady. Couldn't remember the last time he'd been to visit someone indoors. Something told him that this might have once been a regular occurrence in his life, but he couldn't remember when that might have been. Before the war certainly, but when? Jack didn't think about things like that. Didn't want to. Wouldn't. You couldn't make him. He dragged his attention back to Mary. She was saying something about the cookies.

***

"Psst... Hey, Brian. Brian, wake up, honey."

Brian smelled coffee, felt a hand shake his shoulder. Jolie. He opened his eyes to see Jolie looking down at him, a cup of coffee in her hands.

"Here you go. It's fresh."

Brian reached gratefully for the cup as he sat up on the lumpy couch.

Jolie looked as if she was going to burst. She practically hopped from one foot to the other.

He took a long sip of the coffee. "Wow, the star treatment this morning. What's up?"

Jolie sat on the arm of the couch. Her eyes sparkled. "You are never going to believe this. I got a phone call this morning. You'll never guess who it was."

Brian ran a hand over his sleepy face. It was way too early for guessing games.

"Okay, you got me. I'll never guess. Who was it?"

Jolie looked only mildly disappointed and blurted out the answer immediately. "Aunt Jane. Aunt-fucking-Jane!"

"Aunt who? Aunt Jane, Aunt Jane? Bubbles's Aunt Jane?" Brian sat straight up. Jolie had his full attention now.

***

To Daisy's amazement, the car made it all the way across town. Freddy and Toby took her for coffee at Beaterville, a place they'd recently discovered. They pulled up behind the cafe owner's car, which was painted in rainbow colors with a giant shark fin on top. Several older men stood talking in front of a perfectly restored Model-T. The group nodded politely as the three of them passed.

Inside, the little cafe was decorated in a kitschy assortment of old photos, hubcaps, and vintage auto memorabilia. It had a cozy feel, not like the slick new 50s cafes that were fast replacing the old 50s cafes everywhere. There was even a place to tie Fella up outside and a fresh bowl of dog water. Daisy immediately liked the place. After they'd settled in, Freddy reached across the table, took both her hands in his and leaned in toward her. "So what do ya think—is she not the perfect road trip car or what?"

Daisy had a feeling that this question was nowhere near as innocent as it sounded and that her answer could have serious consequences. She racked her brain for the most neutral response she could come up with. "Road trip? I guess. I mean, sometime that might be cool."

"Daze, this car gives us our freedom. We are now officially free to go anywhere in the world. Do you realize that? We can go anywhere we like, anytime."

Toby snickered. "Those oceans could give you a run for your money."

Freddy plowed on. "Okay, maybe not everywhere, but definitely Louisiana and the Black Rock desert. It's the perfect car for that. We take it to Burning Man, everyone will love it. We'll do Mardi Gras, and then head back to the desert—hit all the pre-burn festivals until we get to Burning Man. We won't have to worry about a place to stay or anything. It's perfect."

Daisy stared at him and stuttered out the words, "B-B-Burning Man?" She ran her hand over the ever-growing expanse of her belly. "What about the baby?"

Freddy just smiled. "Don't worry about the baby, Daze. He'll be fine. That's about the best possible place for the little guy to come into the world. What an entrance."

Oh God, there was that he again. Mr. Baby. Daisy looked desperately over at Toby, hoping for a voice of reason. She was disappointed. Toby's face had the same manic expression Freddy wore.

"Come on, Daisy. Where's your pioneer spirit?"

***

Barkin' Jack headed over the little footbridge toward the ducks. He'd showed up at the Greyhound station early and greeted several busloads of folks today. A lot of Texans this morning for some reason. You could tell by the hats.

A dark gray sky hung so low, it felt as if he were inside instead of out. Cutting through the condos, he reached the path to the waterfront and discovered one side had been blocked off. Yellow tape and a cone stood in front of it and the cement looked as if it had been pushed up from underneath. Jack turned in the other direction and headed for the landing where he could see his feathered friends. It was quiet out on the water. Too cold for the little motorboats and pleasure crafts of summer. The ducks were all out and one or two geese. Jack had often wondered why they hadn't migrated along with the rest. Were some animals individualists? Hell no, we won't go?

Jack fished in his big coat pocket for the half bag of potato chips he'd found earlier and tossed them toward the little gathering of birds. He was supposed to visit Mary again today. She'd asked him to come help her clear her rain gutters. Said she didn't trust herself on a ladder anymore. In return, she was supposed to make him something called Frito pie. If he let himself think about it long enough, he might think she was hoping to talk to him about going to that DA again. But as he looked around him at the ducks enjoying their feast and the big hole in the clouds with the sun streaming through like the hand of God—well, he just didn't feel like thinking about it right now.

***

Jane sat in the quiet office space and contemplated her options. She'd spent half the night researching boot camps for teens on the Internet. She'd read the horror stories of the kids and the testimonials of the parents. She'd tried playing devil's advocate, tried seeing it from Eleanor's point of view, but what she'd just read was so disturbing, so scary that she realized she had no choice but to go ahead with the plan she already half-formulated.

There were at least fifteen documented cases of teens dying from dehydration and starvation. Some made to eat their own vomit. Humiliations that went beyond what the actual Army or Marines had tolerated in the worst of times. This was the ammo she needed to get Bubbles free of this nonsense. But would it work? Or was it time for plan B?

There was about a fifty percent chance that Eleanor would change her mind if she knew. Jane didn't like those odds. So she'd put out a feeler—just a feeler—to see what might happen if she contacted Jolie. Trusting her most beloved niece to a Portland stripper wasn't among any of the choices she'd ever anticipated making when Bubbles's care had fallen into her lap. Plan B was certainly risky. But desperate times called for desperate measures.

***

Pony slipped downstairs and out through the kitchen door. She held the knob in her hand and slowly pulled it shut to keep it silent. She didn't want company; she'd had far too much of that. Thirty days and she was allowed out of the house. Allowed a few moments' peace away from the groups, the chatter, the chores, the estrogen.

The house itself was built up against a hillside, with a little path that led up to an expanse that was part garden, part vacant lot. An old cherry tree and a tangle of raspberry vines made it a favorite of the neighborhood critters: birds, possums, raccoons, and squirrels. If you were really quiet and came down at dawn like now, you might see a deer. In her hand, she held the dreaded Feelings Journal they had all been given. You were supposed to fill its pages with your every emotion, an idea that went against everything that Pony had learned on the street. On the streets, you didn't talk about how you felt, and you certainly didn't put it down on paper for anyone to see. That was called evidence. Power. Power in the wrong hands.

***

Jack half-sat, half-lay in the beanbag chair at the little bookstore. He'd sort of scrunched himself in as far as he could go. A cup of chamomile tea was doing double duty as a hand warmer. He'd come here to think this time, but his mind wandered all over the place. He'd wanted to think about his talk with Mary last night. Or more to the point, her talk with him. He was pretty sure she'd talked him into this whole district attorney thing she'd had planned.

According to Mary, he wouldn't have to do very much. According to Mary, she'd get the ball rolling. Make the necessary calls. Talk to the right people. Get the whole thing started so that (according to Mary), he wouldn't have to do much but maybe tell this district attorney person his story in a safe and cop-free office. Could that really be true?

It had started so innocently, with cleaning out the rain gutter and having a really decent pot roast. How did things get so complicated? From keeping the dirty leaves from gumming up the drainpipes to sitting in some big shot's office, talking his fool head off?

Everything in Barkin' Jack's world had been designed to avoid having to do things like this. His instincts told him to get as far away from this situation as humanly possible. But the problem was, that even here in the beanbag, if he listened hard enough, he could still hear Smokey's voice calling out. He could hear those big black shoes going thump thump thump on Smokey's body.

Mary said she could hear it too.

***

Butchie watched Veronica take a tiny sip of her coconut-mango smoothie and thought about carbs. It was one of the better offerings at the juice bar here at 48 Hour Fitness but it could eat up your daily allowance before noon unless you were doing a super-rigorous workout program. He thought about telling Veronica this but she had her "serious face" on. Butchie had learned the painful lessons of not taking Veronica's serious face seriously more than once.

He looked up at the special forty-eight hour clock on the wall. It was either nine or eighteen a.m. Butchie wondered what had brought Veronica out to talk to him so early on a Friday. Friday wasn't one of her regular workout days and Veronica was all about keeping her schedule on track. He waited while she took another tiny sip (maybe she had read the carb count after all), poked her straw around for a while and then slowly looked up and met his eye. "Butchie, you were in the military for a while, weren't you?"

Butchie stopped his surreptitious carb count and looked at her in surprise. "Sure, right out of high school. Up in Fort Lewis, two of the longest years of my life. Why?"

Veronica looked down again. Poke, poke, sip. "They had boot camp there, right?"

Butchie laughed. "Oh yeah, everybody gets boot camp, Veronica. Army, Navy—it doesn't matter."

He watched as her serious face gave a weird twitch, about as much of a frown as the Botox would allow, he guessed.

"Is it really as bad as they say? Is it really like in the movies?"

Butchie shrugged. "I guess it depends on what movies you watch. I sure as hell wasn't crazy about it, but I survived. Why? You're not considering the military, are you, babe? You wouldn't last a...I mean, I don't think you'd—"

Veronica cut him off with a snort of annoyance. "Of course not. You don't have to tell me I'm not exactly GI Jane material. It's Bubbles. My stepfather wants to send Bubbles to a teen boot camp. He's got some golfing buddy who's invested a pile in one of them. Says it'll straighten her right out. They want us to come and help pick her up from Aunt Jane's place out in the San Juans."

Butchie frowned now. The whole full-on scrunched-up face version. "Pick her up, pick her up? Or like the last time? Veronica, I really didn't feel too good about that."

She surprised him then by taking his hand and holding it tight. What she said surprised him even more.

"I know, Butchie. This time I'm not too crazy about it, either."

***

Pony veered away from the caffeinated coffee pot at the meeting. Her roommate had actually gotten snitched out by someone for drinking it at last week's meeting and had lost some of her points. Pony really couldn't see what harm a little coffee could do to someone who'd been abusing their body with heroin and crack cocaine less than a month ago. She chalked it up to one more in a line of bizarre rules the women were expected to follow. She poured herself a cup of decaf and headed out to the smoker's area.

She couldn't help herself from just casually checking out the area at the edge of the lot where Toby had stood in the rain that night. She was just about to turn away when her eye caught a flash of the tail end of Toby's new companion wagging out from behind the tree. She casually sauntered over and carefully slipped into the shade. Toby's face lit up when she saw her. Even the dog's tail wagged harder.

"Babe!"

Pony tried to keep the casual thing going. "Hey, Tobe."

"I really need to talk to you. Is there any way we can do that for more than six minutes?"

There was a vulnerability in Toby's face that seemed new. Seemed different. Pony was tempted to tell her to come to the garden by the house but that would be a violation of everything they were about at Harmony. She just couldn't do that. Even if Toby wasn't really an abuser.

"You got a cell you can talk on? A number?"

Pony held out the little book they gave all the girls to get phone numbers at meetings.

Toby grabbed her pen and quickly jotted down a line of digits. Then she pulled her in for another full strength kiss. Whatever casual front Pony had managed to keep up fell away in an instant and she had to break away before the urge to continue got too strong. She took a deep breath before she spoke again. "I'll call you Thursday. I can get out for a little bit in the afternoon, I think."

Toby gave her the grin again. "Thanks, Pony. Really." She paused as if she wanted to say more and then just reached out and squeezed Pony's shoulder. "Thanks."

Pony nodded quickly and headed back to the church. Her mind reeled with questions. She turned the corner and ran right into Trisha, whose eyes seemed equally full of questions.

***

Pony slipped her cigarettes into her sweater pocket and headed out back. Only nine a.m. and the house was already a buzzing hive: women cooking, women cleaning, women going to groups, to child care, some to outside jobs. Pony had grown to like mornings at Harmony but today the house felt sad, all the activity a little forced. They'd lost one of their own yesterday and it had hurt and confused everyone.

Patty had come into the house only a few weeks before Pony arrived, but she had quickly become a sort of maternal figure for most of the women in the house. Patty had come to Harmony straight from the hospital like Pony, wearing a huge pair of rhinestone sunglasses to cover the double black eyes she'd received from her husband, along with three broken ribs and a dislocated shoulder. With her wild teased-up hair and her armloads of silver bracelets, she was half earth mother, half country-western star and they'd all loved her. She'd seemed so secure in her decision to leave her abuser behind, to start a new life and a new career. Pony knew more than one woman who had looked up to Patty saw her as a model of the strength they all needed.

Pony didn't know what to think. Of all the women in the house, Patty was the last one she'd have picked to flake. What did that say about her ability to read people? She felt sad and abandoned like so many of the others but she also felt a sense of betrayal and more than a little anger too. What the fuck was she thinking? Hadn't she heard all the stories every day in group? Hadn't she read the statistics they'd been given on the likelihood of an abuser changing his ways?

And yet, hadn't she been thinking about going back to Toby just last night? Through all her talks with the counselors, she'd discovered that although Toby wasn't an abuser, the lifestyle they led together had laid her wide open to every form of abuse imaginable. Life on the streets the way they'd lived had just been one humiliation after another, and Toby hadn't even begun to look at the effects of all the abuse in her own past. How could they possibly make such a relationship work?

She was just barely recovering from her treatment at the hands of hundreds of johns herself. How could she help Toby?

***

Jolie waved at the printout she'd just made. "This is incredible. I mean, just when I figured there was no way we could get there—we get an engraved invitation."

Brian reached for the paper. "Looks legit. She really seems like she wants us to come get Miss Bubbles. What on earth do you think changed her mind?" He gave the paper back to Jolie, who set it carefully on the desk. She examined the rest of the papers in the printer, and flipped through them as she spoke. "I don't know, but we better get packing before she changes it again. Have you ever been there? I mean, to the San Juans?"

Brian had disappeared into the little vanity room where he kept his stuff. "Huh?"

Jolie raised her voice. "The San Juan Islands—ever been there?"

Brian reappeared with a stack of neatly folded T-shirts, jeans, and boxers. "Jeez, no need to scream. I have been, as a matter of fact. I've even been to the house, back when Bubbles's grandma was still alive. We went up for Christmas vacation when we were like eleven or twelve. It's really beautiful, but it's really isolated, not one of the big ones. It's not even on most of the maps."

Jolie consulted one of the printouts she held. "It says we have to go to Seattle, take a ferry to somewhere called Friday Harbor. From there, we meet up with the guy with the charter boat. Name's Sam apparently; she says it's all arranged and paid for. She's even sent me a little map with all the various stops highlighted. This is so fucking weird. If I didn't know better, I'd think we were being set up for something."

Brian looked at her seriously. "Do you? Think we're being set up?"

Jolie shrugged. "Well, no, not really. What possible reason could she have? Besides, we can't just ignore it. This is Bubbles we're talking about."

Brian just nodded and fastened the snaps on his backpack. "Bubbles. I guess it'll be an adventure no matter what happens."

***

Mary stirred the white sauce onto the blanched almonds, tasted it and added just a pinch more flour, and then mixed in the freshly shelled peas from the colander on the sink, stirred it up and covered the pot. Seemed like no one made Chicken ala King anymore, least not any worth eating.

Cooking for Jack served a multitude of purposes. It relaxed her and gave her a chance to have the things she never would bother to make for just herself. Eating her food seemed to relax Jack and give him something to do. He sometimes reminded her of an old feral tom-cat she'd taken in as a child, never quite comfortable indoors. Just like the old cat, food seemed to calm him, make him comfortable.

She'd need him comfortable today for sure with the news she had for him. Lord, the whole thing made her nervous, too, if the truth be known. She wasn't used to talking to city officials, never had any call to do that in all the years she'd spent here on earth. But talk to them she had. The wonder of it was how they'd seemed to send her right to the top with very little to-do about it. When they'd taken her information on the first call and told her they'd get back to her, she'd wondered whether that would be the end of it right there and a little part of her hoped that might happen. When she'd gotten the call from the Deputy DA inviting them to come in, well, you could have knocked her down with a feather. The deputy district attorney. If that wasn't straight out of Perry Mason, she sure didn't know what was.

If you looked at it like that, the whole thing was pretty exciting—the wheels of justice in motion—but Mary wasn't at all sure that's how Jack would see it. For one thing, Mr. Porter at the DA's office had told her that someone else would be sitting in on their meeting and that someone was a policeman. He'd be brought in from a different area, probably Washington County or Gresham. So it wasn't like he was from the same department. But still. And if that made her nervous, well, what was it going to do to Mr. Jack?

Mary got up and put the little pastry shells into the oven and set the timer for fourteen minutes. Jack would be here any moment and after that, it was all up to Chicken ala King and the good Lord.

***

Pony had almost reached her destination, an old wooden bench someone had dragged under the cherry tree, when she saw her seat of choice was already occupied.

Trisha sat on the bench and held her journal tight across her chest with both arms. She seemed to stare at something terribly far away. Pony adjusted her step and walked the way people do when they see animals in the woods: slowly and careful not to frighten them. At the snap of a twig, Trisha's head turned and Pony felt the full force of those wild blue eyes on her.

Pony nodded and came to sit beside her. She pulled out her cigarettes and offered one out.

"Thanks." Trisha bent her head toward the light Pony offered.

"This is a cool spot. I come here a lot too," Pony said.

"Yeah, quiet," said Trisha. "That girl, in the parking lot. Is that your..." She let the words fade.

Pony found herself staring out into the distance too, while she considered her answer. A couple of squirrels pounded down the tree and across the lot; the two women watched them with interest. Pony found her voice as they disappeared.

"I guess. She was. Before. We've broken up. I told her to go. I don't know anymore."

"She doesn't seem like one of them," Trisha said. Pony knew just who they were. The ones who put them here.

"No. She's not like that. If she ever hurts anyone, it's herself. She's like me that way. You won't tell anyone you saw her, will you?"

Trisha shook her head. "No. What are you going to do?"

Pony shrugged. "I don't know. I'm still trying to figure it out. She wants to talk." She indicated Trisha's journal. "You making any progress with that?"

"Nah," said Trisha. "I just like holding it."

***

Daisy finished her last pose and rolled up the mat. Her morning yoga practice had been getting shorter and shorter as her belly seemed to get in the way of so many of the poses she'd learned. She knew it was still possible to do them but she just didn't seem to have the energy for it. She'd just padded into the kitchen when Toby and Freddy came in with the dog.

Toby set a paper bag down on the counter. "Breakfast is served."

Daisy opened the bag and took out two coffees, three honey buns, and an orange juice. "Yum!" She placed the pre-packaged food out on the table and arranged it on the place settings.

Toby chimed in, "I actually talked Mr. Freegan into stumping up for treats. You just don't find hot coffee and rolls in a dumpster. Oh, and I figured the orange juice is better for you, right?"

Daisy smiled. Thank God Toby's concept of prenatal care was even more loose than her own. Honey buns had been her favorite wake-up food when they'd lived on the streets together and she still found them irresistible.

Freddy looked at the two women and grinned. "Wow, this is like a regular family meal, huh?"

Daisy and Toby laughed. "You bet," said Toby. "Leave it to Beaver."

Daisy chewed thoughtfully. "Do you think we could ever be normal? You know, like regular people?"

Freddy shook his head. "Who wants to be normal?"

Toby remembered Pony's weary expression the last time they'd been together. "I know what you mean, though, Daze. I don't want to be like, normal-normal, but it'd be nice not to be all fucked up."

Daisy nodded. "Yeah, I guess that's it. I don't want to be like everyone else. But I would love to not have to worry about a lot of the stuff we have to think about all the time. Like cops and money and all that stuff."

Freddy devoured the last bite of honey bun and licked his fingers. "Well yeah, that'd be cool."

Daisy looked at the scene around her. Her two best friends, the white winter sun streaming in from the skylight, the yellow dog curled up under the table. If it could just be like this all the time. The thought fluttered through her like a ghost. She took a sip of her juice. "Yeah, that would be cool for sure."

An hour later, pleasantly full, Daisy looked around the loft. So much about it was iffy. No real lease, just a handshake deal between Freddy and the landlord. Electricity pirated off the place next door. Everything in it was a found object dragged in from the sidewalks. But for the past seven months, it had been home. Now Freddy wanted to hit the road in that crazy car of his. Daisy didn't want to be homeless. She never wanted to live on the street again.

She remembered the first time she'd realized that she had nowhere to go. No one to take her in. That being on the streets could be more than just an expression. She would never forget laying her body down on the cement. The only shelter being the alcove she'd found—a little doorway outside an abandoned building. She had just lain there under it, the pavement at eye level, with her coat over her and her purse for a pillow.

Too frightened to sleep, she'd just tried to keep her eyes from tearing up, tried to tell herself she was free now. No more Dad. No more lies. She'd found Toby a few days later. Toby, who knew all the tricks to living outside.

Now, Toby was perfectly happy to go along for the ride. Perfectly happy to pack up and go. Did she not remember? Did she not remember meeting all those other women who'd lived out there for years? The ones with the croaky voices from breathing in too much dirt, dust, and fumes? Didn't she remember them talking about all the times they'd been raped, beaten, robbed, and treated like human garbage? Didn't she at least remember what happened to her in that van? What happened to Pony? That was the kind of thing that happened to you when you lived on the street. Daisy looked around the loft again and it looked like heaven.

***

Jolie tried to find her balance in the little boat, her second water ride of the day. Friday Harbor was fast disappearing behind them. Man, this was definitely the middle of nowhere for sure. She looked at Sam, their captain. He was incredibly tall, seemed like some kind of Native American with his long black hair pulled back under a beat-up leather cap. Two large silver bracelets with impressive hunks of turquoise circled each massive wrist. Sensing her attention, he turned to her and spoke. "Have you over to Miss Jane in no time flat. You folks been out this way before?"

Brian, who'd been checking things out in his own quiet way, looked up at the big man and answered for the two of them. "This is Jolie's first trip. I came out here years ago, but we took the ferry. It was nowhere near as interesting as this. Have you known…ah…Jane long?"

Jolie had to hide a smile as she recognized his responsible adult voice.

Sam nodded. "Sure. Miss Jane's a year-round lady. Business like mine, you get to know the folks who live here all the time. We depend on one another. She used to run the lending library and the book-mobile. Our winters would have been a lot more boring without her. I got a lot of time for Miss Jane." This last was said somewhat protectively. As if anyone interested in crossing Miss Jane might have Sam to deal with.

Jolie noticed the sound of the motor change and saw they'd slowed their speed. They were nearing one of the little islands.

"Is that it?" She pointed toward the little hump of land covered in pine trees. Large rocks and boulders dotted the shoreline. It seemed incredible to her that anyone actually lived here.

"That's the place." Sam cut the motor and drifted toward a little pier that only moments ago she'd been unable to see.

"Wow," Jolie said.

Brian sat up now, pointing and gesturing too. "Look! It's Bubbles!"

Sure enough, two women were headed onto the pier now. Jolie recognized Bubbles's slouching form, her mass of black hair blowing in the breeze. Next to her, almost identical in size, was an older woman in a long black coat. Little glasses perched on her nose, she peered at the boat and gave them a tentative wave.

Sam swung the boat expertly to the edge of the pier; he jumped out and offered Jolie his hand.

Brian tried his best to hop off cleanly and nearly ended up in the water, which broke the tension a bit. Laughing, Bubbles flew toward the two of them and threw an arm around each.

"Welcome to shit's creek—I thought you'd never get here!"

***

"Well, you clean up right nice, Mr. Jack."

That's what Mary had said as they headed out the door to their appointment that day. She'd pressed a suit of her husband's clothes for him to wear to the courthouse. The neck was a little too big on the shirt and he'd had to make another hole in the belt to make the pants look as if they weren't about to fall off, but Jack supposed he was more presentable, even if he did feel like a horse's ass.

Mary had wanted to spring for a cab and Jack had almost refused until he realized that it might be important for her to get there in some kind of style. He'd wanted to just open the door and leap out into traffic several times on the way there. Mary looked at him so nervously, he had to wonder whether she hadn't read his mind. He tried to settle down after that.

Jack had never thought of himself as claustrophobic before, but that great big building, the tiny elevator that they rode all the way to the sixth floor, and now this tiny office they were in made him want to cut and run something fierce. A secretary took their names and led them to an even smaller room. Jack's breath began to labor a bit. Not enough air.

The door opened and in walked the biggest policeman Jack had ever seen. Jack's feet began to give him the "move it" signal and his body was ready to comply when the door opened again; a woman appeared and something changed. It was like Smokey himself had entered with her. Something about the air.

Jack gave a discreet sniff and realized that along with her perfume he could smell...smoke! Cigarette smoke. Jack almost laughed out loud. He could practically hear Smokey's voice saying, "It's okay, partner. I'm with ya, man. It's gonna be okay."

***

Seeing Jolie and Brian in Aunt Jane's little hideaway felt like some kind of real life example of What's Wrong With This Picture or Parallel Universe. The little Sesame Street jingle went through her head: One of these things is not like the other.

Here were two very different aspects of her life and she'd never entertained the idea of them crossing over. She sure was glad to see them all together, but the whole thing made her really nervous. She wanted them to like one another, to approve of one another. It didn't take much effort to imagine both Jolie and Jane warming up to Brian. But to each other? That was a horse of a different color.

Brian looked good. Although technically, he was a bit less put-together than usual, he seemed a lot more relaxed. Bubbles had once joked about him ironing his underwear and T-shirts and had been amazed to see a flash of guilt cross his face. Relaxation had gone by the wayside now, though; now he was fidgety, bursting with curiosity. And he wasn't the only one.

Jane had made the two visitors welcome, given them coffee and home-made cookies and everyone had done a lot of smiling and head bobbing for a while until Jane finally turned to Bubbles and asked whether she'd like to show Brian the garden while she had a little chat with Jolie.

Now it was taking every bit of integrity (and the likelihood of being caught) for both Bubbles and Brian not to spend all their time with their ears pressed to the kitchen door.

Here it was—the summit. It was like the meeting of the ultimate super powers in Bubbles's life, and it was all going on without her, as usual.

***

Jane and Jolie sat across from each other at the old wooden table in the kitchen, separated only by a plate of cookies and a coffeepot. They'd satisfied some of their initial curiosity by surreptitiously checking each other out while Bubbles had led the group up to the house, bouncing around and setting them all laughing at her imitations of some of the locals they passed on their way up the hill.

Now the librarian and the stripper hoped for a look at something beyond the labels. Hoped they would recognize it when it appeared.

Jane made the opening gambit. "I'm sure it seemed a little strange, my asking you to come all the way out here on such short notice."

Jolie nodded and tried a smile. "Well, it got my curiosity going, that's for sure."

Jane reached for the coffeepot, looked a question at Jolie, who shook her head and then poured a little warm-up for herself. "Bubbles told me about the night you rescued her in front of that club. Did you really fend them off with a tree?"

Jolie rolled her eyes, felt her cheeks warm a little. "It was more of a shrub or sapling, really. It was mostly the shock value, I think."

The two women grinned now, more at ease. Jane continued, "Either way, it made quite an impression. Not only that, but the fact that you brought her along with you, found her a place to stay and looked out for her. I want you to know that counts for a lot with me."

This was unfamiliar territory for Jolie. Not the sort of praise she was used to. She wanted to brush it off but instinct told her that could be a mistake. She went for honesty instead, surprising herself. "Looking back, I think we both really needed a friend right around then. She's become a really important one. It's turned out to be one of the better, ah, choices I've made since I came up North."

"Bubbles has unusual depths and a really good heart. Sometimes I'm amazed, given her upbringing." Jane stopped, looked uncomfortable, and then went on. "I don't want to give the wrong impression about Eleanor, my sister. I feel like I often judge her unfairly. I don't know what it's like to raise a child. I've always been in the enviable position of auntie. The one who can come and go as she pleases. Eleanor's had to take on a lot of responsibility and make a lot of compromises. But this time, I think she's just made a decision that could cause irreparable damage. The kind you can't undo. Damage to Bubbles. That's why I've asked you to come."

Jolie kept her curiosity and impatience on hold, asking only, "What kind of damage? This sounds serious."

Jane removed her glasses and rubbed them with the corner of her napkin.

Jolie noticed how pretty her eyes were even with that strange unfocused look people's eyes had when they wore glasses. They looked very much like Bubbles's eyes. The little cleaning ritual seemed to have focused Jane as well. She looked straight at Jolie. "They want to send her to boot camp."

"Boot camp? She's sixteen!" The words blurted out of Jolie. "You can't make a minor join the Army."

Jane shook her head. "Not a real boot camp. I almost think that would have been better, were it possible. No, this is a private institution. It's designed for minors. And the more I've learned about it, the more it frightens me. There's been eight suspicious deaths at these places in the past two years, one of them at the camp they're about to send Bubbles to."

Jane got up and removed the plate to give Jolie a minute to digest this last statement. She remembered how unbelievable it all seemed when she'd first begun her research. Eying the cabinet above the fridge and the clock over the sink, she spoke her mind. "I know it's a little early, but would you care for a shot of something a bit stronger?" She took a bottle of brandy out of the cabinet and added a neat shot into her coffee.

Jolie held her cup out. "Yeah, this isn't your typical coffee break, is it?" She took a fortifying sip. "A kid died at this place they want to send Bubbles? Damn, Jane, how are they still open?"

Jane came back to the table and brought the bottle along with her. "I know it sounds crazy, but apparently it's been quite difficult to prove. Quite a few of the deaths were suicides and teen suicide seems to be an epidemic now. How do you prove that someone's pushed a kid to the brink? One girl froze to death. The camp says it was an unfortunate accident that happened when she tried to go AWOL but some of the others are saying that she collapsed during an 'outward bound' expedition and was left there because they said she was 'faking it.' The case is in court now, along with all the rest. Apparently there's some decent places out there where they've had good results. But that doesn't make me feel any better." Jane got up and went back to the cabinet to pull out a bag of blue-corn tortilla chips.

"Can I help with anything?" Jolie asked.

Jane shook her head, took a bowl out of another cabinet, and poured the chips in and then sat back down and sighed. "No. This is just so awkward. I'm not used to all this plotting and planning."

Jolie reached out tentatively and patted Jane's hand. "Just take your time." In all the different scenarios she'd played out in her head, this was the last thing she'd expected.

Jane smiled up at her gratefully, took a breath and plowed on. "The only reason I did any research in the first place was that I was looking for a way out. The fact of the matter is that I'm tired of all the lies and meddling. It's not doing any good, no matter how well meant it is. Going along with one more scheme to corral and move this kid is going to make more problems than it solves. It will kill her trust and if she runs and finds herself in trouble, she sure won't look to us anymore."

Jolie looked out the window. Fog had begun to roll in and the long view had disappeared. A squirrel launched itself off the fence to land on the very edge of an evergreen bough, which swayed wildly but held his weight. She felt very far from home.

She turned her attention back to Jane. "So what do we do?"

Jane took in the we gratefully. "I have absolutely no legal standing as far as Bubbles is concerned. She has two legal parents. I did give my sister the information about the camps, but she said I should know better than to believe everything I read on the Internet. After that, I didn't push it any farther. To be honest, I didn't want her to know just how concerned I was in case she should cease to trust me."

"Smart." Jolie's voice held her admiration for this woman. She'd begun to see quite a lot that she liked behind those little glasses.

Jane got up from the table again.

She's a fidgeter, just like Bubbles, Jolie thought. Amazing how these little things translate from person to person, family to family.

Jane pulled a bottle of red wine down from the cabinet and a corkscrew from a drawer. "I don't know why I'm sipping brandy like an old woman with the vapors." Jane laughed. "Care for a glass?"

Jolie laughed. "I'm normally a cocktail girl—but what the hell?"

Jane poured the dark red liquid into a pair of pretty crystal glasses she'd whipped off a shelf, sat back down and looked Jolie straight in the eye. "I know it might seem incredibly arrogant of me to ask for your help and then make ultimatums, but the fact is I'd like to see Bubbles in school rather than a...than—dancing. Perhaps you'd rather do something along the same lines as well? Bubbles has told me how bright you are. That you and your friend have managed to stay clean for a while now. I know she really liked her psych courses; they were the only thing she really cared about in high school. I have some savings tucked away. My mother left me her portfolio, along with the house. Its value isn't what it once was but it's still remarkably healthy, considering. I can't provide the Ivy League education I'd once had in mind but it would certainly see you both through a few years at say, San Francisco City College? I want Bubbles safe and I can't see that Portland's going to be a safe place for her anymore. You know the Bay area."

Jolie broke eye contact. She sat stock-still for a moment to get her head around this last statement. Her lizard brain screamed for solace. She turned to Jane. "I could really use a cigarette—I don't suppose you smoke? You think we might go out on the porch?"

Jane stood and led Jolie toward the front door. "No problem. I quit a while ago but perhaps I might have—just a puff."

***

"I'm sorry to have kept you waiting," the lady of the perfumed smoke said. "I'm Deputy District Attorney Ames and this is Sergeant Tom Hain."

Mary introduced Jack and herself and took in the woman in front of her. Kind eyes over strong cheekbones and sensibly cropped pure white hair, Ms. Ames stood nearly as tall as Sergeant Hain. She had a no-nonsense look about her Mary liked immediately. Still, she wasn't who she'd been expecting. Mary decided she'd better not take any chances.

"I thought Mr. Porter was going to be here."

DA Ames smiled and shook her head. "No, it's Mr. Porter's job to assess the nature of the cases that come our way. He was the one who brought us together. My department deals exclusively with cases involving law enforcement."

"Oh I see," Mary said, although she wasn't entirely sure that she did. Jack just did his best not to squirm in his seat. Ms. Ames came around and sat down at the desk, which took up most of the available space. She leaned forward and made eye contact with Mary. Her voice was warm and sympathetic.

"So I'm afraid you're stuck with me for the duration. Do you have any questions before we get started?"

Mary had a million of them, starting with Could you make that huge policeman go away? but she knew there was no point in asking.

Ms. Ames removed a little black gadget from her desk and fiddled with the buttons. "I'll be recording our session today to ensure that there can be no misunderstanding about any of our communications. Sergeant Hain is here for that purpose as well. I'll have everything transcribed and you are welcome to copies anytime you like. Would either of you care for some coffee, or a glass of water perhaps before we begin?"

Mary shook her head and glanced at Jack trying to get a sense of his feelings, but his face was unreadable. Almost, she thought, somewhat alarmed, as if he hadn't heard a thing Ms. Ames was saying.

Ms. Ames opened a little file folder. "The evidence in this case is primarily made up of eyewitness testimony. The two of you witnessing the same event from different perspectives. I'd like to take a statement from each of you separately. This and Sgt. Hain's presence will help cover us against any charge of collusion."

"Collusion?" Mary asked.

"There have been in the past decade, several high-profile cases regarding the misuse of force in the police department. These cases can reflect poorly on any number of local government agencies. Even the DA's office is not above suspicion."

"Ah," said Mary, hoping she sounded wiser than she felt.

"So," continued Ms. Ames, "who'd like to go first?"

Mary saw no visible reaction from Jack to this question and hurriedly stepped in. "I'm ready."

***

Bubbles came into the kitchen. Brian trailed behind her. They'd been summoned. She noticed the coffee and cookies had been replaced with wine and tortilla chips. The light over the stove was on now.

Jolie and Aunt Jane looked at ease with each other, which allowed one of the knots in her stomach to unhitch. She felt as if she were being called to the adults table now. She crossed to the cabinet, took down two more wine glasses and looked a question at Aunt Jane, who smiled and said, "Okay, but just one, right?"

She put a glass in front of Brian, filled it and sat. After she'd filled her own glass, she said, "Okay, so what's the big news?"

Jane and Jolie exchanged a glance.

"We have a proposition for you," Jane said. "I had an idea, but I wasn't sure it would work until I talked to Jolie." She stopped and nodded at Jolie, who broke into a grin.

"How would you like to start City College in San Francisco next month—with me?"

Bubbles was, for once in her life, entirely speechless.

Later that night...

"Did you tell Aunt Jane I was gay?" Brian asked when they were in Bubbles's room, in bed, warm and safe under piles of eyelet lace and soft down.

"I don't think so. I mean, why bother?"

Brian put on his best Stooge voice and shook his fist at her. "Why you! I oughta..."

The two of them laughed.

"I guess I was just wondering why she was letting her little darling sleep in the same room with me." Brian sighed. "I guess I just don't really look very predatory, do I?"

Bubbles looked over at him, lying there squinting myopically at her in his squeaky clean white T-shirt, perfect teeth freshly brushed. "Um, well...not exactly. Do you want to? Look predatory?"

"Might be nice. At least sometimes." Brian shook off his macho dreams. He sat up. "Damn, you're really going away, aren't you? San Francisco. I'm so jealous."

Bubbles shook her head. "It's all so crazy, I can't believe it. First, boot camp and then when Aunt Jane started asking me all these questions about Jolie, I was really weirded out. At first I didn't want to tell her too much. You know? And then she'd been acting so odd all week. I really didn't see this one coming."

"Aunt Jane. She's a lot cooler than we gave her credit for, isn't she?"

"You have no idea. I'll have to give you the total scoop on that one sometime. Would you even want to go to San Francisco if you could? I mean, you seem to just be getting comfortable living between Portland and the cabin. It seems like it's working for you. You look great."

Brian flopped on his back and stared up at the ceiling. "I don't know. I really don't. It seems like one day we were at Lewis and Clark and every day was exactly like the one before and now...I never know what's going to happen from one moment to the next. I'm in a nightclub, I'm moon-bathing, I'm in the woods, I'm in a strip club, I'm stuck in a van, I'm staying at Jolie's or Daisy's, or now I'm out here. And the crazy thing is I think I like it like this."

"Yeah," said Bubbles. "I know exactly what you mean."

***

They'd moved down the hall to a large conference room. There was a tiny ball on the shiny wooden table—some sort of new camera trained on her while a paralegal typed away on a laptop. The large policeman sat with his tablet in his lap, face stiff as a cigar store Indian.

Ms. Ames's face was taut too, and then seemed to soften when she looked at Mary.

"Okay, Mary, I know it's a little difficult with all of us here with our gadgets, but what I need for you to do is tell me in your own words what happened that day. What you saw out the window."

Ms. Ames went on to note the day and time for the tape and then turned back to her. "Alright, Mary, if you can just start by telling me what you saw that day."

Mary took a deep breath and tried not to think of Jack out there down the hall by himself. She'd promised him they'd do this all together and now here she was in this fancy conference room with the huge mahogany table and the fancy recessed lighting, feeling like a prize hog at the county fair—happy in his blue ribbon, with no idea what was in store for him later. She shifted her attention back to the faces that peered at her and waited for her to begin; she tried to make herself as comfortable as possible under their scrutiny. She was doing it for Smokey. She was doing it because it was the right thing to do. That's why she was here.

She cleared her throat and began. "I was at the sink doing dishes when I heard the sound of a siren. Not going on and on like when an ambulance is going to the hospital. Just one long yelp sound. Like it was getting someone's attention. I could hear men's voices calling out and some kind of commotion. I was curious and went around to the living room window. Just to peep 'round the curtain. They were pulling the little man—I know now his name was Smokey or Joseph—but then he was just the man across the street. They pulled him out of the window. They were rough about it, too. He seemed like he was maybe even stuck a little, but they just grabbed him and threw him down. It might have been funny if everyone didn't look so angry. He kept trying to get up and they kept pushing him down. They were yelling at him, asking him questions—what was he doing, I couldn't hear it all clearly—and then one of them turned to ask his buddy a question and the little man, uh, Smokey, he saw his chance and tried to run. He only got a few steps away, though, and then they was on him, slapping him down and kicking him and kicking him. He wasn't fighting back. They looked so angry. I got frightened, really scared. I wanted to stop it. I wanted to get someone to help him, and then I realized what I wanted was a policeman."

Mary's voice had been getting weaker and softer as her tale went on. She could feel it betraying her now. To her horror, when she'd tried to calm it—to push the words out of her body—the tears came too. She waved her hand at her watchers as if to ward them off.

Ms. Ames got up from her seat. "Stop tape." Then she grabbed a box of tissues off a console and brought them over. The room got very quiet while Mary cried.

***

It took a monumental effort, but Jack waited until Mary, the huge cop, and the lawyer had been gone a few minutes, and then he got up and walked out. His heart raced, his breath ragged. Another minute and he would have had a full-blown panic attack.

The elevator was crammed with people. Jack backpedaled and went down the stairs. He found the front door and burst out onto the street. The fresh air hit him just right, and he stood there and sucked it in. Free.

Jack crossed the street to the park and sat down. Only then could he stop and look around, begin to take in his situation. His heart had slowed but his stomach still twisted. Coward. The crowd around him was oblivious as always, everyone going about their business. He imagined some were on lunch hour; others were returning to work. A group of students—teenagers—waited for the bus, clutching books and backpacks.

A homeless man shuffled over to the bench that faced him. He dug around in a tattered blue backpack he carried, finally pulling a plastic pouch from it. Reaching into his pocket, he began to roll a cigarette. Jack watched as yellowed fingers delicately performed the finite task. The man finished and placed the cigarette between his lips, lit it up, and leaned back. He caught Jack's eye and smiled. The smoke drifted up around him like a halo. He watched it float up, cocked his head and looked at Jack again, narrowing his eyes as if he was calculating odds.

Ah, Smokey, you just won't let me be, will you?

Jack got up and plodded back into the courthouse just in time to make his statement.

***

The morning brought thick heavy fog, made the cottage feel like a secret fairy tale dwelling only accessible if you knew the magic words.

Bubbles had packed her suitcase and tossed the rest of her stuff in a backpack. She was impressed by how portable her life had become.

Inside, Jolie and Brian played "thoughtful houseguest" by helping Jane tidy up the breakfast things, as if they did that every morning, which made Bubbles smirk. She'd lived with Jolie.

She'd come out to say good-bye to the garden, to the little pond, and the Buddha. The good-byes whispered in her head. The trees felt close around her—protective. It was just like she used to do when she was a kid, when she believed every object had feelings. Anthropomorphism, it was called. Weird to think her life would be filled with these five-dollar words for the next few years. Psychology was full of them. Hell, psychology was one of them.

She still couldn't believe Jane would go so far out on a limb for her. That she'd actually help her escape and keep her whereabouts a secret. It was pretty amazing— all of it. She was going to miss Aunt Jane.

She peeped through the French doors and saw them in the living room now. That meant it was almost time. Almost time to leave this crazy chapter in her life.

She'd always felt a little like life was your own book or movie that you watched happen to you. That you wondered whether anyone else would read it, see it, or whether it would just be you.

***

Butchie sat on the ferry boat and thought about metabolism rates. Looking over at Veronica and her mother both sitting ram-rod straight, he'd figured them for high burners. That was a good thing up to a point. Meant you probably wouldn't run too fat as you got older. Of course, you had to be careful, because it could also mean your cholesterol and blood pressure could run high too.

He thought about Veronica's stepdad last night; he had the telltale pink flush that meant he'd be in big trouble if he didn't watch the salts and fats pretty soon.

The man had gone bright red at one point, talking about Bubbles and boot camp and dysfunction and shaping up. Made Butchie nervous; he hated it when people looked as if they were going to explode. He hadn't been too clear or too crazy about the things the guy was saying when he started to talk about family responsibility and one hand washing the other either. It gave him the creeps; made him feel as if the man had all kinds of plans for him that he knew nothing about.

He really didn't know about this family of Veronica's. He felt more and more sorry for little sis every minute.

***

Jane ignored her phone the first time it chimed. She just wanted to cherish these last few minutes with her favorite niece, but it started up again almost immediately and that's when she noticed Sam's name flash on the tiny screen.

Jolie and Brian stood on the porch with Bubbles, all three of them smoking like chimneys. She held up her hand for quiet and answered. Sam's voice came through weakly, a poor connection.

"You wanted me to tell you when your sister called to reserve her boat ride? Well, she didn't bother to call from home. She's on the ferry coming in right now—wants me to be at Friday Harbor in fifteen minutes. Says she's got two people with her. I told her I had another reservation and I'd be delayed.... Hope I did the right thing?"

Jane felt her stomach hit the floor. "You did wonderfully, Sam. How fast can you be at the pier?"

"I'm there now, Miss Jane."

"Oh, thank God—can you take three passengers right away?"

"I'll be waiting."

"They'll be there ready to go in less than five. And Sam? Thank you."

The three of them were all focused on her now. She tossed her car keys to Jolie. "Change of plans—you're driving. Get to the pier, bottom of the hill—Sam's waiting. My sister's on her way right now. Just leave it parked on the waterfront, keys under the front seat. Hurry. I'll do what I can to stall things here."

The three converged on Jane and hugged her. She dug in her purse, pulled out a handful of cash, and handed it to Bubbles. "Take this just in case. You've got the bankcard I gave you?"

Bubbles patted a pocket. "I do." They exchanged one more quick hug, eyes tearing.

"Now go—fly like the wind!" Jane laughed.

Jolie hopped in the driver's seat as Brian jammed the luggage in and Bubbles slipped into the back of the Subaru. The three of them drove off. Bubbles waved out the back window.

Jane took a deep breath and steeled herself for round two.

***

Butchie stood on the pier at Friday Harbor and thought about the difference between strength and cardio training. He wasn't getting much of either unless you counted chasing a sixteen-year-old girl as aerobic exercise. Veronica's mother had been hissing into Veronica's iPhone and now Veronica was working the gadget for all it was worth to find alternate transportation to the island. Their stress level had risen and they were starting to snap at each other. Butchie tried to make himself as scarce as his six three frame allowed.

At least he wasn't that Sam guy they kept bitching about. From the way they were cursing him, Butchie thought they'd have cheerfully ripped his head from his shoulders given half the chance.

The scent of fresh coffee hit Butchie's nose and he noticed a couple of backpackers carrying cardboard cups. His attention was drawn to a little cart at the top of the pier.

Veronica and her mother now both stared at something on the screen of the iPhone.

"I thought I'd get a cup of coffee. Anyone interested?" Butchie asked. Veronica's mother looked up, confused, as if the couch had spoken; Veronica rolled her eyes and flicked her hand at him.

Butchie was getting pretty darn tired of being the hired help.

***

Bubbles eyed the shore as Sam's boat navigated the last mile. "I guess we'll be getting on the same ferry they just got off." She looked at Sam.

Sam looked at his watch. "Timings pretty good for you, I'd say. She leaves in twenty minutes—we'll be there in five."

"Is there anywhere you can drop us out of sight?"

"Ain't gonna be easy." Sam squinted into the distance as he considered the problem. "I can let you off on the far side of the ferry, but it'll be up to you to make yourselves scarce."

He slanted a skeptical look at the three Portlanders dressed all in black. "I'll try to catch their attention, see if I can draw them off."

"Would you?" Jolie grinned and gave Sam a quick hug. Sam's granite features briefly registered alarm as he reached for the coil of rope. "Now get yourselves down out of sight—I'll let ya know when to skedaddle."

***

Butchie waited at the coffee cart and wondered how many extra calories you burned when you were pissed off. He was willing to bet it was a lot more than normal. Just the way his heart beat faster and his breathing changed and got shallow felt like a rack of weights on his chest. He longed for the gym—the boxing room at midnight when he could just wail on the heavy bags, steam in the sauna, shower off, and come out clean, his muscles slightly sore but loose, his pores wide open to the fresh, cold air.

He ordered a macchiato with non-fat milk and dawdled on the pier. He thought about Veronica's waving him away as if he were a trained monkey or something. He wasn't just her personal GI Joe to point at people when she needed them to behave. He thought about little sis again. She looked just like that girl over there with the big eyes and the stripey hair. He squinted and looked again. Sure enough—it was her, dragging her suitcase along behind her two friends. She must have felt his eyes on her, because all of a sudden the two of them were staring at each other. Her eyes were pleading, and she shook her head back and forth, the universal sign for "No." Then she put her hands together like a prayer.

Butchie made his mind up in an instant and gave her a quick nod. Then he sketched a huge yawn and stretch and leaned back against the rail. He saw her grin ear to ear. She pumped her fist once and blew him a kiss. Then she disappeared into the ferry line.

Butchie finished his coffee, feeling better than he had all day, and slowly sauntered back toward Veronica and her mother.

***

Bubbles didn't realize she'd been holding her breath until the ferry started skimming through the water and the air practically exploded out of her lungs. The breath she'd taken in was fresh and full of salt water. She saw Jolie's smile and knew that although she'd never admit it, she'd been sweating it a little too.

"We're free, Jolie; we're really free." Bubbles startled Jolie by throwing her arms around her. Brian had found them a moment later, their arms wrapped around each other, reunion complete.

Back on the island, Jane was having a far less pleasant reunion with her sister.

***

Jane tried to concentrate on her book, a collection of short stories by Jenn Springsteen—one of her favorites. In bed with a good book was generally her favorite place to be, but tonight her brain would not let her relax, enjoy, escape to the world she loved best, the world of fiction. She was being deluged by a rain of fact.

The images played over and over, starting with the one of Eleanor's screaming face. "What do you mean, she's gone? How could you just lose her like that? I don't understand. I don't understand." On and on, over and over.

Jane shivered and tried to concentrate on the page before her. In the happy world of fiction, the heroine was having her own trials. She was alone in the house. The baby whimpered as her son hung off her body, sticky breakfast hands wrapped around her thighs. Things seemed to be getting harder by the moment. Jane felt for this woman and wondered what her life would have been like with a family of her own. A baby to raise, to wake in the night and feed. To stretch the skin of her body to its limits and beyond—to stretch her heart to its limits and beyond. She didn't think she could have taken it.

Just this one episode with Bubbles had stretched her heart, her soul far past the point where she could protect them, far past the point where she could shrug it off, think it through, or forget about it.

Over and over, the thought kept creeping in...maybe Bubbles would be the one to find that magic space between Kitty's life and her own.

Her relationship with her sister might well be damaged beyond repair this time, and she was frightened when she thought about what would happen when Ken found out. Her brother-in law had always struck her as an unforgiving man.

Veronica had been strangely calm throughout, which had surprised Jane. She'd just nodded and stayed in the background with that huge brute she'd brought along with her.

She wondered where Bubbles was right now. She could call, of course, but it was time to start letting go.

***

Coming in from the kitchen, a fresh bowl of chips in hand, Eleni stopped in the doorway and took in the scene in her living room. So much to celebrate between Bubbles and Jolie's San Francisco adventure, Max's tour, and her scholarship. Just now, Bubbles was making little screeching sounds on Gisarra's violin while Gisarra nodded in approval. Jolie was telling a story to a wide-eyed Brian and Toby—one hand waved in the air to illustrate a point, the other buried deep in the fur of Toby's funny yellow hound dog. Nicholas was on the couch, tentatively patting Daisy's huge tummy while Freddy smiled and proudly held her hand.

Bubbles's friends Raven and Alison flipped through her collection of vinyl, occasionally pulling out certain albums reverently as if they were holy relics. Eleni felt Max's breath on her neck as he joined her there and wrapped his arm around her waist; the two of them stood quietly for a moment, thinking their private thoughts.

After a few moments, Eleni smiled up at Max. "Do you remember when we first came here? We didn't know any of these people and now I don't know what I'd do without them."

Max nodded. "We've been pretty lucky, haven't we? I don't think many people would have taken odds on this all coming out so well, do you?"

Eleni shook her head. "No way, honey. No way."

***

Insanity is doing the same thing over and over—and expecting different results. That's what they told Pony repeatedly at the shelter. So was going to meet Toby now an act of insanity? Her counselor had been adamant about Pony starting to take responsibility for her actions. She was not a victim doomed to float from one abuser to the next. She had a say in her life now. So if she felt like hearing what Toby had to say, that was okay, right?

She could hear the yips and barks of happy dogs as she rounded the corner that led to the dog park. It was the first dry day in almost two weeks and everyone in Portland seemed to be out to take advantage of it. She stopped and held a hand over her brow to shade her eyes as she scanned the park. She recognized Fella before she saw Toby. He streaked toward her with a muddy tennis ball in his mouth. Toby chased after him, her hair flying, a huge grin on her face. She looked good. A hell of a lot healthier than she had in their underpass days. Fella recognized her now, and altered his course straight toward her.

"Fella! Nooooo. Watch your paws!" Toby's legs pumped faster now, trying to intercept the dog before he made a muddy mess of Pony's jeans. Pony laughed and held up her hands.

"It's okay, I gotta do wash anyway. Here boy." Somehow Fella seemed to get the message, skidded to a halt in front of her and dropped the ball at her feet.

Toby's eyes widened. "Wow! Good dog!" She turned to Pony. "How did you do that? I've been trying to get him to do that without jumping me first for ages."

"What can I say? I've got the power." Pony laughed.

Toby gave her a quick hug and pointed to a set of picnic tables. "Let's go sit."

After a few attempts at picking up the ball and dropping it in front of them, Fella got the picture and trotted alongside his mistress. He stretched out at their feet as the two women sat on the table.

Toby visibly squirmed for a few moments and then turned to Pony. Her words came out in a rush. "Look, I don't really know how to say this. I've been trying to figure out the right way all week. I know you need to stay where you are for a while and I don't ever want to ask you to just go live on the street with me. I want you to be safe and happy. Um, I've never finished anything I've started. So, I want to go help Daisy have her baby. I promised her I would, and then I flaked on her. Then I want to find a way to get us a place. Get a job or go to school or something. I don't know how I'm gonna do it. I don't know how long it will take. I guess I just want to know if you would ever want to do something like that."

Pony watched as all the air seemed to go out of Toby. Her face was so raw and vulnerable it hurt to look at her. She took a deep breath. The words left her mouth slowly. "As long as we can figure out a way not to hurt ourselves anymore. If we can do that, I could—we could—do something like that. But, it might take a while. I need to work out a lot of stuff for myself. Do you understand what I mean?"

Toby slowly reached for her hand, held it up to her lips and kissed it softly. "I understand."

Underneath the table, Fella's tail wagged.

***

After a mad dash up the stairs, Jolie made it into the apartment and into the bathroom in seconds flat.

Man, there's nothing better than a good pee when you need one. She finished up and pulled her purse toward her and pulled the wad of bills out, uncrumpling them and flattening them out on the side of the sink. Big bills. Thirteen of them.

She'd heard about guys like this before, but she never really believed it. Big, beefy, pink-faced blond guy in a suit. He'd just kept drinking and laughing and stuffing them into her G-string. By the end of her set, she felt like a money tree with all the little green hundred dollar leaves hanging off her. By the time she'd gotten offstage, his table was packed with four other dancers who had scented the free-flowing cash like sharks. She'd just laughed and called it a night.

She still felt the buzz of adrenaline course through her as she tip-toed into the living room, almost tripping over Nicholas's guitar and Gisarra's violin. Bubbles was fast asleep on the couch.

Amazing to think they'd all be gone by the end of the week: she and Bubbles to San Francisco, Nick and Gisarra off on tour with Max. Everything changed; everything different.

She felt antsy, sleepless. Thirteen little whispers floated up from her purse. Just one last fling? She looked toward her bedroom. There was no real rest for her there. Fuck it. The keys to Gisarra's beater lay on the bar. Of course she should ask, but that would mean stopping, thinking. She snatched them up and went out into the night.

At one a.m., the Mexicans were "closed" but her friend Ricardo might just do her this one last favor. She keyed his number into the cell phone and crossed her fingers.

Five minutes later, she was headed down the I-5 corridor, windows down, radio up, wind in her hair.

***

With the car door open, Jolie poured the contents of the beer she'd just bought out onto the ground of the 7-11 parking lot. She kept the metal cap, left the bottle standing there and drove off.

Ahead of her loomed McDonald's. Wow, she thought. Is this the same one I went to my first week in town? Given the universal bright yellow and red décor, there was no real way of knowing. She ducked down the hall to the restroom and locked herself in the stall. She pulled the filter from her cigarette, nipped a tiny bit off and rolled it up.

Rituals, she thought. How many times have I prayed at this altar? Holding the beer cap with her tweezers, she heated the contents of the balloon and dipped the syringe into the cotton, sucking the liquid through. She pulled off her belt, tightened it around her arm, and found a vein.

She felt the familiar warmth run up her arm. Her entire body seemed to sigh, to release all its stress in one clean moment. A wave of euphoria hit, surprising her with its force, its power. Her eyelids fluttered. She felt a dark angel enter the stall, her steel and fluorescent box. Its wings surrounded her and she slumped forward—she felt no more.

***

Bang! Bang! Bang!

Bubbles lifted her head up from the couch in the still-dark room and knew instinctively that it was the police on the other side of the door. She heard Nicholas and Gisarra stir briefly, but neither of them seemed inclined to answer it. She pulled on the oversized hoodie she'd taken to using as a robe and peered through the peephole.

Two plainclothes men stood there, stone faces magnified by the little lens.

This wasn't good news. She felt her stomach squeeze out a hit of adrenaline. Where was Jolie? She'd decided to forget the whole, "Who is it?" fiasco and just open the door.

The two cops adjusted their eye-lines down to her five-five frame. One of them held Jolie's ID.

"Do you know this woman?" the bigger one said.

And just like that—it was all over.

**

Nicholas and Gisarra had gone off to collect her car from the impound, Brian was still at work, and the apartment was empty. Bubbles roused herself from the couch and walked into the kitchen. She washed the coffee pot, dumped the old filter into the trash and located a fresh one. She'd slowly spooned in four heaping scoops and switched on the coffeemaker. Then she'd walked back into the living room and projectile vomited. She curled into a fetal position and tried to control her shaking limbs. The tears poured from her eyes but she made no sound. Her instinct told her that if she opened her mouth, she would no longer be able to control the scream that would emerge.

In the quiet room, as the shakes receded, she became aware of a dripping sound from the kitchen—something off. A closer look revealed the fact that she had not replaced the basket correctly and the coffee poured out of the top of the machine onto the counter and then down to the floor. The black grounds mixed with the dark brown water, swirling, picking up speed as gravity pulled them down. Bubbles just watched as it all slowly flooded toward her.

**

Bubbles looked at the pile of blankets on the couch; the indentation of her body could be seen on the cushions. Now Nicholas and Gisarra were off on tour. Jolie was gone; only Brian remained and the couch was the only place she wanted to be. Asleep was the only place where Jolie wasn't dead. She slept with Jolie's ID in her hand. The one the cops gave her when they came to the door. Jolie wore her Mona Lisa smile. Just a hint of a smile, and Bubbles kept seeing that almost smiling face even when she wasn't looking at the photo. In the dark room, she'd railed at that face, that smile. Why did you leave me here? Why did you have to go and fuck everything up, you selfish bitch? Didn't you realize how much I loved you? How much I needed you? Didn't you care at all?

And then the guilt would come in. How could she be screaming at Jolie, saying these awful things to her? Then, the illogical stream of maybes. Maybe if I was nicer.

Not so needy. Maybe if I'd done something different. Maybe if I'd stayed up late that night. Maybe she wouldn't be dead.

Jolie was almost always there in her dreams now. Sometimes she was aware of the miracle of her presence, aware that Jolie'd been pronounced dead but in that practical subconscious state, there was always a brief and plausible explanation. Oh no, I didn't really die—it was all a mistake. In other dreams, the two of them spent time together, everything back the way it was and no one ever remembered a thing.

Whenever Bubbles woke, she'd have a brief, happy moment of haze where she still had a foot in both worlds. Then her memory would slam home and her eyes would start to tear and her stomach tighten, and she'd be back in a world without her best friend.

So, she'd sink deeper into the couch bed, pull up the covers, snuggle herself into the ready-made contours of the pillows and cushions and try to sleep again. But sleep wouldn't come anymore. It had been three days and her body wanted food and water. Her muscles wanted to move and stretch. Only her mind still craved sleep. Only her soul wanted to curl up again and forget.

***

"Ninety-nine bottles of beer on the wall!" Toby's voice rang out in the quiet car.

"No fucking way—we are not singing that song," Daisy snapped. She'd always hated car songs.

Toby looked at her and shook her head. "Well, excuse me for livin'. Gah!"

"Sorry." Daisy felt awkward and then irritated for feeling awkward.

Toby squinted and looked at her again. "Are you feeling okay, Daisy?"

Daisy was not feeling okay. She could feel every mile between her and the loft, and they had barely gotten out of downtown. She wanted to go back right now. She had no desire to go to Mardi-Gras, Burning Man or the Black Rock Desert, but she was stuck with Freddy's dream. He'd taken her in, loved her and asked nothing of her but this. There was no use crying about it.

"I'm okay. Just a little nauseous." As the words left her mouth, a sharp, painful cramp ripped through her body and she gasped. "Damn, it feels like someone's kicking me in the back wearing giant steel-toed boots." Daisy doubled over as another wave hit her.

Toby turned from the window and looked at her again. "Daze? Daze, have you ever felt one like this before? Daze, do you think those are contractions?"

Daisy tried to gather her thoughts through the pain. The cramps came in waves. Waves. She remembered that word from birthing class, remembered the doctor too: he'd referred to contractions coming in waves. You were supposed to time them. It was all in that book they'd given her, but she didn't remember any of it. Why hadn't she paid more attention?

"I think maybe it is; they are. It's different—it feels serious. Toby, can you find that natural birthing book in the pack there?"

Freddy, who'd been happily tuning them out as he watched the road, sensed the tension now. He'd really been hoping this was all going to work itself out somehow but he could feel the small niggling feeling, the one he'd always thought of as his caveman paleo-conscience: survival, protection, some kind of very old signal from way deep inside. He pulled the car over carefully. Toby was still pawing through

Daisy's backpack to look for the book.

He leaned out over the back seat and looked at Daisy. Her face was covered in perspiration and she looked awfully pale. He reached out and smoothed away a few damp strands that stuck to her forehead. He tried to keep his voice steady.

"Daisy? Babe, is it time?"

Daisy looked as if she were about to answer him when her eyes went wide with alarm. "Oh my God, I think it is. I think it's happening now!" Daisy felt another twist and wave of pain as a real wave of water crashed through and out of her. Her skirt soaked with it and it scared her. She looked at Freddy and Toby as they both leaned over their seats and stared at her open-mouthed. Her support system. She summoned up enough extra breath to scream, "What the hell are you looking at? Get me somewhere, call someone, do something!"

Freddy screeched out of the turnout and looked desperately for the nearest sign of civilization. He spotted a familiar blue FOOD AND LODGING sign and pulled off the highway, looking left and right.

"There!" Toby pointed to a fake-quaint little tavern.

Freddy cut across three lanes and into the parking lot.

Toby leaped from the car.

Freddy took hold of Daisy's hand. "Just breathe, babe. Deep, deep breaths, remember? Breathe. Breathe."

Daisy tried to calm herself and follow along with the sound of his words, of his voice. She took one deep breath, and then another.

Toby raced back and flung the car door open. "They're coming, Daze! Hang on. They're gonna be here any minute."

Daisy took another breath and heard the faint sound of a siren. Help was on the way. "Tobe? Where are we?" Toby looked away suddenly and Daisy realized she was trying to keep a straight face. A small snort of a laugh escaped as she looked at Daisy; her eyes sparkled.

"Well, Daze, right now we're in the parking lot of the Wanker's Corners Bar and Grill."

Daisy felt the world slow down for just a minute as that piece of information sunk in. "Wanker's Corners? You have got to be kidding me."

The three of them had dissolved into helpless laughter when the ambulance pulled in.

***

Brian felt his way into the dark living room like a child playing blind-man's bluff, arms out ahead of him as he felt for familiar objects, walking in a slow stagger to avoid stubbing a toe. He didn't know what time it was—the power went out briefly sometime earlier and all the clocks flashed 12:00. He tweaked the side of the curtain and stood for a moment, entranced.

Bubbles felt the cold as the covers were pulled back. Her arms goose-pimpled and her nipples shrunk under her tiny undershirt. She heard Brian's voice, urgent.

"Bubbles! Quick, come here."

"What the fuck?" Bubbles protested as Brian took both her hands and pulled her off the couch, practically dragging her to the window.

He grinned from ear to ear. "First day of spring and it's a winter wonderland!"

He pulled the curtains open with a dramatic flair.

Outside, Portland was transformed. Everywhere she looked was covered in a blanket of sparkling whiteness. Steps, lawns, bushes: all had disappeared under a coating of pure white snow, and it still fell in glorious fat flakes. The buildings and trees were all edged with it; it piled atop cars and windowsills. The effect was heightened by the complete silence it created. No people on the street; no cars on the road. It felt as if they were the only spectators.

"Seems a shame to leave it now that it's so beautiful."

"Leave? Oh. You're leaving." Bubbles's voice was desolate.

"We're leaving, Bubbles. Both of us. We're going to San Francisco."

"I don't know."

Brian heard the down-scale slide of words, the flat sound that had become the norm for her now. He shook his head. "I do. I know. We're going, Bub. We've got to, don't you see?"

Bubbles's eyes started to prick and she dropped her head as Brian wrapped her in a hug.

"It won't be the same, I know. But Nicholas is gone on tour with Max and Gisarra. Eleni's in the woods, writing. Even Daisy's gone off to Mardi-Gras. The apartment's empty now, Bubbles—no people, no life here."

Brian heard her sharp intake of breath at this last note and continued quickly. "Every day you stay in Portland, you're closer to being swept up by your dad or Veronica and thrown into boot camp. Or maybe just deeper and deeper into that couch. This is what we're supposed to do. It's what Jane and Jolie wanted for you. If it was easy, it wouldn't be worth it."

He felt the pressure of her small body stiffen against his chest and then she went almost limp. As he began to brace himself to keep hold of her, she squirmed out of his arms and stood back. Her small serious face scanned his, and then she wrapped herself back in his arms and spoke one word into his chest.

"Okay."

***

Mary and Jack stood in the busy courthouse hallway in front of the Grand Jury room. Mary stood straight-backed, head held high. She bore little resemblance to the woman who came running out of her house in her flop-mops and house dress the day they met, Jack thought. He was all buttoned up in the court suit she gave him, freshly cleaned and pressed. The wool pants itched; the collar rubbed. He had a fantasy of setting it on fire once this was all over, but he probably wouldn't in the end. He'd never do anything to injure this fine woman's feelings in any way. Maybe he could just misplace it.

***

Mary smoothed the surface of her new skirt, and repeated a childhood prayer over and over in her head. Ms. Ames had told them they might not even have to testify unless the jury decided to ask them to clarify something. She really didn't want to go in there but even more than that, she didn't want Jack to have to go in there. She took a deep breath when she saw Sgt. Hain's form at the end of the hall.

He had two women with him.

Jack heard a small note of surprise escape her lips and cocked his head toward her, interested now.

"Why, Jack, those are my neighbors. That's Mrs. Singletary and Mrs. Nguyen."

They watched as the jury room door opened and swallowed Sgt. Hain and her neighbors before she had any chance to investigate.

Mary shook her head in wonder. "Well, if that isn't the doggone strangest thing?"

Jack just shrugged and shot his brows up; she smiled.

***

Toby looked into Daisy's smiling, sleepy face. She held the baby snug up against her chest while she lay back in the hospital bed. The baby had the slightly squished look of all brand-new members of the human race.

Freddy wore a similar expression common to all men who have just witnessed not only the miracle of life, but the sight of their beloved's tight little hole expanding to the size of a salad plate. It was a lot to take in all at one time. It was all a big fat miracle for sure.

Daisy looked down at the tiny, beautiful little being in her arms. No matter what else happened down the line, right now it all seemed to make perfect sense. This was life. This was how we all started: fresh, and clean, and new. No track records, no woulda-coulda-shoulda. All her fantasies and ideas about what this would be like could not have even come close to what she felt right now. The whole thing was unimaginable.

In so many ways, it had ended up as the perfect compromise. No Mardi Gras birthing for her, and a baby boy for Freddy. She felt uncommonly lucky. Freddy remained here at her side, and Toby really had stuck with her too. She wasn't alone. She hoped the loft would still be there waiting for them when they got back. This child needed a home.

Freddy watched the baby wrap a teeny-tiny fist around Daisy's finger and fell madly in love. Madly in love with this new little guy and madly in love with Daisy all over again. He even felt a pretty huge soft spot for Toby, who sat in the other chair just grinning away at the two of them. Two oldies, "Kooks" and "We're a Happy Family," tangled together and played themselves in a loop in his head.

Toby watched as the little pink face scrunched up and gave a huge yawn. Damn, were all babies this cute? A slow smile crept across her face as she turned to the happy couple. "So what do you guys think of the name Tobias?"

***

Just when Jack was about to make his excuses and get the hell out of the courthouse hallway, the doors opened wide and Ms. Ames appeared, followed by two assistants who held stacks of files and paperwork. She scanned the hall and waved at him and Mary. Jack watched as she sent her minions off. Her face was unreadable as she approached them and Jack's stomach flipped.

"Would it be okay if we stepped outside for a moment?" Ms. Ames asked them.

"Okay by me," Jack said.

Mary just nodded.

Jack could tell she was as nervous as he was.

Ms. Ames cut expertly through the crowd, leaving enough room for Mary and Jack to exit comfortably in her wake. As she hit the sidewalk, she grabbed a pack of Benson & Hedges from her little red leather bag, shook one free, lit it with a sleek gold lighter and inhaled.

In that instant, Jack saw her shoulders drop a little and her whole body seemed to relax.

She looked straight at the two of them with a triumphant grin. "We did it. The grand jury in its wisdom has seen fit to indict the officers involved in this crime. A unanimous vote. We're going to trial."

Jack just stared at her.

Mary asked, "That's it? They don't have to go away and think about it some more?"

Ms. Ames shook her head. "They made their decision in record time. You know, I think we have Sgt. Hain to thank for that."

"Sergeant Hain? What did he have to do with it?"

Ms. Ames leaned against a stone lion. "I guess there's no harm in telling you now. He was very moved by your testimony, Mary. He was really upset by not only your experience, but by the fact that so many people were afraid to come forward after the incident. He canvassed your neighborhood and found Ms. Singletary and Mrs. Nguyen and convinced them to give supporting testimony. I guess he wanted you to know there's more than one kind of cop."

Jack and Mary looked at Ms. Ames in wonder.

Mary shook her head. "And to think I thought he didn't like me! You know, Ms. Ames, I thought at my age I knew everything there was to know about people, but I find I can still be surprised. I can't thank you enough."

Jack just stood there; he seemed to be looking at Ms. Ames's cigarette. She caught his eye and held up her pack. "I'm sorry, I didn't even think to offer you one."

Jack reached out and took one, thanking her.

Mary looked at him questioningly. "Why, Jack, I didn't know you were a smoker."

Jack took the light Ms. Ames offered and lit up, coughing just a little. "I'm not. But this one's for Smokey."

"Ah, right. Well then, I'll take you up on that offer after all." Mary accepted a cigarette from Ms. Ames. She leaned in for a flick of the gold lighter and without the slightest hint of a cough, joined in as they all took another long simultaneous drag, exhaled and watched their smoke mingle together in a cloud, and then slowly disappear into the cold Portland air.

"For Smokey," Mary said.

***

Bubbles looked out the window of the Greyhound bus. Only four more hours, and she'd be in San Francisco. "Riding the dog," Jolie had called it. She'd been dreading the two-day trip what with all the hellish tales Jolie had told her but really, it hadn't been so bad.

Brian was blinking back to consciousness next to her; he'd slept most of the way. He looked at her, his face irritatingly fresh and perky. "Think about it—we can be anyone we want to be there. We don't have all that Longview, Washington, Lewis and Clark baggage anymore. We could change our names, dye our hair and become men and women of mystery."

Bubbles had been thinking along those lines as well. She could finally dump the whole Bubbles moniker once and for all. Go back to her birth name or even change it like Jolie did to something more interesting and exotic. But now that she had the chance she'd been waiting for all these years, it didn't seem as exciting. Bubbles was who she'd been during this entire crazy adventure. It was Bubbles who'd been rescued by Jolie, Bubbles who'd danced in silver boots with her wand, Bubbles who Aunt Jane had nurtured and shared her secrets with, and Bubbles who Brian had followed first to Portland and now to San Francisco.

"Tell you what, why don't we just be Bubbles and Brian this time—that'll really confuse the hell out of them."

END

ACKNOWLEDGMENTS

I'd always thought of writing as a solitary pursuit until I began my own journey. This novel would not have existed without the love, talent, and support of my incredible family and friends.

Starting at the beginning, my wonderful parents, Michael Constantine and Julianna McCarthy, artists who surrounded me with love, good food, beautiful books and music. My brilliant and kind poet brother, Brendan Constantine who has stood by me since day one, and remains a source of strength and inspiration.

Alida Thacher, Jennifer Springsteen, and Kim Taylor of PDX Writers, now my dearest friends who took me under their wing and cheerfully shared their genius with a clueless new writer. My Wednesday workshop clan, who keep me inspired, entertained, and enchanted with their own amazing work.

To Jenn Springsteen again, for her editorial magic. Lesann Berry, the woman of 1,000 talents helped me through my second edit and most importantly, let me know when it was time to stop messing with it!

My dear old friend, the talented Howard Paar, who walked the whole journey with me long distance-- from plotting our books to introducing me to Paul Stewart, the cool breeze behind Over The Edge Books, who with a few clicks of his mouse made a dream into a reality.

But wait there's more!

Ryan Wilson and Ethan Antonucci for running with the first inception of this book as a serial for their Black Boot Magazine, under the name Portlandia.

Eddie Morgan's brilliant photography and instant understanding of the perfect imagery on the cover. Cleo Hehn's fresh talent for creating the Stumptown logo art. Rick Lupert, for his artistry and humor in creating my website. Tony Fried, for twenty four hours of proofing proofs.

And last but not least, Alan Rifkin, and Allen Mac Donell, extraordinary writers who were kind enough to take the time to read Stumptown and write their generous reviews.

ABOUT THE AUTHOR

Thea Constantine was born in New York city to a family of actors and writers. She grew up in Hollywood and spent her youth in the clubs and streets of Los Angeles before finally settling in Portland Oregon. In between adventures, she has worked as an award winning performer, filmmaker, playwright, and giant shrimp. Stumptown began as a serial for the on-line magazine The Black Boot, under the name Portlandia. She is a certified facilitator in the AWA method and does weekly writers workshops with PDX Writers. Her short stories have been published in a number of journals, magazines and anthologies.

CPSIA information can be obtained
at www.ICGtesting.com
Printed in the USA
FSHW020512311219
65614FS

9 781944 082314